THE

MANNEQUIN

MAKERS

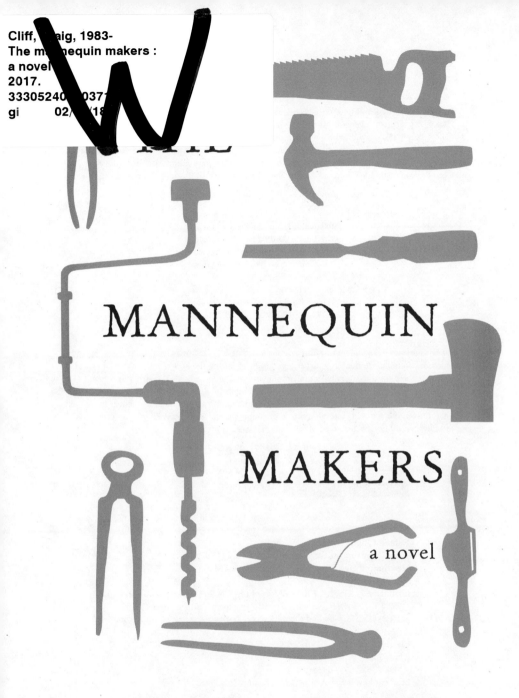

THE MANNEQUIN MAKERS

a novel

CRAIG CLIFF

MILKWEED EDITIONS

Published 2017 by Milkweed Editions
Printed in the United States of America
Cover design by Mary Austin Speaker
Author photo by Darren Cliff
Interior design by Carla Sy
Interior illustrations by J. G. Keulemans
The text of this book is set in Wilke
17 18 19 20 21   5 4 3 2 1
First US Edition

Milkweed Editions, an independent nonprofit publisher, gratefully acknowledges sustaining support from the Jerome Foundation; the Lindquist & Vennum Foundation; the McKnight Foundation; the National Endowment for the Arts; the Target Foundation; and other generous contributions from foundations, corporations, and individuals. Also, this activity is made possible by the voters of Minnesota through a Minnesota State Arts Board Operating Support grant, thanks to a legislative appropriation from the arts and cultural heritage fund, and a grant from Wells Fargo. For a full listing of Milkweed Editions supporters, please visit milkweed.org.

Library of Congress Cataloging-in-Publication Data

Names: Cliff, Craig, 1983- author.
Title: The mannequin makers : a novel / Craig Cliff.
Description: First U.S. edition. | Minneapolis, Minnesota : Milkweed
  Editions, 2017.
Identifiers: LCCN 2017000247 (print) | LCCN 2017006031 (ebook) | ISBN
  9781571311276 (hardcover : acid-free paper) | ISBN 9781571319661 (ebook)
Subjects: LCSH: City and town life–New Zealand–Fiction. | Interpersonal
  relations–Fiction. | New Zealand fiction.
Classification: LCC PR9639.4.C55 M37 2017 (print) | LCC PR9639.4.C55
(ebook)
  | DDC 823/.92–dc23
LC record available at https://lccn.loc.gov/2017000247

Milkweed Editions is committed to ecological stewardship. We strive to align our book production practices with this principle, and to reduce the impact of our operations in the environment. We are a member of the Green Press Initiative, a nonprofit coalition of publishers, manufacturers, and authors working to protect the world's endangered forests and conserve natural resources. *The Mannequin Makers* was printed on acid-free 100% postconsumer-waste paper by Thomson-Shore.

For Margaret Cliff
1925–2013

Notre nature est dans le mouvement;
le repos entier est la mort . . . Rien n'est si
insupportable à l'homme que d'être dans un
plein repos, sans passions, sans affaire, sans
divertissement, sans application. Il sent alors
son néant, son abandon, son insuffisance,
sa dépendance, son impuissance, son vide.
Incontinent il sortira du fond de son âme
l'ennui, la noirceur, la tristesse, le chagrin,
le dépit, le désespoir.

*Our nature lies in movement; complete calm is
death . . . Nothing is so insufferable to man as
to be completely at rest, without passions,
without business, without diversions, without
study. He then feels his nothingness, his
abandonment, his insufficiency, his dependence,
his impotence, his emptiness. There will
immediately arise from the depth of his heart
weariness, gloom, sadness, grief, anger, despair.*

— **Blaise Pascal**

The black-billed gull.

Part
one

———— 31 DECEMBER 1902 – 1 JANUARY 1903 ————

Welcome
to Marumaru

*'We run carelessly to the precipice
after we have put something before us
to prevent us from seeing it.'*

CHAPTER ONE

In which Colton Kemp's wife dies mid-morning, surrounded by misshapen mannequins

---

Another wayward gouge stroke, another chunk of skin from his forefinger. This was always the way once the head had been roughed out, and three-quarter-inch gouge and carver's mallet were exchanged for palm tools. Colton Kemp lifted the damaged digit to his mouth before the blood could surface, and held it there, stemming the flow and delaying the curses he'd hurl at his latest model. He'd named her Ursula but, like all his mannequins, even the men and children, she was modelled on his wife, Louisa. It had taken an hour to sculpt the preparatory clay maquette, but Louisa did not complain, did not move too much, despite being heavily pregnant. He looked at the maquette now, his finger still in his mouth, and could see the impressions of his thumbs in the miniature's features.

He had been at work since first light in the small two-cow barn he'd converted into a workshop three years ago. Despite the sun parading outside it was a gloomy place. A lamp hung from an exposed joist, casting unsteady light on Ursula's unformed face. Friends from Christchurch and Dunedin told him the heads, if a mannequin had a head at all, were usually cast in wax. But this was Marumaru: different rules applied. In any case, he was yet to find the right consistency of wax that would hold up beneath the glare of the gas lamps in the street-front display windows of Donaldson's department store. He'd also tried papier-mâché and plaster of Paris but could not achieve the look of flesh with either. So it was wood—heavy, stubborn wood—and gouges, parting tools, veiners, fluters, sandpaper, nicks, cuts and frustration.

Kemp's shaky hands and rough temperament were ill suited to life as a carver, but it is curious the paths a life can take, the dead ends to which ambition and rivalry can lead a man.

Every new mannequin represented several weeks' work and even then he might uncover a knot or vicious grain when he peeled back the layers of the face. Or, just as likely, he would chip and sand away too much and, no matter how perfect the final expression, the head would be too small for the body he had constructed. His workshop was littered with such failures. Headless Hans holding a heavy canvas sheet in his uneven arms. Eager Mavis, with her lopsided breasts and overlarge mouth, would never don a ball gown. It was best not to think about them as he worked. Instead he held out hope that one day the face he revealed would be Louisa's. Those thin, fair eyebrows that moved with every word, every thought. The cleft in her chin that disappeared upon closer inspection. Those big eyes, green giving way to blue and grey as she passed through the world. But how can you render the kindness of such a face, frozen in a single moment?

It was maddening how her face eluded him in wood, but he had the consolation of finding it in the house whenever he laid down his tools.

He grabbed Ursula's broad wooden jaw between the pincers of his thumb and forefinger. Somewhere, he thought, still sucking the injured finger on his other hand. Somewhere in there is the strong-willed woman who doesn't mind a spot of rain.

At that moment he heard someone shout, 'Rain!', or something very like it. He swung to face the door of his workshop and considered it much as he had the mannequin's face, the puzzlement giving way to discomfort, anxiety, panic—only then did he release the sliced finger from his mouth and set to heaving open the heavy, warped door.

It took a moment for his eyes to adjust to the sunlight.

There, beneath the bare wire clothesline, slumped over a load of washing, was . . . well, it was either Louisa, or her younger sister, Flossie. When Miss Florence had fled the kindness and condolences of Christchurch society and moved south to live with them six months ago, she had taken possession of three or four of Louisa's older dresses. Kemp, despite plying his trade in window dressing, had trouble remembering which outfits were now the younger sister's. He whispered, 'Please be Flossie,' as he took his first step toward the clothesline. That one step was enough, however, to see the larger bulk and know it was Louisa.

He ran to her, raised her gently. A patch of dark blood on the front of her dress had already soaked through to the freshly laundered sheets. The air smelt of soda and iron filings.

'I just wanted to get these on the line,' she said, breathless, wincing.

'For Christ's sake, Lou. Where's Flossie? Flossie!' he called and felt hoarse, as if he'd been yelling all morning. He looked back down at his wife. 'You shouldn't have to hang out the damn washing.'

She winced once more. Her lids came down over her eyes. Her brows lifted and became fixed in place.

'Lou,' he said. 'Lou, stay with me.'

The old lighthouse keeper's dog chose this moment to crawl through the manuka thicket and cross the Kemps' property. She stopped, considered the man and woman sitting on the lawn, before continuing on her way, three feet of rusted chain trailing between her legs.

Kemp felt Louisa's forehead, then stood and hauled his wife into the barn, onto the comfort of a pile of loose hay, wood shavings and sawdust several inches thick. He knelt behind her, propped her up against his own thighs. He mopped her brow with his sleeve, rocking back and forth.

Louisa was silent.

He watched the sawdust turn red between her legs.

'No,' he said, softly, as if afraid of waking her. 'No, you can't take her from me.'

He rocked back violently and knocked one of his abandoned mannequins, which sent a shiver through the ring of limbless, ill-proportioned, inanimate freaks watching over them in what he would later recall, in his bitter, driven future, as a pathetic travesty of the nativity scene.

But in that moment Colton Kemp was lost, oblivious, blubbering. He placed a finger between his teeth to stop the tears and tasted blood.

CHAPTER TWO

In which Sandow arrives in Marumaru, in a manner of speaking

———————

That same morning the train from the north deposited on the narrow platform a dark-skinned youth in shirtsleeves and a plaster statue wrapped in a dirty drop cloth. At Marumaru Station, this was enough to bring a crowd. Within two minutes the platform was thronged with townspeople eager to see what the youth had brought and for whom.

'It has the height of a man,' said Fred Empson, the station-master.

'Perhaps it's an Egyptian mummy,' said the mayor, Big Jim Raymond.

'It must be returned to wherever it came from,' said Mrs Harry Wisdom. 'There's no place for heathenism in this town.'

'It is not a mummy,' said the youth, whose name was Jesse. He was not yet disconcerted by the way that time had sped since leaving Timaru, or the sight of green pastures from the station platform, or the lack of chimney stacks beyond the first few rows of houses. His first impression was instead reserved for the bold colours of the women's dresses and the mayor's hat, which looked as if it were covered with felt from a billiard table.

In his newly acquired performing voice, Jesse announced, 'It is a statue of the perfect human form.' He slipped a knot at the statue's hip. 'It is—'

'Sandow!' shouted Big Jim Raymond.

The crowd cheered and the deflated boy unwrapped the statue to reveal the figure they all expected, the one they'd seen in newspaper advertisements and on the cover of his very own magazine. There were his tight curls and Kaiser Wilhelm moustache, the abdominal muscles like coiled dock line. There the fig leaf covering his manhood, the Roman sandals, the head turned to admire his own bulging biceps. And, if there was any doubt, the pedestal proclaimed in patrician script that this was SANDOW. As in Eugen Sandow, Sandow the Strongman, Sandow's Spring-Grip Dumb-bells, Sandow's Combined Developer, the Sandow Season that had swept through the nation's newspapers, if not all of its drawing rooms, since the muscular Teuton had disembarked in Auckland among survivors of the wrecked *Elingamite*. Indeed, the commencement of his New Zealand tour had not been altogether auspicious. There was a general election in a week's time, meaning there were no politicians to welcome him. Eugen Sandow, the strongest man on Earth, had had to push his way through the shattered survivors, their relieved and boisterous relatives and the silent bereaved to find his promoter, Harry Rickards, who had left Sydney a week before to make final arrangements in the new colony. Sandow would later admit to Jesse that he had expected New Zealand to be nothing more than a collection of wooden huts hastily erected by castaways from the world's four corners, men with wild beards and women perpetually with child who cared not for news from the next hut over, let alone the heart of civilisation. 'But I have been pleasantly surprised,' Sandow had said, 'by the people of your country, the development of their bodies and the commerce evident on every street corner. And of course, they know who I am, which cannot help but make me favourably disposed.'

Sandow was the big draw for Rickards' Vaudeville Company,

which went on to fill town halls and opera houses in Auckland, New Plymouth, Stratford, Wanganui, Palmerston North, Masterton, Napier, Wellington, Christchurch, Ashburton and Timaru. Before each show a life-sized plaster replica of Sandow was sent ahead to heighten anticipation.

But Eugen Sandow was never meant to come to Marumaru.

Sure, the turn of the century had seen the inauguration of the town's first full-time mayor, Jim Raymond, who was rumoured to have shot a man on the goldfields in his youth and now lived and died by the word of the town's first daily newspaper, the *Marumaru Mail*. And it was true that the arrival of a certain strongman signalled one year since the opening of Marumaru's second—repeat: second—department store. But Marumaru was no metropolis: the post office would not bother to distinguish it from the town of the same name in the Hawke's Bay for another twenty years. Rickards' company was not due to perform another show until a matinee at His Majesty's Theatre in Dunedin on the third of January.

It slowly began to sink in for poor Jesse, who had joined Rickards' company in Wanganui, that this was not Dunedin.

'Sandow's shorter than I imagined,' he heard a young woman say to her two friends.

'Why, he's just a man,' said another.

'More than that, he's just a statue!' said the third.

A short man waving his hands and trying to make it to the front of the crowd caught Jesse's attention. He wore an accordion-pleated ascot tie and as he approached he said, in an elevated voice, 'Dear boy, you are bound for the fine establishment of Hercus & Barling, are you not?'

'I—'

'For I am the eponymous Hercus, Emile Hercus, proprietor of the newest, largest and best patronised department store in a twenty-five-mile radius.'

'This is—?'

'Oh no you don't, Emile,' said an older man in a brown

suit that may have once been dignified but now looked merely comfortable. 'You're coming to Donaldson's, aren't you?'

'Donaldson's?' Hercus said. 'The Great Sandow would not be seen dead in that moth-ridden closet.'

The man in the brown suit placed a hand on the plaster Sandow's shoulder. 'It's a good thing Mr Sandow is inanimate then, isn't it?'

'Please don't touch the statue, sir,' Jesse said. 'You'll leave a mark.'

'Quite right,' the man said, removing his hand and wiping it on his lapel. 'Charles Begg,' he said and held out this same overworked hand and Jesse shook it. 'We have a very good window dresser—that term doesn't really do the man justice. He'll rig something up so that you'd swear it was Sandow himself in the window. Where is Kemp, anyway?' Begg asked the crowd of townspeople, who swayed like windblown toetoe, looking for Colton Kemp among their number. He was so often prominent in any scandal, ruckus or commotion. But there was no sign of him.

'I'm sure *my* man is here,' said Hercus, who perched on tip-toe to little effect. 'Has anyone seen The Carpenter?'

A hand went up from the middle of the crowd and they parted. A compact man in a heavy brown checked suit stood there, his large, square hand held out in front of him as if anointing someone or something.

'Over here, my good man,' said Hercus.

'Kemp?' Begg called. 'Where the blazes is Colton Kemp?'

'We stock all of Sandow's physical culture paraphernalia, of course,' Hercus said to Jesse, who was not used to being spoken to with any sort of respect or reverence. 'Quickly, man.' Hercus hurried The Carpenter, whose approach looked laboured. Jesse wondered if it was due to the heavy woollen suit he wore on this warm summer's morning, or simply age. 'I'm afraid he's rather taciturn,' Hercus added.

'Sorry, sir—' Jesse began.

'Oh, don't worry. The Carpenter is the most able man in the field of displays. Just one look at our present window should allay any fears you may have. But why would you have fears? You've come to deposit Mr Sandow's likeness at Hercus & Barling and you're very much in the right spot.'

'A sack of rats for Kemp,' said Begg. 'That's what awaits him, a sack of rats.'

'Come,' Hercus said, placing his arm across Jesse's shoulders, 'let us repair to my store.' He turned to The Carpenter. 'I trust you can transport the precious cargo?'

The man nodded.

'Never a peep, that fellow,' Hercus said. 'Now tell me, boy, what is your name and how long have you been associated with Mr Sandow?'

CHAPTER THREE

In which Colton Kemp keeps mum

The lighthouse, vacant since the death of its first and only keeper, stood at the head of a nameless crag. From the handful of times Kemp had gone fishing with his father he could recall the way the bluff and the land sloping down and away resembled the severed tail of a lizard. For twelve years the gas-powered light had acted as a beacon for ships—Mayor Raymond was still agitating for another townsperson to take up the mantle of lighthouse keeper—but for now the tall white tower and the rocks below attracted only would-be suicides.

Kemp was now a widower and a father of twins—all in the space of a morning. Two lives in exchange for one. But he did not care about those small, squirming things just now. He had left Flossie to deal with the aftermath, hadn't told her where he was going. She was seventeen but had a good head on her shoulders. She had dealt with the sudden death of her parents quietly and had adjusted to life in slower, less accomplished circles. He knew she'd do a good job this time, that she feared and respected him.

The town of Marumaru was further down the lizard's tail, where the cliffs ended and the short beach began. The walk to town was a dry dirt path bisecting a field of sheep-shorn grass that resembled a cricket pitch or, though he tried not to see it, a fairway. Before Kemp's birth, his father had been the greenkeeper of a golf links north of Dunedin. He spoke of it only once: the pride he'd taken in turning scrub into emerald carpets of grass, the thought that went into the placement of each sand trap, the wickedness of a sou'wester on the thirteenth, the difficulties players faced in coming north—the boggy roads, slips and skittish horses—and the slow exodus of members to the Balmacewen course closer to home. The links had been abandoned in the end. In all likelihood it had now been divided into rectangles and was patrolled by Corriedale and cattle beast, though Kemp preferred to think of it overgrown: a shimmering straw-coloured fairway flanked by wild fennel gone to seed and gnarled macrocarpa leading the eye to a perfect circle of Scotch thistle where his father's green had once shone. Kemp senior had been nearly sixty when he moved north to Marumaru and met his wife. His death concluded a roving, eventful life, but left his son with only a handful of memories. Single moments of grace or anger or despair from which Colton was expected to reconstruct a father.

He has been dead so long. Now Louisa has joined him.

This time he had a thousand memories. He had the raw materials to reconstruct his wife. It was impossible to avoid. But it was not enough. He thought of his failure to carve the likeness of her face and knew she was gone.

He stood on the edge of the crag, staring out to the horizon. Looking due east he was faced with over five thousand miles of uninterrupted ocean. All but six of those miles, however, were hidden by the curvature of the Earth. This thought, the concealed distance, the massive isolation, was more fearsome to him than the thought of the rocks thirty feet below. He looked down. The cliff face was vertical for the first half of its descent, then the moss started and the rock stretched out, eager to meet the water. It would take an almighty leap to make the creamy waves.

He did not leap. Instead, he unbuttoned his trousers and

pissed out over the edge, the wind breaking up his stream after a few feet and beating it back into the rock face.

As he headed back down the slope he encountered a black-faced sheep, still heavy with winter wool, standing squarely on the path.

'Hyah!' he said and threw out his hand.

The sheep tilted its head to one side.

'Hyah!' he said again and thrust his shoulder forward in a mock charge.

The sheep turned slowly and began to leave the path, its undocked tail bouncing in clownish defiance. This slow retreat was no longer enough and Kemp ran up behind as if to kick the sheep. No, he truly meant to kick that woollen arse. The beast picked up its pace and rambled down the slope toward a clutch of cabbage trees. He pursued. In his escalating temper he wanted to do the sheep some harm, to feel its neck between his arm and torso, to wrench its head clean off, but the slope was greater than he had first anticipated. His fast wheeling feet hardly seemed to touch the ground. The wool-heavy sheep stopped behind the stout trunk of the leftmost tree, turned to see the man hurtling toward it and, at the last moment, set off in the direction of the town. But Kemp—spirit possessed and momentum unchecked—leapt forward to tackle his quarry. The tips of his fingers brushed wool, but caught nothing.

He lay on the ground, winded, thwarted, miserable.

'Excuse me,' a young voice called from near the path.

He rolled onto his side, wiped his eyes with the meat of his hands and looked back up the hill. It was Josephine Strachan, youngest daughter of the schoolmaster. How old was she? Seven, eight, nine? He was no good at this sort of thing, but he knew her by sight. Flossie had been helping Mr Strachan at the school several days a week. Josephine, most likely starved of attention, had taken a special liking to his sister-in-law. He remembered something about the girl visiting his house unannounced one evening while he laboured in his workshop.

'Why were you trying to tackle that sheep, Mr Kemp?'

The beast, standing further down the slope, let out a tremulous bleat.

He got to his feet and dusted off his trousers. The rush of foolishness made his knees waver.

'I was practising,' he said.

The girl walked gingerly down the hill toward him. 'But it's not football season,' she said and came to a stop a few feet from him. The slope meant that her eyes were level with his. 'And aren't you too old to play?'

'That's rather impertinent of you, Miss Strachan,' he said, hoping to scold her, make her turn and run away crying. But all she said was, 'I beg your pardon,' and continued to stare into his eyes.

He looked away. The sheep, finally bored, turned its head and trotted off, its tail rigid and unmoving this time, as if it were a ferret fresh from the taxidermist.

Kemp grunted and started to climb back up to the path. The girl followed. 'How long have you been up here at the lighthouse?' she asked.

'I'll have you know,' he said without turning, 'I'm not too old for rugby. It may not seem it to you, but I'm still to reach my prime.'

Josephine had raced up beside him. He saw her shrug her shoulders, his vitality beyond her ken.

'You missed it, didn't you?'

'Missed what?' he asked.

'The excitement in town. The statue.'

He had no idea what she was talking about and had little interest in finding out. The two of them rejoined the dirt path and followed it wordlessly back down to the wicket gate.

'Are you going to follow me the entire way?' he asked.

'How is Louisa?'

'She is . . .' he began, intending to say that she was fine, but was unable to continue. He stopped, opened the gate and let the girl walk through. He followed.

'I saw Flossie in town this morning,' Josephine said. 'She said she would teach me piano.'

'Is that so?'

The slope had begun to level out. Soon the dirt path would widen into a dirt road dotted with letterboxes and long, stony driveways until it eventually became Regent Street.

'Father says I am not allowed to go promenading on New Year's Eve until I am ten,' Josephine said, unable to hide her puffing as she tried to match his pace.

He did not respond.

'I wish I could see your new display being switched on.'

'It will be there in the morning.'

'Yes, but that's not the same, is it? Not when it's New Year's Eve *tonight*.'

The properties and paddocks to their left fell away and were replaced with dark green explosions of flax and beyond them a thin strip of sand the colour of camel's hair that stretched to the rocky breakwater of the small harbour. A lone black-billed gull circled the beach in silence. To their right, the first business. Kemp feigned interest in the metalwork gate that read 'J. C. Bannerman, Ironmonger'. It had just gone four in the afternoon and Bannerman had closed his shop for the day, no doubt preparing for a night of revelry.

An approaching buggy forced them out of the middle of the road.

'Are you going to look at the window of Hercus & Barling?' Josephine asked.

'No.'

'Oh, you should. You really should.'

They continued on past Bertie Bush's hardware store, which was desperately in need of a new coat of paint, Padget the watchmaker's narrow shop and the Criterion Hotel, standing proud on the corner of Regent and Albert streets.

'Won't your father be wondering where you are?' Kemp asked as he looked left and right, preparing to cross the street to avoid the window of Hercus & Barling and the lesser evils of Mrs Alves' sweet shop, Mr Borrie's toys and games and the meat pies and coffee of McWatter's cafe.

'No, sir,' Josephine replied.

Emboldened by the girl's sudden bout of manners, he said, 'If you don't leave me alone, I'll tell your father you've been larking about at the lighthouse.' He stepped off the footpath.

'Oh, he won't care.' She ran a few steps to catch him up and jumped over the ridge of horse leavings that had been swept into the centre of the road.

'Well,' Kemp said, 'I'll forbid Flossie to give you piano lessons.'

'You wouldn't!'

'Do you have a piano in your house?'

Josephine turned back toward the lighthouse.

'I didn't think so,' he continued. 'I don't intend to let annoying little girls into my home to use my piano.'

'Flossie says it's Louisa's,' she said, nearly shouting. They stood on the beach side of Regent Street now, both watching the still-circling gull.

'You're horrible,' the girl said after some time. 'I'm going to tell Louisa what a horrible husband she has and what a terrible father he will make.'

She made as if to leave. He grabbed her shoulder and crouched down.

'Listen to me, Josephine. You must not step foot on my property. You *will not* step foot on my property. Do you understand me?'

He looked down at his hand, still clamped to her shoulder, then back at the girl's face: her eyes downcast and blinking rapidly. He released her shoulder and continued down Regent Street, his head inclined a notch too high to seem natural.

Beyond the Albert Street intersection, shops reappeared on the left of the high street, though they too had closed for the day. He turned to look behind him. Josephine was a dozen paces behind, keeping her distance but still following. He stood with his hands on his hips and eventually she drew level with him again.

'What do you think of these windows, Mr Kemp? Aren't they dreary compared with the big stores?'

'Dreary?' he said. 'That's one word for it.'

They walked on, past Professor Healey's store of smoker's requisites and Mr Kriss's bakery, which emitted the heavy tar smell of the black bread that he baked for holidays—his mother's recipe—though no one else in town could stomach it.

'Look at this,' Kemp said, pointing at Sandy Chase's window, stocked with ales, porters, wines and spirits. 'The bottles are still wreathed in tinsel from Christmas. And the McNeils' window . . . Well, a fine coat of dust hardly entices the potential buyer of a pair of boots, does it?'

Josephine thought hard before responding, 'No.'

'Now Mr Ikin, on the other hand,' he said and turned square to the bookseller's window, 'I suspect he wears his dust with pride.'

He looked around and found Josephine in front of the bright white display of the next store over, which belonged to the town's purveyor of pills and sundries, Mr Fricker.

'Have any of these stores ever asked you to rig up a display for them, Mr Kemp?'

'They're above that sort of thing, or so they say. But let's see how long they can hold out, eh? Let's see how long till they're boarding up their windows like the shops on Stirling Road and queuing for a job selling perfume or minding the books at Donaldson's or that other store.'

'You mean Hercus & Barling?'

'I know what it's called.'

The commerce on the beach side came to a halt once more at the grounds of St Paul's, the tallest of the town's three churches. He could smell the fishmonger's shop on the other side of grounds. The reek seemed the final word on religion, no matter how much the vestments, stained glass and ceremony might appeal to the aesthete inside any window dresser.

He leant on the church's wrought iron gate, another of Jolly Bannerman's pieces, and looked across at Donaldson's, square and tall, its black verandah of corrugated iron stretching out to the street. The masonry facade sought to announce quality, class, permanence. The tall windows of the upper floors were bound by Roman arches, each capped with a keystone bearing a white rosette. But he knew it was all for nought without a decent display in his windows, the only windows that counted.

He had started as a stock boy seven years earlier, back when it was Donaldson's Drapers two doors further down Regent Street and old man Donaldson still ran the roost. As the store had grown, expanding the range of goods offered—millinery, gardening tools, sheet music—so too had Kemp's role. He was responsible for all elements of display inside the store and had two stock boys beneath him when Charlie Begg came out from Nottingham in '99 to oversee the move to the new premises. Four storeys, replete with Lamson tube system and twenty feet of plate glass either side of the main entrance. A proper department store, one to rival any in the South Island.

'You say you're responsible for display,' Begg had said at their first meeting. 'What exactly does this encompass?'

'Putting the wares out and making them look nice, sir.'

'Well, we can't have those front windows bare for the grand reopening, can we? Sketch a few ideas and show them to me tomorrow morning.'

Until then, Kemp's idea of window dressing had been to cram as much merchandise as possible into the old store's small dark window and send a boy in there with a feather duster every three months. There hadn't been the space for mannequins. Instead the few that Donaldson's possessed were dotted inside the store. Now he was to come up with ideas to fill the expanse of plate glass and provide sketches? He couldn't wield a pencil for any purpose beyond words and numbers.

At home that evening he'd shared his predicament with Louisa.

'But you must have ideas, Col. You're around the goods all day. Just put them together to make a scene. Tell a story.'

'But half our dummies are missing arms. They look as if they've just come back from fighting the Boers.'

'What about a battle scene?' she asked mischievously.

'That may be in poor taste.'

'If there was some way of hiding the missing parts,' Louisa said and looked down at the threadbare tablecloth. 'Flossie cannot for the life of her draw hands, so her damsels are always holding mufflers, her dashing knights crossing their arms. Perhaps you could hide the missing parts? Prepare a forest scene. The trees could hide the shortcomings of the dummies.'

'A forest? That sounds like a fair amount of work.'

'Not if you're smart,' said Louisa and reached for her sketchbook.

The next morning he'd shown Louisa's drawing to Begg, acting as if it were his own.

'And how much will you need for incidentals?'

'Perhaps one and sixpence?' he'd offered. He planned to cut actual saplings from his own property and install them in the display.

'A miser? My estimation of you grows by the minute, Mr Kemp.'

With time he and Louisa became expert at recognising stories from the newspaper or details from their own lives that could form the basis of a new display. A jail break. A night at the theatre. Bringing home the latest addition to the family—all the while trying to start their own.

Though he no longer had to show Begg his idea before producing a display, he still had Louisa prepare a sketch on a piece of foolscap, which he then replicated in the windows of Donaldson's.

It was Louisa who suggested he carve his own mannequins, sick of his continual complaints about the state of the store's dummies and the cost of ordering new ones from overseas. Louisa who urged him on. Louisa who bandaged his damaged fingers.

He looked across the street at his latest window and saw too much of Louisa in it. The ghost of her face in the four mannequins. The echo of her voice, the shade of her pencil in the layout. The numerals '1902' cut from large shards of broken looking-glass (quite how ladies broke mirrors in the confines of a dressing room was still a mystery to him). The black ropes against the black background, invisible to the casual onlooker, which would hoist the '2' up into the false ceiling and replace it with a '3'. His best mannequins forming happy couples either side of the sparkling numbers, dressed in their finest theatre clothes, who would turn to each other as the '3' descended and almost clink their champagne flutes, thanks to individual turntables concealed in the false floor. All the movement rigged up to the same gas engine that powered the pneumatic Lamson tubes that sent money and receipts around the store.

'I can see the ropes,' Josephine said. He had almost forgotten she was beside him. 'I can picture exactly what will happen, but I want to see it anyway.'

'And you can,' he said, 'tomorrow.'

It was only a short block back to Hercus & Barling. Looking over Josephine's head he could see a small crowd of eight or ten people outside its window. There was no such crowd for Donaldson's.

'Why don't you go look at The Carpenter's window?' he suggested.

'The curtain's still down,' she replied.

Ten people are willing to stare at his blank curtain, he thought, rather than my display. He could feel his skin flush once more.

From the first, the two department stores had not just affected the sole traders—the widow dressmaker, the dealer in golden rings and small trinkets—but had also fed upon each other, undercutting prices, paying exorbitant amounts for shipping to ensure stock was the first to arrive, offering more generous credit terms. Each store had a man dressed as Santa Claus in the week before Christmas and the town delighted in judging whose St Nick was fatter, whose white beard looked the more authentic. But the battle was most evident, and most crucial, in the window. It was not a competition between two stores but between Colton Kemp and The Carpenter, ever since the day the silent sod strolled into town. Kemp had never heard him talk, though Big Jim Raymond swore The Carpenter congratulated him upon his re-election in September. What sort of affectation was it not to speak when spoken to? To always wear the same loud suit with its large houndstooth check and to nod and wave and point before trotting up Pukehine Hill at the end of the day?

But damn the man, his mannequins were a wonder. The story went that The Carpenter walked down from his shack on the hill carrying a wooden mannequin, placed it in front of the entrance to Hercus & Barling two days before their grand opening, and Hercus offered him a job on the spot. Kemp's curiosity got the better of him at the opening and he saw the window display first-hand: dozens of electric lights powered by the store's own generator (Donaldson's, like the town itself, was still to make the leap to electricity), thirteen headless mannequins of the sort imported from Europe (though he suspected they were, like Emile Hercus, second-hand from Sydney) and, at the centre, The Carpenter's serene lady, dressed in a red moirette dress with a blue shawl draped over her left shoulder and arm, the soft hand protruding, palm up. The skin was smooth and bright as porcelain, but looked as if it would give to the touch. What manner of wood had he used? What tools to exact such detail? What paints, tints or stains to flush her with life? What beast had he shorn to create her mane of brown hair, curling as it passed the hint of her ears and tumbled down her shoulders?

The Carpenter's first mannequin was a revelation for Kemp and a sensation for the town. Over the following months The Carpenter produced more figures. The appearance of each was an event that surpassed the excitement of a new window at Donaldson's, no matter how intricate Kemp's mechanics, how timely the scene or artistically it was laid out. The *Marumaru Mail* began speculating about the gender, age, hair and eye colour of The Carpenter's next model weeks before it appeared. No one seemed to care about the masses of blank space in his window displays, the utter stasis of his arrangements, the lack of theme or connection to the town in which the store sat: The Carpenter's window was another world, one on the cusp of coming to life.

Little by little this world began to spill into Marumaru. The ladies of the town, who had conformed to the modest colonial fashion for dark skirts and white blouses, began to step out in the reds and blues and greens of The Carpenter's window. The men stuck with subdued tones for their suits and waistcoats but stuffed silk handkerchiefs of turquoise or magenta into their breast pockets and emerald felt bowlers on their heads. Visitors from the north and from the south often remarked upon the deluge of colour in the town, the women's resemblance to parakeets, the men's to mallard drakes. Perhaps most tellingly, when a visiting photographer set up his equipment at Hercus & Barling the townsfolk chose to be immortalised performing the poses of The Carpenter's models.

Kemp had already thrown himself into the making of his own mannequins before The Carpenter's arrival but he could not breathe life into them in the same way. They remained wooden forms, collections of limbs and blank spaces for covering with cloth and millinery.

An open carriage drawn by two old Clydesdales passed Kemp and Josephine. It was heading toward the wharf, or perhaps out of town. For a moment he considered jumping on the back of the carriage, stowing himself beneath the dirty green tarpaulin and leaving Marumaru forever, but Josephine was sure to give him away.

'Kemp!'

He looked back at Donaldson's and there was Charlie Begg, ruddy with rage, clutching a ledger book with both hands.

'Where the blazes have you been?'

He didn't want to cross the road. He looked down at Josephine, who seemed happy enough to sit on the church fence, dangle her legs and watch the unfolding drama.

Begg slammed the ledger book against an imaginary counter

and stomped across Regent Street. 'Where've you been?' he repeated.

'Wednesday is my workshop day,' Kemp replied. 'The window is all set for this evening.'

'Sandow is here. Well, not here,' Begg gestured back to the store, 'but worse, there.' He pointed toward Hercus & Barling.

'Sandow? In Marumaru?'

'I told you,' Josephine added, though both men ignored the girl.

'Well,' Begg said, 'just his statue at the moment, but you know how they send that ahead of the company.'

'But Sandow isn't supposed to perform here. The theatre's hardly big enough for that pony show.'

'I know. The boy must have got off at the wrong station. Nevertheless,' Begg said slowly, spelling out the source of his ill-temper, 'there is a plaster replica of Sandow the Magnificent in Hercus's window right now and they're selling Sandow Developers as if they were loaves of bread.'

Kemp looked back in the direction of Kriss's bakery. 'Probably outselling bread today.'

Begg hit him on the arm with the ledger book.

Josephine put her hand to her mouth but stayed perched on the fence.

Kemp looked at the ground, trying to keep his anger, lately focused on The Carpenter, from jumping the tracks and ploughing down his boss.

'I get the impression, sir,' he said, mirroring Begg's deliberate pace, 'that you think I am to blame for our misfortune, though I cannot see how.'

'Because The Carpenter was at the train station this morning to carry Sandow off. We could have had him. Donaldson's could have had him. The whole town was there, Kemp. The whole town but you. What, pray tell, was so important that you did not bless us with your presence?'

He couldn't do it. Couldn't say the words that would kill

Louisa once again. Even now it seemed that she would be in the kitchen, struggling to cut a pumpkin, when he returned home.

'I didn't know,' he said. True enough, though he'd later learn that Flossie had seen the commotion at the station and run home to tell Louisa and him of the statue, arriving instead to find her sister limp in his arms in the workshop.

Begg narrowed his eyes. 'One-upped again, eh?' He patted Kemp on the shoulder, causing the flames to rise once more in the window dresser's chest.

Two young women dressed to the nines for a night promenading Regent Street approached from the direction of the wharf. By force of habit, he appraised their outfits and knew an instant later that they were not Donaldson's ladies. He turned to Begg and saw that he had come to the same conclusion. Soon the streets would be crawling with men and women in their finest clothes, sporting parasols and the latest Brazilian and Panama hats. He had delegated to one of his stock boys the task of flicking the switch at midnight to power his New Year's display. If he left now, if he could shake Josephine Strachan, he could avoid the crowds, the tally-keeping, the lies of omission, the revelry of people looking forward without a single fear in their hearts.

'I suppose there's little point in holding a grudge,' Begg said.

Colton Kemp said nothing. He turned his back on his boss and began to walk the mile and a half back to his secluded property, hauling his earthly form as if it were an engine coupled to a dozen freight carriages, every step a fresh battle with inertia. Josephine followed a few yards behind, in silence this time. He would later wonder why she clung to him. What was it she detected?

Eventually she left him, taking the path that ran beside the swamp back to the schoolhouse.

He worried what she would tell her parents when she got home. Not that he had grabbed her by the shoulder, threatened her, but that he had been walking around the town that afternoon as his wife lay dead. Because the news would have to come out. Tomorrow, if he could face it.

Flossie spied him as he walked up their long gravel driveway and ran out to meet him.

'Oh, Col,' she said, 'I'm so glad you came back.'

She lured him inside, fed him, hardly spoke. She had coped well enough. As well as could be expected. Still, the house rang with cries and he found that he couldn't sleep in his bed that night, that it was rendered incomplete without a counterbalance, *his* counterbalance. He soon gave in to his restlessness and stalked to his workshop, lit the lamp and saw the bloody comet trail leading from the base of Ursula, stolid and incomplete, to the heavy barn door. From the muddle of his tool bench, he selected the hatchet he used to chip away large amounts of wood at the start of a new project. Clenching the haft in his right hand, he realised this is how he had felt since the morning: tense beyond all reason but with none of the release of a sweetly placed stroke. Faster than thought, he drove the hatchet into Ursula's unfinished head, braining her as if it were a tomahawk. He had to place his free hand on the figure's right shoulder to free the bit from the wood before swinging again. This next stroke knocked a wedge free from Ursula's head and the heavy wooden form toppled back, coming to rest awkwardly with a trestle against its rump. He turned, eyeing each of the misshapen forms that remained upright before hurling the hatchet end over end into the head of Mavis and her overlarge mouth.

He left the barn, forgetting it would be dark out, and fumbled around the lean-to where he stacked his firewood, searching for his father's heavy, cumbrous axe.

By sunrise he had reduced the mannequins in his workshop to lengths of firewood for the range.

The occasional hand or foot sticking out of the woodpile would unnerve poor Flossie in the coming weeks, but that next morning she bit her bottom lip and placed a firm hand on his shoulder to rouse him. He uncurled from beneath his tool bench, still clasping his father's axe. She looked into his red-rimmed eyes.

'Col, I need you to get some things from town. For the babies.'

CHAPTER FOUR

In which the acolyte makes himself at home

Jesse lay awake as the sun cut through the thin bed sheets that were hung as curtains in his room at the Criterion Hotel. His chest felt expanded and he pumped it like a bellows, lying on his back and watching his breastbone rise and fall. He had hardly slept but his head felt clear. He knew that next to him lay Julia— dear, plump, motherly Julia—that she was a prostitute and that he was no longer a virgin. These facts became soft at the edges and crumbled when he tried to set the night's events in order. Had one of his new friends paid for Julia or had she too been placed on his account (which of course was Mr Rickards' account)? Ah, he didn't care. To Rickards he was a delivery boy, a tagalong. To the people of Marumaru he was a herald, a saviour.

Julia lifted herself onto an elbow and said, 'You know, love, it's not every man I let kip beside me.'

'Was I making too much noise?'

'Not half,' she said.

'Sorry.'

'You've got your own room for huffin' and puffin'.'

'My—?' So this wasn't his room. He was unaccustomed to

the liberties the drink had taken with his memory. All the same, he found it hard to muster any regret that he'd strayed from Sandow's path of moderation.

Julia sat up completely now, making no attempt to shield her large pink breasts with the white sheet. He felt himself get hard again, though there was a dead ache that had not been there last night, an ache he revelled in, the way his muscles used to ache when he started following Sandow's System.

She reached out her hand to pat him on the cheek. 'There's a good boy,' she said, motherly once more, and it set his cock throbbing.

Down the hall, he walked several circuits around his room, laughing to himself and throwing his hands in the air as a maniac might, before stripping to his underwear and settling down to his exercises. He began with the Sandow Spring-Grip Dumb-bell, slowly clenching and unclenching his fist and curling the small weight up to his chin. Ten with the left, ten with the right, thinking all the time about his breathing, his new expanded lungs, the muscles of the chest, the biceps, the triceps, the wrist. He then brought his arm to his chest and extended it in an arc, as if opening a casement window. Ten with the left, ten with the right. On he worked through Sandow's routine, slowly, never taxing a muscle too greatly, never expending excessive energy, focusing his brain in a way that had become second nature to him. He rigged his Sandow Developer to the door and began working his back. He kept noticing muscles he might not normally feel, ones he had employed with Julia. The thrusting fibres in his buttocks. The lower calf that had held him on his tiptoes as long as he wanted and needed. The toes that had grasped for traction on the wooden floor.

After his exercises, he took his sponge to the communal bathroom. He did not fill the heavy grey tub with cold water and fully immerse as Sandow's gospel dictated. He never followed this step at home or when working out with Jarrett. Instead he stepped out of his underpants and soaked the sponge in cool water and proceeded to dab his warm, twitching body with the vital substance.

He dressed once more in his only outfit—short-sleeved shirt, brown waistcoat and thick canvas trousers—donned his cap and headed downstairs. It had just gone seven o'clock and the dining room was empty. The dark carpet of the hall smelt of spilt ale and sawdust. He took a seat at the bar and was happy enough to sit there and read the names on the liquor bottles.

'After the hair of the dog that bit you, eh?' said a voice from behind him. He turned and saw the publican, Ed Coughlin, who slowly made his way around the bar.

'Sorry?'

'You after a drink, sir?'

Jesse smiled. He was still a sir the morning after, though Coughlin forever looked on the verge of winking. 'No thank you.'

'Had your share last night.' It wasn't a question or a jibe, just barman's conversation. 'Dora's in the kitchen,' he said, 'if you're after breakfast?'

Jesse thought of the account the hotel had been happy enough to run up on Mr Rickards' behalf last night. The drinks he had been shouted right there in the Criterion after his second telephone call with Rickards, when he could announce to the gathered crowd that the company would perform in Marumaru the next night.

All of sixteen, a month ago he'd been a schoolboy in Kai Iwi, a two-hour carriage ride from Wanganui, trying to convince his mother that another year of school would not be a waste of time. She had wanted him to find a farm-hand position, bring in some money, put those muscles to use. He did not enjoy school but knew that taking a job would leave no time for training with the troop of boys Mr Jarrett was instructing in the ways of Sandow's System. Jarrett's School of Physical Culture (otherwise known as the Kai Iwi school hall) was the only place where Jesse felt a sense of camaraderie and pride.

When word came that the strongman would stop in Wanganui, Jarrett made a wager with Mr Atkins at the rich boys' school about whose cadets would impress Sandow more. Jarrett picked his six best boys and off to town they went. Jesse and the other Kai Iwi boys were spread among the Collegiate 'Number One Squad', who stood on the football field, topless and flexed as if under inspection by a team of pretty girls. Atkins, their instructor, wasn't even there yet, as he was off meeting Sandow at the station. Even if the Kai Iwi boys had taken off their shirts and vests then and there, it would still have been simple to spot them among the whities.

Jesse had seen plenty of pictures of Sandow in his magazine and on posters beneath the slogans—*Breathe more air and have richer blood*; *Deep breathing is internal exercise*—that Jarrett pinned to the walls of the hall, but the strongman looked much shorter in person. Perhaps it was the three-piece suit, the starched collar, the shiny black shoes that almost came to a point.

'Hello my boys,' Sandow had said, claiming them as his own from the first. 'What an impressive array of young men.' His German accent was strong but did not obstruct his meaning.

Once Atkins and Jarrett had run the boys through a series of dumb-bell and breathing exercises, it was left to Sandow to pick out the best physical specimen. The Prussian had pulled a cigar from the internal pocket of his coat. While Atkins and Jarrett fought over who would have the pleasure of lighting it, he said to the boys, 'I do not endorse cigars for young lungs such as yours. One or two cigarettes is perhaps all right, but none is always better. For me, one small pleasure a day is sufficient.' He sucked as the triumphant Atkins held a match to the end of the cigar. Once the flame had caught, Sandow held the cigar aloft as if inspecting the fidelity of a gun's barrel and said to his two disciples, 'I find it helps me to think.'

Atkins began to shout poses for the boys to perform—The Dying Gaul, Farnese Hercules, Discobolus—and Sandow strolled among their ranks, puffing his cigar, pausing from time to time to look a boy up and down, squinting. Sometimes he would nod, sometimes tilt his head and purse his lips. After five minutes, the boys' posing had become ragged—the Kai Iwi contingent had been making it up as they went along since the first few poses—and Atkins stopped calling out. The Collegiate boys stood at a weary kind of attention. Jesse and his friends each looked down at the circle of trodden dry grass their posing had produced and itched to move. The bet between Jarrett and Atkins meant nothing to them. A perfectly round leather football lay in the distance against a fence.

When Sandow's cigar had halved in size he said, 'Gentlemen, these are the best boys I have yet seen in Australasia. And the best among them? Him.'

'Him?' Atkins asked.

'Him.' Sandow pointed once more at Jesse.

'That's one of mine,' said Jarrett, beaming. 'Jesse Hikuroa. Come forward, Jesse.'

'Excellent chest development,' Sandow said. 'You look as if you could run all day.'

Jesse shrugged and looked at the football.

Sandow turned to Jarrett. 'I wonder if I could use him for my demonstration tomorrow afternoon. I understand that several doctors and other prominent citizens will be in attendance.'

Back at the Criterion's bar, Jesse's stomach rumbled and he remembered that he had not responded to Ed Coughlin's question about breakfast. Coughlin must have heard the rumble, as he gave another almost-wink and called out to Dora to crack a couple of eggs.

'You made the newspaper,' Coughlin said. He produced a paper from behind the bar and slapped it down in front of Jesse.

The front page was devoted to advertising for department stores, hotels and passages aboard the New Zealand Shipping Company's Royal Mail Steamers for London. Jesse opened the paper and was met with the headline stretching across two columns: SANDOW IS HERE, SANDOW IS COMING.

He was mentioned only in roundabout ways in the article. 'Sandow's likeness was delivered to the Marumaru Station on Wednesday morning,' it said, without saying by whom. Later, there was mention of 'Rickards' associates' and 'an advance party', which Jesse took to mean him and him alone. Mostly the article reproduced Rickards' own press for the company.

Rickards was due to arrive on the 9.15 train, along with the props and stage hands, at which point Jesse would be put to work.

His eggs arrived. He continued to leaf through the paper as he ate. On page four, he was surprised to see that he was mentioned by name in the gossip column.

MISS TATTLE'S WORD OF MOUTH

Town is abuzz with the arrival of the plaster brute, Eugen Sandow. My contacts in Christchurch inform me the fleshy version is no more engaging . . . What was J— wearing on her head at the station yesterday? The most likely candidate is a dead possum . . . Young Miss M— seemed quite taken with the plaster brute's companion, a young Maori in possession of perfect health, an acolyte of Herr Sandow no doubt . . . Miss B— was seen down the park eating a whole orange, greedily . . . J— B—'s wife is jolly fed up and beyond wrought with her husband's affair with the bottle. J— is only getting started . . . Elsewhere in the colony, the "cursed drink" is still sending people to the asylums despite the prohibitionists. One ruined publican is the latest victim . . . Miss M— will do well to note the boy's name is Jesse, and to keep such affections a better secret from her father . . . Absent from yesterday's scene was C— K—, which surprised us all. F— was spotted briefly, but we understand she ran away with shame at the state of her dress . . . Those surveyed prior to this edition going to print were eager to see Donaldson's window in action before attending the Watchnight service . . . A— has been to both the big stores and is still to find a glove that fits . . . Sandow's feats include bending iron bars, breaking chains and bursting wire ropes. Constable T— will be in a pickle if Sandow starts having his way with the town . . . The Mayor still writes 189– from time to time, and must then cross it out. To the rest of you, welcome to the New Year. May it be prosperous, scandalous and never dull.

Getting off the train at Marumaru the previous morning had been a mistake and he expected another dressing down from Rickards when he arrived. The extra stop would still turn a profit but the town was small, smaller than any other in which the company had performed since he was asked to join as Sandow's travelling demonstration assistant. But Marumaru was alive, different from any other place he had experienced.

His big night came back to him in a sudden wave: the booze, the bright colours, the handshakes, the gratitude, but also his own generosity. The rounds he had shouted. The toast he had announced at last call, 'To Marumaru, the town that no one wants to visit and no one wants to leave.' He thought of Julia upstairs. With the size of the tab he'd run up for Rickards, the decision to stay might not be his to make.

CHAPTER FIVE

*In which Eugen Sandow performs in Marumaru
and a seed is planted*

————————

Colton Kemp and Jolly Bannerman sat on the damp sand passing a bottle of peaty home-distilled whisky back and forth as the tide receded.

'To the New Year,' Bannerman said for the umpteenth time and held the bottle aloft. The two had spent the afternoon together. Jolly had asked after Louisa several times, but Kemp had not told him she was dead. More than a day had passed and he still had not told anyone. 'She's fine,' was all he'd say.

'And sweet wee Flossie?'

'As sweet as ever.'

'You're a lucky man, Col.'

'We shall see.'

He looked at the ironmonger, slouched forward over his knees, his slender height compressed like a heron about to take flight. Bannerman slapped his long, tobacco-stained fingers on the grey sand. 'Tell me I'm not a good husband, Col? Tell me I don't deserve a little respect?'

Kemp kept silent. Small round pebbles scattered across the

beach shimmered in the soft light of late afternoon. The waves covered them with a thin film on the way up the beach but the receding water took the easier route, parting either side of each stone, creating hundreds of little arrow heads pointing back to town, back to his house. Arrows that flickered a few times and disappeared until the next wave came to his toes and pulled back.

'The likes of which . . .' Bannerman returned his head to his knees without finishing his thought.

Kemp took the bottle from his friend's loose grip. 'I'm not ready to be a father. I can't do it.' He took a swig.

The sloshing sound roused Bannerman once more. He held out his hand for the bottle. 'Hey, are you going to the show tonight?'

'What show?'

'What show? Come on, Col. I know the opposition got one over you with the statue, but you can't tell me you don't have a ticket.'

'When were you ever in a state to get a ticket?'

'Milly got 'em. Just the two I'm afraid. You don't have tickets? Col, my boy.'

'Leave it be.'

'They've got plenty besides Sandow. Singers, story-tellers. Louisa and Floss would love it. Perhaps there are still some tickets left.'

'Louisa is in no state to go,' he said, his lie almost colliding with the truth.

'Right, the baby. Any day I suppose. She looked fit to burst when last I saw her.'

He dug his hand into the sand and squeezed.

'Don't be nervous, Col. You'll be a halfway decent father.' He handed him the near-empty bottle and stood. 'I'm off home. Off to get cleaned up and take Milly to the show like a good husband. A good husband.' He shook his head and patted Kemp on the shoulder. 'Hope to see you there.'

Another wave petered out on the beach and pulled back. The landward arrows flickered. Kemp had not been home since the morning, since Flossie had woken him and sent him to run errands. He'd purchased the supplies she had requested from Mr Fricker and Sam Tong, the greengrocer, but he paid the Chase boy to deliver them. The muscles of his stomach clenched whenever he thought about crossing the threshold. He had decisions to make, so many decisions—funeral arrangements, someone to cover for him at Donaldson's, names for the twins if they could survive on a diet of cow's milk and Flossie's attention—but out in the world he continued to preserve his awful secret.

He looked at the bruised sky, stood and walked up the violet dunes. As he emerged on Regent Street, he saw movement in the window above Bannerman's workshop. He looked down the road: a spoil of dust had been hoofed up in the distance, perhaps at the corner of Victoria Street. Yes, he could see carriages coming from the wharf's direction and turning up Victoria to reach the Theatre Royal. The show would soon be starting. He continued on, down the slight slope. He passed the hushed Criterion, crossed a vacant Albert Street and stood in front of the lawn of the Methodist Church. Unseen silvereyes sang *tweeooh tweeooh* in the black-leafed camellia. A fat thrush toddled a few steps across the sad lawn, stopped and cocked its head before skitting into the bushes.

The Carpenter's window was next. If he had any gratitude for the show, it was that it had cleared the crowd from the front of Hercus & Barling so he could observe the window in solitude. The electric lights that usually ran until nine had been switched off, which meant that he had to press his head to the glass to see the details of the display. At the centre stood the plaster statue of Eugen Sandow, a white spectre clutching one fist close to his forehead and the other down by his hip at the end of a straightened arm. His curly hair and undulating torso were stippled with daylight. Kemp looked at the statue's splayed feet, no doubt a pose struck by Sandow to show off the development of his thighs and calves, and wondered about the weight of the small, square pedestal that managed to keep the likeness from falling over.

Sandow was ringed by seven admirers, all female. Each mannequin was familiar to him: the three blonde nymphs, the dignified dame with the operatic build, the pig-tailed schoolgirl on the cusp of adulthood, the black-haired evil stepmother from a fairy story and the serene lady in the red moirette, though, like the other figures, most of her outfit had been changed to show off the season's latest fashions. The Carpenter's mannequins did not have articulated limbs—his creations were fixed in the one pose as Sandow was—but they were arranged carefully to disguise their odd gestures and give the impression of a crowd clustering around the town's new arrival. To Kemp they were admiring a mere statue rather than a man. It was more than just the difference in materials, the full palette The Carpenter employed against the scuffed white of the Sandow replica. The breath of life granted to his figures had been withheld from the plaster Sandow. He considered the crescent of real onlookers that had occupied the footpath since the display was unveiled and saw how The Carpenter's figures would close this circle. Had he intended this? Was he suggesting that for every person looking through the window there was a better dressed doppelgänger on the other side?

He looked again at Sandow and even in the dimness he could perceive rough edges where he would have made them smooth, blank patches where small but important details—the grain of the moustache, the slight protrusion of a nail beyond the toe, the point at which the earlobe meets the flesh of the face—had been glossed over. He had learnt the importance of such things in the course of his mannequin making, though his hands often muffed these master strokes.

It was clear that this Sandow was a second pressing. A plaster version of a bronze statue from a cast of a showman made to hold the same pose beyond the limits of boredom and pain: a copy of a copy of a charade.

Even now, he thought, I am losing Louisa. Her image is becoming fixed in my head. Those thousand memories, that ever-changing face. All is being sanded down to one, and that will be sanded further until there is no life left.

His forehead pressed against the glass of The Carpenter's window, Colton Kemp felt his desire to see the real Sandow, the living Sandow, grow.

After a long while he left the window and came to Victoria Street, congested with hitched horses, donkeys, drays, buggies and bicycles, but almost devoid of people. On the near corner a boy tossed a silver coin over and over. Even the town's few coach drivers must have had tickets to the show. As he approached the Theatre Royal he saw the 'Sold Out' banner plastered across the placard outside the box office window. The office itself appeared deserted at first, but he made out the rounded form of Burt Tompkins holding his ear to the wall that backed onto the auditorium. Kemp rapped the glass with his knuckles, giving the old man a start that caused him to drop the small metal cylinder he'd been using to listen to the entertainment.

Once Tompkins had regathered himself he said, 'Sorry Col, the house is full.'

'Do us a favour, Burt. Can't I stand up the back?'

'Back's already full of folks standing. The old girl wasn't built to fit the whole town.'

'There must be room for one more.'

'If you had a ticket, perhaps.'

'You know I don't have a ticket, Burt.'

'I'm sorry, Col.'

'Jesus, Burt.'

Tompkins removed his round spectacles and rubbed the lenses with his checked handkerchief.

'I meant to get a ticket,' Kemp said, 'but with Lou—,' the name caught in his throat but he pushed it out with a second effort, 'with Louisa expecting . . .'

Tompkins returned his specs to the bridge of his nose and leant in to the pane of glass that separated them. 'I didn't tell you, but you might be able to get in by the stage door around back. Plenty of hubbub back there, but if you look as if you belong . . .'

'Thanks, Burt.'

'Give my love to Louisa.'

Kemp placed his palm on the glass and nodded.

The rear of the theatre on Market Street was indeed a hive of activity. The backstage area must not have been large enough to house Rickards' entire company and the overflow went about their business in the open air under the glow of several large lanterns. A small-waisted woman with a powdered face sang scales, holding the hem of her blue dress and her many petticoats up from the reach of the dust and dirt. A man in a black tuxedo handed an accordion to a boy standing inside a covered wagon, before inspecting the teeth of two well-fed ponies with jewel-encrusted bridles.

Kemp looked around for an excuse to enter the theatre. Wooden crates were scattered here and there, stalks of hay sprouting from the openings. He placed the lid back on one of these crates, lifted it and made for the stage door.

'Who's that for, then?'

Kemp turned and saw an old man standing near the ponies, a body brush in one hand and his eyebrows raised.

'Fresh chains for Mr Sandow,' he replied.

'Well then,' the man said, '*schnell, schnell.*'

Kemp put the empty crate down inside the corridor and took the stairs two at a time, turning right, away from the sound of a contralto on stage, who was singing what sounded like 'Love's Old Sweet Song', and merged into a crowd of men in the wings. The contralto was joined by the woman in the blue dress he had seen warming up outside. They performed a duet of 'Life's Dream is O'er' which, though sung in perfect harmony, made him grit his teeth. He pressed his back to the wall of the auditorium and tried not to listen to the lyrics. Standing on his toes he could see the twenty-piece orchestra crammed into the theatre's tiny pit and believed he could hear the discomfort in their performance. He scanned the audience, every face familiar, until he spotted Milly Bannerman seated at the end of the very last row of the stalls. Jolly was standing immediately behind, his hands clamped on his wife's shoulders, his eyes closed, head swaying with the music.

The master of ceremonies came forth and shook the hands of both singers. 'Miss Nita Leete and Miss Ray Jones!' he said and clapped theatrically as they skipped off the stage like May queens. The man, dressed in a crimson topcoat, now gestured for the audience to quieten down. Kemp wondered if this was Harry Rickards himself or just another paid performer. It was the kind of question he would lean across and whisper to Louisa. She would know no more than him, but she would find some detail— the frayed hem of the man's coat, the knot of his bootlace—to support a theory either way.

'The penultimate act this evening,' the master of ceremonies was saying, 'is another taste of fine culture. The finest theatre from Mother England's finest poet. A superb vignette from The Bard's great pastoral play, *The Winter's Tale*. A story for the fireside on a chilly January eve—January in the Northern Hemisphere, of course. A tale of jealousy, rage, loss, deception, but also, as we shall witness, magic, transformation and reunion. The perfect apéritif before another statue comes to life.' He raised his hand to his lips. 'But I have said too much. Ladies, gentlemen, I give to you the Gates Family Players and the concluding scene of *The Winter's Tale*.'

The crowd clapped politely as the master of ceremonies backed away from the front of the stage and passed a shuffling figure who, despite being robed in white cloth and sporting a long grey beard, clearly counterfeit, could not have been past twenty years of age. There were a few hoots of recognition from the crowd and someone shouted, 'Atta boy, Jesse!', though this meant nothing to Kemp.

In one hand this figure carried a large hourglass hung from a chain and in the other a book.

Young Father Time stopped at the centre of the stage and began to read off a sheet of paper stuck to the cover of the book:

'I, that please some, try all, both joy and terror
Of good and bad, that makes and unfolds error,
Now take upon me, in the name of Time,
To use my wings. Impute it not a crime
To me or my swift passage, that I slide
O'er sixteen years and leave the growth untried
Of that wide gap, since it is in my power
To o'erthrow law and in one self-born hour
O'erwhelm custom. Your patience this allowing,
I turn my glass —'

He paused to upend the hourglass.

'and give my scene such growing
As you had slept between: Leontes leaving,
The effects of his fond jealousies so grieving
That he shuts up himself. Yea, of this allow,
If ever you have spent time worse ere now;
If never, yet that Time himself doth say
He wishes earnestly you never may.'

With this, the figure shuffled back to the wings and two stage hands rolled out a backdrop painted to resemble the nave of a chapel, with real velvet curtains hung across a niche. Four men and two women, one quite old, the other rather beautiful, took the stage in a jumble of togas, tunics, capes, stockings, sandals and elfin shoes. The largest of the men in the finest of the garments also wore a crown of some heavy metal to which only the last flakes of gilt still clung.

'O grave and good Paulina,' the king began, 'the great comfort that I have had of thee!'

He took the older woman's hand and she spoke to him reverently as they strolled along the stage, the other actors in tow. In front of the curtained niche, the king stopped and spoke solemnly:

'Your gallery have we pass'd through, not without much

content in many singularities; but we saw not that which my daughter came to look upon, the statue of her mother.'

The actress playing Paulina began to describe the statue of the queen, the way the likeness exceeded anything the 'hand of man hath done', before pulling back the curtain. The actors gasped as a woman completely in white, posing on a short pedestal, was revealed. The audience murmured. Perhaps they saw an echo of Sandow's statue—the white powdered face, one hand held up to support a veil of white lace, the other down by her hip.

The actors marvelled at the supposed statue. Kemp thought the use of a veil unwise as the light material showed every movement. He considered the possibility of constructing a new window display based on this scene. He scanned the audience for The Carpenter, who might not be able to deliver such a scene as quickly as him, but would most certainly trump his queen (and that of the poor actress on the pedestal). Yes, there he was, leaning forward in his seat, craning his neck, thinking the very same thoughts.

The king, Leontes, scrutinised the queen's face.

'But yet, Paulina,' he said, 'Hermione was not so much wrinkled, nothing so aged as this seems.'

'So much the more our carver's excellence,' Paulina responded, 'which lets go by some sixteen years and makes her as she lived now.'

Kemp watched Hermione blinking and wondered if it was possible to train the eyelids to behave.

Leontes continued to admire the statue, oblivious to its blinking. The younger actress, clearly the king's daughter both in life and in the play, knelt at the foot of the statue. 'Dear queen, that ended when I but began, give me that hand of yours to kiss.'

Kemp felt behind him for the wall and was glad of its support.

Would a statue of Louisa be a fitting tribute or another painful failure?

When his focus returned to the play, Leontes was saying to another man, 'See, my lord, would you not deem it breathed? And that those veins did verily bear blood?'

Paulina made to draw the curtain on the statue, but Leontes stopped her.

'I am sorry, sir,' Paulina said, 'I have thus far stirr'd you: but I could afflict you farther.'

'Do, Paulina,' Leontes said, 'for this affliction has a taste as sweet as any cordial comfort. Still, methinks, there is an air comes from her: what fine chisel could ever yet cut breath?'

Kemp looked at The Carpenter again, squeezed into the stalls, straining to see over the heads of those in front of him. It seemed an unlikely place for a recluse. But if Begg was to be believed, he'd been on hand to secure Sandow's statue when it arrived at the train station the day before.

'If you can behold it,' Paulina was now saying, 'I'll make the statue move indeed, descend and take you by the hand; but then you'll think—which I protest against—I am assisted by wicked powers.'

Leontes begged her to continue and Paulina, facing the audience directly, said, 'It is required you do awake your faith.'

Stirring music began from the orchestra pit as Paulina urged the statue to come to life. With evident relief the actress playing Hermione began to stir. She reached out for the king's hand and stepped down from her pedestal.

'O, she's warm!' proclaimed Leontes. 'If this be magic, let it be an art lawful as eating.'

The couple embraced and after one last speech from the king the players all left the stage, returning to receive their applause and take their bow.

The master of ceremonies returned, rubbing his hands together greedily.

'And now, fine people of Maru-maru,' he said, pronouncing the town's name as if it were two separate words, 'the time has come for the pinnacle of the performance, the strength of the show. But first I must beg your patience as the stage is prepared for the many feats the Great Sandow will perform.'

The same two stage hands who had rolled *The Winter's Tale*'s background onstage came and rolled it off, though this time they were garbed in white togas and Roman sandals. Joined by four more men similarly attired—two of whom had been in the previous vignette—they began placing wooden crates on the stage in a deliberate fashion. When the boxes were all arranged, the mock Romans removed items with brief flourishes—dumb-bells, barbells, chains, large bands of elastic, lengths of wood—the audience gasping with each revelation. The two strongest-looking men, possibly disciples of Sandow, each carried a large basket on stage and held them still as a third man fixed a steel rod between them. When everything had been arranged the men left and the curtain was lowered.

Kemp took this moment, while the rest of the crowd mur-mured with excitement, to consider again the challenge of a *Winter's Tale* window display: the spirals of artifice of having a wooden mannequin standing in for an actress pretending to be a marble statue (possibly enchanted) of the queen. How he longed for Louisa to be his sounding board, his collaborator. To sketch the scene he saw in his head so that he might see the flaws in the arrangement of the figures. But it would flounder, he realised, without the perfect Hermione. Such a mannequin was beyond his capabilities. He looked at his bandaged forefinger, which began to throb on cue.

The curtain began to rise and the theatre fell silent. At first only the wooden crates at the foot of the stage were visible, then a revolving platform—he tried in vain to see how it might be powered—and inch by inch a man wearing only a leopard skin loincloth was revealed against a purple backdrop.

Though Kemp had seen—had *scrutinised*—the plaster statue in the window of Hercus & Barling, he had still expected the real Sandow to be more imposing. What spun slowly before the people of Marumaru was a fair-headed, clean-limbed man of medium height somewhere in his mid-thirties. The orchestra began to play a swift, upbeat tune. Sandow's clear skin glowed pink under the stage lights. The pose he held—his hands clasped behind his head, his feet at right angles with one heel lifted slightly, his torso in the *contrapposto* of classical sculpture—showed the development and balance of his muscles, the perfect symmetry of his form. Most striking to Kemp was the man's back. It was as if it had been moulded by the hands of a loving god, each muscle distinct and purposeful. It was a tactile thing, begging to be touched. Beautiful in a way that was beyond man or woman, beyond art or life, even beyond the figures that emerged from The Carpenter's gouges.

After two or three slow revolutions of the pedestal, Sandow lowered his arms, making fists of his hands, dropped his head almost until his chin touched his chest and rearranged his pose, making new abdominal muscles prominent that had previously lain flat. It was as if serpents were pulsing beneath the man's skin and he had managed to charm them into performing in unison. Despite the stillness of each pose, he seemed on the edge of being burst open should the charm wear off.

Sandow began to alter his poses more quickly, working up to the pace of the orchestra's accompaniment and giving Kemp less than half a turn to absorb each new perfection before it was erased by another.

In the grief, confusion and anger of the last two days, Colton Kemp had shrunk from the world's many stimulations, had sought and failed to drown his sadness and release his tension, had doubted the existence of happiness elsewhere and in the future, had seen himself confronted with a greyer life untouched by beauty—and yet here he was, in a theatre crowded with almost everyone he knew, excited and overstimulated by this vision of a man, spinning and spinning like a celestial body.

The pedestal came to a stop. Sandow performed a backward somersault from standing, folded his arms and stood perfectly still, his face in profile. The crowd, who had been applauding and exclaiming for the duration of the brief exhibition, responded with a hero's ovation.

'Thank you,' he said and stepped down from the pedestal.

'Thank you. Please, that is quite enough applause.' His voice was deep and guttural.

'I wish to briefly talk to you about how I have attained my strength, the system I am sure many of you are familiar with, before I perform some demonstrations.' He gestured to the props on the stage. 'I was not a healthy child. My parents were not endowed with extraordinary strength. All the strength I possess I owe to my system.'

The boy, Jesse, who had been Father Time, returned to the stage stripped to the waist like Sandow, though he wore a thick leather belt and white tights rather than the master's Herculean loincloth. With Jesse as his model, Sandow—part preacher of the gospel of physical culture, part salesman for his own wares—proceeded to demonstrate how to perform exercises with his Spring-Grip Dumb-bell and his elastic 'developer'. A lot of attention was paid to the development of the lungs and chest—though he pronounced it *schest*, in perhaps the clearest signal of his origins—and at one point demonstrated how he could expand his chest from an already impressive forty-seven inches to a full sixty-one.

He repeated often the fact that a person of any age or gender could undertake these exercises and obtain benefit from them. 'As I travel about the colonies,' Sandow said, resting a hand on Jesse's shoulder, 'I like to hold special talks with physicians and other interested parties of a town. These talks are discussions in the true sense and I much prefer this back and forth to a mere address. Unfortunately, as I will be leaving town early in the morning, I will not have the opportunity to hold such a congress here. However, I will take questions from the floor this evening.' He held up his hand quickly. 'But first, let me conclude the traditional portion of the show with a few feats of strength!'

With one hand he seized Jesse by the belt and lifted him over his head.

The theatre erupted in a pandemonium of applause.

The assistants in togas returned to the stage and the orchestra resumed. Sandow began by lifting a weight he stated was one hundred and thirty pounds, though it looked like a toy as he raised it above his head with one hand. He brought it down and handed it carefully to an assistant, who struggled to return it to its wooden rack. Sandow then lifted a barbell from the floor to an arm's length above his head in a single jerk. 'Two hundred and forty-two pounds,' he said, while still supporting the weight. He then lifted a larger barbell to his shoulder, announced, 'Three hundred pounds,' and proceeded to fully extend his arm above his head.

The strongman began to stalk around the stage, lifting barrels and bursting chains, quickly and quietly. Even as the acts became more and more ludicrous, he maintained an air of grace.

He lay on his side and lifted one of his assistants by the ankle into the air.

Assistants brought forward two trestles. Sandow rested his neck on one, his heels on the other, and began lifting barbells with each hand while four of his assistants stood on his torso.

He lifted the makeshift barbell constructed from the two large baskets and the metal rod, then asked two assistants to stand inside the baskets and lifted the rig with similar ease.

He tore a pack of playing cards in half with his fingers. Then he tore two packs at once, then four, one on top of the other, ripping them as cleanly as if they had been cut with a knife. An assistant fastened the torn packets with ribbons and threw them into all parts of the theatre to be examined and retained as mementoes.

'And now for a feat often referred to as "The Roman Column",' Sandow announced with no sign he was short of breath. He suspended himself upside down, his knees hooked over a horizontal bar protruding from an imitation marble column, then raised himself up in a sort of hanging sit-up. He repeated the feat with a barbell in each hand and again with assistants swinging on the end of the barbells.

Sandow righted himself and the column was removed from the stage. He announced, a little brusquely, 'And now for "The Tomb of Hercules",' and reclined back until his hands were on the ground, his body arched upward, pelvis pointing at the vaulted ceiling. The six assistants carried out a large wooden platform and placed it on top of the strongman. It was so large that one end remained on the ground, forming a sort of ramp, though Sandow's arms and legs did not appear fazed by the weight.

Jesse then led out the two ponies by their jewelled bridles and walked them carefully up the ramp of the platform until it lifted from the ground and the platform was horizontal. The six assistants then retrieved all the weights that had been used during the show and handed them to Jesse, who arranged them carefully, maintaining the equilibrium of the platform. Then, one by one, he clasped the hands of the men in togas and lifted them onto the platform.

Kemp almost forgot that beneath the seven men, two ponies, more than a thousand pounds of weights and the heavy platform itself, was Sandow, hands and feet planted on the stage as if embedded in the firmest of foundations.

As the people of Marumaru cheered, the assistants dismounted with care, removing the weights and lowering the platform so that the ponies could walk down. Once the men in togas had removed the platform, Sandow pushed himself upright with what strength remained in his arms and dusted himself off. He gave a cursory bow and left the stage.

Two minutes later he returned, dressed in a three-piece suit that Kemp would wager had come from Savile Row. He looked almost unremarkable and the audience greeted him with a trickle of polite applause.

'Thank you very much,' Sandow said. 'We have a few minutes remaining if you wish to ask me any questions about my system, or the benefits of physical culture more generally.'

A scatter of hands rose into the hair. 'Yes, madam?' He pointed at Mrs Harry Wisdom in the second row.

'Mr Sandow, what is your view on prohibition?'

'It is my belief, madam, that if a healthy love of physical culture was spread among the young there would be no need of prohibition. Men who study physical culture take care of their bodies and when they have a drink or two have the willpower to say, "No, old man, I have had enough. This stuff does not do me any good if I take more."'

Big Jim Raymond stood without invitation and asked in his booming, mayoral voice, 'What about lunatics? Do you think they would benefit by physical training?'

'Undoubtedly,' Sandow replied. 'They have adopted my system at Coney Island and no fewer than eighty persons have been sent out of the asylum thoroughly cured. It is the body that feeds the brain, the latter consuming twenty-five per cent of the blood in the system. Among businessmen and politicians very often it consumes as much as sixty per cent. It stands to reason, therefore, that if you do not keep the machinery for manufacturing food for the brain in good order something must burst. Many diseases can be cured by physical training of the body, for a healthy state of the mind will not allow the bacillus to live in the body.'

The crowd mumbled in agreement.

'And you, sir, standing toward the back?'

Jolly Bannerman straightened the lapels of his ill-fitting suit. 'Have you received many challenges during your tour, Mr Sandow?' he asked, grinning.

'Oh, a great many,' Sandow said, 'and always from men who have nothing to lose and everything to gain from the advertisement they would get in a public competition with myself. But to accept challenges from every man I meet is not my object in life.' Jolly's face sank. 'I am endeavouring to make other men stronger than I am myself. That is my gospel and I think I have preached it well enough to you this evening. You, sir,' Sandow indicated to a man seated four rows from the front. Kemp recognised him as Mr Fricker, the pharmacist, as he stood to ask his question.

'Have you devoted any time to developing some of the minor organs, such as moving the ears?'

The town chuckled as one.

'I must admit that I have not attained this accomplishment,' Sandow replied. 'Indeed, I do not see its value, unless one wishes to become a professional listener.' This retort was met with widespread laughter, applause and a few ringing bravos.

'But surely,' Kemp shouted, pushing to the front of the men standing in the wings, 'the actress in your company who plays a statue could benefit from learning not to blink?'

Sandow fingered his moustache, grinning as he searched for where the voice had come from. 'Far be it from me to comment on other performers,' he said, looking vaguely in Kemp's direction, 'particularly those more artful than me, a simple strongman.'

'But could the eyelids be trained?' Kemp persisted.

'I do not see why not,' Sandow said, finally eyeing Kemp, who felt as if an icicle had been planted in his chest.

Sandow clapped his hands together. 'What an interesting array of questions. I thank you for your kindness and hospitality and wish you all the best for the New Year.'

The strongman made his way off the stage. The curtains dropped and the townsfolk collected their purses and canes from the floor but Colton Kemp was already out the door and running.

The grey warbler with the long-tailed cuckoo.

Part two

A Mannequin's Tale

'. . . all man's misery stems from a single cause,
his inability to remain quietly in one room.'

26 December 1918

Father looms large in the lives of us all, but my biggest gratitude belongs to Mother for teaching me to read and write. She endeavoured to teach Eugen as well, but he did not see the need. 'Whatever Avis learns, I learn,' he said, back when we were very young and could not imagine a life apart. My brother's diversion, even then, was music. And so it was that I learnt to read and write (for both of us) to the sound of Chopin, Schubert and Sullivan.

It is hard to imagine the world without reading, without books and the stimulating conversations Mother and I have about them. She directs all my reading and acquires from town those books we do not already own. Though there is often a lag of many years between her reading of a tale and mine, she is always quick to recall its details. She says this is thanks in part to keeping a diary. In it she writes of her reading and, she says, whatever else is coursing through her head.

She speaks of her diary often (she has said more than once that it is the only thing that keeps her sane), though I have never seen it. I suspect there are secrets she wishes to keep from Father, though I cannot imagine what they might be.

I am not sure why I did not think of starting my own diary until yesterday. (My Christmas gift from Mother was this very notebook . . . It seems a shame to mar these crisp pages with my poor penmanship.) Unlike Mother, I am not concerned about my sanity. What I fear is forgetting. There is much to learn in life and there is no time to waste relearning. Now that Eugen and I are almost ready for the window (it is only a matter of days!) I am possessed by the urge to record everything for posterity. Life has been leading up to this moment. Life will never be the same . . .

Goodness. I have been thinking about setting pen to paper all day, but now that I am done with all exercise routines and household duties I am at a loss to know what to write here next. My whole life has passed so far unrecorded and it now feels somehow irretrievable.

I mustn't panic.

I suspect writing a diary takes practice. I shall return tomorrow bursting with things to say and the power to say them. For now I hope I have not made too many errors. Perhaps I will give it to Mother to check.

27 December

Mother has been most helpful. She says that I should not worry too much about the past. She promises there is much to write about in any given day. Should something from the past be relevant to the day's events then it is easily incorporated.

She also said it was unusual to give one's diary to another to read. I long for a day when I might have an exciting life that contains events I might wish to conceal from even my closest family, but until that time I shall continue to let her proof my entries. It would seem a shame for a later generation to uncover this diary and conclude that I was uncouth and had no desire to better myself.

So let us focus on the events of this day, which was a Friday.

Eugen and I rose at six a.m. and performed our morning routines, which are identical, unlike afternoon exercises, which differ according to our genders.

My brother frequently tells me girls have it easy. I do not agree. Granted, we are not expected to attain the same brute strength, but I must work equally as hard. The fruits of my regime, however, are not as easy to show as flexing a biceps. While Eugen can compare his development favourably with Father, who has never gone in for exercise and eats sparingly, I can only compare myself with Mother, who is much younger than Father and is quite beautiful without seeming to work at it. Not that Father would ever acknowledge this. His focus is solely on Eugen and me and preparing us for the window. He is vigilant in monitoring our progress. With Eugen it is a push for greater growth, greater change. With me it is a matter of not progressing too far and losing the feminine edge. Much can go awry with the female body. For example (ah yes, I see how this might be done): the time shortly after my eleventh birthday when my golden locks began to darken to a troubling dun. To correct this, Father had me wash my hair in lemon juice and instituted a regime of sun exposure in the summer months. I had to be careful, however, to ensure only minimal skin exposure as this would cause blemishes and a degeneration of skin tone. (Father has a piece of a seashell, sanded down to a small disc, that he places against the flesh of my neck and forearm to ensure I maintain the perfect complexion.) He rigged up a splendid contraption for the purpose of lightening my hair: I lie on a bench fitted in the workshop with only the top of my head and my hair protruding through a hole in the wall and into daylight. I must wear a special calico visor (it is in many ways a skirt for the forehead) to protect the upper reaches of my face. Preparing for the window is a great balancing act, I tell you. This method was successful in lightening my hair again, if it never quite returned to the shimmering gold I remember.

Eugen, on the other hand, is free to roam around the property in his breeches or with no clothes at all, tending the vegetables, maintaining the high macrocarpa and manuka hedges that enclose our property, taunting Juniper, our nanny goat—as his skin is less susceptible to the sun's degrading rays.

Not that I am frail or idle. I assume many tasks inside the house and out, but must don a large bonnet when out of doors and cope with the encumbrance. Today, following morning routine, I did just this while picking peas and broad beans for our lunch. It was a pleasant summer's day and I could feel the warmth of the sun through the protective layer of my blouse and white cotton gloves.

We grow all our own vegetables and have our own cow. Only our meat comes from town. Mother and I take pride in the variety of meals we prepare for the table. Of course, as I am still a few days shy of sixteen I have not yet ventured there. I am counting the days, I assure you. Mother is doing her best to dampen my expectations, but I fear it is a difficult task.

It is hard to believe that if everything goes well I will be engaged to marry at the end of next month.

Eugen shares my anticipation for the window, but he is restless rather than eager. He truly has the fidgets, which is perhaps the worst affliction one could hope for when confronted with the window. We know so much hinges on this short period, not least Father's happiness (and doesn't everything hinge upon this?), but I fear Eugen's unremitting pride might see his feet swiftly taken from under him.

But just try to tell him this and prepare to be beaten back.

He is a special creature and I love him dearly.

28 December

Three more nights to pass until the window. I am tempted to lay down my pen and go to bed (it has just gone seven in the evening) to hasten our coming out, that moment when I can see and be seen. The first thing I will do once my fate has been arranged and I can step down from the window is run to the sea. Mother says our house is quite close to it and sometimes she can smell it, but to me it is a wonder from a storybook.

But I mustn't get ahead of myself. I know I will regret not writing down the happenings of this day if I do not do so now.

Firstly, I should add that last night Eugen spied me scribbling in this diary when he grew tired of the piano.

'What are you writing?' he asked with a single lifted eyebrow.

I stared at him directly. 'A diary.'

He closed the lid over the piano keys.

'Would you like to take a look?' I asked. I still hope that one day he will be enticed to learn to read so that I might converse with him about *Treasure Island* and *Pamela* and *Oliver Twist* as I do with Mother.

'Read it to me,' he said. He gestured with his head at the clock, meaning that Father would not be home for several hours, it being a Friday night.

After listening to my entry for that day Eugen remained silent.

'Mother says it is not common practice to share a diary,' I said, 'but if you wish I will read you my entry every night.'

He shook his head. 'Why do I need to hear about my own life?'

So it seems this diary will not be subject to masculine eyes or ears. (Father has never approved of my reading—'fanciful distractions' he calls my books—and takes little interest in the goings on inside the heads of others.)

All the better.

Today we rose at six as usual and performed morning routine. Until recently I could not foresee a time when I would ever forget a single aspect of this, having carried it out every morning since I was the smallest child. However, this afternoon, while laid out on the bench in the workshop, my hair bleaching in the sun, I finished a book entitled *Twice Upon a Double-Cross*, in which a man loses his memory after a blow to the head. Mother suggested it to me after reading of my great fear of forgetting. For much of the book I was cast into deep agony as the man, Roland Crumb, stumbled through his unfamiliar life. However, with the help of his wife, Roland was able to slowly recover his memory and avoid falling into the same trap set by his covetous business partner, Webster Wattle. Father, Mother and Eugen might be able to stand in for the character of the helpful spouse (and soon enough I may have one of those!), but I also see the value of committing these details to paper should I ever suffer from amnesia (so long as I do not forget how to read!).

I will also do my best to avoid any blows to the head.

Morning routine: rise at six, then bathe in the large basin that extends from the washhouse. This is the worst part during the colder months, but it is quite pleasant at the moment. The air is crisp and still. Several pairs of grey warblers have constructed their pear-shaped nests in the manuka thicket nearest the house and at this time of morning I can see the nests wobble, though the birds dart around so swiftly I can never catch a decent sight of them.

When Eugen and I are both cleansed, our muscles relaxed and pores open, we begin to work through the gentle dumb-bell and developer exercises. These are meant to awaken the muscles rather than provoke them and to reacquaint our brain, that most crucial muscle, with every part of the body so that we may determine any weakness or imbalance that exists. These may then be worked upon in the course of the day and corrected over time.

Having warmed up completely, Eugen and I have a little breakfast (porridge in winter, bread and butter in summer) before taking to our pedestals in Father's workshop.

Two years ago Father rigged up electric lights in the workshop to prepare us for the reality of the window. We still rely on lamps in the house and only pose under the electric lights two times a week. We would do so more often but Father says the generator is costly to run and he does not like the noise.

Father used to observe us throughout morning routine but these days he comes and goes. There are always things in town that he must attend to, though I am never privy to them.

When it is time for me to help with the lunch we step down.

Afternoon routine is less rigid and Eugen and I go about our tasks separately. These last few weeks Eugen has spent every minute of daylight working on his muscles and will only touch the piano keys after supper. I am as excited about the window but my time is often better spent posing in costume or with my nose in a book.

As the thirty-first approaches, I have been thinking more and more about the customs observed in countries depicted in my novels and our own unique customs here in New Zealand. It is hard to imagine 'school life' as described in books from the Northern Hemisphere. Perhaps it is easier on the parents in these countries. Caring for Eugen and me, instructing us, preparing us for adulthood and marriage, has been a time-consuming task for Father and Mother. But there must be a great variety in the quality of teachers in these schools, many of them beastly places, and I cannot say I would like my child exposed to other children before his or her personality is fully and rightly formed. I also wonder what sort of bond exists when a parent is not fully responsible for their child. Our antipodean custom might seem quaint to visitors from Europe or North America, but I truly believe, as Father does, that it is the best situation. Parents can freely appraise the prospective partners for their own offspring. By the age of sixteen a person's outward appearance should indicate their physical health and suitability for procreation. The manner of presentation, 'the window' in which the new adult must remain perfectly still, is a test of fortitude, grace, dedication and mental strength, which are important in determining the worth of a marriage partner.

I am well aware that twins are unusual and Father reminds us often that we will create a storm in Marumaru. Great crowds will gather at our window, scrutinising us for flaws and family resemblance. Some, Father says, are likely to watch for hours waiting for a slip-up. If that should happen, our prospects would be severely damaged.

Though Father has never read to us, he used to tell us bedtime stories about boys who sneezed in the window and never got a bride, or the girl who smiled when a man blew a raspberry on the window pane, sentencing her to a solitary life without laughter.

The stir we will cause as twins in the window will bring added scrutiny, but it is also a blessing. We will be together in the window, Eugen and I. This not only provides a great deal of comfort, but it increases the variety of poses and stories we can present with our tableaux.

The window would be a frightening proposition without Eugen there beside me. I try not to think too much about what will happen once our matches have been settled.

29 December

Two nights until the window.

One thing I failed to mention yesterday regarding morning routine: every so often Father will teach us a new tableau to add to our repertoire. He moulds us, planting our feet in the correct spots, twisting our torsos, raising or lowering our chins. He will often stand there with his hand on my chest until he cannot detect my breathing. (As he is fond of saying, 'If you can fool the hand you can fool the eye.') He also instructs us on the characters of the tableau, the inner feelings we must transmit through our outward appearances. Our characters are not always happy siblings or young lovers. This morning Father taught us one of these more vexed tableaux. It will certainly be the last we learn before the window.

In the new tableau I am a respectable young socialite who has previously rejected Eugen because of his poor prospects, only for us to be reunited once he has made his fortune. Some of the story-telling can be conveyed by wardrobe (fine clothes in the newest fashion for Eugen, respectable gown for me) but for morning routine we pose unencumbered. As Father says, if a bare pose is convincing it can be enhanced by clothes, but nothing can save an unconvincing pose.

The first day of a new pose is always the hardest. It is taxing, both mentally and physically, but after so many years of morning and afternoon routines, we both look forward to the challenge.

It is always humbling (for me at least) to move from a perfected pose to a new one and learn that the stillness you had achieved so completely is not easily transferred. You must interrogate where each body part is positioned, which muscles are required to hold everything in place and where the cheats are: those parts of the body that are idle or obscured in the pose and thus require less attention. With time and much effort, and under Father's watchful eye, Eugen and I have learnt to subtly rearrange our weight to draw on the untapped strength of these cheats without making any perceptible movements.

In the moments when I could disengage my mind this morning I pondered whether this would be the first tableau we use for the window, or if it was too great a risk to attempt it with only three days' practice. I thought about the gown I might wear, something plush and feminine like the orange velvet dress Father brought home one night in October.

One positive aspect of the new tableau is that Eugen and I are facing each other. Sometimes, I am turned away (such as when I am the young maiden refusing a diamond ring, though my face must express that my heart will soon melt and I will turn around and accept) or Eugen's back is to me (when we are farm hand and farmer's daughter caught in a sunshower and running for the shelter of the barn). I must fix my gaze for the duration of the tableau and I much prefer to look upon Eugen's face than his shoulder or a knotted rafter. Eugen is not much of a conversationalist in the traditional sense, but I treasure our silent exchanges when posing.

This morning as I looked into Eugen's eyes his face contorted into a cold and satisfied expression. I was reminded of the scene where Edmond Dantès reappears before Mercédès, although he is now the Count of Monte Cristo and she the Countess de Morcerf. As I recalled the scene in greater detail, Eugen's face began to resemble the vendetta-driven count's all the more. If I were to walk up to him now as he plays 'Fantasia in F minor' (I can see the heading on the sheet music from here) and ask him about the scene he constructed around this morning's tableau, I am certain it will match that of Dumas' novel, though Eugen will not be able to give any of the correct names.

30 December

Father has had one of his dark turns. Of all the days. We are to appear in the window tomorrow. Tomorrow.

Eugen and I bathed and limbered up this morning as usual, unaware of Father's condition. Mother did not wish to say anything over breakfast but it was clear on her face. (When you spend so long standing still and scrutinising one person's face you suddenly find yourself fluent in the language of all faces.) When he came to the table, he did not look at us and said nothing. He is a kind of ghost at such times, liable to drift away, pass through walls, leave the property, only to reappear and unleash sudden bouts of terror. This morning he left the table less than a minute after taking his seat. He'd touched nothing on his plate, of course.

I am not sure whether it was seeing Father this way, or my own nervousness about the window, but I felt quite queasy myself and couldn't finish my breakfast. I excused myself from the table and went in search of Father, but he was no longer on the property. Oh, that I could have left to pursue him.

There was nothing to do but take to our pedestals and play Dantès and Mercédès, though it was hard to strip the concern from my expression or keep the dew from the rim of my lower eyelids. The burrowing worm in my gut was no help either.

Eugen, holding his pose perfectly, tried to tell me not to worry. We were ready for the window. Father would be recovered tomorrow.

Where does his confidence come from? He has never been to town, never been in the window. Our experiences have been identical since birth and yet sometimes I feel we are two different species left in the same nest by chance. He is the cuckoo and I am the tiny warbler chick.

It is approaching eight o'clock and Father has still not returned. He has spoken about the window at length, the things we are likely to see (depending on the pose and the direction of our gaze, of course), but my head is awash with practical questions I have never considered. How are we to get to the window? What happens when the curtain is lowered once more? When will we return to the property? Will we ever return? When will we see Mother again?

Our lives are directed toward this one moment, but what next?

31 December

Oh Diary, what a lot I have to record.

It has long since passed midnight so technically it is January the first. A new year: 1919, like a pair of twins (though Eugen and I would be better represented by 1616). But I must first return to the evening of the thirtieth (when we were still 1515).

Eugen and I had been in bed for a long time but neither of us was sleeping. For all the time Eugen spends standing still, he is a restless sleeper, turning and turning, even once he has fallen fast asleep. But last night I could not hear anything, not even his shallow breathing. I was listening so intently it is no surprise I heard the scrape of the workshop door being opened. I ran outside in my nightgown and bare feet and saw Father's face, lit by the candle he held. He looked quite ill.

'Fetch your brother,' he said and entered the workshop.

I returned to our room, its darkness more profound after my brief glimpse of candlelight. 'Eugen,' I said, 'aren't you coming?'

A sigh came from his bed. A moment later I heard it creak as my brother rose.

Outside once more I could hear the gentle growl of the generator and see the electric light shining through the gaps in the workshop walls. The wide glow from the open door stretched out upon the path like a golden tongue.

Inside the workshop, Father was sitting on my pedestal. Two green canvas bags with drawstrings lay empty at his feet.

'Pack what you will need, each of you,' he said.

'How long will we be gone?' I asked.

'We are leaving in twenty minutes,' he said. 'You might like to say goodbye to Flossie.'

'Father?' I said. The dew was settling once more in my eyes.

He picked up one of the bags and tossed it to me. Eugen leant forward and picked up his own.

'Go,' Father said and raised his head. Only then did he look at me properly. 'Don't worry. We will go through everything for tomorrow when we get there.'

I ran inside and could see the glow of a candle from the drawing room. Mother was up, sitting in her armchair, looking at the volumes in her bookcase. I thought it a most beautiful pose: her face in profile, lit softly by the candle, her fine chin tilted upward, tightening the muscles of the neck, her kind hands crossed upon her lap. I wished to commit this pose to memory forever but she turned slowly and her red, swollen eyes extinguished any sense of beauty.

'Come here, child,' she said. I ran to her and threw myself at her feet, my head buried in her lap. I felt her hands upon the back of my head, stroking my hair.

'I don't want to go,' I said.

'You must,' she said. 'Think of all the work you have done.'

'But what will happen? When will I return?'

She continued stroking my hair.

'When will I see you again?'

'I will come to you if you do not come to me,' she said.

'Oh Mother.' I wrapped my arms around her waist. I could sense Eugen standing behind me, watching.

'Keep an eye out for me in the crowd,' she said. 'Both of you.'

'Come on,' Eugen said. 'You will want to pack your diary at least.'

'Will I have time to write?' I asked. I was in a panic. Things I had been told before, hundreds of times, had slipped from my mind. 'Will I have time to read?'

'Go and pack a few clothes,' she said. 'I have a book in mind for you to take.' She stood and ran her fingers slowly, lovingly, over the spines.

Eugen guided me to our bedroom. He was so calm.

'Don't you care for her?' I asked.

He shrugged. 'This is how it was always going to be. There's no point getting upset.'

I knew he was right. But it seemed to be happening so suddenly.

'What about the piano?' I asked. 'Oh Eugen, how will you survive without your music?'

'It'll be all right,' he said, touching my shoulder.

Back in the drawing room, Mother handed me a book with a faded red cover. 'I've been saving this book for you, for this very moment. Look after it, Avis.'

We embraced for a long time. I could feel Eugen just behind me. Mother reached out her hand and rubbed his cheek.

Outside, Father had a covered wagon hitched to Emily and Charlotte, Father's two horses (though the names were Mother's doing). He asked Eugen to help him lift our wooden pedestals into the wagon. Mother stood beside me, clutching my hand.

'All right,' Father said, 'in you get.'

'Good luck,' she said brightly, though I could see the strain on her face.

Eugen helped me into the wagon. There were several hay bales arranged around the sides. Father threw a blanket to Eugen. 'Both of you lie down and put this over you. You mustn't be seen.'

We did as instructed and waited.

'Right,' I heard Father say, eventually. 'We'll be off then.'

We were rocked side to side as Emily and Charlotte led us down the drive. This was to be the first time Eugen and I had ventured beyond our front gate. I expected us to pause for Father to open it, but we soon lurched to the right, meaning the gate must have been left open and we were now on the road.

'So this is the wide world,' Eugen whispered, mischievously, for we knew we mustn't talk. His hand felt for mine and found it. He gave it a squeeze.

We were jostled left and right as the wagon made its way into town. I tried counting the turns but after a short time beneath the blanket I lost all sense of direction and my head filled with other thoughts. Eventually we came to a stop. Eugen and I lay perfectly still, the blanket over our heads, waiting for Father's instructions. I felt the wagon dip as he stepped up and leant over us.

'Quickly now,' he said, pulling the blanket off in one quick tug. 'Inside.'

By the light of his candle I could see that the wagon had been backed up against a large double doorway. Father hopped down and held out his hand. 'Duck your head,' he whispered.

Eugen followed without Father's assistance.

Father led us along a dark corridor and into a large cavernous space that smelt of perfume, though different from Mother's. It was much stronger and seemed to assault me from every direction. The light of Father's candle did not reach the ceiling, but as we made our way deeper into this space, past racks and racks of clothes and hats and gloves, I decided it must be a giant wardrobe. Perhaps we would have the choice of all of these items for our costumes? The thought delighted me.

We came to what I assumed was the back of the giant wardrobe. Father felt around for a keyhole and having found it, he opened the door.

'In here,' he said.

Eugen entered first and I followed. For a moment it was pitch black until Father came in and the room was suddenly illuminated with bright electric light that made us all rub our eyes.

Father blew out his candle and laid it on a small dresser. I can accurately describe what I saw when I looked around the small room as this is where I reside at this minute. The room is narrow (Eugen has measured it with his feet and says it is fifteen by six, though I am not sure how his feet correspond with the imperial measurement) and it was quite a squeeze with the three of us inside. There was a second door to our left, which was closed. Two stretcher beds were stacked one on top of the other against the far wall, with a pile of blankets and two pillows on them. A small wooden stool stood alongside. In another corner there was a chamber pot, a wash basin and two jugs of water. Apart from the dresser by the first door, which I have already mentioned, and the single electric bulb that dangled from a brown cord in the centre of the room, that was all in the way of furnishing. The Spartan appearance was lessened only by the posters of Mr Sandow on the cream walls.

'Through there,' Eugen said, pointing at the second door, 'is that the window?'

Father nodded. He went over and unlocked it.

'This door should always remain locked when I am not here,' he said before opening the door to reveal a heavy black curtain. 'We can't turn the lights on in there now. We don't want to attract any attention. You never know who might be around, even at this hour. Eugen, come and help me with the pedestals.'

'Can I go through?' I asked.

'You can but don't touch anything.'

They left me alone and I approached the black curtain slowly. I held out my hand to part it, but I could not find an edge. I had to step forward into the curtain and slide along the wall until I found where it ended and I emerged into another space, dark and silent. I felt around behind me and lifted the curtain to let in the light from the bulb in the first room. Three walls were draped in black and the fourth was covered by a different sort of curtain lined with yellow silk. Just now, as I looked up from writing this, sitting cross-legged on my stretcher bed in the first room, I noticed a winch in the corner which must raise the curtain at the beginning of our performance.

'Pull this thing right back,' Father said as he backed through the black curtain, holding one side of my pedestal. They carried it to the far wall and placed it down. Father drew back the curtain nearest him to reveal a small storage space and they pushed the pedestal inside this recess. Eugen placed his hands on his hips and inspected the space. He shrugged and followed Father out the door to fetch the second pedestal.

'When do we go on?' I asked when they returned. 'Which tableau will we do?'

Father grunted. Once they had slotted Eugen's pedestal on top of mine, Father retrieved a heavy-looking pole with a glass capsule on top. 'Keep the light coming in,' he told me sharply and I pulled the curtain back further.

Father laid the pole down in the centre of the room, lifted a small hatch from the floor and began to connect wires that protruded from the bottom of the pole to something inside the hatch. With Eugen's help, they carefully hoisted the pole upright.

'I'll have to test it,' Father said, apparently to himself. Beside me were three switches on the wall that had been obscured by the curtain. He flicked the farthest one on for an instant and the bulb at the top of the pole lit up the room. I noticed in that brief burst of light that the floor had been painted in stripes of grey and brown.

Father ushered us back into the first room and locked the door behind him. 'Get some rest,' he said. 'The curtain will not come up until eight o'clock tomorrow night. There is plenty of time to prepare. I will visit later in the morning.'

'Food?' Eugen asked.

'There's some bread and biscuits in the top drawer. I'll bring something for your other meals.' He looked at me. 'Relax. Don't let nerves or emotions ruin this opportunity.'

'Yes Father,' I said.

'You mustn't make any noise. I am the only one with a key to either door. Don't, whatever you do, try to leave this room.'

'Oh Father,' I said and hugged him, forgetting myself.

Once he had left we lay the stretchers out and arranged the bedclothes.

When we were ready Eugen took pleasure in switching off the light bulb (Father never let us touch the switch in his workshop) and climbed into bed.

'What time is it?' I asked.

'I don't know. It was still dark outside.'

'There are no windows,' I said.

'There's one,' he said. 'The only one that matters. Concentrate on that.'

I am not sure how long we slept but we were woken by the electric light coming on. I realise now that this was the first time I had ever woken anywhere other than our bedroom, excepting the handful of times Eugen and I had been allowed to camp out under the stars, which helps to explain the terrible confusion I experienced.

When my eyes had adjusted and I had my bearings I entered the window room, where Father had parted the back curtain to reveal a painted scene of stone buildings and large glass windows.

'Get your nightgown off and wash down,' he said.

'Morning routine?' I asked.

'It is morning,' he said. 'Don't think of today as any different.'

'Can we please have a clock? It is hard to keep track of time without—'

'Yes, yes. I'll bring you a clock this afternoon.'

Back in the first room Eugen was already rinsing himself with a brand-new sponge. He handed it to me when I had undressed and I ran it over his back.

A pile of new clothes rested on top of the dresser. A cardboard box on the floor contained our dumb-bells and developers from home and a single pack of playing cards.

'The worm is back,' I told him.

'In your stomach?'

'Yes.'

'Don't be nervous. Nerves will only hinder your performance.'

Oh dear. Eugen has just asked me when I will be finished writing as he wishes to turn the light off and sleep, so I must hasten things along.

Father managed to answer all of my questions and allay my fears during this visit and his next and in the minutes before the curtain rose at eight o'clock I could not have felt more comfortable. Once we were in our costumes, Father asked me to lower my head and he slipped a necklace over my head. I looked down and saw the seashell disc he uses to check my complexion, hanging down as a pendant on a single strand of fine silk.

'You are perfect, Avis,' he said, with a trace of tenderness in his voice that made my entire being pulsate. 'No one will notice this,' he said, fingering the necklace, 'but we know it is there. It will be our secret.' Over the top of this he placed a large silver necklace with green and red gems, which seemed gaudy in comparison with Father's gift.

'I've waited a long time for this,' he said, returning to his usual solemn, almost threatening, self.

I nodded and walked through to the next room where Eugen was already waiting.

Our tableau was one we had practised many times and seemed the obvious choice: we were two young lovers out promenading on New Year's Eve. I wore a flowing dress of vibrant emerald silk voile, which Father says was very much the rage in Paris during their summer. Eugen wore a flecked tweed suit with the golden chain of a pocket watch emerging from his waistcoat. We both stood on the painted pavement (no pedestals) with our feet placed to give the impression of a moment captured mid-stroll. My hand rested in the crook of Eugen's arm and we both faced forward, looking at the yellow lining of the curtain and the imaginary street that extended from our tableau.

Oh, what a sight it was once the curtain rose. Faces were pressed to the glass, with rows and rows of people behind, stretching back to the other side of the road. Beyond: the pointed spire of what must have been a church, my first church. The sky was an orange flare fading quickly. Iron poles topped by flickering electric lights, resembling the one in our tableau, sprang up from the middle of the crowd. Oh, the clothes they wore. The variety of heights and faces, all of them agog in that first moment but each expression unique. I longed to shift my eyes and see how far the crowd stretched to my right, to turn my head completely and take in every detail of the street. I wished to close my eyes tightly and reopen them to test if that would wash away this hallucination or prove it real. But I had practised too long to falter so soon. Too much was riding on a perfect performance. A perfect season in the window.

After some minutes those further back began to push through the crowd to get a closer look. Those nearest the glass seemed unwilling to give up their positions, no doubt wishing to catch us out, but they were pushed aside by the general swell. The crowd continued to move and rearrange itself, but its overall number did not alter greatly as the hours passed, even when midnight came and the fireworks were let off from the churchyard. Eugen and I had observed these fireworks from our house on birthdays past. It was strange that being so close to the marvel reduced the spectacle rather than enhanced it. The street filled with smoke that slowly pushed up against the window, reducing everything to blurs and smudges.

The townspeople were singing 'Auld Lang Syne', a song Mother taught us, when the curtain was slowly lowered on our first performance. We continued to hold our poses until we heard the door open and Father announced, 'Bravo!'

I have not had any time to consider it more fully, but I suspect this is only the second piece of praise I have ever heard from Father's lips, the first occurring earlier in the evening. It finished off what has been a night that lived up to and exceeded all expectations.

Seeing Father so happy is heartening, but Eugen seems unmoved. I suppose, if you expect success to the degree he does, it is hard to be delighted when it arrives.

Speaking of poor Eugen, I must let him get his beauty sleep.

1 January 1919

We gave a matinee performance today, posing in the same New Year's Eve tableau as the night before from eleven in the morning until three in the afternoon. The worm still made his presence known this morning, but aside from this I felt less nervous before stepping into the window.

The crowd was less numerous today and dressed in a smaller variety of colours, but they were no less interested. I could see Father moving among these people. The men all shook his hand vigorously. The women preferred to dip their heads.

The disturbing thing about today's crowd was the number of children. Some so young that they seemed to have recently learnt to walk were allowed to wander and stumble among the adults of the town. Men lifted children on their shoulders so they might get a better view of our window. I managed to keep perfectly still and maintain my promenading countenance, but it perturbed me greatly. I feared for these children's prospects in life if they had already been spoiled for the window.

Once the curtain was lowered I asked Father about them.

'Yes,' he said, slowly, 'it is a terrible shame. They are all orphans. By necessity they have had to enter the world prematurely. If they are lucky they might wed another orphan, but they will never be a true member of society.'

'How tragic,' I said.

'It's not too late for your fortunes to diminish. Best you keep vigilant out there. Less thinking about what's beyond that pane of glass and more about what's in here,' he pressed his finger into my chest, 'and here,' he said as he touched my forehead.

Father says we will perform another matinee tomorrow and after that will move to two performances a day with an hour interval for lunch and to refresh ourselves.

We are to remain in this anteroom whenever we are not performing. I already miss Mother greatly. I have not seen her through the glass but that is not to say she has not been out there. Her hand is evident in the meals Father brings us and for now this will suffice.

My eyes are not accustomed to so much electric light. I feel it is worse due to the size of this room and its dark walls. No doubt the exertion of controlling my eyelids while in the window adds to this strained feeling. I understand that we must be confined to preserve the impact of our performances, but I long to dawdle through the garden. I miss the shy morning routine of the warblers when we are going through our own, their trilling call and swaying nests.

At least I have my diary, which is proving a useful diversion. Without any means of making music, Eugen spends his time clenching spring-grip dumb-bells and staring at the posters of Mr Sandow. In terms of physical development, Eugen is the equal of his namesake (with the exception of the moustache). I have not seen Mr Sandow in the crowd, either, or anyone who might match his development. How strange.

2 January

I love performing in the window with a passion that is equalled only by the distaste I feel for the time we spend cooped up in this anteroom. It is either too bright or too dark, it seems to trap every moist exhalation and it is cramped to a ridiculous degree, even when it is just the two of us. It is perhaps no wonder I feel ill when I wake each morning. I miss Mother. I miss walking in our garden. I miss the sun rising as we bathe outside. I miss the smell of the dew lifting from the grass and the sound of the birds. I miss my own bed (these stretchers are so rigid and Eugen makes such a racket every time he turns). I know that we must be kept from prying eyes when not in the window, but it is so trying.

Eugen doesn't seem to mind, which only doubles my torment. He just stares at the posters of Mr Sandow while tapping complex rhythms on his thighs, or else naps or performs dumb-bell exercises. He scoffs the meals that Mother has prepared for us and Father brings in paint tins lined with tea towels. In the first few days the shepherd's pie or mutton and rice were not tainted by the smell or taste of paint, but today it was as if the roast chicken, potatoes and kumara were merely props never meant for consumption.

The only distraction I have (besides putting my complaints in writing) is the book Mother gave me before we were parted. I have inspected it enough to know it is another novel by Mr Dickens, *Nicholas Nickleby* to be precise, but I cannot bear to open it. I cannot bear the thought of another story about street urchins like those I see through the window, nor can I concentrate on anything in this soupy atmosphere. I feel as if my eyeballs would explode after reading a single sentence.

It is with great effort that I rouse myself from self-pity and return my attention to the window. Today we presented a new tableau. We were dressed in the same promenading costumes as for our New Year's Eve scene, to convey the idea that this new tableau is a scene from later on in the evening. Father constructed a cobblestone path that ran alongside the electric lamp post and deposited moss and fallen leaves on either side of it. He brought a new backdrop from home that depicted trees in splashes of paint. Eugen posed on one knee, offering me a small felt box, its jaws open to reveal a large golden ring with a stunning sapphire surrounded by small diamonds. I was turned away, of course, but had enough of my face to the window to allow onlookers to sense my imminent change of heart. The small sliver of the outside world I could see allowed me a better view of the comings and goings of the townspeople, on foot, bicycle or horseback, in carriages or even the odd motor car. I remain largely unimpressed with their fashions or physical development and continue to despair at the number of orphans who are consigned to a difficult adult life, one without laughter, though they seem mercifully unaware of their fate and play chasing games in the grounds of the church opposite. Whatever the prospects or appearance of these people, however, I cannot help feeling pangs of jealousy at their freedom. I know I will soon be free to walk among them, to walk barefoot on the sand

and even into the breakers and, if I continue to hold my poses as I have thus far, I can expect to marry into a successful family and lead a life of comfort and happiness.

But oh how I loathe this tiny room!

3 January

Today we gave two performances for the first time. From nine until midday we presented the proposal tableau from the previous day. We then had an hour to tend to our bodily demands and for Father to alter the window before posing from one o'clock until five, or 'closing time' as Father called it. During this second performance, Eugen and I donned different outfits and presented what I have come to think of as our *Count of Monte Cristo* tableau: Eugen contorting his features to appear older and more distinguished, taking my offered hand with formality . . .

The benefit of two performances is that we spend little time in the anteroom during the day. The worm still gnaws my innards from time to time, but I find him easier to vanquish in the window, with so much else to think about. It is not as warm in here during the evening and the electric light is less grating. I even had the energy to open *Nicholas Nickleby* after supper tonight.

The hero has just been forced by his unscrupulous uncle to take up a teaching position at Dotheboys Hall, where, as expected, young children are severely mistreated. They are not all orphans, it seems, but their parents or step-parents care so little for them that they are willing to place them in the care of beastly, duplicitous Wackford Squeers, which is an equally depressing fate. I am left wondering why Mother selected this book for me at this moment. Perhaps to prepare me for the abundance of wasted childhoods beyond the window? Or perhaps the true connection comes later in the story?

Yesterday, in the depths of my despair in the anteroom, I told Eugen I missed his music.

'Where would a piano fit in here?' he asked.

'I miss our home.'

'If you want to go home you can break pose tomorrow. Walk laps around the window. Father will have to take you home and you and Mother can talk about all the books you please. Just know that you will not only disappoint Father, possibly destroy him, but you will have wasted all of your training and might damage my chances of finding a suitable match as well.'

'Eugen, I would never dream of such a thing—'

'Then there's no use complaining, is there?'

4 January

_____

I was touched by someone from the outside world today.

During our morning performance (the proposal tableau again) I noticed Father talking to a man in a top hat on the edge of the crowd. He was the sort of respectable older gentleman that I imagined I would see in the outside world but had so far been missing among the onlookers. I thought nothing more of this man until the interval, when Father informed us that he would be letting someone in to inspect us during the afternoon performance.

'In the window?' I asked.

'Yes. He's very impressed with you both and wishes to appraise you up close.'

'Does he have a daughter or a son?' asked Eugen.

'Better than that. He's come all the way from Christchurch.

He runs the windows up there. He says you two might be of city calibre.'

'Will he send parents down from Christchurch?' I asked.

'No, we'll go up there. They have the best windows in the South Island and the most people. It is a great honour and will significantly increase your prospects.'

'When?'

'Let's not put the cart before the horse. He must inspect you first. You mustn't move a muscle. He might touch and prod you, but you must hold your pose.'

Eugen crossed his arms confidently.

After a lunch of ham sandwiches and a costume change we returned to the window and assumed our poses for the *Count of Monte Cristo* tableau. When everything was set, Father locked the door and turned the winch in the anteroom to raise the curtain. Eugen and I were left staring at each other, unsure when the visitor would enter. We could hear Father banging about in the anteroom for some time and then silence. I am not sure how much time passed before we heard the door being unlocked once more (an hour perhaps?), at which point I felt every fibre of my hand longing to squeeze Eugen's, but I resisted. It was enough to be staring into his eyes and he into mine.

'After you,' I heard Father say.

The sound of the man's hard soles on the wooden floor reverberated in the narrow room.

'Yes,' the man said from somewhere behind me. 'Oh yes. Marvellous.' His words were punctuated by tiny coughs, as if he hoped to expel the tickle in his throat as he spoke. 'Just marvellous. The detail. You'd swear they breathed.'

My heart sank, but Father said, 'Thank you,' quite graciously.

'May I?' the man asked and gave another little cough.

'Of course, but please be careful. They are delicate.'

I felt his hand on my hair, just below my shoulders. It was an odd sensation to be touched by someone other than Father, Mother or Eugen. The man stroked his hand down the length of my hair and bounced the very tips on the palm of his hand. 'Is this human hair?' he asked, which seemed a strange question.

'A magician does not reveal his methods,' Father said, which seemed an equally strange answer.

The man moved closer to Eugen and into my field of vision. It was indeed the same man I had seen Father talking to during the morning, though he was clutching his top hat in one hand, pressing it to his chest as if to catch his heart should it burst from his ribcage. His head was bald except for a few dark strands that had been slicked over his scalp with some kind of grease.

'A fine specimen,' he said, passing around the back of Eugen. I saw him lift my brother's coat-tails, presumably to inspect the development of his gluteus muscles, though I am not sure how well they would show through his trousers. I wished we were posing unencumbered so that we might show off the true extent of our development. I knew that this was not the custom, that costume and pageantry were as much a part of a successful season in the window as muscles and skin tone, but this inspection differed from a crowd of people looking from the other side of a pane of glass. I knew that Eugen was thinking exactly the same thing.

'This pose is quite different to the one this morning,' the man said.

'Yes. The limbs are fully articulated. The facial expressions are achieved through a variety of subtle changes.'

'Make-up, lighting . . .'

'Yes, yes,' Father said.

'I was told you bring the curtain down at night also. Why is that?'

'To maintain the interest and encourage visitors to return. There's little point drawing crowds once the store's closed. But also because I need to change the display often. I work alone and it takes many hours to paint a new backdrop, select costumes and arrange the models. To do this in the open, well, it would destroy the illusion.'

The man had rounded the front of our tableau and was now looking intently at my neck. I worried that he would detect the seashell necklace that sat beneath the gaudy silver one, but he prodded a finger into my flesh, just above my collarbone.

'It gives to the touch?'

'It must if the eye is to be convinced.'

The man ran his finger along the line of my collarbone, sending shivers down my spine.

'Do I detect warmth?'

'Ah, that is from the electric lighting. The materials are mildly conductive. Quite like the flesh in that sense.'

I looked deeply into Eugen's eyes, searching for a hint of the same frown I wore internally. He seemed perfectly at ease.

The man hooked a finger inside the neckline of my dress and pulled it away from my flesh. I had to quickly and imperceptibly shift my weight further back to avoid being pulled forward and ruining everything. A most difficult challenge but one I am pleased to say I rose to.

'Anatomically correct?' He coughed in a higher register than before. 'My, my.'

Father kept silent. The man withdrew his finger and stepped back and to the side, now standing somewhere just behind my right ear.

'And balance? How is this maintained?'

'By modelling the figures as close to life as possible.'

The man made an unconvinced *huh* sound.

'There are also iron rods that connect them with the floor.'

'I see. Well, you have thought of everything.'

'It was a long time coming,' Father said.

'I can imagine.'

'Years.' It was Father's turn to give a nervous cough. When the sound died away, Father and the man remained behind us, both of them still and silent.

'It will depend on the fee and the term of the contract, of course,' the man finally said, 'but I'd like very much to see these mannequins in the window of Ballantynes.'

'I'm glad,' Father said. I heard him opening the door to the anteroom. 'Perhaps we could discuss the finer points in my office.'

'Of course.'

I heard their footsteps recede, the door shut and Father turn the key.

There was still a long time to go before the curtain fell on our afternoon performance but there was so much to discuss with Eugen. We have perfected the exchange of emotion while posing, but our connection is not such that an entirely new concept can leap from one mind to the other. In this case, I wanted to know about the term 'mannequin' that the man had used, which I could not remember ever hearing or reading before. I wanted to know why Father had talked about our 'materials' and lied about iron rods connecting us to the floor. I understood the need to preserve our performance to demonstrate our strength and character, but it was as if Father's pretence stretched to the point that we truly *were* statues.

Eugen was not worried by the man's visit. He was excited and proud, ready to move on to Christchurch, the city to the north that Mother speaks of sometimes as the place of her birth. She never says much about her family, however. Perhaps she reserves these memories for the pages of her diary.

I wonder sometimes how a match was made between Father and Mother. He is clearly older than her, and much less handsome, which seems at odds with what I know about the window and the matches it produces. Equally, I have read of affection between parents but never seen so much as a handshake between Father and Mother. They can go days without speaking directly to one another, passing messages through Eugen or me. 'Tell your father dinner is ready.' 'Tell Flossie to mind her own business.'

What do I conclude from all this? Perhaps *conclude* is too strong a word, but I do *suspect* that this is not Father's first marriage. I have never been brave enough to broach the subject with him, or cruel enough to raise it with Mother, but such were the thoughts that plagued me this afternoon as I waited for the curtain to fall.

I was not completely blind to the goings on beyond the

window, however. I noticed, for example, the old man standing on the flank of the general crowd that, even five days into our season, never seems to number less than twenty, although my view of the street is often quite limited. At first I thought he was an orphan dressed in adult clothing, so short was the figure. But I soon saw the wrinkled skin of his face and the large, rough hand he used to dab the corner of his mouth with a bunched handkerchief. I am poor at guessing ages, as one might expect with my limited exposure to the outside world, but he was a good deal more hunched and shrunken than Father. I did not recall seeing him in the crowd before, though that is not to say he was not there. What made him remarkable was the way he was positioned, beyond Eugen's left shoulder. It was as if this old man were staring into my eyes just as my brother was. I worried that he, too, could penetrate my thoughts. That he was trying to catch me out in a way Father had not warned us about.

He was still standing there when the curtain was finally lowered and Father unlocked the door.

'So,' Eugen said as soon as we were free to move, 'when do we go to Christchurch?'

'Soon. A week perhaps.'

'A week? And what do we do until then?'

We followed Father back into the anteroom. All the furniture had been shifted into the corner where the chamber pot and basin sat and a large sheet was draped over the top of everything. Father ripped the sheet off and started to reconstruct a stretcher bed.

'We're wasting our time in this window, Father,' Eugen continued. 'You see as well as I do that the people of this town are sickly and ill-proportioned. Their children cannot be that much better.'

Father looked up from the stretcher, his face contorted into a rare and faintly disturbing smile. 'You're right. You've both worked too hard to end up in Marumaru. But I must go to Christchurch first and ensure everything is in place.'

'When?'

'In a few days. Until then, you must keep performing as you have.'

'Father,' I asked, 'what did he mean when he called us "mannequins"?'

'It is just another term for performers.'

'Is it complimentary?' I asked. 'It didn't sound so.'

'It's fine, Avis. You are doing so well.'

Not every new sensation this week has been unpleasant. I could become quite accustomed to Father's compliments and encouragement.

5 January

The short old man was out there watching me again today. Both morning and afternoon performances. Standing there in his thick woollen suit.

Last night we helped Father prepare the window for two new tableaux. He drew the outline of a field of corn and a barn in the corner, then Eugen and I painted in the colours while Father rigged up a series of pipes in the false ceiling of the window to create the appearance of rain (though it would fall between us and the window, allowing us to remain dry throughout the performance).

In this morning's tableau I was being dragged along to the barn by Eugen as the first spits of rain started. These spits were caught in a gutter recess at the front of the window that Father had constructed in advance. I marvel at the amount of planning and ingenuity he has invested in our season. I still miss Mother very much (and am yet to spot *her* in the street) but I am coming to understand why Father was as he was while Eugen and I were growing up. Each day I become more grateful for everything he has done for us.

When I mentioned the old man in the heavy suit to Father he gave a coarse laugh (coarse, perhaps, because he is so unaccustomed to making the sound). 'Don't worry about him,' he said. 'He's just racking his brain trying to figure out how it's done.'

'The rain?' I asked.

'Everything.'

'The fact we are twins?'

'Everything,' he repeated. 'He's from a different generation. He doesn't understand the new ways.'

For the afternoon, Father brought in a number of hay bales and we posed as two young lovers waltzing to the music inside their own heads. I now was facing the other way up the street and yet the old man was standing square in my line of sight again. He stayed there the entire four hours. The only difference between the two of us was the occasional dab of a handkerchief to his mouth and his frequent and undisguised blinking.

But enough about my strange companion. I am now about a third of the way through *Nicholas Nickleby* and see another reason Mother may have chosen this book for me. Nicholas has entered a company of actors managed by a Mr Vincent Crummles. There are many similarities between the stages Nicholas and I tread. Of course, Mr Dickens sees fit to introduce a degree of humour and outlandishness that we will do well to avoid. In particular I am thinking of Crummles' daughter, 'the infant phenomenon', who has been fed gin and water from an early age to keep her looking ten years old when she is well beyond that (though the added years have not done much for her acting).

Perhaps Eugen is a better stand-in for Nicholas Nickleby and I am supposed to sympathise with his sister, Kate. She is beautiful and seems quite virtuous, but I feel I have little in common with her situation. All of us, I suspect, male and female, feel we will be the hero of the tale when the book of our life is writ.

6 January

———

Father will journey to Christchurch tomorrow. He has enlisted Mother to deliver our meals and work the winch that raises and lowers our curtain. I could hear him instructing her in the anteroom as Eugen and I performed this afternoon, but she was not there once we had finished. I asked Father why she had not stayed behind and he made a poor excuse about there not being space for all four of us in the anteroom. I must say I am perplexed and not a little hurt by this. Why have I not seen her on the street, if not to satisfy her own curiosity then to give us encouragement? Why did she rush back to our house, that little world unto itself, before we had finished our performance? Perhaps she feared the commotion our reunion would precipitate. I have so much to tell her and so many questions to ask.

In addition to the old man who continues to stand in my gaze for the duration of morning and afternoon performances, I am beginning to recognise a number of other characters on the street.

There is the poor orphan boy who stops his bicycle in front of us every afternoon for the final two hours of our performance. He seems more interested in Eugen's development than mine, which is to be expected, I suppose. (I wonder if they have dumb-bells at the orphanage or if their deprivation stretches further than I care to think.)

There is the finely dressed, rotund gentleman with dark skin, though he does not much resemble the drawings of Indians or Africans in the books I have read. He is frequently on the street, but pays our window little attention. His interest is in shaking the hands of the adults and engaging them in conversation. When he laughs, which is often, he places his hands on either side of his large belly.

And there is the woman with her hair in a bun who addresses the crowd with her back to us and is roundly ignored. The plate glass dulls and distorts her speeches so that I cannot understand what she is saying. She is always clutching a book and points often at the sky.

I caught Eugen looking at my torso as we washed down following our afternoon performance.

'What is it?' I asked.

'You've been neglecting your abdominal muscles,' he said. 'Being in the window is no excuse for idleness.'

'Eugen! I have hardly been idle. I do as much as you.' I looked down at my belly and could detect no change in it. 'You've seen how little I have been eating.'

'Perhaps that is the problem.'

'I promise I am no longer nervous. If only we had better ventilation.'

'The window is a test, Avis. It is not meant to be easy,' he said, looking up at the poster of Mr Sandow showing off his chest expansion.

Is it any surprise I preferred the company of Mr Dickens for the rest of the evening? Having said that I have little in common with Kate Nickleby yesterday, I feel greatly for her predicament: a pawn in the schemes of her Uncle Ralph and Sir Mulberry Hawk. It was with much delight that I read of Nicholas' return to London to come to the aid of his sister and the sound thrashing he gave to Hawk.

I must remind myself that to stand in the window and look upon the people of our town would have been the height of stimulation for me but one week ago. I am not as restless as poor Eugen, who does not speak unless to utter the word 'Christchurch', but I would not refuse a new adventure.

7 January

This morning Father unlocked the door to the window and raised the curtain on our tableau before setting off for Christchurch. We have been instructed to present the same scene for the duration of his absence: I am standing on my pedestal in a white dress, posing with one hand held to my forehead, the other at my hip, while Eugen is admiring me from the ground. I am a statue and he is my sculptor.

'You must keep the pose identical at each performance,' Father instructed.

'But why?' I asked.

'Because,' interjected Eugen, 'we can't waste anything else on this town.'

Father gave a gentle cough and added, 'I won't be here to help change the backdrop or rig up any lighting or waterworks. This tableau is a classic. It will tide everyone over until I return.'

A few minutes after the curtain rose and Father left the anteroom he appeared on the street. This time he did not stop to shake people's hands. He did not even meet their eyes. He shuffled to the centre of the window and stood there, looking at us through the glass, for a minute, perhaps longer.

The expression on his face is difficult to describe. There was no smile or frown, no pallor or flush. His eyes were no more bloodshot than normal, though his lower lids looked as if they were weighed down. This may be my own invention as I grasp for something of note to preserve in my memory that expression so blank and yet so full of some emotion—pride? Nervousness? Affection? Sadness?

He left, as I say, after a minute or so, and I expect he is now in Christchurch.

When the curtain was lowered three hours later and the door unlocked, it was Mother standing in the anteroom. I rushed to her and we melted into each other's embrace.

'Why have I not seen you in the street?' I asked, my cheek pressed into her shoulder.

'I couldn't bear it, child.'

I lifted my head and looked at her. 'Why ever not?'

She placed her palm against my cheek and turned to my brother. 'Hello Eugen.'

'Hello.' He dipped his head slightly. 'Did Father get away all right?'

'Yes.'

Eugen nodded, satisfied.

'Now, you two must be famished.'

I noticed for the first time that an array of cold meats and condiments had been arranged atop the dresser. Eugen stepped over to it and began to load his plate.

Mother was wearing a black skirt with constellations of flour particles near the hem and a white blouse that had yellowed slightly at the cuffs. I thought it strange as she had always taken such pride in her appearance. I had been waiting for an opportunity to talk to her about *Nicholas Nickleby*, which I was now more than halfway through, but I was struck dumb by sadness. It is strange, but I missed Mother more in that moment, with her less than a foot from me, breathing the same musty air inside the same tiny room, than I had at any time during the previous week. I was reminded of our past conversations about books, the way she would prompt me to recall the events of the plot, interjecting with questions about whether I had taken to such-and-such character, or whom I suspected of being the murderer, or did I know what a convent or a catacomb was. The old Mother would have been itching to hear about my reading of *Nicholas Nickleby* and would not have delayed broaching the subject. But today she seemed reticent and withdrawn.

I picked at the food on offer (mealtimes are still a struggle for me; the worm persists) and readjusted my costume in preparation for the afternoon's performance, waiting all the while for Mother to speak. But she sat on the stool, her legs crossed and her mouth wearing a rigid smile, saying nothing.

Soon enough the hour was over and Eugen and I had to return to the window. I felt so silly and wished to recant my silence and spend the hour over again, this time in conversation with Mother, but it was not possible. Instead, I retrieved this diary from beneath my pillow (I am not hiding it from anyone but there is so little space in the anteroom that this is the best place to keep it) and thrust it into Mother's hands.

'Do read it,' I said. 'It may help to pass the time.'

Eugen and I returned to the window, took up our poses and the curtain rose. When I am standing upon the pedestal, my shoulders are square to the window and a large section of the street is visible to me. The old man was not there when the curtain came up, but within moments he had stepped into view. He stood on the far footpath, his eyes interrogating mine, the gaze broken only by a passing carriage or motor car. When I am away from the window I feel shaken by this man and am certain I should fear his motives for he intends to catch me out and ruin my prospects, but while we are together (oh, even the phrase seems ridiculous) I am strangely at ease. It is as if I can see through to his intentions as I can divine Eugen's emotions and in those long moments I'm confident he means me no harm. This confidence fades, however, as soon as the curtain lowers and I am left, as I am now, in a muddle of anticipation and anxiety.

During the afternoon I could hear Mother making bangs and clatters in the anteroom, with long pauses when I imagined she might be reading my diary. When we returned to the anteroom at five o'clock, it was evident she had been there all day. She had prepared a hot meal with only a lamp-stove. Her hair had frizzled and her forehead glowed like a Christmas ham left on the table too long.

'It is not much fun being cooped up, is it?' I said.

She gave a weak smile. 'We must humour your father.'

'It is for our benefit,' I said, 'in the end.'

'It is how it must be,' Eugen said, lifting the lid of the cast-iron pot and dipping his little finger into its contents. He gave a yelp as it was promptly scalded.

'Have you reacquainted yourself with my diary?' I asked.

'I have.' She swept the hair from her face, lifted the lid and began to ladle the stew onto three plates. 'I see you are getting through *Nicholas Nickleby*?'

'Yes, I hope to finish it before we leave for Christchurch. What strange creatures the brothers Cheeryble are,' I said, hoping to draw her into conversation, but her eyes remained downcast. 'They seem so kind and generous. You remember them, don't you, Mother? The brothers Cheeryble,' I prompted, 'who have given Nicholas a job, and their clerk, Tim Linkinwater, who seems the very model of loyalty and dedication.'

'Did you notice the inscription?' she asked, her glance still directed at the food.

'Inscription? No, I began the story immediately as I always do. Should I have?' I placed my plate beside me and went to retrieve the book but Mother told me to eat while my dinner was still hot.

'You'll have time enough to inspect the book this evening, once I've left.'

The three of us ate and afterward took out the cards and played Kuhn Khan until it felt quite late. It was a pleasant way to pass the evening. A nice change from me reading or writing in this diary (though I've still found time to do that now) and Eugen lifting barbells while staring at Mr Sandow.

'I must be off now, children,' Mother finally said and stood to go. 'Be good.'

She opened the door to the giant wardrobe and shut it behind her.

On the blank first page before the frontispiece of *Nicholas Nickleby* I found the following handwritten message:

To my dearest Colton on his 23rd birthday
Yours absolutely
Louisa

Colton is Father's name. I do not know anyone called Louisa, but that is not surprising. In my sixteen years I have only ever known Father, Mother and Eugen. I have read enough romances to know that anyone who writes 'Yours absolutely' is not a family member or an acquaintance. Did Father have an admirer in the town? Was this the source of Mother's recent unhappiness and the thing she was trying to alert me to? Should I have been paying more attention when Father mingled with the onlookers in those first few days, shaking hands and shrugging his shoulders? How many years have passed since Father's twenty-third birthday?

I closed the book and turned it over in my hands, inspecting the worn cloth binding. This, I concluded, was a gift from Father's first wife.

'What do you make of this?' I asked Eugen, and read the inscription aloud.

'So who is Louisa?' I asked. 'And when did you ever see Father read a novel?'

'He has devoted his life to us, Avis. Perhaps he hasn't had time to read since we were born.'

'Yes, precisely,' I said, becoming animated. 'You know my theory that Mother might be Father's second wife.'

Eugen sighed.

'But I haven't considered who the first wife might have been. It must surely be this Louisa. Not only that, but I suspect she was our mother. Who else would write "Yours absolutely"?'

'Another dreamer like you? Or your wrinkled admirer out there.'

'Oh, be serious, Eugen. Haven't you ever wondered about how distant Father and Mother are?'

'Yes, of course I have. Though I wonder more at how distant we are from them. The question you should be asking yourself is: Is Father our father?' He looked up at the poster of Mr Sandow.

'But he is, obviously.'

He gave a dismissive laugh. 'You are so ready to rid yourself of one parent, but not another. Don't you think, Avis, when you look out of the window and see all the skinny, weak, powerless people, that Father is just another one of them?'

'Father has had his own trials,' I said, which seemed true enough.

'Wouldn't it make more sense if our parents were more like Mr Sandow? If Mr Sandow *was* our father?'

'You are being ridiculous,' I said. 'Why would Mr Sandow deposit us with Father and Mother?'

'He must be a busy man. Perhaps he didn't have time enough to devote to us. Father, on the other hand . . .'

I thought of the poor children left at Dotheboys Hall, but shook the image from my head. 'You're talking nonsense, Eugen.'

'Let us see what Christchurch brings,' he said and began to undress at the basin.

My head has not stopped spinning from these speculations, even now that Eugen's hand hovers over the light switch.

10 January

Three full days have passed since I committed anything to the page, but the gap feels closer to three months or three years. I do not know if I will ever regain my old diary, which was left under my pillow in the anteroom, or the inscribed copy of *Nicholas Nickleby* under my stretcher with a hundred or so pages left to read. There will be other copies of Mr Dickens' book to supply the ending of that story, but I may never recover my diary and so must start afresh.

I have much to cover. Fortunately it seems I have little other call upon my time. No performances to give. No one to converse with, at least not in any balanced way. The only limit is my own stamina and the amount of ink I have in this hut.

It is difficult for me to recall particulars of the morning of the eighth of January, despite the fact it promises to have been my last performance in the window.

I know ~~Mother~~ Flossie arrived late and flustered, leaving us only a matter of minutes to eat breakfast and no time for me to raise the subject of the inscription.

I know my old admirer was out there, penetrating my gaze as I stood atop my pedestal in an exact replica of the previous day's pose.

I know Eugen was kneeling in wonder before me. The sculptor in love with his own creation.

I know that when the curtain was lowered and we returned to the anteroom, I had been stewing over the question of our parentage for three hours (in addition to all of the previous night) and came right out and asked Flossie, 'Was Louisa our mother?'

She did not seem taken aback by my forthrightness. She nodded.

Eugen entered the anteroom behind me and I grabbed the sleeve of his loose white sculptor's shirt. 'It's true, Eugen.'

His bottom lip disappeared beneath his front teeth and he shrugged his shoulders. It would clearly take more to discourage his fantasy of being Sandow's heir.

'Is she alive?' I asked her.

She shook her head.

'I knew it.'

Eugen had stripped off his shirt and was running cold water over his hair.

'She died giving birth to the two of you.'

'Oh my.'

'Your father loved her very much,' she said with care, as if she had rehearsed this moment often, 'and was greatly changed by her death.'

'You knew them both? Before . . .?'

'She was my sister.'

Her face was whiter than my seashell pendant.

'Oh Mother,' I said, 'that makes you my aunt!' I gave her a hug. 'I knew we were blood. Why ever did you keep us in the dark about this, about our mother?'

'Your father, he couldn't bear to hear her name spoken.'

'It must have been so hard for you both.'

'I,' she said and her hand reached around her head, as if the back of her skull were about to lower like a drawbridge. 'I was only your age. I should have been stronger.'

'Oh Mother.' I embraced her again. 'I mean Aunt. Oh, what should I call you?'

'Flossie is fine, my dear.'

Over her shoulder I met Eugen's eyes. He was standing shirtless in the corner of the room, his abdominal muscles tense, his eyes piercing and pitying all at once. I saw he didn't believe her. That he couldn't let himself believe. He wanted so badly to be linked to another family, to Sandow. To be a prince. To be special.

I never got the chance to tell him that he was special. If there is anything my time in the window and the last three days have taught me, it is that Eugen is one of a kind.

The hour was soon over and I returned to my pedestal, Eugen to his pose below me. I had gained a dead mother and a living aunt. If I thought my head was spinning the night before . . . But the curtain was rising and I quickly fixed my pose, stilled my chest and let my eyelids fall into their regular rhythm.

The old man stood on the far side of the road, looking on. The hours passed. Eugen's young admirer arrived on his bicycle. I had learnt to approximate the time by judging the light in the sky. I began to expect the sound of the door to the anteroom opening, the sound of the winch starting and the curtain falling, but it did not come. The aches in my back, the arm I had raised to my forehead and the arch of my left foot told me we had indeed posed for longer than normal. Eugen tried not to show any discomfort, even to me.

Outside, the usual flux of passersby continued around the constant old man and the boy with the bicycle, though pedestrians began to stop and comment among themselves more frequently.

The boy with the bicycle pedalled off, no doubt for his dinner, and I heard Eugen's own stomach grumble.

I began to worry that something had happened to Flossie. Perhaps she had fallen ill or been involved in an accident on the roads. Or perhaps Father had returned from Christchurch and they were both on their way.

The daylight began to soften and fade. The woman with her hair in a bun arrived, looking harried. She paid us both a longer glance than she usually allowed herself before turning to face the street, the back of her white blouse pressed to the plate glass and her hands upon her hips.

The hubbub on the street began to increase until it was nearly as packed as on the first few days of our season. The gentleman with the large belly and brown skin arrived and began to make his way around the townspeople, shaking their hands as if he were working a butter churn. The electric street lights came on and the last light drained out of the sky. Orphans and their minders stepped right up to the window, ignoring the woman, to peer at us. With only two small lights illuminating our side of the glass, we must have been getting very hard to make out, which was just as well as we had both begun to falter after so long in the one position. The rearrangements Eugen undertook to ease the weight on his kneecap sent tiny shivers around his body, terminating in his eyebrows. I had developed a slight wobble that was proving difficult to still. We had never posed for so long, not in the window, not even in the comfort of Father's workshop. We had no alternative but to grit our teeth behind closed lips and maintain the tableau. Perhaps it was another test of our mettle. One last trial before we graduated to the great windows of Christchurch. This is what Eugen seemed bent on convincing the both of us. It will be all right, he told me with his eyes.

When night had completely fallen the townspeople began returning to their homes. The orphans peeled their foreheads from the glass and followed their minders to the orphanage (I tried not to think about the meagre meals and cruel treatment they might receive once there). Only the old man remained, standing on the far side of the road as he had been since the curtain rose. I could make him out in the glow of the street light but evidently he could not see me well as he soon crossed the road and stood a foot away from the glass. He seemed changed. His tongue made frequent forays out of his mouth to moisten his lower lip. His customary handkerchief was nowhere to be seen. He frequently glanced to his left and to his right, breaking our gaze, checking if he was alone on the street.

And then he slunk away.

At first I suspected he had only stepped to the side of the window and would leap forward once more to catch us as we yielded to our bodies' demands for rest and relief. But the street remained perfectly deserted for some time.

Eugen continued his encouraging looks. There was no way he was breaking pose while the curtain remained up.

I longed for Flossie to open the anteroom door. Not just for the relief of our bodies but the relief of my heart and mind, for I feared (and still do, at certain moments) that she was badly injured or worse. What else could have prevented her from lowering the curtain?

My thoughts continued to oscillate between the pain in my limbs and the pain in my heart.

Then, at last, I heard the door between the giant wardrobe and the anteroom open.

Eugen's eyelids fluttered in an involuntary round of applause.

I let out the first full breath I had breathed in what must have been ten hours. Ten long, torturous hours.

But who had entered the anteroom? Why had they not worked the winch to lower the curtain? The thought of an intruder suddenly crossed my mind and leapt over to Eugen's. I thought of the man from Christchurch weighing my hair and prodding my flesh, the way he clutched his top hat to his chest. I heard footsteps approach the door to the window. We both held our poses as best we could.

The door opened. No one announced their arrival, not even in a whisper. Eugen and I were both turned toward the glass. I could only hear the rustle of the curtain and the creak of the door between the window and the anteroom and feel the slight breeze that suggested the first door had not been shut and locked securely according to Father's protocol.

I heard the curtain that concealed the door to the anteroom being pulled back and the light from that room mingled with the two small bulbs in the window. Eugen and I had altered our poses by degrees since we commenced our session at one o'clock that afternoon, but in that moment we kept perfectly still. I was staring ahead at the reflective surface of the window. The world beyond was no more, but I could see Eugen and me and the shuffling form of the intruder.

It was my admirer.

He placed one cold finger on the calf muscle of my right leg. The sensation was infinitely more testing than when the man from Christchurch had inspected my 'materials'. One finger was followed by the entire rough hand, which clamped on my calf and gave a gentle squeeze. Eugen kept looking up into my eyes. It was clear that he too had caught a glimpse of the intruder and that his identity was no great surprise. It made perfect sense that my admirer would be the one to bring an end to this ordeal, but what sort of an end would it be? Was he the dark figure who lurks throughout a novel only to reveal his benevolent side at the climax and remedy all of the heroine's misfortunes? Or was he the dark figure who lurks throughout a novel only to bring the final misfortune upon the hero's sister?

I had no choice but to hold my pose as I felt his hands on my hips. I focused every last ounce of energy on contracting my muscles so that I might hold everything in place as I was hoisted from the pedestal. For a small, old man, his strength was surprising. He managed to take me down and bring me horizontally against his hip. In the moment, I believed I was keeping my entire body rigid, but now I cannot be sure. After posing for so long, where did my strength come from? But the man did not act as if I had given myself away. He carried me through the tiny room that had so tried my patience and into the giant wardrobe, for the first time in nine days. It was completely dark, as it had been the night Father brought us in to the window. My nose was assaulted once more by a thousand exotic odours. The elbow of the arm I held to my head brushed against clothing on the racks as we made our way along a row. As we turned, my feet collected a few items that then fell to the floor. The clatter of the wooden hangers against the hard surface of the floor reverberated in the giant wardrobe.

We continued to twist and turn among the rows, taking a much less direct route than when I had come in with Father. I wondered if my abductor was making evasive manoeuvres. Perhaps Eugen was giving chase. But I knew deep down that whatever Eugen felt for me, he would not break pose. This realisation hurt in the moment but with three days to think on it, I know that my brother thought little harm could come to me. We had lived such cloistered lives, away from crime and depravity and death. He could not have conceived of a fate worse than a spoiled season in the window and one's prospects being dashed.

Dear, sweet Eugen. When will I see you again?

We finally made it to the double doors and my admirer pushed slowly through with his free arm, careful to protect me from any knocks. The wind was up outside and the cool night air was like a razor. I could feel my skin turn to gooseflesh: this is one bodily function Father did not teach us how to control and I wonder if it is even possible. But I kept my limbs as rigid as possible and maintained, as best I could, my horizontal attitude to the ground, seesawing slightly against the pivot of my admirer's hip with every step, as I imagine a real statue might.

We rounded a corner and I was set upright once more. He spread a rug out across the flat bed of a wooden cart that was hitched to a single grey horse not much bigger than a dog. I was hoisted once more and slowly slid onto the platform so that I was lying comfortably (a relative term in this case: I still held my pose in a manner, but did not have to support any weight). Another rug was then drawn over me completely.

I heard the reins being whipped and the small horse began to trundle forward.

As before, I tried to follow the twists and turns to keep some measure of where we were and where we might be heading, but it was hopeless. I know so little about the town of Marumaru beyond the stretch of street I could see from the window and the pocket of our property, which lay somewhere further up the hill and away from the sea. The cart soon began to incline so that my feet were lower than my head, suggesting we were going uphill. For a moment I considered that we were heading toward home because ~~Mother~~ Flossie needed me, but we plodded for far too long. No, we were well beyond our home and, perhaps worse, we were moving further and further from the sea!

After some time the exhaustion and the repetitive swaying motion of the cart got the better of me and I fell asleep.

When I awoke the top rug had come down from over my head and I had broken pose completely. The cart was stationary, and tentative morning light trickled through the leaves of a tree. I could hear what sounded like running water. I tried to look around without moving my head but I could not see enough to know where my admirer was. Slowly I lifted my head to see the small horse that stood patiently, still hitched to the cart. We were almost enveloped by the branches of a large tree, which hung down with the weight of their narrow green leaves. Through the foliage I could make out the dirt trail we had evidently been following and the old man, still in his heavy suit, crouched beside a stream some twenty or thirty yards distant. The water was a strange, milky, opalescent blue. When I lifted myself higher the stream turned out to be a strand of a much larger thing—I hesitate to call it a river because in my mind a river has always been a single line of water, larger than a stream, straighter than a creek, with two sloping banks. This river, if that was the correct term, was more a series of shallow streams braided together by nature's haphazard hand.

I saw my admirer stand up from the smooth grey stones at the edge of the water and I lay back down, though I was unsure what position to assume. He had surely seen me sleeping, but I was less mortified than I might have been. It was hard to imagine the rules of the window applied any longer. Even so, I decided to pretend I still slept and shut my eyes. I heard the sound of his boots on the stones and felt him pull the blanket up over my shoulders. Then we were off again.

Lying on my side I was able to observe some of the landscape we were passing through. It seemed we were on a kind of plain or plateau, relatively flat with only a slight incline which the trail ascended. The braided river was to my back and I faced grassland dotted with scrub. The hills shimmered brown and red in the distance. As we continued on the trail they appeared to approach and recede, approach and recede, as if in a kind of dance.

The sun reached its apex and signalled twenty-four hours since I had eaten or drunk. The worm traced a figure eight inside me. I found it harder and harder to keep my eyes open. The hills felt closer now, ready to embrace me. My lips were dry and cracked. My head pounded. If I had had something in my stomach it would have come back up.

Late in the afternoon we finally came to a stop. I felt the blanket being cast aside and the cart bounce as my admirer climbed up to collect me. I did not have the strength to hold any sort of pose. I could not straighten a leg if my life depended on it. I was carried limp and half-conscious up a path. It must have been uneven or unstable as I remember my head being jolted several times, my thoughts being thrust back into my body before drifting once more, out into the blues, greens, yellows, browns and reds of the wide, windowless world.

I was taken into a small wooden hut and placed carefully on a bed that later inspection would deem quite modest but in that moment felt like a giant marshmallow. I felt my lips being pried open and cold water—the coldest—being poured into my mouth. The water hit the back of my throat and made me cough and splutter over the man's hand and the bedding. I looked up weakly and met his gaze for the first time since the previous evening. His eyes were moist. In them I saw kindness. I let myself relax, relent, drift away.

This morning I awoke at my usual hour. Six o'clock. There is no timepiece in this small hut to verify this, but I could recognise this time of the morning, its smells and sounds and subdued colours. The man was slouched in a sitting chair, his suit coat draped over his shoulders, his head cocked awkwardly to one side, his eyes closed. I surveyed the small hut. It was not much bigger than the anteroom and seemed smaller still, owing to the pitched roof that started four feet or so from the ground. A small peak protruded above the doorway in order to accommodate its greater height. The walls were made of vertical slats of wood, similar to Father's workshop but with even more gaps to let the daylight knife inside. There was no ceiling, just the blackened underside of the shingles and the supporting timber frame. My bed lay at one end of the hut and at the other there was a bench with a basin recessed into it. There were no taps over the basin (I have since learnt there is no plumbing whatsoever). Behind the old man's chair was a fireplace constructed from bricks that looked so porous they might float. A cast-iron pot sat in the ashes and a smaller one hung from a hook inside the chimney.

I rose from the bed that had been such a comfort. Despite the strain upon my muscles of posing for so many hours I felt no pain in my limbs as I stood, but when I moved forward it felt as if my brain were sloshing inside my head like soapsuds in a bucket. I made my way slowly to the door and eased it open. The hinges gave a creak but the man did not wake. Outside, I surveyed our destination for the first time. To my left a curving wall of rock rose up to a height of thirty feet. The rock was yellow with black tarnished edges and greenish-black vertical stripes. A collection of square-sided boulders lay at the foot of this cliff, their surface brownish-grey with pocks of the same sandy yellow. Dry, thorny bushes and larger trees with waxy green leaves sprang up from gaps between the boulders but I stood on a sort of plain with knee-high grass that swirled in the breeze like some diaphanous material. The grass was bound by another curving wall of rock perhaps forty yards away. It was as if I stood between two cupped stone hands.

I stepped forward, letting my fingers run through the grass as I walked. The sky was bluer than anything I had seen in

Marumaru. The few patches of white cloud were stretched thin as cotton wool so that the blue still shone through. Every few steps I stopped to inspect some new discovery. The tiny flowers, dried and brown like Cape gooseberry skins, that sat atop thin red stems tangled among the tall grass. The small brown and orange butterfly that alighted on the top of a boulder. In the distance a range of mountains rose up, dusted white with snow even in these dog days of summer.

I wished to keep walking, to explore, to take on the world, but I needed food and water. (I felt properly hungry for the first time in days.) Still, I stood amid the grass and rocks and chicketing cicadas for some time, absorbing everything, feeling my strength return with the soft glow of the sunlight on my bare white skin, until I heard a clatter of activity inside the hut. The man burst through the door to find me not ten yards away, in the same white dress and silken slip as yesterday and the day before. With my hand up to my forehead to shield my eyes from the sun I must have resembled the marble statue I had been in the window.

I let my mouth curve into a smile.

'Hello,' I said.

The look upon his face! Which was the greater surprise to him: that I had not run away or that I spoke?

'Do we have any food?' I asked. 'I am quite famished.'

He nodded and gestured with his hand for me to come inside.

I sat on the bed while the man started a fire. He took a bag of oats from a potato sack slumped in the corner of the kitchen and poured some into the small pot, added water from a canteen and placed it over the fire.

'What is your name?' I asked.

He turned around, held out his hands, one of which gripped a tarnished spoon, and shook his head as if to say, 'I'm sorry.'

'But what do I call you?'

He shrugged.

'Is it that you cannot speak, or you will not speak?' I asked.

He scratched his head and raised his eyebrows, then opened

his mouth and emitted a croaking sound. I could not decipher any words, but I grasped his meaning.

He turned back to the porridge.

'Well, this might be difficult. I have many questions. Do you write? Perhaps you have some paper and a pen.'

He patted his hand down beside his hip, telling me to be patient.

When the porridge was ready he spooned it into two crockery bowls and came to sit beside me on the bed, though there was space enough for a third person to sit between us. The oats were hot and a little dry, but it was a great relief to have something to eat, and I was able to keep them down.

'Did Flossie send you?' I asked.

The man continued to eat in silence, looking intently at his bowl.

'Are you a friend of Father's, perhaps?'

He smiled but shook his head.

'What happened the other night? Why did the curtain not come down at five o'clock? How did you get into the window? Wasn't the door locked? Where have you brought me?'

He gave a meek look, and I let out a yelp of frustration.

'You're no use. No use at all.'

He seemed hurt by this. He took my empty bowl and went to the sink. I lay down on the bed and covered my head with the pillow. When I looked up again he had gone. I got up and inspected the contents of the hut once more. There were a few books lined along a single plank that was braced high on the wall nearest the bed. Beside the fireplace sat a wicker basket with a few splinters of wood at the bottom. I looked inside the sack of provisions sitting on the floor near the door. From the small amounts of tea, sugar and milk powder, I got the impression he had not planned to stay long (though the bag of oats was large enough). Or perhaps he had expected to be alone up here? Next to the front door was a small cabinet which I greedily inspected for writing materials. My first thought was not to recommence my diary but to find some way of communicating with my nameless companion. I found a fountain pen but no paper.

I moved the chair over to the shelf of books and ripped the blank or nearly blank pages from them to compile a stack of papers. I was careful to check each book for inscriptions. Most had a name on the inside cover to indicate ownership. There was a Thomson, a Billick, a K. Herbert and a J. P. Staves, but there were no Coltons or Louisas, no Yours Absolutelys. The books themselves covered a wide variety of topics. There was a book on native plants, an almanac of tides and the passage of the moon dating from the last century, a seafaring novel called *The Voyage of the Penobscot*, another titled *Carmelita: A Romance* and a few small books of English verse.

I readied the pen and paper for my companion's return. I even wrote my first question, 'What shall I call you?', in advance, but he had not returned by midday. I went outside to look for him. The small horse was gone, though the cart remained. I went back inside and made another bowl of porridge for lunch.

After eating, I sat down in my companion's chair and wrote a few more questions, should he ever return, leaving space for him to write his answer. Then I started writing this entry.

I see that I have already chewed through most of my store of pages. The man is yet to return. I hope he comes soon, if only because I do not fancy another bowl of porridge.

What shall I call you?

They call me The Carpenter, though I am more of a carver.

Where are we?

The back country.

Is this your hut?

Yes.

———————

Why did you take me from the window?

I am a fool.

What do you have planned for me?

I have no plans.

———————

Why can't you speak?

It is a long story.

Can you write it down?

No.

Please?

No.

Why not?

Because it is of little consequence.

Surely not. At the least, it will pass the time.

We do not have enough paper.

**Perhaps you could fetch some. I won't run away.
I promise.**

———————

Do you have any questions for me?

Are you hungry?

Not that sort of question.

Are you real or have I dreamt you?

———————

You are still here.

I said I would be.

I suppose I should start my story then.

Please do.

———————

The erect-crested penguin.

Part three

The Carpenter's Tale

'The eternal silence of these infinite spaces frightens me.'

8 November 1890

I was lashed partway up the mizzenmast when the noonday sky grew dark. I had been up there for four days. I was weak. My eyelids were heavy as sodden sails and I had long since given up trying to keep them furled, but the changing light was enough to rouse me now. I heard the crackle of the unseen spanker as it was sucked in a new direction by the shifting wind, and the loud report when the sail was flicked to its fullest stretch. With great effort I lifted my head to observe the sails above me shiver and slap against the sheets and spars. The constant chill at this height and in these latitudes became a polar assault. The movement of my pendulum grew more erratic, more violent. A rash of white crests spread across the sea. The sailors on the deck below moved like bees about a flowering honeysuckle, walking in strange arcs, pausing over winches and davits, scuttling up ratlines and down hatches. I wished to spit upon them but my mouth was parched. If not for the occasional cloudburst I would have been reduced to a husk already.

Four days. Four entire days. Long enough to contemplate death, to reconcile it and to welcome its arrival. My rope burns had surpassed burns. Images of flame meeting flesh were fitting only for those first few days. Now my ankles, shins, wrists, elbows, upper arms and neck had been gnawed by rodents, attacked by cutlasses, my flesh opened and raw for the blotting bluebottles that had arrived that morning, lured up the timbers to the mizzen top by my fresh decay, my fetching stench. Now these flies struggled to hold fast to my prickled skin in the wind that came rushing from the south.

I spied Ruskin, Boag and the apprentices of their watch clambering up the mainmast to stow the sails so that the ship might weather the coming storm. As they climbed, sailors below hauled on the lines, raising the sails and permitting me my first glimpse of the storm off the windward side of the bow, thick and dark as charcoal. It was less a storm than the entrance to a massive cave, a black insatiable mouth.

And so it ends, I thought.

I wished now that I could lose consciousness once more, but the mizzen top jerked without rhythm, dashing my head against the mast and running the ropes across fresh skin. The world was too alive for me to drift back to sleep, eternal sleep. My last breath would not slip unnoticed from slack lips as I dreamt of the looping flight of the albatross. No, more than likely my last breath would be thwarted by the icy water. It would be a desperate gulp—salty, unforgiving and full of fear.

The storm was soon upon us. When would the mizzen sails be hoisted? Would anyone dare to climb my mast or would Sepsey fell it like a lumberjack and be done with me?

Off the starboard side I observed with delight that the water really did look as if it were boiling, as it was always described in the accounts of shipwrecks I'd read as a child. So too the wind howled, the decks groaned and waves worked themselves into mountains.

I felt a hand press upon my bare foot but could not see past the coil of ropes that encased me. The hand became a shoulder pressing into my shins and then the figure came up to my face.

'Young Tim,' I managed to say with a measure of equanimity.

The youth cast his eyes down, grabbed for the shrouds that led further up the mast and pulled himself onward.

'I'd cut you down,' Tim said, one bare foot resting on my shoulder, 'but you're safer tied up for the minute.'

It was probably true. If I were cut free I wouldn't have the strength to stand, let alone climb down to the deck in this gale. I would fall to the boards like a bag of sand. A corpse. I recalled my brief fancy four days ago: that Sepsey had climbed to the yards in his drunken frenzy and fallen to the deck.

'Perhaps on the way back,' I said, but Tim was already edging along the footline that ran beneath the topgallant yard.

Swenson was the next to drag himself up to the mizzen top. Rather than bring his face level with mine, he edged around the side of the mast, making a point of grinding the sole of his boot into my bare toes.

'What do we have here then?' Swenson asked, as if he had an audience. I couldn't see him, but his voice was equal to the squall. 'A strange couple, if ever I seen one. You will beg my pardon, madam, won't you?'

The wind dropped for a moment as if waiting for a reply.

Oh, that Vengeance could strike this fiend.

But all was silent around the mizzen top. Swenson's face appeared before me, the skin of his cheeks finely bristled as the stem of a briar rose. 'She's a quiet one, i'n'she?'

From the main top I heard Dhalla's cry of 'Land ho!'

Swenson swung away once more, but I could see no land.

'Land ho!' Tim confirmed from the tip of the topgallant yard. Jarrell and Burton had joined him on the yard—they must have passed while Swenson had been holding court—and they had managed to bundle their half of the sail. Tim was struggling to fasten the farthest gasket, which would hold the sail in place. Somehow he managed to extend his right arm to the north. I followed the line until I struck a row of sheer black cliffs. In that moment the ship must have been broadsided by a large wave as the world was tipped to one side. I smelled the ocean once more, as if I'd been on land these past four days. I heard Swenson groan behind me as he struggled to keep his grip. The ship's tilt was finally checked by the cargo in the hold and the mast was whipped back towards vertical but all too quickly for young Tim, out there on the thin footrope they called the Flemish Horse. He lost his grip and entered the white water without a ripple.

'Canny bastard,' I said.

Jarrell and Burton clung to the yard as children cling to their mothers' legs when they are to be left with relatives. Each had lost hold of their portion of sail and were being whipped and jostled by the lively canvas. They clung for dear life, however cheap it was down there in the Southern Ocean.

And Swenson? I turned my head as far as I could manage in both directions as the mast continued to sway, but saw no sign of him. Down below men from all directions were converging on the quarter deck, presumably to the bag of sand that had been Swenson.

The basalt cliffs loomed ever larger as the rain began to sluice down from its heavenly trough. I could feel the ship wearing to starboard when a lurch of angry wind rushed unimpeded through the bare rigging of the ship's first two masts and met full on the mizzen royal and the partially furled topgallant sail. The very top of this third mast snapped as if it were a twig, its swift retreat only slowed by the forestay that ran to the main top, which strained a moment before bursting loose. The recoil of the stay must have caught the topgallant yard as it passed and undone the gasket, undone Tim's final act, and let the sail unfurl completely. I felt the ship rear back, the bow lifting into the air as if climbing a massive wave. I was tilted back, my shoulders pressed hard against the mast. The sky fell open before me. The black magic of the storm clouds seemed close enough to touch, if only my arms were free. Far from fear, I felt enticed, though I had no choice but to resist the siren's call of the storm.

Jarrell and Burton had managed to make it off the yard and descend the mast without a word to me. I heard the whishing sound of the remaining forestays as they were cut free by the men on deck. The mizzenmast began to shudder in the search for the point of least resistance. I could hear the creaking of the timber over the wind and rain that pummelled me and the topgallant sail.

And then my mast snapped once more, somewhere below the mizzen top this time, and I was lifted free of the infernal ship, the remaining lines giving way like cobwebs, and my giant crucifix splashed down into the waves.

Here was the salty water, the final bath. The cold shot down my spine. My raw wrists and ankles screamed with pain. I found myself holding my breath in the calm underwater world and gasping for air whenever I breached the surface and returned to this other wild, roaring world. The mast must have landed with its yards square to the water. It seemed a wonder they had not snapped. Perhaps they had and it was only a matter of one or two waves before the great log rolled over and I was pitched into the water for good, but for now I found myself lying with my nose to the sky and being dunked into the water less and less. I thought about my companion, lashed to the other side of the mast. The side that did not see the surface.

Oh, to trade places with her.

A mass of canvas was washed over me, covering me like a bed sheet. The topsail and its spars must have come away with this section of mast. The sail was pulled back as the mast swung slowly to leeward. I managed to lift my head and catch one last glimpse of the ship as it tottered near the horizon before I closed my eyes and lowered my head to the mast. The wind was not as fierce down at this level. The length of mast to which I was attached must have been at least forty feet long and further stabilised by the yards, canvas and rope that stretched from it.

I felt myself being lulled back to sleep, despite the noise and the biting cold. *Sleep, eternal sleep . . .*

Why did you start there?

It is how stories like mine tend to start. In the middle of things.

But you survived, you must have. Why were you tied to the mast? How did you get to Marumaru?

As I said, it's a long story.

Beginnings

My name is Gabriel Doig. I was born into a family of ships'
carvers on the banks of the River Clyde in Scotland. I grew up at
the feet of my father and grandfather in a shower of sawdust and
wood shavings as they made their figureheads: bold ladies in
flowing dresses bound for the grandest barques and the fastest
clippers. My mother, Agnes, would often pose as a model in
the early stages of a new carving, but she preferred to pass her
time in the wee office that fronted Dalrymple Street, the main
thoroughfare between the custom house and the shipyards. Her
chief task was keeping the books, but she was seldom alone.
Shopkeepers, fishermen, *Evening Times* paper boys, women
with the finest parasols or the tattiest tartan shawls across their
hunched shoulders—they all found time as they went about their
business to stop in and say a word to my mother. She knew
everything that was happening along the docks although she
never seemed to step beyond the threshold.

The four of us lived above the workshop. The living quarters
were cramped, but it was handy being only a flight of stairs from
your work. From the upstairs window you could see the bare masts
in the graving dock and beyond these the off-white sails of world
trade coming and going. I was an only child raised in a world of
adults. When I was a wean my family called me precocious. As I

grew older the terms they preferred to use were: brash, bull-headed and contermaucious. I was a handful, all right. I can't count the times I told my father I was running away, that his figureheads and trailboards and whetstones and invoices could go hang.

But I am getting ahead of myself.

My grandfather, Robert Doig, had been lured down from his croft in the 1830s by the promise of steady wages and the extravagances of kippers, salted salmon and apples. He was one of seven novice carvers apprenticed on the *Jupiter* and he quickly worked his way up to carving the figureheads for a dozen merchant sloops and brigantines. When my father, Duncan, was old enough he joined the firm of Doig & Son, doubling its workforce. At the time, the banks of the River Clyde were home to dozens of shipbuilders who catered for the best shipping lines in Britain and a good many European firms. Clydeside ships were taking coal, coke, textiles, tempered glass and settlers to strange corners of the Earth and bringing back to the motherland tea, cotton, flax, gum, gold, wool, stuffed birds, shrunken heads and tales of wonder.

I was given my first carver's mallet when I was old enough to walk, though I preferred to gnaw its handle rather than put it to work. Sometimes I sat at my mother's feet as she talked the ear off a police constable or supercargo. Her talk was constant, compulsive, as if she would die should a minute of daylight pass in silence. When it was just the two of us in the office, she told me stories about beings from the Unseelie Court: the spunkies that steal children from their beds and leave ugly changelings in their place, or the Glastig, who resembles a beautiful woman until you are up close and realise she's made up of animal parts— goats, horses, hares. According to my mother, the Glastig liked to seduce near-sighted men and drown them in the breakers. She would laugh and slap her thigh at the most gruesome parts, as if she didn't believe in the old stories, though she still insisted on pouring a wee jug of milk over the cobblestones on the night of Samhain for the 'auld Hairy Ones'.

I was only a bairn and believed it all, of course. The world was a scary place, a magical place.

The only helpful beings my mother ever spoke of were the brounies, who liked to complete unfinished chores. At the end of the day, when my father and grandfather retired upstairs, she'd say, 'All right, Gabriel, time for the brounies to pick up their broomies.'

I was five years old when my grandfather began his sudden decline and I was expected to do more around the workshop. But my head was filled with fairy stories. My father would often catch me dreaming, pausing as I rubbed crocus powder and tallow into the leather strops and taking a long, satisfied sniff, or leaning on my broom, the workshop half-swept, and inspecting my red and swollen hands, the result of another calamitous expedition to retrieve the beeswax we used to seal the carved taffrails that were left unpainted.

Around this time my mother taught me to read so that in time I could handle purchase orders, invoices and remittances, though I preferred to put this skill to use perusing *Reynolds's Miscellany* for true accounts from castaways or following the fortunes of Dick Turpin in the penny dreadfuls. I learnt early on that people spoke differently on the page than in real life. If I were to open my lips right now—if I could speak—I'm sure I would sound quite different. But this is the voice I have on the page, the only voice I've left.

I spent my time in the workshop acting out feats of the highwayman with my band of imaginary friends, hiding behind great blocks of yellow pine or lengths of elm before leaping out, wielding a parting tool like a pistol and telling the passengers of the coach to keep still 'Or I shall have a snap at you'.

Soon enough, my imaginary friends took up residence in the figureheads my father was producing. I gave them all names— Betsy, Mirabelle, Rosanna—and could not hide my tears when they were carried out of the workshop, laid flat on a cart and shrouded in bed sheets, to ascend to the bow of a ship and never return.

My memories of childhood ring with four sounds: sandpaper on wood, steel on wood, steel on slipstone and my father's voice berating me: 'The workshop is nae place f'dreaming!'

Just as you have many questions for your father, Avis, I am left grasping for answers when it comes to mine. I look back now and wonder if he was so eager to put me to work simply so I could pick up the slack left by my grandfather, or if his father's demise had affected him in other ways. Did he ever stop and think about the trade into which I was being ushered? As he passed me my first carver's mallet in lieu of a rattle he must have had an inkling that a ship's carver mightn't fare as well over the next two decades as he had in the last two. My father was not unaware that the steam engine had already changed the world. He called the steamers that ran along the Clyde 'puffers' or 'toy shippies'. He claimed they were no good out on the ocean and couldn't match the grace and beauty of a sailing ship (he was right about this last point, at least). Perhaps he really believed that sailing ships would endure. That he was offering me as good a life as the one he had led. If this is true, all I can say is that he was subject to the most human of self-deceptions: that he and his profession were necessary and infallible.

Whatever grudge I bore the man, it has long since dissolved. But as a child I ignored his remonstrations and continued larking about the workshop. As I soaked the day's paintbrushes in turpentine and massaged the last traces of pigment from between their bristles, it was hard to resist the urge to think about the places to which my figurehead friends were travelling, out in front of their vessels. I imagined myself cast below the bowsprit and cutting through the waves, through the pea-soup fogs and icy storms of the world's wild oceans, the eyes of the ship, its proud mascot, clutching my breast and staring defiantly at all who sailed past.

My mother was fond of telling me how much I resembled my father and grandfather. That even at the age of six or seven it was apparent that I would grow to the same modest height, would share their stocky build and square, paw-like hands. I already had their thin auburn hair and would no doubt grow a fine rust-coloured beard in time. I did not like to hear this. I wanted to grow up tall and blond, a fitting mate for whichever of Doig & Son's Nordic beauties miraculously returned to the workshop, animate and amorous, after being struck with lightning out there on the ocean.

Though I found enough wonders inside the workshop of Doig & Son, the town back from the docks seemed a dull place to spend a life. I dreaded the days my father sent me to collect scrap leather from the back of the saddlery or buy paintbrushes from blind widow McTavish, errands that led me into the network of narrow closes and lanes where the walls of the buildings were rough and uneven, the paving stones small and jumbled, the air thick and close with smoke. The tenements struggled to conceal the lives they contained: washing hung from wooden poles fastened to walls with guide ropes; rough rugs were draped over railings for beating; solitary old women wrapped in cloth and blankets as if they were bandages stood sentry every few yards; children huddled in twos or threes fast against walls, sheltering from the rain or the bucket of suds likely to be tossed by the upstairs neighbour. They would always break off their chatter or pick up their ball of tightly wound rags and stare at me as if I were a ghost. I suppose I was looking at them the same way.

Despite the yellow bills plastered to the side of some of these tenements proclaiming, 'Town Improvement Bill: These Premises Coming Down', the closes never seemed to change. Time refused to pass. All the movement and enterprise seemed to be around the docks or on the water: the constant stream of carts around the huge brick cone of the bottle works; the chugging chimneys of the sugar refinery further along the river; the puff of white from the paddle steamer that puttered up and down the river like a gosling that has lost its mother; the derricks of the shipyards, the masts rising in their midst.

I began avoiding the lanes and closes, taking circuitous routes along the river and the major roads to accomplish my errands. On reflection, such actions scream of cowardice and timidity and run contrary to the image I held of myself at the time as some kind of brave adventurer trapped in a life of drudgery. But if there is one thing I have learnt in the course of my life it is that proximity seldom improves perception.

Time passed and I graduated from tales of highwaymen and pirates to *Journey to the Centre of the Earth*, the *Odyssey* and the *Aeneid*. But my father did not give up on me.

'If you want to daff with gods and goddesses,' he said one day, 'then you had better learn how to make them.'

He drew the rough shape of a figure in pencil on four planes of a block of yellow pine and instructed me to rough it out.

'Leave plenty of fat on the banes,' he said. 'It's for me to find the final shape and there's nae way to fatten her up if you go too far.'

The final figure was to be a full-length female with a long dress trailing down below her ankles. Other ships' carvers formed their blocks by laminating several smaller lengths of timber together—sometimes they even carved heads and limbs separately before affixing them to the trunk—but the preferred approach at Doig & Son was more akin to that of a carver working in marble. This new figure was cast diagonally on a great block of yellow pine that was much taller than I would ever be. I pulled up a stool and began by knocking off the four top corners with the hatchet and was soon immersed in the fantasy that there was a woman trapped inside the block and I was working to set her free. Was it Circe or was it Dido? The pleasure I felt as the form slowly took shape and the woman emerged from the wood was better than any burst pimple or whiff of treated leather.

When I came to the lower half of the figure, I had to hold her blocky chin with one hand to keep her from toppling forward as I chipped away down below.

'You'll be wantin' to lay her down,' my father said, chuckling.

I dropped my hatchet and placed my other hand on the figure's chin, but could support only the weight of the wood and nothing more.

'Aye, you'll need to work on those muscles if you're to be

much use to me,' he said and drew out two sawhorses from beneath the far workbench. 'You mind her head.' He ran one end of a chain under the wood and pulled it up until he could slip the final link over the large hook hanging from the ceiling to which the other end of the chain was already attached. He pinned his right hip to one of the block's remaining flat planes, pulled the leather strap that hoisted the chain with one hand and directed the figure with his other hand until it came to rest on the sawhorses. 'Just hoy when she needs turning.'

When I had done all I could safely do with the hatchet my father gave me a large gouge and took up one himself. 'You take the backside and I'll take the front,' he said and gave me a wink.

The figure became slimmer as the day wore on, but was still more golem than siren at day's close. As I swept up our shared shavings, I revelled in the glow of my father's good mood and admiration.

'A good day's work, my son. And about time you did your first.'

After another day of roughing out, I had to lay down my tools and look on as my father set about removing the last of the woody rind to reveal the raw grain of the figurehead's hair, skin and clothing. I'd never seen anything so beautiful and he still had another week of work feathering the hair, bringing out the veins in soft relief and detailing the lace and brocade on her dress, before sanding and treating the wood and painting the figure in polychrome. While my father worked, I copied acanthus scrolls onto a length of mahogany that would become one of the trailboards.

When a cart arrived the next week with three more enormous pre-dried, square-cut blocks of pine, my father translated a sketch that was attached to a purchase order onto the first block and asked me to start roughing out, beginning the adventure anew. Except it was less of an adventure the second time around. By the third, it was just another chore. Anyone could slough big chunks of wood off with an axe. I wanted to keep going, to feather the hair and sand the skin, but instead I was stuck practising my gouge work on decorative panels while my father carried out the master strokes he had learnt under his own father and perfected in time, but seemed unwilling to share.

I'd badger him as he worked. 'How come I cannae do that?' 'I'm nae going to learn anything this way.' 'You're just afraid I'll be better than you.' He told me I was going as fast as I could expect, that it was not a race and he couldn't afford to waste any timber.

'It might grow on trees, Gabriel, but wood doesnae come cheap.'

I was surprised my father did not come down on me harder— if I couldn't get my way, the least I could do was make him lose his temper—but I think he was pleased that I was showing an interest in his craft for the first time and this must have softened his mood.

Time passed. My father was true to his word. With every new figurehead, I took on another task: treating the wood, painting the base coat, colouring the clothing and finally the skin and eyes. In the months leading up to my fifteenth birthday, I learnt how to make larger blocks for stock figureheads by laminating three-inch-thick lengths of pine together with linseed oil putty. On the day of my birthday, my father removed the clamps from a five-foot-high block and handed me a pencil.

'There you go,' he said. 'Your first figurehead from scratch. There's enough here for a bust, possibly a full torso.'

I had been waiting for this moment. A piece all of my own. I stared at the laminated block, pencil in hand, but could not imagine the shape of the figure submerged inside.

'Dinnae worry,' my father said, 'it's just for stock. Take your time.'

I spent the entire morning and most of the afternoon sketching and resketching on a piece of paper and then on the first plane of the block itself until the surface was a grey, indecipherable map.

'Come on, lad,' my father said. 'I said take your time but you cannae take forever.'

'But I dinnae know who's inside,' I said.

'Ach, it's nae hard. Will it be a lad or a lass?'

'A lass.'

'Aye, good choice. Dinnae waste time on a man unless it's a commission. Is it a bust, or will you go for everything above the waist?'

'Everything.'

'Long locks or a bunnet?'

'Long locks.'

'And what's her name?'

I hesitated. 'Penelope.'

'Och, that's nae good. You cannae give her a lassie's name, you have to give her a *ship's* name. Venus o' the Seas, Perseverance, Faith, Valour, Glory.'

'But Pa, there are plenty of *Marys*.'

'Aye. And this lass'll end up on a ship with a name like *Big Ben* but that's nae the point. Think of a virtue and bring it to life, that's the secret, Gabriel.'

I thought about Penelope being bothered by all those suitors in Ithaca, holding out hope that her husband, Odysseus, was still alive and might one day return. How he did return, disguised, and won Penelope's hand by stringing his bow and shooting an arrow through twelve axe heads before turning his arrows on the suitors.

'All right,' I said. 'What about Vengeance?'

He chuckled. 'You've been reading more of them stories. But aye, Vengeance will do. You dinnae have the wood for a raised arm, but will she have both arms crossed or by her side?'

'Crossed in defiance.'

'Good lad. That's your figure there.' He grabbed the block of wood and rotated it a quarter-turn so that a fresh plane faced me. 'Now sketch her profile and get roughing out.'

I worked slowly the rest of the day and all of the next, careful that there were no rash strokes to limit my future choices. Vengeance emerged from the wood, her shoulders square to the world but her head turned to the side, demurring in unsanded pine though I'd make her cheeks burn once they were painted. I was able to change the position of her arms so that they were no longer crossed: one rested on her ribs as if she were about to make a low bow, while the other was positioned behind her back.

At the end of the second day, my father paid Vengeance an inspection.

'Is this the neckline of her dress way up here?' he asked.

'Aye.'

'Och, she'll need to show more flesh than that. One breast at least.'

I felt my face redden. I knew that sailors believed a naked woman could calm the seas—I'd sanded and painted dozens of bared breasts that my father had produced—but I was hoping to avoid carving my first breast entirely by myself this time. I hadn't seen or felt a real breast since I was a bairn.

Before I could respond my father had turned the figure and asked, 'What are you doing around the back here?'

'She's clutching a knife.'

'Aye, but her back'll be bolted to the bow. Dinnae waste time on the back, lad.'

'But Pa, if she's for stock, willnae a shipowner give her a full inspection?'

He brought a hand to his beard. 'Aye, perhaps. But it willnae do to spend a day's work for a ten-second keek.' He picked up a veiner and his carver's mallet. 'The story needs to be told out front. This arm needs to say, "I'm holding a chib 'gainst me back," but you dinnae need to carve it.' He set in a faint line with the veiner on the outside of the arm, making the angle at which it protruded from the shoulder more dramatic. 'Aye, that's an arm with something to hide.'

'Thank you,' I said begrudgingly.

'A carver doesnae makes mistakes, Gabriel, only adjustments.'

I took his advice, lowering the neckline of Vengeance's dress to reveal one breast and leaving the back blocked out while I worked the final layers of wood from her flesh and got to sanding her down. I was back in familiar territory now, having painted dozens of my father's figureheads, but the blank back continued to bother me. It was true that when Vengeance was pushed against the wall she looked as if she clutched a knife to her back and as soon as she turned her face to you she'd strike. But pull her out from the wall a couple of inches and it was too much not to peek around the back and be disappointed.

'She's nae a bad first effort,' my father said, inspecting Vengeance the morning after I had applied the final coat of paint. His hand ran over the folds of her dress and up to the smooth mound of her exposed breast, coming to rest as the webbing between his thumb and forefinger pushed up against the slight rise of the areola. Still gripping the breast, he turned the figure around, paused and turned her back.

'She's a bracing design all right, and may nae be to many tastes, but a good first effort.'

I may have spent my childhood separate from others my age, shut in the workshop or off on some adventure with Dirk Turpin or Captain Nemo, but I see now that I was typical of most fifteen-year-old lads in that I thought myself deserving of more praise than my father granted. I could see a few imperfections in my handiwork, of course, but I felt that I was only one or two figureheads' practice from equalling the skill of my father.

One or two figureheads became four or five, yet I was still spending days on the fingers of each hand or perfecting the nostrils. My father seemed resigned to the process, which did little to improve my mood.

'It took me a few figures to get to where I am now,' he'd say. 'Your scroll work is barrie and your figures are getting there.'

'I'm sick of carving for stock,' I told him one afternoon when I decided this was what was holding me back. 'When can I do a commission?'

'When you're ready.' He cast a purposeful glance at the far wall of the workshop where Vengeance stood alongside Fortitude, Courage, Lightning and Passion, all awaiting a second-rate shipowner to select them for their latest bow.

Enter Agathos Rennie. He came in through the workshop's

large back door, which we left open to Drummer's Close to let in air. Rennie was well known along the docks as an upstart who had inherited a one-third share of his father's shipping business and, thanks to a campaign of half-truths and intimidation, had managed to unburden his younger brother and mother of their stock and claim control of the firm. On the afternoon he entered Doig & Son, his first big commission, an unnamed two hundred-foot clipper, was nearing completion.

'Hard at work, I see,' he announced stiffly, in the kind of sanded-down accent that frequent visitors to London seemed to acquire. He was tall and lean but a wee bit stooped, as if he'd crammed himself into a coat two sizes too small. Rennie pressed a finger to the bridge of his pince-nez, despite the fact it appeared to be pinned hard against his face as it was. He couldn't have been more than twenty-five years old and I questioned whether the eyeglasses were necessary or an attempt to seem older.

'Mr Rennie,' my father said, 'I wondered when you'd stop by.' He laid his rasp down but gestured for me to keep working.

'Aye, Doig,' said Rennie. ''Tis a figurehead I'm after.'

'Your father was a good man but you're cutting it fine if you want his likeness,' he said, 'or your own.'

'I'm aware of that. What have you got,' Rennie paused and made a show of inspecting his fingernails, 'in stock?'

'A fine selection.' My father placed a hand in the small of Rennie's back to guide him to the wall where half a dozen of his own figureheads stood.

'I don't fancy spending much on what is, in the end, a trifle to please the crew and nothing more.'

'In that case,' my father said, wheeling Rennie to the left and directing him to my figures, 'we have a selection of busts and torsos. Perfect for a clipper. Keeps the weight down and,' he slipped into a whisper that was still audible to me at the back of the workshop, 'easy on the pocketbook.'

At this I placed my gouge down on my piece of inlay and crept forward. I saw Rennie bring his hand to his chin, appraising my feisty maidens.

'Are they all the same price?'

'Aye. We can work something out for a firm such as yours, Mr Rennie.'

The shipowner ran his eyes along the row once more before stepping forward to inspect Vengeance. I wished he would not peek around the back, but so he did.

'She's all ready to be fitted,' my father said. 'Perfect size for a clipper bow.'

'What is the meaning of this arm?'

'She's clutching something back there, in'she?'

'But what?'

'It's best left—' he began.

'A knife,' I said in my loudest, clearest voice.

Rennie and my father turned, one face a mixture of surprise and derision, the other all vexation.

'And who do we have here?' Rennie asked.

'That's my lad, Gabriel. A fine carver hisself.'

Rennie pulled his pince-nez from his nose and squinted at me. 'Did you carve this, boy?' he asked, flicking a thumb dismissively at the figurehead.

I didn't like the way he had spoken to me, so I said nothing.

Rennie turned back to survey Vengeance. He stepped forward and ran the back of his fingers along the cheek of her turned-away face. I liked how she refused to meet the shipowner's gaze. It was easy to imagine that she bore a grudge against this snoot. That she would creep into his room when he was fast asleep and slit his throat.

'I see you are trying to foist your seconds on me, Mr Doig. Bup!' Rennie raised his hand to silence my father. 'Whatever you were going to charge me, halve it and we have a deal.'

My father looked down at the long-fingered hand that was offered him. For a moment I imagined him clamping his hand down on Rennie's wrist and telling him that he'd not stand for a body treating any of Doig & Son's wares with such disdain. But he took the hand and shook it firmly.

I had sold my first figurehead, though the circumstances left a lot to be desired.

The next day we took Vengeance to the shipyard where Rennie's clipper was near completion, me pushing the barrow and my father striding ahead, telling the fishwives and bootblacks to mind the way. The harmless grey sky was obscured by the rigging of ships large and small, old wooden barques that had rounded the Horn for the last time and freshly painted iron-hulled vessels that had yet to leave the Clyde.

'She's a fine-looking craft,' my father said when we came to the yard of Rennie's shipbuilder. 'She'd trim a day off the *Ariel*'s time, though I fear we will nae see too many more like her. Shame young Rennie's too tight to deck her out properly.'

I looked down at Vengeance, wrapped in sheets.

'I didnae mean your figure, lad. The inside. I suspect even the captain's doorknob is without a flourish.'

He patted me on the shoulder and went to speak to the chief shipwright. Soon enough a wee crew of men was working to winch Vengeance up to the bowsprit. I accompanied my father down into the dock and up the tall wooden ladder that was lashed to the gunwale.

'Shouldnae be too much to fix her on,' my father said when we were both on deck. 'Just a few notches and a few daubs of paint.'

'The paints,' I said. I had left them sitting in the barrow at the end of the dock.

'Aye, you'll have to get down and fetch them.'

It was hard work climbing the ladder a second time: the rungs were spaced with taller men in mind and I was clasping my father's wooden palette box. I made it to the bow and leant over to find my father sitting on a network of ropes, his feet dangling through the bottom while he positioned Vengeance against the wooden trenails that protruded from the prepared surface of the stem.

When the figure was held fast, he looked up. 'You took your time.'

'Aye. It is a decent ladder, that one.'

He laughed. 'How about you pass me the paints and climb over?'

I pushed onto my tippertoes and peered further over the edge and to the ground.

'That's it. Take a look down. There's nocht to fear. A ship's carver must have a head for heights.'

'I'm nae scared,' I said, though of course I was.

I passed the box to my father and gingerly lifted one leg over the gunwale.

'That's the way. Now grab hold of my hand. Aye, that's it. Ease yourself down. Aye, aye, that's the lad.'

And there I was, standing on the rope netting, one hand pressed hard against the bowsprit, the other white-knuckling my father's fingers.

'You'll need a hand, or two, for the painting.'

My body gave a sudden shudder as the lines moved beneath my feet.

'I can do it,' I said through gritted teeth, more to myself than my father.

'Aye, but nae when you're shaking like that. You'll settle.'

He hoisted himself to a standing position and, leaning his head against the bowsprit, opened the palette box and began to mix a small amount of paint to match the deep blue of Vengeance's dress. He then placed the brush between his teeth, folded the box shut and placed his free hand on my shoulder. I looked up at him. He raised his eyebrows and bared his teeth, prompting me to take the paintbrush from his mouth.

'Aye, that's the lad.'

With my father's hand on my shoulder, I soon forgot the precariousness of my position and was transported back to the workshop, giving Vengeance her last touches before she set off to see the world.

'How does she look from down there?' my father yelled to two men at the bottom of the drydock. They gave a hoot of agreement.

Our work complete, we climbed back onto the deck and descended the ladder.

We were standing at the cutwater, paying our last respects to Vengeance, her head turned to the Clyde's dredged channel as if eager to commence her exploits, when a cold voice sounded from behind us.

'I guess that will do.'

I turned to see Agathos Rennie, as thin and stooped as he had appeared in the workshop, though in the weak light that filtered through the heavy clouds his skin looked paler; it was hard to imagine blood flowing beneath it.

'She's a perfect fit,' my father said.

'Does your ship have a name yet, Mr Rennie?' I asked.

Rennie frowned and looked at my father. 'She's to be christened on the morrow. The *Agathos*, that's her name.'

On the way back to the workshop, my father said he'd expected nothing less from Agathos Rennie. 'She might be a grand ship but she'll have a miserable crew so long as it's doing the bidding of that beetle.'

Little did I suspect I would one day experience such miseries first hand.

I am enjoying your tale very much.

I am glad there is pleasure in it for some.

I haven't read the Odyssey, though I have seen it mentioned in other books. Would you recommend I read it?

I will see if there is a copy for sale when next I go for supplies.

To Marumaru?

No, that would be unwise. There's another town to the south. Much smaller. No department stores. But it will have enough to sustain us.

You mustn't forget more writing paper.

Of course, my dear. I will fetch something for your stomach as well.

9 November 1890

When I awoke it was as if the inside of my skull were being chiselled out. My body convulsed with cold. Weak daylight filtered through my eyelids. An oily, cludgy smell filled my nostrils. The sound of breakers and the screech of strange birds entered my ears. I brought a hand to my forehead and felt the crust of salt below my hairline, opened my eyes and looked at my hand. The palm and fingers were white, the wrist a mess of reds and browns, but it was free. I could feel the pitch pine mast pressed to my back, but ran my hand against it just to be sure, knocking twice, as if for luck.

I lifted my head and saw that the ropes sat limply around my waist and legs. The mast lay perpendicular to the breakers. Beyond my feet and the battered mizzen top I saw green, land-green, a slope covered in vegetation leading up and away from sheer rock faces. I sat up, keeping the surf to my back. The cliffs did not seem as high as I had supposed during the storm the previous day. Perhaps this was a different island. Still, if I was to reach this green slope I would have to make my way along the rocky foreshore and find a way up the cliffs. I wriggled my legs free of the ropes, swung them around so that my feet might touch terra firma once more, but hesitated. The margin between the sea and the foreshore was alive with a tangle of thick kelp. The narrow beach, if that's the term, was a blanket of rock riddled with thin seams, jagged edges and wee boulders making their hundred-year journey from the earth back to the sea, all of it given a marbled appearance by the thousand-thousand white streaks of bird droppings. My bare feet were numb. They resembled cakes of delicate soap. I mightn't feel it at the time but the rock would tear them to shreds. I lifted my feet up to rest on the mast and hugged my knees to keep warm.

The sense of abandon that had gripped me while fastened to the mizzen top had vanished. I was cold and weak but no longer wished to die. The melodrama of it all had seemed fitting in the moment of my life that most resembled the stories I'd read as a child—stories where women would swoon in equal measure at the sight of a pistol, the revelation of a true identity or the simple avowal of love. I rolled onto my chest to feel beneath the mast. Rock. Pressing one hand gingerly against the ground I lowered my head. Bits of dry brown kelp, fresher, slimier strands of yellow-tinged weed, rock, ropes and tattered canvas, but no sign of *her*. She must have slipped free during the night. It would explain the looseness of the ropes. I marvelled at how I could have stayed perched atop the mast and out of the waves.

I scanned the beach that curved like a crescent moon. A number of birds were gathered around one patch of kelp in the distance. I thought of them as gulls, though they could have been nellies, those dark-feathered birds the sailors liked to take pot shots at from the gunwales, or any number of other birds for which I did not then know the name. I didn't even know where I was. Could it be Tierra del Fuego? It seemed too soon to have reached the Horn, but perhaps I'd lost count of the days. There must have been other islands littered in the Southern Ocean, but I knew nothing of them. I knew the State of Victoria better than I knew this ocean and could recite all the stops on the Melbourne to Albury railway line, despite the fact I never got to board my train.

I wished to lie back down and sleep, but I knew that I would catch my death. I ripped two strips of canvas to wrap around my feet, gathered the loose pieces of timber and rope that were scattered near the mast and went in search of food and fresh water. I set off in the direction of the gulls, still in the same spot on the foreshore. As I drew closer I discovered the source of their curiosity tangled in the kelp. I picked up a rock and threw it at the feasting birds, but it fell well short of the corpse. I let out a scream, but the gulls seemed unafraid of me. They seemed, in fact, to regard me with greedy interest. Tossing another rock underhand, I managed to strike the corpse square on the chest, pushing up its arms, and the gulls took fright. I quickly threw another rock and approached waving and shouting.

'Get gone. Away with you!'

The birds withdrew a few yards, some to the air, some to the rocks, screeching all the while.

I grabbed a boot and hauled the corpse free of the kelp, so that it lay on its back, arms outstretched. The eye sockets had already been pecked clean, but I could recognise young Tim well enough.

'Ach, it's nae right,' I said. 'It's nae right at all.'

I crouched down. The gulls had already worked the waistcoat and shirt open, nudged his vest upward and had been in the process of pulling his insides out when I had interrupted. I reached inside the waistcoat and removed Tim's grimy spoon, a splinter of wood and his pocket watch.

'Half past four, as always,' I said.

I searched the trouser pockets next, finding a coarse needle that looked as if it had been whittled from the bone of some seabird, and a little wooden cardinal, one of Sepsey's carvings.

'No matches,' I shouted to the waves. But why would the lad have matches on him? And even if he did, they would have been sodden and useless now.

I stood and tossed the little cardinal into sea.

There would be no fire that night.

My clothes were still damp and clung to my skin. The sailcloth around my feet was coming undone. I looked at Tim's boots. Though the lad had been but a spirl, he was close to my height.

'Aye, they're no use to you now,' I said, patting him on the shoulder. I untied the laces on the left foot—the right's were already undone—and removed the leather boots.

'Ach, you're nae wearing any hose. What would your mammie say?'

I rewrapped one of my feet in cloth and tried jamming it into a boot, but it wouldn't pass through the narrowest part of the shaft. I removed the cloth and tried again. This time my toes were able to touch the insole and with a bit of wriggling the rest of my foot slid inside. I did the same with the next boot and stood. The fit was tight. Without stockings I would be plagued by blisters but I knew this was better than leaving my bare feet at the mercy of the rocks.

I noticed one of the gulls had returned to its perch on Tim's forehead. It had managed to open the mouth and work its head down the lad's throat.

'Hoy!' I shouted, but the bird either couldn't hear or chose to ignore me.

I crunched over and considered kicking Tim's jaw so that his teeth would sever the bird's head, but hesitated. Perhaps it was the fear of desecrating the corpse, or the thought of kicking Tim with his own boots. Or perhaps I knew deep down that these birds were not so different from me. They were just making do with what the sea provided.

The dull brown bird removed its head from Tim's mouth. It was cloaked in an executioner's hood of dark red blood. A strip of meat trailed from its beak and I tried not to consider the origin of this morsel. I tapped the bird under the breast with my boot and it took flight.

I set about removing Tim's clothes. Waistcoat, shirt, vest, trousers. I considered removing the drawers. Every thread would be useful. They looked as if they were made of decent cotton. But I wondered how a ship's boy had come to have cotton drawers.

Perhaps he'd run away from a wealthy family. Perhaps he was the youngest son of a merchant who was friendly with Captain Bock. Or perhaps he'd come from poverty as I had always assumed and these drawers were the only gift his widow mother could give him before he set sail.

It was no good. I couldn't take the drawers.. Even though I knew the birds would find a way beneath their hem.

I found three smaller rocks, placed two in Tim's eye sockets and wedged one in his mouth.

'I'd bury you, but I dinnae have the tools,' I said aloud. 'Could use my hands, I guess, but then I might as well be howkin' my own grave.'

I trudged further along the beach in my tight boots, squeezing the lad's clothes in my arms, looking for more flotsam, following the flight of the seabirds in case they led me to another corpse. I noticed movement in the distance. A wee, wobbling form making its way across the rocky shore to the kelp. As I approached, the shape of the bird became clearer. A penguin, about two feet high, with striking yellow eyebrows a couple of inches long that stood erect on its head. My stomach rumbled and the bird turned its entire body to face me, cocking its head to the side. Its snowy breast was marred by an irregular maroon patch, not unlike a large birthmark, though my first thought was that even the penguins on this island stooped to defiling corpses.

The penguin showed no fear of me and after a few moments of contemplation, turned back to the sea and waddled forward, its black flippers held out to maintain its dainty balance. I thought about giving chase, but my feet were already warming up and had started to ache. I could hear more birds nearby and spotted a few penguins on ledges protruding from the cliffs. If these little, awkward creatures could ascend the steep face, I must also be able.

I walked swiftly along the bottom of the cliff looking for the rock fall or terraces that the penguins must have used. I rounded a small promontory that required me getting my boots wet. On the other side I found not just the imagined rock fall but a small, brown stream of fresh water. I fell to my knees and brought cupped hand after cupped hand to my mouth. If I had stopped to taste the water, it might have been the foulest thing to have ever passed my lips, stained with peat and penguin effluent as it was, but it made my body sing. It was only once I'd had my fill that I stilled my hands and saw the reflection in the shallow water. Sunken eyes, blotchy skin, rust-red beard.

My father's reflection.

A Family Complaint

I was eighteen and my father forty when it happened, though not all at once. The first sign was him complaining daily of a wammlin stomach and pounding head. He was forever running out into the close to relieve himself.

My mother began to spend more time in the workshop fretting over her husband than in the office minding the books and trading gossip.

'It's nae good, Duncan,' she'd tell him. ''Tis your father's affliction.'

'Blether. There's no similarity. The old man was a drunkard. I never touched a drop since he met his end.'

'Aye, but I never saw your father touch a drop neither.'

'Ach, away with you, woman. It's just me wammlin stomach. A wee dram would probably do me good.'

Soon after this exchange his hands began to tremble and he found it difficult to work a gouge.

Then his ankle went. It was as if, unbeknownst to him, he had been a marionette his whole life and suddenly the great puppeteer in the sky had snipped the string attached to the end of his left foot. He would lift his leg and the foot would hang down like the head of a dead duck, the toes dragging along the ground. Unlike the aches in his stomach and head, my father did not voice any complaints about his ankle, though his distress was plain enough to see. He walked by moving his left foot out in a semicircle to avoid lifting the leg and having the toes drop. To see him coggling towards you on the street you'd swear he was drunk, but I never did see him have that dram of whisky.

He descended into a deep depression, armed with the knowledge of what became of his father and the injustice that the affliction had set in ten years sooner this time, cutting him down at the peak of his powers. Unsteady on his feet and easily distracted, he was little use in the workshop and spent most of his time shut away in the upstairs quarters, leaving me to finish his commissions and keep Doig & Son afloat.

I had become a proficient ship's carver without ever developing a passion for the craft. My antagonism towards my father had spurred me on, the desire to prove his equal, his better, but I still dreamt of leaving the Clyde, setting sail on a ship bound for the Pacific, making my fortune capturing exotic birds for sultans and zoological societies or absconding to become the chief of some scantily clad tribe. But I didn't run away. With my father consigned to bed, I knew I couldn't leave my mother. Not yet. So I picked up my tools and tackled my new responsibilities with the confidence of youth. I'd show my father. I'd show everyone. But each figurehead presented a new challenge. How to produce a valkyrie's spear that wouldn't snap in the first gale. What colours to mix to produce the flesh tone of an Indian maharaja. Finding the right blend of symmetrical swirls and natural chaos for Neptune's beard.

When I went upstairs at the end of the day I found circuitous ways of asking my father's advice.

'Och, I'm nae use to anybody,' was his only response. 'And it'll happen to you in time, mark that. It'll happen to you.'

The family physician, Doctor Stanley, who'd overseen the demise of my grandfather, was equally baffled by my father's illness. After the first few visits and the abuse my father hurled at him, the doctor refused to return.

Four years I laboured in the workshop alone, joined only by

my mother at the end of the day to sweep the floors. In quieter moments, the occasional groan from my father might sound through the workshop ceiling. The figureheads that filled the workshop were no longer my friends—I needed to sell them too much to form any sort of attachment—but I used them as stand-ins for my father when rehearsing the blazing rows that always seemed to end with me turning his own words back on him: 'Och, you *are* nae use to anybody.' But the sight of my father's twitching, writhing, waxy form whenever I ventured upstairs sapped whatever spite or courage I needed to attack the man and he expired without that knot of bitterness in my gut ever getting untied.

The year was 1881. New sailing ships were no longer being built along the banks of the Clyde. The Suez Canal had been open a dozen years, providing a faster route to China and undercutting the chief appeal of the fast but unpredictable tea clipper. The screw propeller and triple expansion engine meant steamships could do everything a sailing craft could without being at the mercy of the winds. I was only twenty-two—younger than my grandfather when he had come down from his croft—and could easily change trades, change towns, change countries, but I worried about what my mother would do away from her office and its window.

Commissions were harder and harder to come by. The projects I carved for stock, though of the highest craftsmanship and refinement, found no buyers. I had no friends my own age and, unless the old fantasy of a bolt of lightning bringing one of my figures to life came true, there was little chance of me finding a woman to share my bed and give me a son. The ratio of wooden breasts to flesh ones I had seen since I was a child must have been several hundred to two (both of these belonged to Claire, to whom I paid a single visit out of a sense of obligation, hoping it would kickstart my entry into manhood—but I found myself comparing her unfavourably to my figureheads and was unable to bring myself to touch her uneven, overworked chest). Perhaps it was for the best, I thought, given the curse that afflicted the men in my family. How many years would it be until I too was struck down with the wammlin stomach and wayward ankles? No, I would not go out of my way to bring an heir into the world.

And so time passed. I was waiting for that one decisive incident that would let me lay down my father's tools and start my own life. I berated myself for my cowardice. Dick Turpin or Odysseus didn't let their mothers hold them back.

Of course, I now see the virtue, however minor, in my inaction.

A trickle of commissions kept me afloat over the next decade, most for replacement figureheads. Having affixed dozens, first with my father and then in sole charge, I wondered how the originals had been lost. I would always ask the shipping company clerks who placed the orders but they knew as little about life at sea as I did. The figures inevitably met their end in 'a storm' or 'a collision'. With the luxury of time to lavish upon each piece I went to great lengths to replicate the old figurehead, if that's what the owner was after, and then exceed it, thanks to the small measures I'd learnt from my father or improvised myself.

Late in the autumn of 1889 my mother caught cold while sitting in the office with nothing to do. For years I had been telling her to leave the books to me. It was enough that she cooked and cleaned for us. We had made an art of living frugally: no salmon or kippers or apples for these Doigs. I could go a day on a single potato; my mother only needed a half. But Agnes Doig was not about to retire to the upstairs quarters she claimed still rang with the moans of my forebears.

'I prefer me window,' she said.

'But there's a window up the stairs.'

'Aye, but I dinnae fancy staring down on hats and umbrellas. It's the faces, Gabriel. They dinnae stop in as they used to, but I still keep an eye on them all.'

Doctor Stanley, however, ordered my mother to bed when she became ill. She didn't last out the week.

At the age of thirty I was alone in the world, free of filial responsibilities, and yet I still did not shut the doors of Doig & Son. I was, deep down, that same boy who was afraid of going into the closes. The longer I delayed my entry into the Byzantine world beyond Dalrymple Street, and the wee stretch of the River Clyde I knew, the harder it became to make that plunge.

I was not much use in the kitchen, nor could I afford to pay someone to cook for me. Those first nine months without my mother I ate a lot of oats.

'You sure keep that horse of yours well fed,' Mrs McLaren told me one fateful morning in 1890 when I purchased another twelve-pound sack from her stall out the front of the bottle works. I will forever remember the date: it was the second of August.

'Aye,' I said, breaking into a smile. 'Aye, that's right. My horse.' I began to laugh and removed my cap. 'My horse.'

The other stallkeepers began to stare, but I couldn't help myself. I gave a wee wave to Mrs Guigan, who made a living teasing oakum from ropes salvaged from ships that were to be broken up, and young Fanny Balfour, who was selling the whelks she'd collected at low tide. I understood for the first time the enjoyment my mother might have found in the faces of others. No one really has any idea what anyone else is thinking, I decided. It's one of life's great jokes, don't you think, Avis?

I returned my cap to my head, hoisted the bag of oats onto my shoulder and set off towards the pier, paying little heed to the ships at port or their rigging, concentrating instead on the faces I passed, treating each to the manic grin I could not remove from my face. As I approached the custom house the run of familiar faces was replaced by strange ones. A man with dark skin, wearing a thick canvas shirt that looked as though it had once had sleeves, who screwed up his nose as if the land itself carried a stench. A lady of the country, in full bustle, who thought herself unobserved, stretching her legs between the carriage ride to the coast and the steamer journey that would take her to her destination. A team of wee boys and a single, red-cheeked lass calling 'Barley, barley'. Two of these lads were so enraptured in their pursuit that they failed to part and both collided with me, making me drop my sack of oats. The lads rose to their feet, brushed themselves off and exchanged gap-toothed smiles before sprinting to catch up with the pack, only for one of them to run square into a large bollard, collapse onto his back like a stricken beetle and bawl until his comrades quit their game and gathered around him silently.

I lifted my sack once more, dusted it off and continued my passage along the quay. Near the custom house, two sweating men were standing with their hands on their hips, looking with pleasure at the row of barrels, stacked two high, that was kept from rolling off the pier by a single wooden stock. A woman in a grey dress and black bonnet passed me a handbill with the heading 'The Lips That Touch Liquor Shall Never Touch Mine'. I flashed my manic grin and she shrank away.

Further on, I came across two men having an argument beside a docked sailing ship that looked liable to sink into the Clyde at any moment.

'I know I said I'm not comin' bag on that rattlebones,' shouted one of the men drunkenly, 'but I left somethin' aboard.'

'Get away, hound.'

'I ain't no hound, convict. You convict, you soulless,' he paused and his shoulders wobbled as if his feet were planted on a tightrope, 'convict hound.'

The sober man stood with his arms crossed and his back to the vessel. It looked as if its wooden hull had seen its last coat of green paint several voyages ago. His fair brown hair was pulled behind his head in an old-fashioned sailor's queue and he wore an unbuttoned leather waistcoat with a clean-looking white shirt beneath.

'If it's grog you want,' he said, 'buy it like any other man. I won't let you come back aboard and steal my ration.'

'It wouldn't be your ration, hound.' The drunk gave a half-hearted howl at the invisible moon. 'We're pals, ain't we?'

'What am I, a hound or a pal?'

'You're a man's best friend, in't ya?'

The other man gave him a firm push in the chest, starting

him on a backward tumble that seemed to gather momentum, bringing him closer and closer to me, his feet tracing wide circles to avoid each other. There was time enough for me to move out of the way, but I had forgotten myself and was involved in my second collision in a matter of minutes.

The drunken man clasped his hands on my shoulders. 'Beggin' your pardon,' he said, then added in a lower tone, 'you dirty hound.' His teeth were flecked with what might have been wheat husks, his breath heady and pungent.

'Leave that boy alone, Ruskin,' the other man cried before I could respond.

It had been some time since I had been called a boy and it conjured up the ire that I used to feel towards my debilitated father.

I dropped my sack of oats.

'You will do well, sir,' I said, adopting the firm cordiality of a highwayman, 'to remove your hands from my shoulders and crawl under the nearest bench until you have recovered yourself.'

The man appeared frozen so I took it upon myself to knock his hands from my shoulders, turn and walk back up the quay. I was met, however, by a scene much changed. Of the barrels that had been stacked with such care, only one remained, held by one of the sweaty men. The other man was grabbing his head and peering down to the waters below. The woman with the handbills was nowhere to be seen.

The oats. I had left them in front of the ship. I turned back towards the bedraggled vessel and noticed for the first time the familiar figure on its bow.

Vengeance. My Vengeance.

Like the rest of the ship, she was in a poor condition. The deep blue of her garment had been slaked. Long vertical cracks traversed her form. The arm clutching the imagined knife was reduced to a splintered wound at her collarbone. Her face was turned away from me, as if she were embarrassed by her wretched state, her once burning cheek now bare and grey. But I also noticed deficiencies I could not attribute to fifteen years of squalls and neglect. The inadequate distance between the indentation of her navel, visible through her dress, and her breasts. The limp, lifeless way her hair sat upon her remaining shoulder. No hint of an ear beneath the locks that covered the side of her face. It had taken me more than one or two figures to perfect my craft, but I now stood before Vengeance a man with the ability to do her justice. I could return to my workshop that minute and turn my last, untouched block of yellow pine into the figure of Vengeance that I'd seen in my mind as a boy but did not have the hands to execute. And then what? Even if the carving was flawless, it was unlikely to sell. I could not afford to buy any more timber. Doig & Son would be finished. I would be finished. At last, at last, at last.

I walked back towards the gangway. There was no sign of the drunkard. The sober man stood with his arms crossed once more.

'I'd like to repair your figurehead,' I said, forgetting my highwayman voice and sounding like an eager boy.

'That thing?'

'Aye.'

'There's no money in it. Besides, this old girl's days are numbered.'

'The ship is to be broken up?'

'Not exactly. The owner wouldn't benefit from that. But she's bound for the Horn.'

'In this condition?'

The man nodded.

'But that's suicide.'

'Perhaps. But a well-paid suicide.' The man's voice rang with what I thought might be courage.

'But the owner—' I began, then remembered Agathos Rennie, his long fingers and stooped shoulders, his theatrical pince-nez.

'The owner would like nothing more than a wreck and the insurance monies that'd flow in its wake. He's all for steam, is Mr Rennie.'

'Is he here?'

'No. Rennie's based in London. Do you know the firm?'

'Aye. Their office used to be along this very quay.'

'Is that so?' The man turned to look at the ship. 'The old girl limped back here after meeting a hurricane off the Azores. Snapped the foremast. She's been in the graving dock these past two weeks getting enough repairs to send her to her doom.' He gave a laugh. 'We're setting sail on the morrow if we've crew enough by then.'

'You might struggle on that account.'

'One trip around the Horn will net you the same as three trips in a fitter ship.'

'Aye, if you survive.'

'It's mostly looks. She's still a fine craft. Sleek and fast. Ah, she's fast. It is a good life to see the seven seas on a clipper. Better to die aboard such a vessel than in a puttering tin can that your mother could tend.'

'Why did that man call you a convict?'

'Oh that. I'm from Australia.'

'You're not—?' I began.

'I'm a free man, if that's what you're asking.'

'Of course. I'm sure you are. I've never met an Australian before, that's all. My name's Gabriel Doig.' I offered my hand.

'Basil Porter.'

'What would you say, Mr Porter, if I came back this afternoon to touch up the lass out front? Gratis, of course.'

Porter let out a light, high-pitched *ha-ha*. 'You can touch her up, all right, but it may be me who should be charging.'

I returned to the *Agathos* with a barrow of tools, paints, resins, copper nails and small blocks of new timber from my workshop. Porter, evidently the ship's first mate, led me across the gangway and onto the deck. I surveyed the timbers I had trodden half a life ago. The decrepit impression cast by the exterior of the ship proved misleading. The boards were firm and freshly swabbed. A new coat of paint would liven things up no end. Porter laid a long plank of wood down as a ramp so that I could take my barrow up to the fo'c'sle deck.

'This is no shipyard,' he said, leaning out over the gunwale to inspect the figurehead. 'Are you happy for me to belay you over?'

'Aye, I'm used to it.'

'You any good up a ratline?'

'That I've never tried.' I looped a rope below my buttocks and tied an overhand knot.

'Really?'

I swung down below the bowsprit, placed one foot on the bobstay and the other on the thick chain of a bowsprit shroud, and began to inspect Vengeance. Close up, it was clear that I needed to remove her. I asked Porter for my mallet and a wooden wedge from the barrow and began to work Vengeance away from the wooden pegs my father had used to affix her to the stem.

When she was nearly free I called for Porter to pass me the end of another rope, which I worked around the elbow of Vengeance's remaining arm and her other side.

Once Vengeance and I had been hauled on deck I started sanding back the rough edges, fitting fresh timber shims in the cracks that had opened between the laminates and fashioning a new right shoulder and upper arm. I worked quickly, inspired by the opportunity to resurrect one of my own pieces after so many years improving the work of others, conscious of the limited daylight remaining and the fact the *Agathos* intended to set sail the following day.

Porter alternated between watching me work, leaning over the gunwale to survey the docks and standing sentry at the edge of the gangway.

'You're handy with a chisel,' he said as I quickly turned a block of yellow pine into Vengeance's missing arm.

'It's a gouge, actually. A carver doesnae have much use for chisels.'

'But it's all woodwork.'

'Aye, I suppose.'

'You know we're in need of a ship's carpenter?'

I laughed and looked up from the arm. 'What happened to your last carpenter?'

'He'd have been a wealthy man if he'd held his nerve.'

'Och, that's rich. I'm nae a greedy man, Mr Porter.'

I returned my eyes to the new arm, but inwardly my mind

was racing. Here was the chance I had been waiting for. What did I have tying me to the Clyde? I had no family and virtually no business. But at the same time, the ship scared me. Look at what it had done to Vengeance. Even Porter, who seemed a level-headed sort, acknowledged the suicidal nature of taking the *Agathos* round the Horn.

Porter read me as if I were a spirit level. 'I don't imagine there's much call for figurehead carvers these days.'

'I make a living.'

'Oh, I can see from your fine trousers, so fine I can see your knees through the weave.'

'I'm dressed for work.'

'Of course, of course. And I'm sure you're so bony and pale from always being indoors. You'll get three hot meals a day aboard the *Agathos*.'

'Salted gull and scurvy are not to my tastes, unfortunately.'

'Please yourself. But you say you've never been to sea, can that be right? Never felt the sting of old briny once you leave the harbour?' Porter turned away and leaned out over the headrail to face the slow-flowing Clyde. 'Never seen the water black as tar and clear as glass? Never crossed the line? Never seen the sun so close you'd swear it was a giant peach dangled by the Almighty? Never lived a minute of your life?' Porter turned back to me. What could I do but shrug? 'A sailor's life might be a short life, especially aboard the *Agathos*, but it is a man's life.'

As the sun set I had not yet begun to repaint Vengeance. Porter brought me a lantern but the slight breeze that had picked up meant the light shifted too much to continue working.

'Are you still set on making way in the morning?' I asked.

'That's the master's call. Now there's a man who has seen this world and a few more besides. He'll be none too pleased with me if we don't have a carpenter on board, but he's eager to set off. The bosun can pick up some of the slack and I've spent my time as a carpenter's shadow. But if we're to make it through the Southern Ocean we'll need a full complement of hands.'

Despite Porter's strong persuasion, I was still in two minds. My gut seemed equally torn and my heart, well, it was too busy waking from its long slumber to take sides.

'I will come back in the morning,' I said, 'and paint her if there's time. If not, I suppose I'll just fix her back on.'

'There'll be plenty of time for painting aboard. A ship's carpenter near enough sets his own time. You'd have no watches in fine weather and you'd never have to swab the decks or clean the heads.'

I smiled politely and began to load my barrow.

Porter picked up the lantern and led me down from the fo'c'sle deck once more and across the gangway. I hadn't noticed the slight movement of the ship while on board but the cobblestones of the pier felt hard and unforgiving.

'The crew will appreciate the work you've done,' Porter said and shook my hand. 'Till the morrow.'

'Aye, till the morrow.' I set off for Doig & Son. When I arrived I lit the lamps inside the workshop and surveyed my stock of unwanted figureheads: the commissioned figure of homely Mrs Abigail Havanagh, which Mr Havanagh reneged on purchasing after he discovered, to everyone's surprise, his wife in bed with the wax chandler; an effort to copy my father's valkyrie, just as the fad for Norse figures went on the wane; the figure of Courage, the third piece I carved from beginning to end, which had sat unwanted all those years. At least Vengeance has a story to tell, I thought, running my thumbs over Courage's eyes as if to close her lids.

I left the lamps burning and used money I could scarcely afford to part with to purchase a hot meal of roast beef, potatoes and carrots from the Anchor Inn. I sat alone at my table, which rocked slightly as I carved my meat. I removed one of the unneeded wedges of wood I'd fashioned for Vengeance from my trouser pocket and placed it beneath the offending table leg. The tavern rang with the sound of sailors, shipwrights and customs inspectors telling stories in the private languages of their trades, of young men with shining pocket watches and brightly coloured handkerchiefs seeking to impress plump-cheeked young ladies whose thick skirts bunched halfway up the backs of their seats, of the men playing cribbage in the adjoining room, their shouts of 'Losh!', 'Ya bandit!' and 'Muggins!'

Back in my workshop I began to sort the pieces of scrap timber into piles according to their size. I took the biggest pieces and laid them out in a rectangle, large enough that a young boy might fit inside. I took up my hammer and a handful of copper nails and began constructing a box. When it came for the lid, I did not have any hinges to hand, so removed those from the door that led to what I still thought of as my mother's office. For a latch, I went upstairs and unscrewed the gilt locker from the heavy oak chest that used to store the Doig family valuables but had long since been emptied. When my chest was complete I lifted it onto my trusty barrow and began to fill it with my favourite tools, my leather-bound sketchbook, a few novels, my clothes, boots, oilskin hat and cutlery.

I arrived at the dock at sunrise the next morning, conscious that I looked like a timorous boy but unable to take better control of my quaking knees. Sailors nudged past to get up the gangway or disembark, reeking of rum, tobacco and human excrement. I was on the verge of lifting the handles of my barrow once more and retreating to the safety of my workshop when I heard a familiar voice call from the deck, 'Is this a carpenter I see before me?' Porter slapped his large hands on the gunwale. 'Why, I think it is.'

He leapt over the edge of the ship, his boots making no sound as they hit the cobblestones after a fall of five feet. 'Make way, make way, you dogs,' he cried, picking up my sea chest. 'We've a carpenter after all. We might make it round the Horn in one piece.'

The sailors offered their imperfect, conniving smiles as I followed Porter aboard the *Agathos* and forward to the petty officers' deckhouse. 'Carpenter sleeps here,' he said, placing my chest down and sliding it beneath the bunk nearest the door. I couldn't see beyond the third bunk in the dimly lit space and wondered how many men slept there. 'You'll catch the first spray whenever the door opens, unfortunately. You might do well to intimidate one of the apprentices, once you've found your feet. Best stay on Slushy's good side, though.' He indicated the bunk adjacent to mine. 'And Meiklejohn too, while you're at it. And not just because he's bosun and you'll need his help, if you catch my meaning?'

I nodded, though I wasn't sure I did.

'Come, I'll show you the storeroom.'

We made our way down a steep flight of stairs that was almost a ladder and along a narrow passage. I had been below decks only a handful of times and always in new vessels that had yet to take their maiden voyage. The air inside the bowels of the *Agathos* was damp and smoky and I wondered how it would be after the men had been crammed below deck for a month at sea. I ran my fingers along the blackened teak of a bulkhead. It gave slightly under my touch, like the skin on your heel. No oak, I thought to myself, a pity. But it was pleasant to be surrounded by so much wood, fashioned for new and different purposes and aged in mysterious ways.

As we came to the door of the storeroom I was reminded of my father's declaration about the *Agathos* that day we installed Vengeance: 'I suspect even the captain's doorknob is without a flourish.' The storeroom door, which Porter was working to unlock, was certainly plain. It would be a few days before I had cause to pass the captain's door, but my father was right: not a flourish.

'We're below the deckhouse now.' He opened the door. 'Stores are all in here. You're the master of the ship's chest. I expect you've brought some of your fancy gouges? You can keep them here, it's safe. There's much more for me to explain, but as we're about to set sail, I reckon you should get to work fixing your lass to the bow. Can't have the *Agathos* running blind.'

I gathered the necessary implements and emerged above decks once more to be met with the light of a thousand lamps. One of the sailors must have noticed the way my face contorted in the daylight and announced, 'Seems we have a pollywog in our midst.'

'And it's this tadpole,' Porter said from somewhere close behind me, 'that'll keep your foremast from snapping. You'll be glad of the work he's done on your missus with the missing arm, too.'

'Is that so?'

We proceeded to the fo'c'sle deck where Vengeance lay on her back, covered with dark green canvas. Porter removed the cover and I set to work sanding back the small ridges of resin that had issued from the crevices I'd sealed the day before and priming her for painting. A crowd of sailors gathered to observe and provide a running commentary of proceedings.

'She looks twenty years younger,' one announced.

'Like her own daughter,' another added.

'Aye, just as stuck up but half as knowing,' said a third.

'If that's the daughter, has anyone told the father? Mr Swenson,' the second voice called, 'Mr Swenson, your love child is aboard and the men are eyeing her already.'

'Well, I trust you're the expert in children, Boag, seeing as how you leave a new bastard in every port.'

I couldn't help but grin at this exchange.

'Look here,' one of the men said, 'you've gone and made Slimy smile.'

'Aye, 'tis a sorry reflection on our capability as sailors. He should be in tears by now.'

'There's just no sport in it, ever since poor Tim came aboard. The lad's never stopped spouting.'

'I'll show you,' said an adolescent voice.

'Are you sure young Tim here's not another son of yours, Boag?'

'Now don't go and make me cry,' Boag replied.

I was fanning the white undercoat dry when Porter came to check on my progress.

'There won't be time to colour her today, Carpenter. The passengers are all aboard and the captain's ordered us to set sail in half an hour.'

'But that's barely time for me to get her fixed out front.'

'You heard the carpenter,' Porter said to the gathered men. 'He needs a hand fitting the lass out front.'

Two men lifted the figure that instant, two more wrapped ropes around their wrists and jumped over the bow, while young Tim walked up the slight incline of the bowsprit before pirouetting, kicking out his feet and catching himself with his hands before any serious damage was done to his groin. I remained on deck, directing the men as they placed Vengeance against the trenails. I handed Boag my mallet and a cloth to dampen the blows.

'That's a queer-looking mallet,' he said. 'All rounded like that.'

'It's a carver's mallet. It's rounded so you strike your tool in the chosen spot.'

'Whatever you say, Mr Carpenter.'

'My, my,' a voice sounded from behind us, 'what a lot of commotion.'

Tim, still straddling the bowsprit, saluted. I turned to meet the eyes of a compact man about my height wearing a thick felt coat with gold buttons and gold fringing at the shoulders. Atop his head sat a black bowler hat more suited to the driver of a hansom cab than the captain of a sailing ship.

'Captain Bock, sir. We was just helping out the new carpenter,' explained Tim.

Bock let out an unimpressed grunt. 'Can someone explain to me the worth of a carpenter who requires the assistance of half a dozen men for decorations?'

Porter appeared at the captain's shoulder, short of breath. 'This,' he began, 'is the new carpenter, Captain.'

'Thank you, Porter, we have already established that.' He continued glaring at me as he addressed the mate. 'I was just registering my doubts about the crew you have assembled. A carpenter who won't work and seamen who prefer to dangle from the rails rather than dwell amongst the yards.'

'Yes, Captain, sir,' Porter said. 'I expect it will take a few days for the carpenter to become familiar with his duties, after which I am sure he will be a credit to this ship.'

'This ship?' Bock said, arching his top lip and turning to Porter. 'This ship is not worth a damn and has been crewed by madmen and incompetents on a fool's errand. But I'll be damned if this will be my last commission. We are due in Melbourne in eighty-two days and I shall see that we return to Great Britain in a further ninety as richer men deserving of great encomia.'

The tassels on the captain's shoulders flew out as he swung around and descended to the main deck, where a dozen men in stiff collars and two women in heavy dresses—one the colour of ivory, the other a faint blue—had gathered, presumably the passengers Porter had mentioned.

'Is she fast?' Porter asked the men still slung over the side of the bow.

'Aye, she'll hold,' said Boag.

'Then scale the yards, men, we're setting sail.'

'What should I do?' I asked.

'There's no time. Besides, Meiklejohn has inspected the masts and yards already. We'll ease you in, Carpenter.'

I was left standing on the fo'c'sle deck as the last hurried preparations were made for the departure of the *Agathos*. Considering how close I had come to turning my barrow homeward on the dock, I had very few misgivings as the moorings were loosed from the bollards. The sailors were as bawdy as the best pirate ballad, the captain as mysterious as Nemo and ahead of us waited an adventure that Homer would be proud to set to verse.

I was no longer a landlubbing figurehead carver, a copy of my father who was a copy of his father. My footsteps from now on would be my own.

Such were my thoughts as a steam-powered tug cruised into position and the tow-line was fastened. Soon I felt the bow ease away from the dock, heard the rumble as the foremast's topsail was spread, saw the gap emerge between the starboard side of the ship and my home town, between me and terra firma. The *Agathos* made her way out into the channel under tow, towards the firth, the waters brown and reflective as bottle glass beneath a soft, measured sky.

I am feeling much better of late. Thank you.

You understand why you must stay here a wee bit
longer, don't you?

**Yes. I can't leave without reading the end of
your story.**

That is not what I mean.

I know what you mean, Gabriel.

Good.

23 November 1890

I walked up through the squawking, reeking yellow-brows once more. I was not there to fill my larder. This time I was heading for the ridge. Exploring at last. If a chick stumbled across my path, of course, I might snatch it up, twist its neck and toss it in the sailcloth sack slung over my shoulder. I didn't know how far I would walk this day and having a snack for later couldn't hurt. Maybe the penguins were right to squawk. It was hardly fair. Me five feet tall, feeling massive for the first time in my life, able to cover a yard in a single stride. Them with their pot bellies and inquisitive red eyes.

'Just passing through,' I told them, already short of breath.

I had no compass but had learnt where the sun rose and set, knew my east from west and north from south, or so I hoped.

It was surprising how swiftly my first fortnight as a castaway had passed. Day upon day was devoured by the search for the necessities of life—food, water, shelter, warmth—and the struggle to maintain them. An overhanging bluff at the northern end of the rocky bight had provided some shelter from the sleet and rain on my first night. Every day since had been spent improving this imperfect space: rigging a portion of the sailcloth so that it might impede the prevailing wind that burrowed into the shallow cave, collecting tussock from the fringes of the penguin colony to weave into mats for the floor, rerigging the sailcloth after a westerly gale, collecting peat to soften the ground beneath the tussock, rinsing the tussock in the breakers in an effort to rid the cave of its flea explosion, learning to sleep with lice in my beard and hailstones charging through the latest tear in the canvas, learning to survive with the constants of the subantarctic castaway's life: chattering teeth, growling belly, stinging fingers, numb toes, wet clothes and tired, watering eyes.

After the second day I had removed every piece of rope, cloth and metal from the section of mast that had saved my life and stashed them in my grotto. The mast itself would have made a nice wind stop if it could have been placed across the entrance but I was unable to move it by myself. I tried rigging up a system of pulleys but did not have enough rope or suitable anchor points. Through these efforts—and quite by accident—I managed to wedge one end of the mast so completely inside a crevice in the shore that it did not wash away, even in the highest of tides.

I discovered early on that I was too late for a feast of penguin eggs. The shallow indentations in the rock that passed for nests were occupied by downy chicks and their rowdy parents. That first night I made do with limpets plucked from rocks at low tide. They were cold and rubbery. After several dozen I felt as hungry as when I had begun.

The next day I had returned to the yellow-brows. At the cost of a pecked shin I was able to grasp an adult bird by the neck and dash it against the rocky floor of the colony a few times amid the strangled, high-pitched skreigh of several hundred of its neighbours. With no fire to return to, I tore into the white breast right there with the blade I had fashioned from the metal eyelet of one of the topgallant clews. The thing was more talon than knife, only two and a half inches long and curved, but it sliced through the penguin's skin and presented the oozing, pinkish flesh. I retched this first time, covered my mouth and nose with the elbow of my free arm and, pinning the carcass by placing my boot across the broken neck, tore off more of the skin. I had soon liberated a chunk of breast meat weighing about a pound and held it, slimy and skinless, in the palm of my hand.

My hunger had grown to such proportions that the walls of my stomach felt as if they were eroding, collapsing in upon themselves, and soon my outsides would follow, caving in until I was a pile of dry rubble. But still, I hesitated. This was no bowl of oats or boiled potato. It wasn't even a rubbery limpet or a ladle of slumgullion, viscous and suspect. But it was protein. I brought the flesh to my mouth and drove my teeth in. It was warm against my lips, surprisingly warm. My jaws, tense from the cold and out of practice, struggled to push my teeth through the meat. I was forced to gnaw and twist the breast in order to liberate a piece that might fit in my mouth. The taste. My thoughts were shot through with images of fish guts and castor oil. After swallowing three mouthfuls, a heroic amount in my estimation, I took the remaining portion and the flayed carcass down to the water line. I battered the cutlet flat against a rock with the heel of my boot and left it there to dry in the sun. The carcass I wedged between two rocks beneath the water line in the hope the salt water might improve the taste. When I returned at dusk the escallop of penguin was lousy with flies, the carcass nowhere to be seen, and I made do with more limpets and a few wee mussels.

I was now three-quarters of the way up the yellow-brow colony, on my way to the ridge and whatever lay beyond, but I had to rest. I hunched over, hands on knees, head slung down, waiting for my breath to return. I felt a peck on the back of my head, rose and saw a smaller adult on its nest, the black feathers between its yellow brows standing erect, its flippers extended and chest jutting forward in a sign of aggression.

'Good day,' I said, doffing an imaginary hat. 'I hope you dinnae mind me stopping by unannounced.'

The penguin pressed its flippers hard against its sides. With its shut-tight beak and its round red eyes fixed upon me, the creature appeared to be seething. The white feathers of its lower belly began to ruffle. It rose slightly to reveal the tips of its pink feet and the twisting head of a soft black chick. I had learnt by this time that the chicks were more appetising than their stouter, tougher parents, though the layer of fat between the skin and flesh on the adults proved tasty enough. If only I had a slice of bread to spread it across! Even a ship's biscuit. Such farinaceous cravings were another constant of island life.

The chick edged out from beneath its parent, presenting itself for the snatching. It cheeped once and looked at me with its black eyes, smooth and wee as apple pips.

'Och, you'd make a meagre mouthful, you would. Eat up. I might come back.'

I set off again, though my breath had not returned in full.

Each day on the island I had placed a new notch in the mast with my clew talon, vowing that the next day would be the one I cleared the ridge behind the colony and truly surveyed my situation. But for all the lack on my beach there was no shortage of excuses. I didn't have the strength. The fog was too thick for exploration. I would catch my death in the icy rain.

There were fourteen notches on the mast as I staggered through the last nesting bowls, all of them deserted. Presumably these belonged to the last penguins to arrive, the juveniles and grandparents, the ones that had already returned to the sea to fatten up for next season or to die. The morning was overcast and the habitual westerly wind blew, though with diminished intent. I was warm enough, wearing Tim's vest and shirt beneath my own. I'd left Tim's trousers and waistcoat back in my grotto so that I might have something dry to put on if the weather turned.

'Keep gangin',' I told myself as I passed an untouched crown of tussock, which marked the farthest I had ventured since my arrival on the island. I had not allowed myself to consider what I might find over the ridge. No sight would be without its pangs. If there was any sign of human habitation, even a tiny, unoccupied shack, I was a fool for lingering so long on the foreshore. If there was nothing but a stretch of windswept tussock, I would most likely die there, surrounded by limpet shells and penguin skins.

The wind picked up and pushed against my back. An albatross swept overhead, its wings still and broad as a topsail yard. I turned to see it corkscrew out across the white-capped water and dissolve into the distance.

A few more laboured steps and I was in waist-high tussock, the ridgeline still twenty or thirty yards up the slope. The ground was hard and dry beneath my boots, despite it having rained or worse every day I had been on the island. The sound of the yellow-brows back down the slope carried on the wind. My boots, Tim's boots, felt as if they were lined with lead. I stopped once more to catch my breath and saw an emerald flash in the tussock ahead, followed by another flash close behind. A small parrot? This far south? I scanned the clumps of tussock and soon spotted the brighter green of the bird against the dull blades. The colour seemed fresh from my father's palette, the green of Caesar's laurel or a valkyrie's eye. I felt my excitement grow at the prospect of what lay beyond the ridge. A few yards further I saw another parrot—or were they parakeets?—dashing from my left, though this bird appeared to have a splash of red atop its head. I thought of the gull's head cloaked in Tim's blood and my imagined sanctuary beyond the ridge was exchanged for a hellish Eden with carnivorous polychrome parrots and shiny, poisonous fruit. I shook my head and continued on, almost in a rush, clutching my sailcloth bag in one hand and dragging it through the tussock and sedges.

The wind was fierce now, pushing me on until I stumbled and fell face first into the tussock. I rolled onto my back and let the wind rush over me, pinning me down as if it were the lid on a coffin. A light grey opening broke through a cleft in the clouds and disappeared just as swiftly. I rolled back onto my stomach and lifted my torso. I was nearly there. The crest just a few feet away.

I hauled myself forward on my hands and knees and caught my first glimpse of the other side. There was nothing there. The land dropped away swiftly after the ridge, terminating in high cliffs that ran the entire length of the island. I turned and looked back down the much gentler slope I had ascended but could not quite see the rocky beach that had been my home these past two weeks. From the crest it appeared that I had found the only shelter the island offered. That I was stranded in the Southern Ocean on a slab of rock that resembled a wedge of lemon lying on one side. I looked over the eastern edge, the steep rind of the island, and out across the endless ocean. To the north, at the tip of my island, there was another smaller island that might have been the size of an upturned ship's hull. I might be able to make it across the gap between the islands, but what chance would I have there? To the south, I saw nothing at first with the wind blowing in my eyes and the late morning fog rolling in. But were those breakers I saw? And a black mass like a giant limpet on the surface of the water? An island? Yes, I became more certain by the moment. An island, much larger than the one on which I stood. I thought of all the things it might hold, chief among these wood. Besides the tussock, the sedges and the moss, I had seen no other plants on my island—no trees, no woody shrubs, nothing to fuel a fire if I managed to light one, nothing to carve if I was to spend the rest of eternity marooned here, nothing but what had washed ashore with me. This meagre haul was all I had to fashion a raft that might ferry me across the mile or so of rough, frigid water to this bigger island.

I shut my eyes, felt the tingle of tiny mist particles hurtling into my eyelids and wished the temptation would disappear.

A Sailor's Life

Contrary to the jovial, gibing atmosphere I had experienced among the crew that first morning as they helped to mount Vengeance to the bow, I found myself ignored or worse by my fellow sailors once at sea. I was 'Slimy', 'Polly' or 'Porter's Parrot' to the men before the mast. When they sidled past me in the narrow passageways I was treated to a sneer or a malicious, unsettling wink. At first this resentment puzzled me, as did so much of shipboard life, but in time I understood. I was untrained in the ways of the sea and yet Porter had enlisted me as an officer, circumventing the usual order of things. Some men had to take on extra duties while I was taught the ropes, none more so than Meiklejohn, the bosun. He never said a word to me or acknowledged my presence, but took great pleasure in shaking off his oilskins beside my bunk whenever he came in from a rainy watch. The other men spoke behind their hands as I entered the galley to receive my portion. My inexperience was no trifling matter for the crew: it could one day put their lives in danger.

During fine weather, I was called at daylight and worked at my trade until the sun set. Every day I was to pay the ship and its boats a full inspection and carry out any necessary repairs. During the first fortnight I relied on Porter to instruct me in what to look for, how the various booms and winches worked and how repairs might be made to ensure a seaworthy, watertight vessel. I was also expected to take frequent readings of the ship's draught and report to Captain Bock if the results were of concern. Should a leak spring over the stores or the sail room, it was up to me to stop it. When the weather allowed, I spent my free time above decks, fashioning plugs for such eventualities.

As carpenter, I was stationed with the larboard watch but was not expected to handle the light sails or go above the topsail yards unless repairs were needed. When all hands were called, however, I had to pull and haul about the decks with the other sailors and, if necessary, reef and furl aloft. The call to go up into the rigging invariably came in foul weather or when the *Agathos* was carrying a heavy press of sail. The head for heights my father had instilled in the drydock was found wanting that first time Porter took me up the modest distance to the main top. The added motion of the waves set the mast oscillating like an inverted pendulum. Keeping your balance was difficult enough without having to handle the sheets or carry out repairs.

'It's the world that's moving,' Porter shouted from his side of the mast, this first time aloft, 'not the ship.'

'That's daft,' I said, clinging to the shrouds that led further up the mast.

'It mightn't be true, but it helps.'

I looked down and saw that I'd been swung out over the water—to fall at such a moment would mean certain death—before being pulled back and pushed beyond the vertical once more, so that Porter was dangled over the eager waves. The mate swung one leg out over the water and maintained his puckish grin.

I considered the ridiculous proposition that the ship was a fixed point beneath which the Earth was moving and remembered the hawker who was sometimes on the Princes Pier with his trained seal. The way the seal balanced its colourful ball on its nose. Was it the seal's nose balancing the ball or was the ball balancing the seal's nose and, by extension, the entire seal, the entire world?

'See?' shouted Porter.

I raised one hand, palm up, to question what he meant.

'It helps.' Despite Porter's comfort above the mainyard, I thought the effort to hang on made his winning smile appear more of a grimace. 'You wouldn't have been game to loosen a hand a minute ago.'

I looked down at my palm and we both began to laugh, though the sound was drowned out by the whipping sails and creaking deck.

From that moment on there was always a touch of the absurd in my relationship with the ship and with the sea. A flight of fancy about the Earth pivoting at the ship's centreline could improve your balance. The thick-skinned and foul-mouthed sailors showed no fear racing up a ratline or untangling a rope and yet they filled their days with superstitions to appease the waves. Ibanez, the Spaniard, would cross himself each time he ascended the companionway and always took the last step facing backwards. Young Tim kept a pocket watch that had stopped at half past four hard against his chest at all times. The sailor's calendar was a mess of inauspicious dates when journeys could not be commenced and certain words or phrases ('good luck', 'drowned') could set the crew against you.

I took my meals in the same mess as the men in the fo'c'sle. The first few days after leaving the Clyde, we were treated to fish stew and fresh bread, which the sailors called soft tommy and took great relish in. When I asked about the origins of the name the other men grunted and looked away. After a time, Boag said in a hoarse voice, 'If you don't want your tommy, Slimy, there're plenty of takers. It'll be hard biscuits till doomsday soon enough.'

I looked down at my half-eaten crust of bread. My stomach was still not used to such food and in such proportions as the sailors greedily inhaled. I shrugged and offered the crust to Boag, who snatched it as a toad might snatch a fly. The other men seemed stricken with stomach pains at the sight of Boag's increased portion. Mantzaris, the sail maker, bit the handle of his wooden spoon. Dhalla cracked his knuckles. Kulke bared his teeth. I decided to divide my bread among the men evenly at the next meal, but it just so happened that we had seen the last of the soft tommy.

On receiving my first hard biscuit that evening, I laboured to break it with my hands to divide among the men, but it might as well have been teak. I tried placing it between my molars but only ground a few unsatisfying crumbs from the edge. I looked up to see the men sneering as they soaked their biscuits in the day-old fish stew. After a time they each brought their biscuits to their mouths and scraped off the softened layers with their haphazard teeth. Defeated, I could only dunk my own biscuit and work away at its sawdusty substance until I was alone outside the galley and could toss my half-gnawed biscuit overboard.

Thereafter the barrels and tins of salted beef and pork and pickled vegetables were opened and the contents fashioned by the cook into burgoo or slumgullion. The only difference between the two that I could detect was the speed at which the stew slid from my spoon.

It was a rough, dangerous and confusing life those first few weeks at sea, but I found wee pleasures where I could. My chief diversion was keeping my tools and the ship's axes sharp. I used the same mixture of crocus powder and tallow to treat my strops as I had done in the workshop of Doig & Son. After spending time in the rigging or being shunned by the crew, I would retreat to the stores. The smell never failed to transport me to more tranquil times.

The friendship I hoped would develop with Basil Porter never did. I expect he was disappointed by how few of my skills as a figurehead carver were of use as ship's carpenter and came to begrudge me the time he spent teaching and reteaching me basic tasks and pieces of ship's etiquette. He had shown his inexperience as first mate in enlisting me as carpenter, throwing out the harmony of the ship, and I gathered he was paying the price in his dealings with Captain Bock. Equally, his estimation in my eyes slowly diminished. I had been drawn to him when the *Agathos* was still in dock because he spoke of the very things I thirsted for: change, adventure, self-determinism. But I soon learnt that Porter was little more than a salesman: he had the talent of knowing what to say to people and, when this failed, the sound of his own voice was enough to sustain him.

'You think you've seen the sun?' he said one afternoon when his monologue drifted to his Australian homeland while I repaired a chicken coop that had been damaged in a passing squall. 'You haven't seen the sun unless you've seen it rising red and round over the earth back home, its light running over the backs of dusty sheep and rusting iron. The black cockatoos squawking in the marri trees. An emu patrolling the perimeter.' He placed both of his hands on the gunwale and leant out over the sea. I could've used another pair of hands to hold down the new wire mesh for the coop but Porter was on the other side of the planet. 'As far as I know, both my parents are still alive and kicking, though news to the contrary would struggle to find me.'

As the days passed, I needed to be shadowed by Porter less and less and was eventually left to my own devices. I now reported to Captain Bock, but he was seldom on deck. He preferred to spend his time with the paying passengers. The *Agathos* began to feel like the narrow, winding closes back home: the men stared at me as the children of the closes did, as if I were a ghost. But I was no longer the same child who stuck to the main thoroughfares.

'What is it about me you so despise?' I asked Swenson one day as I handed him a new brace block I had carved, which he was to install aloft.

'You're not a sailor,' he said.

'And what does it take to become a sailor in your eyes?'

He laughed coarsely. 'We'll talk once you've crossed the line, eh, Tenderfoot?'

As the *Agathos* entered the doldrums, those humid, windless latitudes, I found time to remove Vengeance from the bow to complete her refurbishment. Once she was back on the fo'c'sle deck, I noticed the new shoulder I had fashioned and affixed before we set sail had already become jagged and raw. The sailors gathered in a circle around me once more and something of that light-hearted mood from the docks returned.

'Time for some rouge and lipstick, is it?' the cook asked.

'I'll have to fix her shoulder first,' I said.

'Anything to soften her embrace,' said someone behind the first ring of onlookers.

'While you're at it,' another voice said, 'could you address her . . . anatomical deficiencies?'

The men roared with laughter.

'Aye,' Boag added, 'it's a long time between drinks out here.'

'It is the least a lady could do,' Kulke said.

'I'm afraid she'll not stand up to such alterations,' I said, adopting the false airs and rising inflexion of the crewmen.

''Tis a shame, 'tis a shame,' Boag said and pummelled my shoulder with the heel of his large hand.

'Why waste your time on the shoulder?' young Tim asked from beneath the arm of the cook. 'We'll only pick it fresh.'

'You all did this?' I asked.

'Aye,' the men proclaimed.

'But why?'

'For luck, of course,' Boag said and produced a splinter of pine from his trouser pocket. The other men reached into their trousers and waistcoats and socks and retrieved their splinters, holding them out to me as if they were gun sights and I the target.

Even Meiklejohn was there holding out his splinter, though his eyes were focused somewhere over my head.

'All of you—' I began.

'I'd be surprised if Captain Bock doesn't have a chip himself,' said Tim.

I looked around but saw neither Bock nor Basil Porter. I was angered by the injury inflicted upon Vengeance, but also, I suppose, because I had not been invited to take part in the superstition. I still wanted dearly to become a sailor, despite the pageant of grotesques and madmen that went by such a title aboard the *Agathos*. Once I was a sailor, I thought, my hardships would ease and the adventure would truly begin.

'Go on, Carpenter,' Boag said, as if reading my mind, 'take a chip yourself. You'll need the luck when we cross the line.'

Tim held out a grimy spoon, which must have been the tool he'd used to acquire his own splinter, but I shook my head. 'I'll use my own tool, thank you.' I took up a gouge with a shallow curve and pressed it inside one of the vertical grooves until I lifted out a piece of wood the thickness of a matchstick. I took the splinter and put it in the breast pocket of my shirt and the men let out a cheer before bursting into song:

> Oh, the sea's a fair old mistress,
> The land's a withered shrew,
> Oh, the sea's a dainty mistress,
> And we're just passin' through.

> Oh, the sea's a fair old mistress,
> We have our own a'bow.
> Oh, the sea's a dainty mistress,
> But our lady'll do for now.

I ran into Porter later that day as he ascended to the quarterdeck for the evening watch.

'I finally got Vengeance painted,' I said.

'I heard a rumour. I'll have to take a look in the morning.'

'She took longer than I expected,' I said slowly, looking to the bow. 'The repairs to her shoulder . . .'

'Ah,' he said and began his salesman's shuffle. 'I didn't want to agitate you when we were just setting out. It's a tradition. Would you rather the men threw their earrings and acorns and wren feathers overboard and abandoned hope? We'd be done for, Mr Doig.'

'Aye, dinnae fret.' I reached inside my shirt and withdrew my sliver of Vengeance. 'I need all the luck I can get.'

Porter gave his singular, high-pitched laugh and for the first time I noticed the tinge of nervousness in it.

The next day, my nineteenth aboard the *Agathos*, a pack of soft, low-slung clouds had been dealt across the sky. The ship sat on the surface of the water, its close-reefed topsails the only canvas out to catch the breeze. From time to time a darker cloud would pass over us and let go its contents. These downpours would last a minute or two, the rain falling in vertical streams rather than individual droplets. The men ran out into the showers to wash, some stripping to the waist, others taking the chance to eke the salt from their clothes while they were still on their bodies and wringing out their rough laundered vests and shirts and trousers when the rain stopped.

I stood beneath the eaves of the deckhouse, alongside Jarrell and Burton, the two apprentices who, like me, had never been this far south. After the first two showers, we joined the men on deck. The water was warmer and softer than any rain I had felt before, but still a wee bit salty.

Our shirts, vests and waistcoats were draped across the gunwale and the sun was shining bright as new copper when Porter emerged from the 'tween decks, sweat beading on his brow.

'Waterspout weather, if ever there was,' he said.

I looked out to the horizon. Aside from two lighter patches where the rain was falling, the sea appeared slick, harmless.

'Aha,' Porter said and made for starboard. I gathered up my clothes and followed.

'See that darkening, there, a mile off? Just you watch.'

Before our eyes a dark triangle began to descend diagonally from the cluster of nimbus clouds. The corner of the triangle then stretched out into a thin white finger that pushed down to the surface of the water, becoming thinner and thinner until it was no longer a finger but a scalpel, poised for the first incision. I noticed now that the sea itself was not a flat plane: a small cone of water and mist was rising, twisting up to meet the descending cloud. The *Agathos* must have been drifting towards this phenomenon, or the clouds were edging towards the ship, as it appeared to grow, its form becoming clearer with every passing moment. When the sky cone and the sea cone connected, a white, ghostly veil was whisked up at the base of the vortex.

'See the wake it traces?' Porter said. The spout was indeed tracing a rippled line across the oily water, not unlike the wake of the *Agathos*, though its edges were parallel rather than V-shaped.

'There,' Porter said, pointing over the bow, 'another one.'

The funnel of this new spout had not fully formed and I turned back to the first, interested in its movement across the water. By concentrating on its base, I was able to observe the halting rhythm of its motion. The spout would cover a good distance in a smooth sweep before pausing over one spot, as if catching its breath before continuing. The rhythm was instantly familiar. It was a carver's rhythm: gouge stroke, pause, stroke, pause, adjustment, stroke. Perhaps it was the superstition of the men surrounding me but a shiver ran down my back. It seemed a sign.

The veil of mist at the base died down and the connection was broken. It looked as if the spout were being erased from the bottom up, scrubbed out like a sketch another soul was never meant to see.

'Crikey,' Porter said. I turned and saw him pointing through the rigging at three dark funnels that had already formed and the finger of a fourth reaching towards the water less than a hundred yards from the ship.

'Trouble?' I asked.

Porter grabbed Burton's bare wrist. 'Sound the bell.'

The mate directed the sailors on deck to hoist the topsails. I threw on my shirt, leaving it unbuttoned, and dropped the rest of my clothes. I uncoiled a buntline and released the belaying pin that held it in place, but before I could haul upon the rope a waterspout collided with the port side of the *Agathos*, causing her to jerk from side to side. The sound of the vortex itself was no more fearsome than the beating of a fly's wings, perhaps a few dozen flies, but it was accompanied by the cracking of braces and stays against spars and the zip-zoot of the topsails being rent to shreds. Fortunately the funnel passed across the deck in a single stroke and did not pause to consider its next move.

'You men get aloft,' Porter shouted over the flutter of the spout as it meandered away. 'We'll need to get these sails down. Tim, fetch Mantzaris. There's work enough for him now.'

'Should I—?' I asked, my eyes slowly moving up to the topsail yards.

'Carpenter,' Porter said in the same storm-piercing voice, 'survey the decks for damage.'

I nodded and hurried to the storeroom to retrieve my tool belt. When I emerged back on deck the waterspout that had passed over the *Agathos* was all but erased. The dark cloud at the top of the funnel had developed a lighter bulge. On cue, this gave way: the water that had been sucked into the sky was free to return once more, falling in a single crumpled sheet that smacked the surface of the sea and disappeared.

The spout had passed amidships, leaving the boats and the chicken coop untouched. One of the chests that sat hard against the base of the mainmast was missing its lid and two of the dead-eyes that braced the foremast shrouds had come free from the base of the bulwark, but the decking and the bulwarks themselves appeared to have withstood the test.

The damaged chest stored spare sets of oilskins and I found a few items strewn about the deck. Its lid was over at the foot of the quarterdeck steps, hinges still attached. Back at the base of the mainmast, I had to move the lid to the left to avoid the chewed-out holes left by the screws when they were wrenched free, which meant I'd have to make further adjustments to ensure the lid would be watertight. I gave a sigh, looked aloft and saw the men working to untie the robands that bound the sail to the yards. The topsail was torn in at least three places but it hung limply in the still afternoon air. There were no signs of further waterspouts. I could hear men whistling, others talking in a rattle of vulgar words. Everyone was glad to be occupied after two days becalmed with little to do.

I returned my attention to the final hinge. I did not enjoy carpentry: the need for measurements, spirit levels, all that metal to bind and separate wood. The rhythm of the waterspout had crystallised my thoughts: where carpentry fought against nature, carving sought to work with it. A carver learnt to understand every piece of wood, to follow its grain deep into the heart of a block and find the shape the wood wanted to become. Carving was an art, carpentry a collection of chores—often fiddly and mathematical, but chores nonetheless. My father had randered along similar lines when I was a child in his workshop. When Porter had carried my sea chest across the gangway and I followed in his wake, I did not expect to dislike the work to this degree. I was working with wood, after all. And I was at sea, experiencing the world in a dozen different ways every day. Such were the thoughts, Avis, that jangled in my head when the sky went dark and I was laid out flat.

The next thing I can remember was being in a bunk, grasping for consciousness. It felt as if time were sluicing through the hole in my head. That I was being pummelled by the unremitting passage of time and if I were to ever get up from my bunk I would be greatly aged. Perhaps this was the onset of the Doig family affliction, hastened on by external forces. Perhaps it was my time.

I recalled Porter beside my bunk at some stage in the night, perhaps more than once, but the effort to recall his words was too much for my aching head. What had happened? How long had I been laid out?

When I let my mind unclench a tide of phrases rolled in and receded.

Rest. As long as you need. Rest. A heavy blow. As long as you need. Rest. Didn't know you were there. As long as you need.

Others came. A man with a wolf's head. The cook's assistant with hard tack and grog. Doctor Stanley. Tim with fresh bandages.

You'd best recover smartly. Rest is my prescription. The men are talking. Best get above decks smartly. I don't believe it's serious. The men, they grumble.

Where were the others, the apprentices, Meiklejohn, Mantzaris, the cook? I was not in my bunk, I realised, not in the deckhouse. I was below decks. Some kind of infirmary.

The men are talking. A heavy blow is my prescription. Recover smartly. A smarting blow. Och, you are nae use to anybody! The men, they grumble.

Eventually, the flow of time began to relax and no longer coursed through my head.

I was on deck, I thought, fixing the chest. A waterspout had crossed the deck, a spiral swarm of flies, the airy finger of the Almighty. The Doig affliction. No. I was fully awake. Aware to the point of heightened consciousness. I was alone. There was no one snoring in an adjacent bunk. No one picking at a Jew's harp. I was alone. The door at my feet remained closed, untested by wind or spray. A ribbon of light cut through beneath it. I was enclosed in this wee space, an envelope of wood alive with the sounds of wood. From the slightest mouse squeak to the deepest rolling groan. I fought hard to banish the ghosts and woodland creatures that the creaking ship conjured in my mind and tried to focus on the wood itself. What part of the ship made such a noise? Where was the pressure coming from? In what strength and at what velocity? What sort of wood or woods? How might the grain affect the sound?

My head effervesced but my body ached, felt encrusted, as if a skin of bark were forming, a coarse grain trickling through my flesh, knots taking shape, my form hardening.

Footsteps above. Hard leather on teak and tar, the vibrations passing through the layer of softwood and the dark space to my ears. Footsteps on the teak treads of the companionway, the creak of the teak handrail and the brass fixings. The give of the pine door against the teak jamb. Pine, I thought. It mustn't catch the spray.

'You're awake.' It was Porter.

'What happened to me?'

'The memory still no good, eh?' He sat down on the edge of the bunk. 'You were struck by a brace block that came away from the yard. It was a heavy blow, but softened some by the sail that came away before it.'

'You've told me this before.'

'That I have, Carpenter.'

'I should get above deck. The men must be talking.'

'You need to rest. You'll need your strength when we get further south.'

With great effort, I hoisted myself into a sitting position and, as if it had been waiting for this very moment, time rushed back into the hole in my head.

It was four days before I could walk on deck and a further two before I resumed light duties. I'd been forewarned about the chilly reception I might receive from the men, but I assumed it would make little difference. What I hadn't accounted for was the fact we were now in the Southern Hemisphere and I had missed crossing the line, the ceremony, the ritual humiliation of the first timers at the hand of the ship's Neptune. In time I got the story from Tim: Jarrell and Burton, the two apprentices, knelt on the poop deck, the rusty razor, the two buckets of piss, the pledge to Neptune and the Order of the Waves—but I knew it all the instant I saw Jarrell: his downcast eyes, the cherry-red seam running down his cheek.

The men's contempt for me, unvented, began to take on physical dimensions. Shoulders were thrust into me as I queued outside the galley, feet were left dangling to trip me as I exited. Hot tar was 'spilt' on my ankle as I crossed the deck.

The brace block had knocked nearly a week from my life, but I had suffered below decks, unseen. I never found out if it was the same block I had carved and Boag installed a few days earlier and, if so, whose fault it was that it had come away with the canvas. To the men, I had been standing in the wrong place. What fool would work at the base of the mast while the men replaced a damaged sail?

It was no use trying to argue with the men, to bring their resentment to a head and move on. They just sat there, grunting or wiping their nose upon their sleeve, leaving their rebuttal for the next time I wandered in range of the jib-boom.

The *Agathos* entered the ice zone in mid-September. Her bow was pointed eastward and the Roaring Forties whipped her through the thick, scrambled ocean.

'I suggest you keep your mouth shut with the men,' Porter told me one night. We were standing near the stern, in the shelter of a deckhouse. I was in my oilskins, Porter in shirtsleeves. He had summoned me, was counselling me as a first mate rather than a friend. Should things get out of hand he would be responsible. I was back to full carpenter's duties and performing them as best I could, given my limited experience and the antagonism of the crew—should I be laid out for any period of time, it was Porter who'd have to ensure my tasks were covered.

'I see,' I said. 'I'm causing you trouble.'

Porter waited until I lifted my head and trained his eyes on mine. 'I'm leaving the ship in Melbourne,' he confided. 'I've done my dash. I don't want anything to go wrong the next few weeks, all right, Carpenter?'

I admired his honesty, though later I wondered if it was another calculated act.

'Does Bock know?'

'No. And he won't, will he?'

I shrugged. It was not as if I had a regular audience with the captain.

'I've got a cousin in Geelong. It's not so hard to slip away from port. Or sign onto another ship that departs before the *Agathos*.'

'I see.' I began to unbutton my oilskin coat. 'I've been thinking about my stramash with the brace block.'

'Forget about it, Carpenter.'

'I understand what happened.'

'If you think there's some conspiracy—'

'No, nothing of the sort.'

'If you want to avoid their attention, you could start by getting a little spray on your brow.' He gestured at my cap.

'It's fine,' I said and stuck my hand inside my coat. From my shirt pocket I retrieved the splinter I had taken from Vengeance. 'Such a thing might be good luck for a sailor,' I said, holding it up high to catch the flickering light of the quarterdeck's lantern, 'but I am no sailor. I am no sailor,' I repeated and tossed the splinter into the ship's dark wake.

14 March 1891

I worked my clew talon across the pitch pine to complete another tally of five days. I considered making that day's mark in advance but decided against it. There was no guarantee I would see out day one hundred and twenty-six as a castaway, not with the channel crossing I had ahead of me.

When I had first glimpsed the big island back in November, I considered building a raft, but my resources seemed so meagre, the channel so broad, that it was not worth the risk, especially as there was no guarantee this new island would be any more hospitable. As the days and weeks passed I returned to this scheme and abandoned it a dozen times until—three days ago—I saw the steamer.

I'd been up at the ridgeline, foraging for Hell's Cabbage, my name for the large flowering plant that was dotted around Lemon Wedge. I often lay awake at night craving the runnelled green leaves or the sugary root that I chewed raw, in small rationed chunks so that I could enjoy it over several sweet days. I'd found another patch and was digging at the earth with Tim's trusty spoon to reach the roots when I noticed a puff of steam floating across the sky. It was one of those rare days when neither mist nor fog clung to the island. The wind blew from the west with unceasing glee and the weak sun barely registered through the steady sheet of clouds, but it was a glorious day by island standards. A day on which white puffs between sea and sky were not easily explained.

I stood and saw the steamer easing towards the big island. It was close enough that I could make out the white hull, the two bare, raking masts and the yellow cylinder belching steam at the centre of the ship. I squinted, trying to make out any men on deck, but the distance was too great. If I were to be seen, I needed to act and act quickly. A fire would be best, but I still had no way of lighting one. I made my way back down to the beach, juggling speed and safety, and gathered up all the canvas and wood I could carry. On the way back up I needed to stop several times.

When I made the ridgeline I couldn't see the steamer or its steam. I walked south along the crest, dragging my bundle of canvas and spars like a tiller. When I reached the southern cliffs I saw the ship, a white speck just off the northern edge of the big island. Its chimney was no longer chuffing steam and the ship appeared motionless, suggesting it was at anchor.

Terns and smaller albatross flew across the face of the cliffs and overhead as I set to work lashing the lengths of pitch pine and white spruce together with blades of tussock and precious rope to form a pole some ten feet high.

Oh, Avis, what I would have given for a nail!

I stopped often to poke my head up and check the steamer's position. It remained anchored for the hour, perhaps longer, that it took to attach the largest run of sailcloth I had to my flagpole. The wind had almost dropped away by the time I managed to hoist my flag. The canvas seemed impossibly heavy and my hopes of it striking out into a broad, rippling banner seemed foolish. I held the pole and its limp flag aloft for several minutes but when the steamer showed no sign of making way I laid it back down.

The sun passed across the sky in its ever more oblique orbit. The wind continued to lie low. From time to time I would hear the hollow knocking sound of albatross clapping their beaks together as a pair changed places on the ledges below, one moving onto the nest, the other taking to the sky.

In late afternoon the ship began to send steam into the air once more. I lifted my flagpole and watched the ship wheel around. 'Please head north,' I muttered. 'There's nocht south but ice. That's the way. Aye, there you are. Aye, here I am.'

The ship seemed to be heading directly to me. I worked the flagpole back and forth to spread the sail, lifting up the soil at its base. About a third of the way across the channel the steamer suddenly beat to the north-east, a path that would take it close to Lemon Wedge but, ultimately, past it. They hadn't spotted me yet. Surely they would as they drew nearer. I continued to work the flag, which seemed happier to tangle around the makeshift pole, its edges snagging where the pieces of wood were lashed together.

'Would it be too much trouble for a gust of wind?' I asked. 'You can blow till kingdom come for all I care, but you'd better start now.'

The steamer continued to carve its wake across the calm channel. For the first and last time, this part of the world reminded me of the time in the doldrums before my accident.

When the steamer was five or six hundred yards off the tip of Lemon Wedge Island, I could see the entire length of the port side. I could see men moving about the deck, ducking their heads to avoid the hanging lifeboats as they moved aft. 'Ahoy!' I shouted, letting the flag drop and waving out my free hand. I could even see the captain standing atop the T-shaped upper deck, staring straight at me, or so it seemed, a pipe in his mouth, while another officer manned the wheel.

'Ahoy! Up here! Ahoy!' I shouted, feeling myself grow hoarse but ignoring the pain, pushing for more volume with every shout. I beat the pole back and forth but the steamer continued on its course, moving further east until it was clear that it had passed as close as it would come. I saw the captain release his hands from the rail, take his pipe from his mouth as if emerging from deep contemplation and walk to the opposite side of the wee deck.

I continued to scream, louder than the skua gulls, louder than the yellow-brows, louder than the strongest gale, but the ship carried on, puffing its jolly clouds of steam as it slipped further and further away.

I woke the next morning with a throat so raw I might have guzzled boric acid. The wind was up, of course, and the rain came in heavy sweeps. I disassembled my failed flagpole, wrapped myself in canvas and started working on the thick section of mast marooned on the beach. I traced a line around the middle of the log with the sharp tip of a gull's beak and began sawing it with a piece of seal jaw studded with teeth. I'd found the beast washed up on the shore, a small wound on its belly being excavated by the seabirds. Its decaying flesh had been difficult to eat raw, but I'd managed to make use of the creature in other ways.

After several hours of hard labour I had cut a groove two inches deep and worn the teeth away to pearly nubs. I placed a wedge-shaped rock in the furrow and struck it over and over with a section of spar that had become my favourite cudgel.

At the end of the day I had managed to turn this section of topmast into two five-foot lengths. These would be the pontoons for my raft.

The next day I dragged everything to a spot on the beach where the kelp was at its sparsest. I used every piece of wood at my disposal, first fixing a block to the end of my cudgel to form an oar, then using the rest to brace the two pontoons. I strung lengths of canvas across the pontoons to form a taut platform. That night I had to make my bed beneath the raft to ensure it did not drift away with the tide, though I did not sleep a wink.

It was moulting season at the yellow-brow colony and the shiftless morning wind lifted thousands of soft white feathers into the air. Two weeks ago the adults had grown blurry at the edges and stopped going down to the water, stopped feeding. The stench grew worse than ever. The rocky slope rang with ever more impatient squawks as the birds fluffed up and became helpless. The bumps and scrapes of colony life—and the constant nuisance of the nellies and skuas—gave them a mottled, almost rabid, appearance. The chicks had grown into stouter, disgruntled-looking juveniles. Their only remaining fuzz was a rough mane stretching across their haunches. They continued to gather in their nurseries, groups of five or six brown-black birds around a foetid puddle. To me it always looked as if these youngsters were organising a mutiny.

The wind shifted and the soft, white blizzard descended on me as I worked on the beach. Tiny feathers found their way up my nostrils and between my eyelashes.

I would not miss this island.

I retrieved Tim's pocket watch, which I had managed to repair at a cost of three weeks. The brass cover of the timepiece was scratched and dull, but I could still make out my reflection: my matted hair and coarse ginger beard appeared newly bleached, as if I had aged overnight. Then I remembered the feathers and swept both cheeks angrily with my free hand. I flicked the watch open. Nearly eight in the morning. It promised to be a long day, but there was no time to dally.

I returned to my grotto—it had developed its own stench, a melange of penguin blubber and my own musky scent that my nose seemed unable to ignore—retrieved the bladder I had fashioned from seal hide and trekked up through the yellow-brows to collect water from the freshest point, a trickle between the pedestals of tussock far above the nesting bowls.

While the bladder filled I kept an eye out for parakeets. I'd learnt that the red patch on the heads of some of these birds was formed from a crest of bright red feathers rather than the blood of another creature. At one time it had been of great importance to prove that these beautiful birds were not carnivorous. I had brought hunks of penguin flesh up to the tussock, placed them on the ground and waited to see if the parakeets would take my bait. They never did, probably because there was nowhere to properly conceal myself and still keep sight of the meat. Weeks later I observed one of the completely green parakeets picking at the corpse of a penguin chick at the edge of the colony.

Needs must, I told myself, but the fact these beautiful birds were scavengers like the rest of the island's inhabitants had been a great disappointment.

On my way back down to the foreshore with a bladder full of fresh water, I stopped to pluck two gloomy-looking juveniles from their nursery so that I might have something to eat, either on my crossing or once I had made it to the big island. I didn't know what sort of life it harboured, or how far I'd have to trek to find fresh water or shelter. Whatever the answers, I was better off there than on this fingernail. The steamer was anchored in that bay long enough to suggest there was work on the island. Perhaps they were trading with the inhabitants, or were hunting wild pigs to fill their larder. That particular ship might not return, but others must. I would be there to greet them. I would not be overlooked this time.

I carried the last of my possessions from my grotto: the woven tussock mats, the sailcloth sack containing my spare clothes, bone needles, fish hooks and other improvised tools. I laid the mats across the canvas platform of the raft and lashed the sack next to the sealskin bladder and my boots, each of which contained the carcass of a penguin chick.

The tide was now lapping at the rough tips of my pontoons. I stood alongside in my bare feet, my trousers rolled up to my knees, waiting for the first big wave that would allow me to push the raft out into the breakers. I looked out at the sea, beaten into thousands of small white peaks by the wind. The leathery blades of kelp throbbed on the surface, crowding into the wee gap through which I intended to launch before pulling back to show the cool green water and the rocks beneath. The hardest part would be this first section, paddling through the breakers, against the current and the wind, to get to the southern tip of Lemon Wedge. Once I had rounded the headland, I would have sight of my destination and could make my way into the channel in the lee of the smaller island.

A large wave broke over my shins and I felt the raft lift slightly before it settled back on the rocky shore. I moved around the rear of the raft and placed a hand on each pontoon, my arms nearly at full stretch. Another wave was rolling in. I took a deep breath. The water rushed up to me, lifting the raft, and I pushed. The effort made my shredded throat sizzle. The raft was moving, I was moving, the water to my knees, my crotch. I felt a slimy arm of kelp brush against my bare calf. I jumped. My hands grasped the rope that ran around the midsection of the raft and I hauled myself aboard. I pulled the oar from where it had been lashed and began to paddle madly. The wind cut into me but the low profile of my craft meant I was able to make way. The waves broke over and through the raft but it remained upright, remained intact. I lost a tussock mat, then another, but it was no bother. Big jaups of sea water sloshed into my face, my open mouth, but I didn't stop. I couldn't stop.

Finally I was clear of the breakers and dug my oar into the water at the back of the raft, turning it southwards, making for the headland.

The sun was at its sheepish apex by the time I rounded the point and caught that day's first glimpse of the big island, though the name seemed to overstate its size. From my vantage, a few feet above the water and a mile or so to the north, it was little more than a dark mound. Water plashed over the pontoons and settled on the canvas in pools which I scooped out from time to time with my oar. I didn't know how I would cope if rain arrived.

After what seemed a long time, but could not have been more than twenty minutes, I noticed myself being pulled off course. Whether by the wind or the current, I was being taken to the east. If I continued to steer straight for the big island I would be taken past it so I shifted my position on the raft and began paddling towards a spot just to the west of the island.

The raft was constantly jostled by the whitecaps, the spray fizzing against the canvas deck and my own flushed face. In moments when the wind dropped, I could hear the spars rubbing against the pontoons but holding, holding.

I was parched, but needed to paddle due west for ten minutes to buy myself the time for a drink of water and to check the pocket watch. Half-past two. I plunged my oar into the water again, turning my head with the stroke to look back at Lemon Wedge, then forward to the big island. Perhaps another hour and a half, if I had the strength.

As I drew closer to the big island it began to look as inhospitable as the one I had left, simply larger. Above the cliffs it appeared that a high plateau of dead grass surrounded the peaks at the centre of the island. The beach I was aiming for began to take shape. It was rocky, but possibly sheltered, the slope up to the plateau manageable. No wonder the steamer chose this anchorage. Then I noticed something almost white on the northeastern end of the island. Above the shore, about a hundred feet up, there: the first new straight lines in one hundred and twenty-six days. Yes, a pitched roof. From my low angle I couldn't be sure if it was a house or some sort of storage shed. Part of me stood distant, noting that I was exhausted, had possibly been driven mad by my diet of raw penguin and loneliness. Books were full of stories of desert wanderers being fooled by mirages. I shouldn't get my hopes up. But I stuffed this nay-saying down and paddled as furiously as I had when I first set out.

A few minutes later the wind shifted so that it blew from the north, which meant I needed only to fight the current. Every breath was another draught of acid, but I battled on, the island growing larger with every stroke. Soon I could make out grey birds flying around the cliffs, birds I had not encountered on Lemon Wedge. The occasional wave formed behind the raft and shunted me onward, closer and closer to the beach. My arms felt as though they had been stretched and stretched, that they would never assume their previous form, never regain what strength they had possessed. But I was in the breakers now. The hut had slipped from view, obscured by the bluff above which it sat. My faith in its existence was unshaken. I could have abandoned my raft at this point and bounded through the waves but could not be certain how easy it was to reach the hut from the shore, how much strength it would require. Light was draining from the sky and I might need the wood, ropes and canvas from my raft if I was to make shelter on the beach, just as I needed my bones unbroken and head clear if I was to get warm after being wet through for so long.

I made land with about an hour of light remaining, hauled my raft into the lee of a small bluff and stood for a moment, hands on hips, looking back at Lemon Wedge. How unremarkable, I thought. No wonder the steamer crew had paid it no attention. I drained the last drops of fresh water from my sealskin bladder and stuffed it into my drenched sailcloth sack and set off for the hut. A few yards up from the shore I came to a band of thick tussock. The crowns were up to four feet across and stood atop pedestals up to six feet high—much bigger than I had encountered on Lemon Wedge. I tried forcing my way between the clumps, but the balls of tussock were so tightly packed, their leaves knitted together so completely, that it was impenetrable unless I crawled on my hands and knees. A few feet into the thicket and it was completely black. After fifteen minutes, I came to a rock wall and decided it might be quicker to walk over the top of the tussock.

Bracing myself against the wall, I managed to shimmy up to the top of a crown of tussock. I could see now that I had made it only a dozen yards from the shore. I lunged forward to step onto the next crown, which swayed but held my weight. It was similar to crossing a stream via a series of stepping stones, except these stones did not stand still and they ran uphill. The light was fading fast. The hut remained hidden. I thought it a good thing that no one was around or else the whole business would be quite humiliating. After two more steps I could no longer be certain where to place my feet. I lowered myself down until I was lying prone on a bed of tussock several feet off the ground, my sack of meagre belongings still strung to my back, and began to crawl like a snail.

Dark had arrived, the day had ended and yet I was still on the move, still fighting for the clearing. I hadn't eaten since daybreak.

Hadn't drunk since I'd left the shore. But there was a hut on this island.

At the edge of the clearing the crowns were half as high as elsewhere and I was able to roll onto the ground without injuring myself. I rose to my feet, looked to the sky in the hope that the moon, so seldom seen for all the clouds and mist, had deigned to appear on this night. I saw wisps of orange and violet light, as if I'd been closing my eyes shut too tightly, but no moon.

I kept the tussock to my left, running my hand through the coarse leaves as I edged towards where I thought the hut sat. I tried to call out, but my throat couldn't manage a simple hello. Any sound I tried to produce came out as a mangled croak. I might have recovered my voice in a more hospitable climate, perhaps, but it was not to be.

After twenty yards I felt the wind drop as I entered into the shelter of some rocky nook. I knew I was in the right place. The hut would be sheltered to the south but with a view to the north. I pushed forward, feeling the space with my hands, grasping at the black until I felt it. Wood. The delicate topography of its grain. The straight edges. The wee depressions around the nails.

I ran my hands across the weatherboard until I came to an upright. A door jamb. A galvanised hinge. The vertical boards of the door. I knocked but heard nothing in reply. My fingers found a metal knob. I wrapped my fingers around it and turned. A slow cloud of musty air enveloped me as I stepped across the threshold. I smelt the tang of tinned mutton and gunpowder, but my hands had found the frame of a bunk, the thick warmth of a woollen blanket. My stomach could wait. I dropped my sailcloth sack and lowered myself onto the thin mattress, tucked my knees up to my chest, pulled the blanket over my head and slept.

And that is the story of how I lost my voice. Not that I had much need for it at the time.

You are going to continue, aren't you? You must bring the strands of your story together at least.

Must I?

Of course! Do not tease me, Gabriel. I have told you everything about my life.

Everything?

Quite everything. You, on the other hand, have much left to explain. How did you come to be tied to the mast? How did you ever get off the big island? How did you end up in the window that night you took me away?

Is a girl in your condition up to hearing more of an old man's tale?

Please don't call me a girl. And I am fine, now that I know the reason for the worm in my stomach.

The Second Leg

The *Agathos* made Port Phillip on the seventeenth of October. 'Four nights you have,' Captain Bock instructed me. These were the first words he'd directed my way in weeks.

'Is there nae any work needed while she's in port, Captain?' I asked, well aware I was tempting fate.

'We are here long enough to fill her hold with cargo, Carpenter, nothing more. Then it's on to the Horn.'

Four nights was a short layover, considering we'd been at sea for seventy-five days and the journey back to Europe would take another hundred. But, as Porter had explained when we first met, the *Agathos* was being run hard in the hopes of making her crew rich—or freeing up some capital for the Rennie, Chambers & Bishop Shipping Company to invest in a steel and steam monstrosity.

I didn't intend to return to the *Agathos* on the twenty-first. I wouldn't receive my full pay until we made London, but I had been advanced £1 6s when I first joined the crew and a further £2 once we reached Melbourne. I left the ship in my oilskins— fortunately the sky was grey and promised rain—beneath which I wore as many of my clothes as I could manage, though I had to leave my tools and sea chest aboard. I felt no guilt in abandoning ship: I had fairly worked my passage to Australia. Besides, I was not so great a ship's carpenter that I could not be easily replaced.

I found a room in an unnamed boarding house up a short lane that my fellow crew members had walked right past. The proprietor was a rail-thin woman with a plum-coloured bruise cupping the right side of her chin. I suspected her of colluding with the ships, so I lied and said I'd be returning to sea in four nights' time.

'Rooms are rented by the week,' she said, 'and just because you're stayin' only four days, don't expect an extra rasher for breakfast.'

The boarding house was full of sailors intent on drinking their fill of undiluted rum, gambling with people they had every hope of never meeting again and sleeping with women whose kisses tasted of cigar ash.

I spent a lot of time that first day and night in bed, groggy, disoriented, one particular sea shanty the crew had sung in recent days running through my head.

And we'll all go ashore
Heave away! Haul away!
Where we will drink with girls galore
And we're bound for South Australia.

The afternoon of the next day I ventured outside, my head a wee bit clearer. I was no sailor. There was nothing for me back in Scotland, no real reason to risk my life rounding the Horn in a hard-run clipper with a crew of bullies. I walked along the waterfront, from Town Pier to St Kilda, dodging tear-shaped puddles and shaggy dogs dragging daydreaming men. When I looked out upon the harbour it was as if all the old sailing ships, the last of their kind to be built, were gathered in this one place at the bottom of the world. I wondered how many of Doig & Son's figureheads graced these bows, but decided I was better off not seeing what had become of them. No one would pay me to repair another figurehead, not enough to live on. And yet I found myself scrutinising the sign of every warehouse and workshop I passed, hoping for a ship's carver—so much for a fresh start—but it was all ironmongers, muntz traders and boiler works.

I caught a tram heading north to the centre of the city. The roads were lined with large stone buildings and terraced housing. When I alighted, I stood outside a long brick building covered in scaffolding. At the far end there was a square clock tower, while teams of tilers worked to cover three more conical towers spaced along the roof. This was a town of stone, I decided, not wood.

Trams jostled past every few minutes. The people walked so quickly that I expected them to stumble at any moment. I had never been to London, but I imagined it was like this: hectic, imposing, impersonal.

A man could disappear in Melbourne.

Having paid for a week's stay, I returned to my boarding house and passed another queasy night.

I must have been a miserable sight at breakfast the next morning as an extra rasher appeared on my plate. I looked up but the proprietor did not turn around as she returned to the kitchen.

She had seen my kind before, no doubt.

I walked around Melbourne again that afternoon, waiting for lightning to strike as it did that day I saw Vengeance on the docks. I could become anything. I could go anywhere. But a man cannot make a choice when presented with infinite possibilities. I began to understand the appeal of spending one's shore leave in a drunken stupor: a sailor's life does not stand up well to interrogation.

> When the she-oak's gone to our head
> Heave away! Haul away!
> The girls can put us all to bed
> And we're bound for South Australia

My boarding house was crawling with such men. Three in particular were fixtures in the dining room, nursing their sore heads and forcing down greasy mouthfuls. From overheard snatches of conversation I gathered they were Americans. Two had signed on with a new ship; the third had decided to stay in port a while longer.

I tried to catch the proprietor's eye as she entered the dining room with plates for the Americans, but she avoided my gaze.

'Excuse me,' I said when she returned with my own plate. She plonked it down, turned her back but paused, waiting for me to speak. 'I was wondering if I could stay the rest of the week.'

'I'm not in the business of hiding runaway sailors, Mr Doig,' she said, addressing the doorway, and left for the kitchen.

One of the Americans lifted his head from his hands, narrowed his eyes and began growling. I looked down at my plate: just the one rasher of bacon. The American barked and I looked up to see him baring his impossibly white teeth.

I decided I should head inland to a town without sailors. One with no need for a figurehead carver. A place like the one Porter described, where the sun rises red and round over the earth. I would return to the land, become a crofter like my grandfather's father, though the terrain was surely different to the Highlands. I would have to work my way into some land, shearing sheep and building homesteads. Perhaps I could marry well.

I spent a long time in front of a large map at Flinders Station and settled on Wadonga, two hundred miles to the north-east. The next train didn't leave until ten the next morning so I purchased a ticket and returned to the boarding house for my final night.

The world no longer swayed as I lay in bed. The shanty that had wormed its way inside my head had softened to a whisper. I slept and slept well. A glorious night, all things considered. I lay there long after the sun had risen, listening to the groans as the men made their way downstairs and the clinks of crockery on the breakfast tables. In time I rose, gathered my coat and hat and looked at my smoky reflection in the tottie window. I made my way down the stairs, thinking about the woman I would marry, the children I would have, the dry stretch of red earth I'd leave them when I died. I was so occupied by this fantasy that I didn't see

Swenson and Boag waiting outside the boarding house, one either side of the door. Before I could take in what had happened, they each had me by an elbow and were pulling me towards the docks.

'What are you doing?' I managed to say.

'You signed on for a return voyage,' Boag said.

'Don't think because we got a proper chippy now you can abandon ship,' Swenson said. 'You can earn your keep this time.'

'There's a new carpenter?' I asked. I stumbled as I tried to look into Swenson's face and my hat fell off. Boag stooped to pick it up in one swoop and plugged it back on my head.

'Aye,' he said. 'And a new mate.'

'Keep your trap shut,' Swenson said, craning his neck to talk over me. 'I had a hard night and he's stronger than he looks.'

I tried to resist but our progress towards the *Agathos* continued until her masts were visible, her hull, her figurehead—Vengeance looking away, unable to face another reunion—and soon we were up the gangway. The men on deck stopped rolling barrels and coiling rope to stand and cheer. For a moment I thought they might be happy to see me. That this was all some kind of hazing. That the torment of the first leg had been a test and now that I was back I would be treated as an equal.

Someone shouted, 'Three cheers for the smallest press gang I ever saw!' The men hoorayed and I understood my fate.

'So you're my new dogsbody?'

I turned and saw the American from the dining room, his white teeth shining. He raised his hands up near his chin, unfurled his large pink tongue and began to pant.

In time I learnt how Randik, the other American, had signed on as the new first mate and recommended his friend, Joe Sepsey, a ship's carpenter with years of service, to Bock. The captain had leapt at the chance. I'm sure his heart didn't even flutter at the thought of demoting me to an apprentice—in truth, my rightful station—but Randik and Sepsey understood straight away the virtue in casting me once more in the role of scapegoat and punching bag.

Sepsey was true to his word. I was his dogsbody. Hauling spars up from the storeroom onto the deck, then stowing them away once more when he figured out 'another way to do it'. Climbing the masts to inspect yards and spreaders at dawn and dusk while the carpenter whittled his little wooden birds on the deck below.

There was something off about Sepsey. The left corner of his mouth would twitch, as if he were chewing a plug of tobacco. Even at his most serene he would curse unlike anything I had ever heard—'Massive cocksnot!' 'Punch the clock fucking asslick!'

One day in the galley, waiting for my ladle of slumgullion, I overheard Jarrell and Burton talking about my new master. The two apprentices, inseparable since their experience while crossing the line, continued to shun me, but from their raised voices it was clear they knew I was behind them.

'I heard he was a castaway on a desert island,' Jarrell said.

'Not a desert island,' Burton said. 'It was down Antarctica way.'

'Desert island don't mean sand, I don't think. It just means deserted.'

'I heard that's the reason his teeth are so white.'

'What?'

'Being a castaway. They say it makes your teeth go white.'

'What does?'

'I don't know. It weren't no cocoa-nuts.'

'How long was he shipwrecked?'

'Long enough for that screw to come loose.'

'Ah, but he's a good sort,' Jarrell said. 'Knows what he's doing all right.'

'Best person to be wrecked, in a way. No wonder he survived.'

In less than a week the entire crew was under Sepsey's spell. During the day he'd regale the men with tales of his shipwreck, his sixty-four days 'against the elements' on his uninhabited rock, all the while whittling his cardinals and jays while I installed new benches in the ship's boats and sanded them down. At night, Sepsey led the revelry in the petty officers' deckhouse. He never seemed to sleep, always seemed to have a jug of grog to his lips.

The voyage, for him, merely extended the sea-oak bacchanal that took place in port.

Captain Bock, true to form, was never spotted unless in the company of the paying guests. These new passengers, bound for England, wore clothes as fine as those on the southbound leg but something always seemed to have gone awry in the dressing: the narrow section of a man's neck tie protruding beneath the wider part, a button missed on a shirt, a brooch pinned upside down, the live flowers on a woman's hat wilted and browning.

The weather grew wild as the *Agathos* dipped down once more into the Southern Ocean. The passengers replaced their parasols and ties with fur stoles and oilskins, if they dared venture above deck at all. Inside the deckhouse, Sepsey told his tales of coracle construction and seal hunting, leaving me to inspect the bulwarks and clear the scuppers.

On the first of November a family of icebergs was spotted off the starboard bow. They appeared benign—a small flock of sheep grazing on the surface of the water. The ship never passed close enough for this image of mine to be challenged.

That evening the rain began in earnest and fell for the next three nights. Sepsey's revellers continued to pile into the deck-house between sodden shifts on deck, the floor of our cabin perpetually slick with a film of water and ringing with the jeers and barks of my tormentors. Each night the party became more raucous, until on the third night Sepsey began barking, 'A woman!' in the same manner as his curses. 'A man needs a woman. This man needs a woman.'

He tore off his shirt and ran outside, clutching his whittling knife.

The men cheered and charged their near-empty vessels and I pulled my blanket back over my head. The others soon grew quiet without Sepsey. Some returned to the fo'c'sle. Others crammed onto Jarrell and Burton's bunks or slept on the sloshing boards.

The next morning the sun was out, bright and cool, and the men slowly roused themselves, untangling their limbs and wiping off the worst of the grime.

'Where's Sepsey?' Kulke asked.

'Did he not come back?'

The men filed out into the light, leaving me alone in the deckhouse, the door swinging with the swell. When I got up to shut the door I noticed the men in a circle on the fo'c'sle deck just before the bow. Curiosity got the better of me and I went to see what had become of Sepsey. Perhaps he had climbed the foremast and fallen. Perhaps he had simply passed out on deck.

'Don't wake him,' I heard Swenson say. 'Look at the smile on his face.'

'Look at the smile on hers!' Boag replied, and the men nudged each other with elbows and hips.

I drew closer, catching glimpses of the forms that lay on the deck.

'A fine addition,' said Kulke.

'I think you mean subtraction,' said Jarrell.

'Ho!' said Swenson, 'make room, men. The apprentice is here to see the master's handiwork.'

'What's a matter, Polly?' Boag asked. 'You look a little pecked.'

I forced my way between Jarrell and Burton. There, undisturbed by the commotion, lay Joe Sepsey, flat on his back, his pants around his ankles, his penis red and shrivelled. Next to him, Vengeance sat at an odd angle, her head tilted back to the sky, having been removed from beneath the bowsprit by Sepsey in a display of superhuman strength. Just above the base of the figurehead, where Vengeance's waist merged with the ship's stem, Sepsey had carved out a vertical crevice.

'I cannae believe you people,' I shouted.

'How deep does it go, you reckon?' Boag asked the others.

'I'm not about to stick my hand in there to find out,' said Mantzaris.

'It's not made for fingers,' Swenson said, 'eh?'

'Young Tim's keen,' said Boag.

'He's sanded it,' said the boy.

'Nothing worse than getting splintered, I guess.'

I grabbed Sepsey's bare shoulder, which was so cold it made my fingers sting. 'Wake up, Sepsey. Wake up.' I slapped his face with the back of my hand.

'Easy now, Slimy,' said Boag.

'Yeah, let the man sleep it off.'

I let Sepsey drop, his head banging against the deck with a satisfying thud. 'And you, you degenerates. You cannae go on like this, surely? This man is an animal. You're behaving like animals.'

One of the men produced a deep growl and soon the circle rang with the sound of rutting stags.

I put my arms around Vengeance's shoulders and hoisted her up, understanding the dark pit from which Sepsey had drawn his own strength, but the men's hands were upon me.

'Where do you think you're takin' my wife?' Swenson asked.

'And my mistress?' Boag added.

'And my sweetheart?'

'And my one true love?'

'And my *lass*?' This last voice belonged to Sepsey, who had rolled onto his side and was looking up at me, his white teeth flashing between blue lips, his cheeks a contorting mass.

'You'll nae touch her again,' I said.

'He's cutting in line,' said Jarrell.

'Wait your turn, Slimy,' said Burton.

'Keep away,' I said, backing towards the bow.

What did I expect to do? I wondered about this later, once I'd been tied to the mizzen top, facing forward, with Vengeance lashed behind me, facing aft. I couldn't overpower them all, no matter how enraged I felt.

Indeed, the struggle was brief and humiliating.

'We'll nae touch her again,' Sepsey shouted from the deck in his mock Scottish accent while Swenson, Boag, Jarrell and Burton carried me and Vengeance up the shrouds. 'You two will be close for eternity, but you'll nae see her again.'

15 March 1891

Wind eased beneath the door and daylight followed, illuminating a band of whirling dust above the floorboards. I rolled onto my back, draped my forearm over my eyes and composed myself. Despite the excitement of crossing the channel, traversing the tussock and, in the perfect dark, finding this hut, I'd managed to sleep soundly. My first settled night since leaving that dingy Melbourne boarding house, a room that had been transfigured by months of deprivation into the height of opulence. But here I was: inside, sheltered, nearly dry. My body shivered, a habit that would prove hard to kick, but my teeth were not chattering. Wisps of air rustled unseen pieces of paper and metal fixtures, but it was silence compared with the wind and rain that had raged outside my grotto on Lemon Wedge. My ears felt both clogged up and cleaned out. As if I were losing my hearing as I had lost my voice. As if I could hear a twig snap a hundred yards away.

I lowered the arm from my eyes and looked up at the underside of the top bunk. Into one of the slats someone had carved:

STELLA, JULY 1889, CPTN'S ORDERS

I ran my fingers across the letters, feeling the tiny ridges pushed up by the scribe's implement. What had he used? The corner of a chisel? No, the lines were too thick and imprecise. More likely a screwdriver, something close to hand when the vandal's impulse struck. And what was this wood? Tidy parallel grain. Long knot-free sections. Light in colour, though this was possibly the sapwood. It would hold a fine edge, whatever it was. I looked closely at the wall beside me: a tongue and groove panel of this same wood, each piece a uniform six inches wide. The work of a skilled builder. Someone with a decent saw, at least. Perhaps it was all pre-cut and brought to the island. These wallboards were slightly darker than the slats, more honeyed, with tiny reflective flecks like mica in a slab of granite. I pushed my cheek hard against the wood and inhaled deeply. I closed my eyes and saw the timber's silvery speckles transposed on the dark of my lids.

I'd slept fully dressed, feet still inside my decaying boots, just as I had every night on Lemon Wedge, though the layer of salt crust, sweat and peat that caked my skin felt inexcusable on this particular morning. I swung around slowly and placed my boots on the floor. The boards rumbled like an empty stomach as I stood, careful not to knock my head against the overhang of the top bunk. The place was tiny. A single room, perhaps fourteen feet by nine, crammed with wooden crates—cheap pine if I was not mistaken— stacked on top of each other, tantalisingly nondescript. The roof was corrugated iron, pitched from a high stud on the back wall down to just above the lintel of the door, and supported by a series of rafters and purlins of the same attractive wood as the rest of the hut. Not only would it be wonderful to carve, a log of it was bound to make a decent mast. I hoped the tree that produced this timber was a native to the island. I even considered leaving an inventory of the contents of the hut until later and running outside in search of trees, so that I might climb among their limbs, pick their strange, antiscorbutic fruits, shed my soiled clothes and live a life in Eden.

There was a wee window to the right of the door, covered by a square of red and blue flannel that was nailed to the frame. I pulled the nearest corner free from the powdery nail and pushed my face close to the glass. It seemed to frost before I'd let out a breath. I wiped the glass with the meat of my hand. The scene outside remained unchanged: complete white. My hand was on the door knob in one step.

The outside world rushed to greet me, the surging wind leaving pricks of water on my cheeks and beard. I shielded my eyes and squinted. Dark shapes to the left and right showed through the gauzy mist. Hills perhaps. Low down the knee-high sedges were being threshed by the wind, thick droplets of water jumping from clump to clump. I tightened my grip on the door as the wind pulsed against it, eager to snatch this new toy from me. I turned to look back inside the hut and spotted an oil lantern resting on the bench against the eastern wall. There must be matches, too, I thought.

I stepped back inside, closed the door and struggled to see in the sudden gloom. I pulled the flannelette curtain from the window and heard the tinkle as one of the nails bounced on the floorboards. I blinked a few times and edged across the small, unoccupied patch of floor towards the bench and the stacked crates. Next to the lantern I found a dusty bottle with a cork half-inserted down the neck. I gave it a shake and heard the rattle of matchsticks loose at the bottom, removed the cork and tipped the contents onto the smooth surface of the bench. In addition to two dozen matches there was a wee piece of flint. The lantern felt heavy, as if there were oil in it already, but I gave it a sniff anyway. Penguin blubber. I would know the smell anywhere.

I held a matchstick down by the head to ensure it did not snap and struck it against the surface of the bench. A blue-orange flame fizzed to life and I quickly lit the lamp. In better light the room was no larger, the wooden crates just as inscrutable. I hung the lamp on a nail that protruded from a nearby rafter and lifted the first lid. Inside were two containers of red metal, possibly zinc, about eighteen inches high and twelve inches square at the top. Both had pieces of softly yellowed paper with scalloped corners pasted to their lids.

The first read:

Flannel shirts, 12 count (six blue, six grey)
Woollen vests, 12 count

The second read:

Trousers, 12 count

A sudden itch coursed down my back. Fresh clothes. I hadn't eaten since the previous day, but I was no stranger to hunger by this time. I slipped my battered waistcoat from my shoulders and undid my shirt in three rough tugs. I leant forward to look more closely at the lid of one of the tins. It was welded shut. I scanned the bench, the tops of the crates. There must have been some kind of opener, a knife, something to get into these stores. On the far wall someone had written:

GOOD WATER IN SWAMP CLOSE BY

I noticed another message painted in thin black lines on top of the crate nearest the door.

> *The curse of the widow and fatherless light upon*
> *the man that breaks open this box, whilst he has*
> *a ship at his back.*

I paused a moment to decode this message. These supplies were not for men with a ship at their backs, therefore they must be left for castaways like me. The next logical step was to conclude that if there was the need for a provision depot such as this, I must still be a long way from civilisation. Perhaps it would take many days to cross the island and find a settlement. Perhaps there was nothing to find. I took a deep breath and tried to focus on the blessings these boxes and this well-made roof over my head represented.

I lifted the lid with the curse painted on it. Sitting atop one of the zinc containers was a can opener. I took it up, the bulbous wooden handle cool against my flesh. Before pressing the sharp prong into the zinc I weighed this tool in my hand. It was well balanced, pivoting at the gold-coloured ferrule that hid the point at which the tang of the blade recessed into the neck of the handle. It wouldn't take much to adapt this tool for woodwork. There were bound to be stones against which I could increase the bevel. And leather, there was surely leather—boots, belts, the latches of bags—among this bounty. Perhaps there would be no need to alter this tool. There might be carpenter's tools in one of these boxes for the castaway to repair a boat or craft a new one. I pressed the blade into the box and worked it around three sides before peeling back the lid. *Cabin bread*, proclaimed four identical cardboard boxes. I lifted one out of the container, but they were all the same. Boxes and boxes of cabin bread. I tore open the first of these boxes and the dusty, mealy smell of the biscuits plumed into the air and my stomach turned in a mixture of delight and disbelief. My teeth were weak, but I managed to break off a corner, using the molars on my right side. One hundred and twenty-six days on Lemon Wedge, nursing my farinaceous cravings, and here I was dissolving a lump of cabin bread in my mouth. I tell you, Avis, there are not many sensations in my life, these past few weeks notwithstanding, that can compare to that moment of succour.

By midday I had opened every box in the hut and arranged my provisions. Beneath the bench I placed my food: four cases of preserved beef and mutton in four-pound tins, one hundred pounds of beef dripping, twenty-five pounds of tea, fifty-six pounds of sugar and twelve hundredweight of cabin bread. I also had a kettle, a frying pan and a camp oven, but no flour or yeast, meaning no fresh bread.

The provisions were better than raw penguin flesh and limpets, but it was clear that a castaway was supposed to supplement his diet with the island's bounty. To this end there were two sheath knives, six fishing lines and thirty-six fish hooks of assorted sizes. If I could not fish easily from the shore I could use my raft, which

I could now improve thanks to the saw, hammer and file that lay swaddled in hessian beneath my bunk. I also had ten pounds of wire nails of assorted sizes, two skeins of twine, one packet of sewing needles, six sail needles, one seaming palm, twelve reels of strong white cotton and four packets of white tape.

If I injured myself among the waves or clambering over cliffs I had a crate bursting with medical supplies: one pint of castor oil, one pint of carbolic acid, one jar of zinc ointment, ninety-nine laxative pills (I'd already greedily popped one into my mouth as if it were a boiled sweet), lint and wadding, a reel of silk for sewing wounds, a packet of surgical needles, one pair of scissors and fourteen pounds of yellow soap.

Whoever had left these supplies had envisioned more than one castaway occupying the hut at a time. In addition to the two bunks, there were two Bibles and a draughts board with the requisite number of pieces. I wondered if I could fool myself into playing both sides. And then there were the dozen three-piece suits of the thickest wool, sporting brown fingernail-sized houndstooth checks against a dull black background. On closer inspection the brown was flecked with grey, red, light blue and reddish orange. The lining of the single-breasted coats was dark brown with a greasy sheen and featured deep internal pockets. Of course, this will all be familiar to you, my dear. They had been packed into zinc containers like the rest of the supplies, with layers of sacking and cardboard between each item. Some of the coats and waistcoats still bore their price tags (49s 6d and 4s 9d respectively). I could not imagine anyone stepping out in such a suit in any city, its loud checks and heavy fabric, the waistcoats uniformly tight, the coats and trousers long and baggy. And all those deep pockets. They seemed purpose-made for the castaway's life.

I looked at my new wardrobe, laid out across the lower bunk, and sighed. So much and yet no footwear. There were thick woollen socks and underwear, but nothing to replace Tim's tatty, too-wee pair of boots. I had double- and triple-checked the boxes, underneath the bed, even climbed onto the top bunk to make sure there was nothing stored in the rafters. Still, there might be more stores outside. Perhaps this hut was one of several in the vicinity.

The whiteness still pushed against the window. I clenched and unclenched my toes as I weighed my choices. The excitement and exertion of opening and cataloguing my supplies had flushed my cheeks, despite my being bare-chested since uncovering the first container. I had resisted putting on any of these new items, wanting to wash with the yellow soap in the 'good water close by' once the mist had cleared.

I picked a fresh woollen blanket from the pile at the foot of my bed, pulled it over my shoulders and headed outside.

The cold took a bite from each cheek as if my head were an apple. I regretted not putting a shirt on beneath the blanket but hunched lower and hustled around the side of the hut.

Nothing.

I looked in the direction I suspected was east. Nothing but mist. Not even the dark shapes in the distance I'd seen that morning. There was no telling what I'd walk into, or walk off, if I left the hut in these conditions. I considered retrieving the lantern from inside, but the light would settle on the pinpricks of moisture that surrounded me and go no further. And the wind. I couldn't risk it catching the lantern, smashing it, the flames reaching the hut that was stuffed with wool, wood and beef dripping. Wouldn't that be something, I thought. Finding this bonanza and seeing it go up in smoke having traded two shirts, two vests and one waistcoat for a single blanket. I placed my hand on the wall of the hut, both to reaffirm its existence and to steady myself. I took a step towards the rear of the hut, tracing a line on the weatherboard with the tips of my fingers. As I rounded the corner I let my hand drop. There was something leaning against the hut, almost as tall as me. It took a moment to decipher the form, the odd angle, the fact I had become resigned to never seeing her again. I stepped forward. Yes. I didn't know how, but it was her. It was Vengeance.

I placed a hand on her right cheek. It was cold and damp, scarred by her journey.

I picked her up, calling on that same charge of adrenaline I had used to carry her away from Sepsey and the other sailors that day in November. How could any man carry her up from the shore, through the dense tussock? It must have been a team of men. But still, it would be a great effort. And for what? It was as if she had worked her spell on the men.

I remembered the stories my mother used to tell me about brounies and the Unseelie Court. Perhaps there was a spirit inside Vengeance. It would explain a lot.

As I carried her inside the hut—her back, pocked with round trenail holes, pressed against my chest—she could be smiling. I hoped she was smiling.

Once we were both inside, I placed her against the far wall so that her head was turned to face my bunk. The wound Sepsey had inflicted at her base had let the rot in. She was mouldering, being eaten from the inside.

It's a good thing we cannae talk, I thought, *the tales we have to tell. Better to move on. Make a life here. Make a home.*

A new month begins tomorrow, did you know that? We've been up here three weeks. I am not sure how much longer this can last.

Keep writing, Gabriel. Oh, do please keep writing.

I fear we will be interrupted any day. Any minute. I wake at the slightest sound outside. Your father will come for you. He is coming for you. This cannot last.

But while it does, you must write!

Adventures in Solitude

Do you know what the morra is? I asked.

The seventh of November?

Aye, but—

Day number two hundred and thirty-nine on the big island?

I stopped on the path to consider this, running my hand over the browned tips of bracken leaves. *Aye, you're right—*

Of course I'm right.

Well, all right. But it will also be one year since the Agathos *was dismasted and we were cast away.*

An entire year, she said, the appropriate note of wonder in her voice. *How many albatross do you think you've killed in that time?*

Och, you know that's a sore spot.

And yet here you are, skelpin' up to snap another's neck.

I swung around to face the hut, now more than a hundred and fifty yards behind me.

I'm nae like you. I cannae make do with a light breeze and a coat of dust.

I understand that, Gabriel. Take as many of the tube-nosed numpties as you please. I merely object to the black mood it'll put you in for the next two days. You never take the strunts when you kill a penguin—

Aye, but there're thousands of them.

And there are hundreds of albatross.

At this moment a large, dopey adult started to run down the path towards me, its huge webbed feet slapping the ground, its impossibly long wings flapping, head bobbing as if convincing itself that yes, it will happen, a gust of wind will come and lift me into the air and take from me the great burden of gravity. I leant face-first into the ferns to avoid a collision. When I pushed back and looked behind me the albatross was gliding over the corrugated iron roof of the hut and out to the cold blue channel.

You know how I feel, I said to Vengeance, who I'd left, as always, propped in the corner of the depot atop a layer of flattened zinc boxes, a thick wool blanket across her shoulders. My voice had not returned since I tore my throat to shreds screaming for the steamer on Lemon Wedge, but Vengeance couldn't talk either so we were on equal footing.

You're a fool, Gabriel, she said as I resumed my progress higher up the plateau.

I know. But I cannae face another bite of penguin.

They've only been back a couple of months.

We have been cast away too long when we're saying 'only a couple of months'.

You made do on oats back home.

Aye, oats and tatties. I could go weeks without a strip of meat. But that was different. I cannae do what I do down here without some meat to charge me up.

The albatross pathway led up along a wee ridge in the island's central plateau. When I first discovered it I thought it was the work of man, that it led to more huts, to civilisation, but I had scoured the island and found it deserted. The few signs of previous visitors I came across did little to suggest I'd be rescued any time soon. Up from the landing place I'd found a teak headboard with a faint inscription, its letters disappearing after seven decades of moss, frost and wind.

*To the M— Foster, Chief Officer of the Schr. Prince
of Denmark, who was unfortunately drown— —ke
the Board Arbour—14th Day of December in
the—1825*

Closer to the depot, but later in my stay, I'd found a pine board
buried under a layer of peat. Into the wood someone had carved:

*Brig Amherst, in search of castaways, March '68;
by order of the Government of Southland*

I knew I was in the Southern Ocean, but had no clue where this
Southland might be. I still referred to the island I was on as the
big island, though with every walk it became a little smaller, a
little more comprehensible. What I needed, I decided, was to
leave my mark as the men from the *Prince of Denmark* and the
Amherst had done. But I didn't fancy carving my own epitaph
just yet.

What about a sign on the front of this place? Vengeance had
suggested.

Doig's Castle, you mean?

*If you must. From what you've told me, this depot is a stately
home compared with your grotto on the other island.*

*Aye, that it is. Castaway's End might be a better name. But I
havenae got the wood for a sign.*

Then carve it directly onto the door.

Will it even—? I said, and drew a gull's beak down one of the
timbers in a straight line. *Perhaps this splinter*, I said, holding up
the sliver of wood I had dislodged, *will bring me good luck.*

You are the master of all that you survey.

And you are the lady of Splinterlands.

Unfortunately, the grounds of Splinterlands were not flush
with game. On another of my long walks I'd found the skeleton
of a cow at the bottom of a cliff on the southern coast. I couldn't
be sure if it had fallen or if it had jumped after walking four

miles from the landing point and finding not a blade of decent grass on the island. Once I was rescued, I was asked repeatedly if I'd seen any livestock: cows, bulls, goats, sheep. I wrote that I had only seen this one skeleton and the odd scratch of wool suspended in the tussock that at the time I'd thought was the work of a hardy spider.

On the north-west of the island I'd found a scatter of timber and tin, the remnants of a blown down hut. A sealers' hut, I surmised, back when the beaches were thick with the creatures. I'd seen a couple swimming just beyond the breakers—their whiskers held above the water, the rest of their light-giving, hut-warming blubber a dark mass below—but they were too wary to come onto the shore. Near the sealers' hut, in a tangle of shrubs, I'd found a spruce spar, possibly once the mast of a boat. It was too heavy to lug back to Splinterlands so I carved it on the spot. Once finished, I placed it upright on a nearby knob above this same north-western beach. Rather than a beacon for potential rescuers, this totem was like the patterns I was working into the tongue and groove walls of the depot, the rafters, the beams and struts of the bunks—a kind of vandalism, *Gabriel was here*, a marker of my existence and my quiet acceptance of the fact I might never see another living soul. Vengeance referred to it as my *island style*: the dense network of arrow-headed bracken leaves, unfurling fiddleheads, bursts of tussock, the 'm' silhouette of gulls and hundreds of tiny, distinct human faces poking through the overgrowth, their eyes cast this way and that.

It helps to pass the time, I'd say to Vengeance when she tried to draw me on the subject.

The only woody plant on the island was a kind of shrub with waxy leaves, never more than a few feet high. The gnarled and twisted branches were no thicker than my own scarred wrists. The wood burnt poorly and couldn't be worked in any civilised way. Fortunately I could keep my makeshift fireplace running on peat and my lamp on penguin blubber. The yellow-brows had disappeared from their colonies for the winter months, during which time I survived on tinned beef and mutton, Hell's Cabbage, another wee creeper that tasted of celery and the occasional albatross or burrowing petrel.

When the yellow-brows returned in spring I ate them salted, wind-dried, smoked and boiled, but the greasy, fishy-mutton taste was barely altered. For the past six weeks I'd had their eggs as well, though the initial bounty was over. Any egg left on a nest now would be addled. My cache of two hundred eggs would have to last me until next October.

I had a soft spot for the albatross, their combination of grace and awkwardness. Their flesh was slick and shot through with dark veins, but as each day passed the memory of it moved closer and closer to chicken until, as on this day, I pushed aside my thoughts about their hard life and gentle nature and trudged up the plateau to pluck another from its nest.

Well, go on then, Vengeance urged.

There were several species on the island. The smaller ones, the ones with the dramatic eye makeup or sooty mantle, made their nests on, or near, the cliffs, but the largest sort—their bodies big as bull terriers, their white plumage sprinkled with brown sugar—preferred the plateau. They did not go for much in the way of nest making. They might scrape at the sedges and dead leaves with their feet before squatting down, or prune a nearby tussock with their beak once seated, but on the whole they seemed happy to let their mass and time combine to form a comfortable indentation. With no mammals on the island, I could see why these birds had become so cavalier about raising their young, though I had once seen the skuas engaged in a tug of war over an albatross chick. But these foul birds were nothing compared with me.

Most of last season's chicks had fledged by this time and the adults were busy tapping their beaks and bobbing their heads in their intricate pre-mating ritual, which meant I would have to break up a happy couple. It would not be difficult. When nesting with a chick, they would happily rise to let me snatch the shock of white feathers they were working so hard to rear. They might clap their hollow beaks together—*tock tock tock tock tock*, like an agitated grandfather clock—or nudge me with the side of their heads, but this was the extent of their defence.

There were dozens of heads visible above the sedges, ferns and tussock and I soon found a solitary bird. As I approached, it stared at me through one eye, then the other. It was madness but I felt as if she were trying to remember whether I was her mate. I was right beside the nest now, kneeling down. Satisfied I was not her mate, she faced forward, stoically. I stroked the top of her head, which was larger than a door knob and soft as velvet.

All right now, Gabriel, Vengeance encouraged.

I stroked the head once more and continued the motion down to the middle of the neck, placed my other hand across the throat and squeezed hard, once to crush the windpipe, then twisted, once, twice, to break the neck and stop the flapping. Two birds about ten yards away stopped their dance and stared at me, then began to clap their beaks together. To this chorus, I stood, lifted the albatross carcass and began my trek back down to the depot.

I knew when I started talking to Vengeance that it was all in my head. But since I had lost my voice, my thoughts were all I had. Then there was the question of Vengeance's unlikely reappearance in my life. The inkling that she was more than met the eye. That she had a spirit or a spirit dwelt within her. She never let me catch her blinking or scratching her nose, but she seemed to be engaged in mischief. Her expression of stern forbearance and poorly suppressed rage had softened until it was almost a smirk. *Guess what I've got behind my back?* she seemed to be saying. It was no longer a chib she clutched, it was a magician's top hat or a silvery salmon. And since we communicated without words, like those mentalists who advertised in the boys' magazines I'd read—*Learn the secrets of telepathy! Read your mother's mind! Your teacher's!*—we were never apart.

Vengeance was ever vigilant about the threat of scurvy. She

suggested brewing teas and broths from the leaves of herbs and green coprosma twigs to ward it off. She reminded me how long it had been since my last bite of Hell's Cabbage and proposed where on the island I might find another patch. She suggested collecting whelks, mussels, limpets, chitons and hermit crabs on fine days. She understood the tides. She knew when it was time to change into another of the identical houndstooth suits and insisted I boil the swamp water before I washed my clothes. But she was strangely silent about the men who had intruded upon our world as I carried the dead albatross back to Splinterlands.

In a year on these islands I had become accustomed to the sound of strong winds and the frantic, shimmering movement they caused, which meant I could now detect something different, something foreign, further down the slope.

What's going on, lass? I asked, but got no reply.

Instead of continuing down to the hut I diverted to the right at the end of the albatross pathway to the top of the hillock that sheltered the depot. There I placed the bird under a crown of tussock, got on my belly and crawled to the edge.

Two men were standing in the clearing with their hands on their hips. They wore thick flannel shirts, brown trousers and sturdy-looking boots. *Och, those boots*, I said. *What I wouldnae give for a pair of new boots!*

A third man arrived, carrying a heavy hessian sack on his shoulders. Despite the fact I had now made the trek through the tussock to the landing point dozens of times, I still marvelled at the strength of the men who had carried up the provisions. The other men began gesticulating, pointing at the hut. They'd been inside, seen the boxes emptied and flattened, the bench with all my tools laid out—orderly, as my father had taught me—and the mad network of fern fronds and faces I'd carved on every available surface. I felt ashamed, as if my mother had walked in on me with Claire, the prostitute, then felt ashamed again because until then I'd kept this memory cordoned off from Vengeance.

Even if I had a voice, how could I explain to these men what I had done inside the hut?

And then she spoke to me.

Are you coming down, Gabriel? Or are you just going to play hidie up there?

The third man dropped his sack to the ground and followed the others inside the hut. I stood and walked back down the hill, entered the clearing and light-footed my way to the back wall of the depot. I pressed my ear to the wood and listened.

Are you not coming in? Vengeance asked.

Shh.

The men's voices were low and muffled through the weatherboard, but I soon began to make out words and phrases.

'— vandals?'

'She's been raided all right.'

'— whalers?'

'I don't know who—'

'— Splinterlands?'

'How'd *she* get in here?'

'They brought her in, didn't they?'

'For company?'

I heard a brushing sound and then felt the vibration rattle through my head as one of the men knocked on the other side of the wall.

'A lot of work has gone into this. Look at it.' I heard the brushing sound again, imagined the third man running the rough tips of his fingers over the grooves of my scrollwork.

'They bloody near cleared the place out,' another man said.

'But left the tools.'

'And most of the clothes. I think there's one suit missing.'

'Then we'll hear about it if they ever set foot in town, won't we?'

'It could have been a castaway, though, couldn't it?'

'— so. We'd have heard if they got picked up. There haven't been any ships reported missing since we last visited.'

'I supposed you're right. Bloody —'

Gabriel? Vengeance said in a sing-song voice. *These men would like to talk to you. They have a lot of questions.*

I removed my ear from the weatherboard and placed my shoulders square against the wood. I lifted my eyes to the grey blanket of clouds. It would rain soon. I needed to get back to the albatross carcass before the skuas found it. I had to worry about the parakeets, too. Then I realised what I was thinking. I was worried about a single dead albatross when rescue was on the other side of the wall. There'd be hot meals on board the ship—real chicken, perhaps—and cake and oranges and fresh bread and questions, endless questions. The world of man was complicated. The world beyond these islands no more hospitable and just as inscrutable. What would I do back in the world, a mute thirty-two-year-old figurehead carver in a world of jabber and steam?

I began the walk back to the top of the hill, to join the albatross beneath the tussock and wait for the men to leave.

I regretted my decision as soon as I returned to the hut, found it stocked with new provisions and smelling of the sweat of other men. It felt strangely empty, deserted.

I was alone.

They had left a note, another hex upon the soul of looters. 'Reprobate,' they called me. 'The miseries of the world' they wished to heap upon my living soul.

The note was signed, GSS *Hinemoa*.

Cowardice of the highest order, I heard Vengeance say. It was as if she had been speaking for some time. I crawled into my bunk.

Fair gauperie, she said.

Aye, aye, I said and drew the blanket over my head.

A dowfart, you are.

Aye, I hear you. But what can I do now?

Eat your damned albatross. Maybe start carving the floorboards? I would expect nothing less, Gabriel.

They'll come back, I said. *They've been twice now. The day I lost my voice on Lemon Wedge and today.*

You're banking on that, are you?

I said nothing.

And what if they do come and you play hidie again?

We'll walk that bridge when we come to it.

And so I slid back into my old routines, using those few moments every day that did not revolve around the getting of food, its cooking or consumption, to find new patches of wood inside Splinterlands and inscribe them with my island style.

Despite the grand name, my stately home felt smaller than ever. It seemed to be closing in upon me an inch or two every day. My existence felt hollow, artificial, as if I were a street peddler who demonstrated the sharpness of my knives by cutting through iron bars that were not really iron and lengths of wood that had already been part-sawn. I might be leading a hard life, but the world was not heaping misery upon me; all this was now by my own hand. I had stepped aboard the *Agathos*. I had failed to disappear in Melbourne. I had played the sort of victim every crew desires. And now I had turned my back on men who could have plucked me from all of this. I chewed these events over as if they were Hell's Cabbage roots, grinding every last grain of sweet regret out of them.

In time my thoughts turned to Vengeance. If she had not appeared on the quay that day I would never have crossed the gangway, never heard Porter's words, never left the Clyde. If she could survive the dismasting and end up stashed behind the provisions depot, perhaps she had engineered the arrival of the *Agathos* that day, calling forth the storm just past the Azores that snapped the foremast and rid the ship of its appointed carpenter. *Och, the coincidence of it all. Cannae you get any new tricks!*

With that, I stopped talking to Vengeance. She kept her peace as well.

And so I spent the island's short summer in the kinch of my regrets and bitterness, the time seeming to pass swiftly and not at all.

Along with more tea, sugar and cabin bread, the men from the *Hinemoa* had added to my meagre library—the two untouched Bibles—with copies of Brett's *New Zealand and South Pacific Pilot*, Norie's *Complete Epitome of Practical Navigation* and a three-week-old copy of the *Otago Daily Times*. I thought about the return of these men, all of the things I must explain, the game of charades that would ensue. If I was able to write everything down in advance I could avoid any confusion, but they had not left any ink or writing implements. If Vengeance had been talking to me she would have chided my feeblemindedness: *What is a quill, Gabriel? And what is that red ink that so readily stains your hands?* When I finally twigged I ripped the flyleaf from the Norie and started writing responses to the questions I would surely be asked.

Can you speak?
What ship were you on?
Were there any other survivors?
Where are you from?
Did you carve the interior of the depot? Why?
How long have you been here?
Did you not see us when we came last? Why did you not make your presence known?

This last question proved difficult to answer in the quarter-inch remaining on the back of this first page. I tore another from the book but after half a page I grew frustrated, crumpled it into a ball and tossed it near the fireplace. After two more false starts I decided it was the fault of the question.

Why did you not make your presence known?

I looked around the depot, every inch of it changed by my hand since I'd arrived in March. I thought of the male albatross that returned from the ocean to relieve his mate on the nest only to find her missing, the lost generation of yellow-brows from which I made my morning omelettes, the bare patches where once Hell's Cabbage had grown, the rock falls I had caused and the spongy, iridescent moss that would bear the imprint of my boot till kingdom come.

I was in bed when the men returned to Splinterlands that morning in late January. I had started to lie in later and later, devoting less time to foraging and growing weaker as a result. It took me a moment to realise what was happening when the door opened and the watery daylight entered the hut.

'We've got him, John,' I heard a man call.

I felt the same rush of shame and discomfort I'd felt back in November, though I hadn't killed another albatross since then. I wished to go back to sleep and wake up when the men had gone once more.

I heard the door hinges creak and felt the hut grow darker. 'You see this,' the first man said, 'he's carved the outside of the door now. Look at these. Boots, everywhere.'

A second man laughed. 'I'd like to meet this man.'

'He's in bed.'

The door opened again and a slightly built man with a full but well-trimmed beard entered.

I was sitting up now, my head leant forward slightly to get out from under the top bunk.

'Hello there,' the man said.

I nodded.

'I'm John Bollons, first mate of the *Hinemoa*. Who are you?'

Two men crept into the hut and stood behind Bollons.

I pointed to my throat and shook my head.

'Are you unwell?' Bollons asked.

I shook my head again and stood. I made my way over to the pile of books that sat on the bench, next to my tools.

'Gently. We won't hurt you.'

I picked up the Norie, retrieved my prepared pages and handed them to Bollons.

'What's it say, John?' one of the others asked.

'Hold on, I need more light.'

The three of them went outside and I moved into the doorframe.

'He says he lost his voice. In March.'

'How long's he been here?'

'Hold on. Cripes. He must have been on Horseshoe Island to begin with.' Bollons looked up into the sky. 'By my count he's been down here over four hundred days. Three hundred on this island.'

'Cor,' said one of the sailors.

'Why did we not find him in November?'

Bollons turned the first page over, then counted out the five pages that remained. 'I suspect, Charlie, the answers are all here.'

'He don't look so chipper,' Charlie said.

'Nor too pleased to see us,' said the other sailor.

'It is odd,' said Bollons. 'Normally the first thing a castaway does is give his rescuer a hug. Every man I ever rescued has done that.'

I held out my hand for Bollons to shake, keen to remind the men that, though I could no longer talk, I could still hear well enough.

'You are a strange one,' the mate said, but took my hand and shook it firmly. 'All right then. Charlie, you take, uh,' he paused and looked down at the pages in his hand, 'Mr Doig back down to the ship, get him some fresh clothes and a hot meal. Ted and I will take stock here and we can send some more lads up with supplies after.'

Charlie placed a hand between my shoulders and made to lead me down through the tussock and to the ship, but I brushed him off. I stepped forward, snatched the pages from Bollons' hands and shuffled them until I found the right section. I handed the page back to Bollons, pointing at the spot where he should begin reading. As he read, I returned inside the hut to collect my suit coat. I wish I'd thought to grab Tim's pocket watch from the floor beside my bunk, but I suppose the next castaway would appreciate it.

'He says he wants the figurehead to come with him.'

'The old girl we brought up last time?' Charlie asked.

'Time before,' Ted corrected.

'It says here,' Bollons said slowly, 'that Mr Doig carved her.'

'He's batty, though, isn't he?' said Charlie. 'Look at what he did to the depot.'

'Says he was a ship's carver in Scotland,' Bollons said, not looking up from the pages.

'It is some fine scrollwork,' Ted said.

'All of those faces. Gives me the willies.'

'I'd like to see you spend four hundred days on your own down here and not go a little potty.'

'That's enough, men.' Bollons folded the pages in half and handed them to me. 'You keep these, Mr Doig. I expect Captain Fairchild will have all of these questions and more. We'll have you on the mainland by Monday.'

I had not thought to write down any questions I might want to ask my rescuers, but was suddenly possessed by the desire to know where I was and where 'the mainland' might be. I ran inside the hut and grabbed my quill. I normally wrote with fresh penguin blood, not having found a way to store it without it congealing and drying overnight. I looked around but saw nothing else I could use as ink, so I removed the albatross-bone needle from inside my jacket pocket and poked it into the tip of my left index finger. Across the title page of Brett's *Pilot*, I quickly scrawled: *Where am I? Where will we go?*

I returned outside and handed the book to Bollons, who gave a single, emphatic burst of laughter.

'Why man, you're on Antipodes Island, part of the Colony of New Zealand. You're bound for Port Chalmers, the South Island, New Zealand, the Pacific Ocean, the world.' He gave another laugh and slapped me firmly on the upper arm. 'Get him down to the *Hinemoa*, Charlie, and get him some bloody ink!'

Arrivals

It occurred to me, as the *Hinemoa* bore us away from the Antipodes and back to civilisation, that this was the point at which true tales of shipwreck survivors ended, at least the ones I'd read as a boy. There might be a sentence or two about returning to a forsaken wife or finding a bride, taking up a trade or returning to the sea, but then it was on to the next *true tale of adventure*.

John Bollons had mentioned other men that had been saved by the depots and on the third day of our voyage north I asked him, in my steady handwriting, whether he had kept in contact with any of them.

'No,' the mate replied. We were the last men left at the rectangular mess table. Bollons had wiped his bowl clean with a chunk of bread and was eyeing my nearly untouched portion of stew. I pushed my bowl towards him, but he said, 'Oh no, you need it more than I do, Mr Doig.' He pushed back from the table and rotated his shoulders as if his hunger were somehow linked to tension. 'Our timing has not been too good of late. Last year, we visited the depot at Erebus Cove looking for survivors of the *Kakanui*. We found nothing, but a month later the *Campadre* goes down in that same cove. The crew of seventeen men found the depot and a note from me saying, "We've just called. We will see you in six to nine months!" They lasted three and a half before being rescued by a bloody sealing ship. We never did find a trace of the *Kakanui*.' His fingertips traced the line of smooth skin just above his beard. 'So no, I haven't had much chance to talk with survivors lately. The *Campadre* lot never even thanked us for the provisions, not that I heard.'

I nodded.

Bollons leant forward. 'Don't worry about what will happen in port. You'll be looked after. I think you'll find the New Zealand people are a generous lot.'

I wrote: *I am sure they are. Thank you. I only wondered whether you knew how well castaways made their way once back in society.*

'You will do well enough, Mr Doig,' he said, chuckling. 'You will do well enough. God knows how you kept your sanity on that island, but it seems you have.'

I thought of my conversations with Vengeance.

My compulsive carving of the depot.

Bollons stood from the table and walked to the doorway. He stood there for a moment, looking out to the silver band of the horizon, his hands clasped in the small of his back. He said, 'I do remember reading something Alexander Selkirk, *another* famous Scottish castaway, said a few years after his return to society, as you put it. "I am now worth £800," he said, "but shall never be so happy as when I was not worth a farthing." I hope this is not the case for you, Mr Doig.'

I took one last mouthful of beef and gravy, picked up my bowl and handed it to Bollons on my way out. He nodded his thanks and pointed with his forehead at the horizon.

'The Snares,' he said. 'Just the one depot to check here, then it's on to Port Chalmers.'

I watched the islands grow larger as Bollons devoured my stew. None of the islands was as big as Antipodes, but above the surging fringe of kelp and the familiar ridges of yellow-brows, the islands were blanketed with tree daisy, leatherwood shrubs and a tree, a *bona fide* tree, covered in pinkish-red flares.

'The rata,' Bollons said. 'It's almost finished blooming. You should see them at Christmas.' I had to grip the rail to keep my hands from shaking. The mainland, I told myself. There will be better trees on the mainland.

The brick and stone buildings of Port Chalmers seemed something less than solid through the steam-fog that drifted in from the wee harbour. Reporters and government officials were waiting for the *Hinemoa* to dock, though neither group seemed prepared for a speechless castaway. In the five days it had taken the steamer to reach the Otago Peninsula, the crew had grown quite fond of me. It was only natural, I suppose, given the care and effort they put into stocking the depots, that I should represent a kind of vindication for them.

Bollons spoke for me on the docks, talking of my four-hundred-and-forty-five-day ordeal, explaining how I'd lost my voice calling for rescue—though he omitted the fact that it was the *Hinemoa* that had passed me by and that I had actively evaded rescue in November.

'Mr Doig is a private man,' Bollons said, 'and does not wish to be unduly hounded.' It was true, though I don't think I ever wrote anything to this effect.

The next day a subscription was started, 'in recognition of a great feat of survival', according to the article in the *Otago Daily Times*, 'and to provide funds to assist another Caledonian son to settle in this great province'.

I wasn't sure about settling in Otago, but I was penniless and had no choice but to wait out the month until the subscription closed and the government supplied me with new identification papers.

I was given free lodging in Dunedin, eight miles to the south-west, at the head of the harbour, by a hotelier named McLintoch, who never appeared without a piece of his family's red and black tartan somewhere on his body. The town was many times larger than Port Chalmers and seemed both eerily similar to Scotland—its architecture, the names of the people, the dreich summer weather—and utterly unreal. It was as if I had stumbled into a town of ships' figureheads come to life: the inhabitants simulating the actions of living men and women, approximating the way they spoke, but somehow falling short of the real MacKay.

Vengeance, however, the one true figurehead in the town, remained silent and frozen. I kept her wrapped in a spare set of bedclothes and stashed in the closet of my hotel room, though I got up from time to time to check she was still there, even going so far as to peel back a corner to ensure that her expression had not changed.

The *Hinemoa* went back to ferrying government officials around the colony and patrolling its far-flung islands for sealers and castaways, but before departing Captain Fairchild had inquired, on my behalf, about the fate of the *Agathos*. I was told news would reach me at McLintoch's. Yet another thing to wait upon.

A local barber offered to tame my wild hair and beard and I accepted. Though I had seen my reflection in puddles and streams on the Antipodes, these images were as true to life as a half-developed daguerreotype, only hinting at colour and wantonly warping forms. When I first encountered a mirror on the *Hinemoa*, it was not the shock of red hair and whiskers that surprised me, but the whiteness of my teeth. I had Sepsey's gnashers. A castaway's smile. Much later I would learn it was from chewing the roots of Hell's Cabbage, though no one else called it that. *Stilbocarpa polaris*, that was its scientific name.

McLintoch arranged for a doctor to visit me in my room twice a week. Was this another philanthropic gesture, I wondered, or had the hotelier decided, after seeing me in the flesh, that this was necessary to avoid the bother of a castaway's corpse in one of his rooms?

I, too, had a worm in my stomach. The cramps had begun almost as soon as I set foot on the mainland. I blamed the rich and varied food I had received on the *Hinemoa*. Perhaps the kinder climate was also responsible, plunging my body into a form of shock after the prolonged trauma of fifteen months in the subantarctic. I'd wake in the night, my pillow covered in slobber, craving the taste of salted penguin flesh. I could manage no more than a single bite of soft tommy before my throat closed up, as if the morsel of bread were an enchanted sponge that could sap all moisture from a man.

As I lay on my hotel bed, holding my clenched midriff, I wondered if this was how my father's wammlin stomach had felt. What if this was not related to my time as a castaway? What if this was the onset of the Doig affliction? I was thirty-four—six years younger than my father had been when he was struck down. But then he had been a full decade younger than his father when the affliction arrived. And who was to say my southern travails hadn't hastened the onset of my own suffering?

Galbraith, the doctor sent by McLintoch, was in his late twenties. He wore an undertaker's frock coat that was buoyed slightly by the addition of bright buttonholes of scentless native flowers. He came every Monday and Thursday to take my temperature, peer down my throat and offer pills. I gave no indication of my stomach troubles. My experience of doctors—Doctor Stanley, that is, the man who could save neither my grandfather nor father and sent my mother to bed to die—meant I felt safer tipping Galbraith's elixirs down the drainpipe.

I recalled Alexander Selkirk's words—*I am now worth £800, but shall never be so happy as when I was not worth a farthing*—as I sat alone in my hotel room in Dunedin, hungry, nauseous and contorted inside. I didn't expect to receive £800 at the end of February, but I hoped it would be enough to start a new life, a happier one, should my stomach ever adjust.

To pass the time and quell my doubts, I decided to research the lives of other castaways. I learnt from McLintoch that Dunedin did not yet have a public library.

'There was a poll back in November,' the hotelier said, 'at the same time as we voted for mayor. Unfortunately, those against a free library were in the majority. What I wouldn't give, Mr Doig, for another hundred and twenty men in this town who knew the value of a bleedin' book.'

McLintoch, however, had many connections, one of whom was a retired ship's captain who lived on Cargill Street and possessed an impressive collection of books, mostly on nautical themes. After a single ten-minute interview with the captain, in which time my honest answers and careful handwriting convinced him I was not a true seaman and therefore of little further interest, I was free to come and go from his library as I pleased.

I hoped to find evidence that happiness could enter a life after a stretch of solitude, but the results were less than encouraging. One of the accounts seemed particularly ominous. It told of a native woman who was left behind on San Nicolas Island after missionaries removed the rest of her people to protect them from Russian sea otter hunters. She survived alone for eighteen years. Perhaps it was no great wonder, the island being her home, a place she understood and that had resources enough to sustain a great many more people. Still, when she was discovered in 1853 by another sea otter hunter—I was not aware of there being a great demand for sea otters in my lifetime, though my stretch as a castaway had taught me the manifold uses of an animal carcass—she was living away from the old settlement. She was clad in a dress of cormorant skins roughly sewn together and living in a shelter made from whale bones. She was taken to live with the otter hunter and his wife in Santa Barbara, California, where no one could understand her language. Had she gone mad? It was impossible to tell. She suffered from dysentery almost as soon as she set foot in California and died after seven weeks. You can understand how such stories did little to loosen the knot in my stomach.

At least, I told myself, my trips to the captain's library got me out of my room and among the locals, however distressing these meetings were at the time. No images of me had been published in the papers—merely a description: 'Mr Doig is short in stature and emaciated'—and yet everyone in the town seemed to recognise me, even once I was clean shaven and my hair cut short. They waved from buggies and trams, shouting, 'Good day, Mr Doig.' They stopped me in the street to ask how I liked Dunedin, how it compared with 'back home'. At first I thought it was my bright white teeth that singled me out, but learnt soon enough it was my suit.

'You're about the only man in the colony who can pull off such an outfit,' a man told me one day as I bustled along Princes Street to the captain's library. He had thin brown hair pasted down with what looked like penguin blubber, though I knew it must have been something else.

By this time I carried a number of index cards in my pockets that bore prepared phases—written in black ink this time, rather than blood.

Yes.

No.

I'm fine, thank you.

Dunedin is a lovely city.

I removed from my pocket the card that said *Why?* and showed it to the man.

'I am a tailor, sir. Bernstone, the Paris Tailor,' he said and offered his hand. His accent was not French. He seemed to be another figurehead brought to life but getting certain crucial details wrong. 'You, sir, are wearing what we in the trade call a "looter's suit". That pattern, oh,' his hands flew into the air, as if attached to his wrists by hinges and lifted by a sudden gust of wind, 'just hideous. Instantly recognisable. What man in his right mind would pilfer such a thing? Though I suppose it's all you have, poor soul.'

I looked down at the stack of index cards in my hands. I had two more of these looter's suits back in my room, hanging in the wardrobe next to Vengeance. The crew of the *Hinemoa* had offered items of their own clothing, but I had grown accustomed to the thickness of my suits, the warmth of the wool. After all those months in the teeth of the Roaring Forties I never wished to be cold again. Instead, the men had given me two brand-new suits of the same design from a box of provisions intended for the depot on the Snares.

'You must come with me,' said Bernstone, the Paris Tailor, and led me by the hand—a fiercely intimate gesture that made my eyes fog. I was whisked up Princes Street and through the town square, which the locals called the Octagon for the sake of geometric correctness, and into the tailor's shop in George Street.

The man let go of my hand once inside and ushered me deeper into the shop. 'This way, Mr Doig. We'll get you measured up.'

In the week and a half I had spent in Dunedin, I had avoided stepping inside shops wherever possible. The interior of Bernstone's shop was a jumble of cabinets and tables buried beneath chalk-lined trousers and rolls of fabric. In the window, I noticed a headless mannequin in a tight-fitting suit. I thought it rather gruesome.

'Tip top.' Bernstone brushed his hands together twice, making a light clapping sound each time. 'Arms out,' he said and retrieved a yellow tape from the top of a cabinet and began to take my measurements.

'They tell me you're a woodworker?'

I nodded.

'Keep still please. I bet you would have done a better job than Harrison. I told him to make the fittings in kauri and he goes and uses pine. You'd know all about wood, wouldn't you?'

I resisted any movement this time. Bernstone pulled my feet apart and began to measure my in-seam.

'Went to court, we did. I wasn't about to pay for pine. Look at that skylight,' he gestured with his eyebrows. 'It leaks. I could have used your testimony, Mr Doig.'

Bernstone, still on one knee, looked up at me expectantly. I forced a smile.

'Right,' the tailor mumbled. He stood. 'Fabrics. What takes your fancy?'

I inspected every roll of woollen suit fabric in the store, the colours ranging from mouse grey to peat brown, as well as several tweeds and a roll of thick, tightly woven fabric that was diagonally ribbed on one side and smooth, almost shiny, on the other.

'Ah,' Bernstone crossed the shop in two quick strides to place his hand on the top of the roll, 'that's gabardine. Straight from Europe. You won't find that anywhere else in the colony.' He stopped and shook his head as if trying to cast out another, more persistent voice. 'What I mean to say, Mr Doig, is that this isn't suiting material. It's for outdoor wear, all-weather apparel.'

My eyes widened. It was not as thick as my looter's suit, but the promise of waterproofing was too much to resist. I nodded and pointed at the gabardine.

The tailor's eyebrows shot past what must have once been his hairline. He began to protest, suggesting that this was either the most expensive fabric in his shop or the hardest to work—perhaps it was both. But I was quickly discovering how to win arguments without talking.

'Are you sure,' he asked slowly, as if I were some kind of imbecile, 'that you want this fabric for your suit, Mr Doig?'

I nodded, trying hard to suppress my first real smile on the mainland.

A week later I returned to collect my new suit and found a crowd of more than a hundred men, women and children waiting outside Bernstone's to see yet another example of southern hospitality.

As my month of waiting wound to a close, my stomach began to unclench. I was able to stand up straighter, could eat more—though without the need to hunt or forage for food, my appetite remained modest. I was strong enough to carry Vengeance down a flight of stairs when the time came.

On the first of March, I was presented with a thin envelope in front of another crowd of locals and reporters. I tried to act grateful and honoured, but was a wee bit disappointed that the subscription hadn't mustered more than a few bank notes. I'd heard nothing of the *Agathos*, had put that ship far from my mind, but as I stood on the improvised stage next to the statue of some Scottish settler in the centre of the Octagon, turning the envelope over in my hands, I heard the mayor mention that very ship.

'The lone survivor of the ill-fated *Agathos*—'

The lone survivor.

The ill-fated *Agathos*.

Had she not made it round the Horn? Had Sepsey inadvertently saved my life by lashing me to the mast? Perhaps things would have happened differently if Vengeance and I had not been up the mizzen top when the storm struck: the *Agathos* might not have been dismasted and would have made it back to Europe.

My head swimming with questions, I retrieved a pencil from inside my gabardine suit jacket, which would last one or two more outings before the seams gave way. I wrote: *Was the* Agathos *ever found?* on the back of my envelope and passed it to the man standing next to me, his face speckled with rosacea. I guessed he was the deputy mayor, or perhaps the postmaster.

'No,' the man whispered, his breath rich with the burnt stench of coffee. He looked down at the envelope in his hands again, surprised. I snatched it back and wrote: *Insurance?*

'I don't know. I suspect you'll have to talk to London.'

The mayor stopped his booming address, turned and frowned at the two of us. I bowed my head to obscure an irrepressible smile. The *Agathos* had sunk into the depths of the wild ocean and the only things I cared about—me and my figurehead—were not on board. Good riddance, I thought, half-conscious of a door opening to ever more wicked thoughts.

After the ceremony, when I was alone once more in my hotel room, I finally opened the envelope. It contained no money, just a single leaf of paper folded in thirds, though this page bore the details for an account in my name at the Bank of New Zealand. The people of Otago had raised £245 16s for this Caledonian son. A tidy sum. Enough to disappear.

The next morning I withdrew £100 from the bank and bought a second-class train ticket to Christchurch for 25s, plus 2s to place Vengeance, still wrapped in sheets from McLintoch's, in the luggage carriage. I chose to head north as the further I got from the subantarctic, the less likely anyone associated with the castaway depots—be they looters or provisioners—would be around to recognise my suits, my teeth, me.

The tar-black locomotive hissed and steamed at the end of the platform like a caged beast. It promised to be a different journey to that on the *Hinemoa*, which seemed to scythe serenely through the nastiest chop, or the rocking *Agathos*, already growing misty and spectral in my memory. The train's progress, however, was much slower than I had expected. We stopped at every station—Waitati, Seacliff, Waikouaiti, Palmerston, Hampden, Herbert, Maheno—to offload and collect mail, leaving little time to work up steam. And what strange names these places had! The three and a half minutes the train had spent in Waikouaiti was not enough for me to form the sound of the word in my head, let alone wrap my tongue around the name if I had the power of speech.

The railway weaved between the coast and the hinterland, flashing bare, mustard-coloured hills, dense patches of dark scrub and tree ferns, wooden town halls and tumbledown sheds no bigger than my castaway depot. Near the coast the tracks were lined with flax and tall grasses gone to seed, their blond heads like the manes of stallions. Every time I caught a glimpse of beach the sand was a different colour: modelling clay, fresh spruce shavings, old teak with shimmering veins of crushed shells and smooth wet stones.

The train stopped in Oamaru for a twenty-minute 'luncheon', despite the fact it was already four in the afternoon. I was not hungry, having done nothing but stare out the window all day. Oamaru was not just another town for stonemasons, but a kind of heaven for them. The tall columns and ridged pediments I'd caught sight of as the train passed into the station suggested the work of ancient Greeks or Romans, not rough-handed men on the underside of the world. I almost left the train, curious to explore the town, to understand what natural bounty had afforded such extravagant designs, though that would take longer than twenty minutes. I was in no rush. I had funds enough for another train fare should the town disappoint once I got down from the platform. But I worried there were too many people, that I wasn't far enough north. Even so, I began to walk down the carriages to where Vengeance was stowed. I found her beneath a thick woollen blanket, not unlike the kind I'd had in the castaway depot. I placed my hand on her shrouded head, hoping, just once, that she'd talk again, tell me what I should do, what I actually wanted.

The conductor blew his whistle, though I knew from previous stops there would be another two blasts and a toot from the engine before we pulled away. Even if my suit doesn't give me away, I thought, my appearance on the platform with a figurehead wrapped in bedclothes will attract attention.

The whistle blew a second time.

'Waitaki North, Marumaru, Studholme Junction, St Andrews, Timaru,' the conductor called and blew his whistle once more.

The engine performed its deep, percussive toot.

The train began to pull away, leaving Oamaru and its white stone buildings behind. I slumped down on a pile of suitcases, disappointed at another loss of nerve. If Oamaru was too large a town for me to disembark in, how could I handle Christchurch? I'd have to leave the train before then, though there were many more hours before this final destination.

I hung out the door of the luggage carriage, watching the hills approach and recede.

The train crossed a wide but shallow river by means of an iron bridge. The water was a colour I had never seen in nature, something my father might have concocted on his palette, two parts white, one part blue, stirred briefly with the wooden tip of his brush rather than blended completely.

We stopped for less than a minute at Waitaki North. The next station would be Marumaru. The name seemed a jumble of nonsense to me. The sort of sound my mangled larynx might be able to produce if I attempted to say a real word or phrase: *Are you untrue? Maintain-top view. I believe you.*

The town was on the coast. The inhabitants seemed in the process of building a breakwater, so I thought it might be a fishing village. The houses were generously spaced, the wide streets deserted. The sun would not set for another hour or so but there was already a twilight feel to the place. The hills were close, as if this point along the railway was the eye of a needle, the narrowest point between the sea and the ranges.

This is the place, I thought.

The Carpenter

I didn't cope well with Marumaru when I first arrived. No one seemed to recognise the significance of my looter's suit or white gnashers, but I was pushing a ship's figurehead in a wheelbarrow, and that was enough to cause a fizz. The townspeople fired question after question at me but I kept my index cards in my pockets.

I lasted one night in the Criterion Hotel before buying my first horse—Galahad, a clod-hoofed beast that could carry me and my weathered companion—and heading west, into the hills. After a full day in the saddle I was drawn from the trail by the sight of straw-coloured cliffs and the promise of a cave in which to shelter for the night.

Dense shrubs and cabbage trees sprang out of the gaps between the boulders that clustered at the foot of the cliffs, but otherwise the land had been cleared of scrub. Further along, I discovered another terrace of rock facing the first. I was in a kind of narrowing crevice. Near the head, the cliffs suddenly parted again, creating a bowl of grass reminiscent of Dunedin's Octagon, though perhaps half as large. In place of severe, Presbyterian buildings I was surrounded by rock walls two or three storeys high, their sandy colour marred by dark stains that ran down from the edges like penguin guano. In some places the cliff face was scarred with holes and scrolls, as if it were riddled with borer.

You are no doubt familiar, my dear, with the place I describe and the hut I found at the head of this clearing.

There was nothing to indicate who had built it or why. It was empty: no furniture or benches, no fireplace, no carving. I claimed it for my own by scratching *New Splinterlands* across the door. I didn't have the tools for a proper sign. Not yet.

Those first few years I lived with the nagging dread that at any moment the person who had cleared this land, or their ancestor, would return and cast me out. It never happened, but that feeling has returned this past month, only the fear has multiplied a thousandfold.

Some mornings, when I got up and stood in the doorway, surveying my domain, I would think it a shame there were so few trees. On others, it added to the magic of this place. I admired the zeal of the pioneers who had tamed this land, though it seemed their descendants had not prospered. They certainly had not overpeopled this stretch of hinterland. A few farmsteads, a few barns, windbreaks of pine and macrocarpa and the old bridge over the stream—these were the only signs of civilisation. The farmers kept to themselves, but their sheep roamed freely, often visiting New Splinterlands to trim the grass and break the silence with their bleats. The occasional skylark or goldfinch visited too, twittering their familiar tunes.

After three years, Scotch thistle began to appear in the clearing. I wondered if it had taken this long for the seeds to be carried here by the wind or if I had acted as my own Acclimatisation Society, carrying them back pinned to my suit or trampled into the soles of my boots.

But this was not Scotland. It was not home. It could not be. It was temporary. I knew that.

There was something about the sky up in these hills—there *is* something about the sky. You have surely seen it: the persistent blue that bears its traces of white so lightly, as if the great artist behind it all has run his paintbrush against the firmament to clear the last of his pigment before dipping the bristles in turpentine. This is no place for a mortal man, certainly not a man alone.

In the end I stayed in this hut six and a half years and never had another soul knock on my door. I would venture into Marumaru once a month—twice at most—for supplies, my order pre-written on a scrap of paper. I made do with the subscription funds in my bank account and the meagre interest they accrued. It was not a princely sum, but after I'd bought Galahad, some basic tools—a handsaw, an axe, a mallet—and some seed potatoes, there wasn't much else for me to spend my money on.

From a stable two hours to the south-west I pilked a farrier's anvil and a set of tongs. Poor Galahad, that anvil weighed a ton. The journey back to New Splinterlands took twice as long and he wouldn't let me on his back for the next fortnight.

I built my own forge from an old oil drum and learnt to make my own charcoal to fire it. I collected scrap metal from behind barns and stables to make more tools. It was time-consuming, but time was in plentiful supply. Before making my first gouge I had to make a floe to split timber for the handles. I spent many an afternoon scouring the countryside for new trees: totara, miro, red pine, matai—though I wouldn't learn all the names until later. Once the wood was felled and hacked into logs, Galahad and I dragged it back here for seasoning. I learnt how best to work these timbers in the only way I knew how: by setting a bevelled edge to the wood and striking.

After a year or so, I began writing letters to John Bollons, care of the New Zealand steamer service. A month after I posted the first of these letters I went back to the post office in Marumaru and flashed my index card: *Any mail for Gabriel Doig?*

An envelope was waiting for me.

I learnt Bollons was an amateur botanist, a 'student of the natural world' as he called it. His letter was full of questions. He wanted to know what I had eaten on Antipodes Island besides the provisions in the depot. Had I discovered any plants with medicinal qualities? What birds had I seen? What had I killed? He told me how he'd spent only one night on the island while constructing the depot in March 1886. The rest of his visits were confined to daylight hours and most of this time was occupied trooping up through the thick tussock with more provisions for the depot. On the other hand, I had lived there and unwittingly amassed valuable knowledge about the flora and fauna.

I began to look forward to my trips down to Marumaru, as a new letter from Bollons usually awaited me. I learnt a lot in return: the scientific and common names of the plants I had sketched in my previous letter, the cause of my white castaway's teeth and, little by little, the customs of New Zealand.

The town of Marumaru seemed to be growing with every journey down to the post office. A theatre was constructed on Victoria Street, another hotel, a Methodist church. The windows of the high street were crammed with products: locally made shoe polish and the latest boots from Europe, German spinning wheels and New Zealand wool. There were more people walking the streets, but not enough to make me feel uncomfortable. It was almost as if the town were growing with my needs.

Bollons was interested in more than just my time as a castaway. He asked about my family, my childhood in Scotland, how I came to be in the Southern Ocean. Much of the story I have given you I rehearsed in letters to my friend.

In one letter I told Bollons of the sudden declines of my father and grandfather, the wammlin stomach and floppy ankles. A month later Bollons wrote back with another series of questions, some about the sorts of shellfish we got along the Clyde and some about the job of a ship's carver. 'And regarding the Doig Affliction, as you call it,' he wrote, 'I wonder what kind of paints you used on your figureheads?'

In the month I spent waiting for his next letter I turned this question over and over in my mind. Did the paint we used—specifically the white paint, which relied on lead for its pigment—have anything to do with the deaths of my father and grandfather? Of course it did. There seemed little doubt in my mind, despite the fact I'd never considered the link until Bollons' letter. Lead poisoning was not unheard of when I was a lad. I remember switching to a new brand called Patent Zinc White in 1879 or 1880—one of those years when my father was laid up in bed, clutching his stomach and cursing the world, while I toiled alone in the workshop. I'd chosen this new paint not because, according to the newspaper advertisements, it was free of poisons, but because its covering power was twice that of standard lead paint. I look back now and marvel at how blinkered I was to the world, the simple connections that were screaming out to be made.

Such are my feelings when I look back upon other moments in my life, in this tale of mine, some of which are still to come. Just as I trod over Antipodes Island, killing creatures and ripping up plants without truly understanding them, I have walked blindly through the world, narrowly missing pitfalls and swinging blades by luck and luck alone.

And yet here I am, a few weeks from my sixtieth birthday, in this ricklie hut with the most unlikely ally and friend I could suppose. It is no exaggeration, Avis, to say that this past month has been among the happiest of my life.

Of course, I have not been alone in my ignorance. My grandfather, my father, my mother, Doctor Stanley—they all overlooked the tins of paint dotted around the floor of the workshop. And I think about how the town fell under the spell of you and your brother, there in your father's window. Credulity and ignorance are, perhaps, different sides of the same coin.

Bollons became captain of the *Hinemoa* in 1898. By this time I'd told him everything about the Antipodes, about my childhood, about Joe Sepsey and Basil Porter—everything I have presented here for you, my dear—and our correspondence began to peter out quite naturally.

My quiet existence was hardly full of drama, but I had something to show for it: a full set of hand-forged carver's tools (the tools I use to this day). It filled me with pride to survey them: the gouges of every sweep I'd need, deep gouges, spade and front bent gouges, parting tools, a veiner, a selection of flat and bent chisels, two corner chisels and a macaroni tool. Every shank had taken weeks to complete, getting the fluting perfect, the bevel of the cutting edge just right. The handles, which I have seen you admire, I made from kanuka, one of the few natives that grows within walking distance of these cliffs. Each tool was made for my own hand. Each so well balanced that it is almost weightless when held the correct way. You cannot achieve this feel with a set of gouges from a factory, especially when you have hands as boxy as mine.

I began doing odd jobs for the townspeople in return for money. Up here I carved balustrades, newels, table tops, door-knockers, gargoyles and bird baths and carried them into town lashed to Galahad. It got that I was spending two days of every week on horseback, heading down to Marumaru and retreating to New Splinterlands. I no longer needed total solitude—I no longer had it. And so I struck a deal with old man Donaldson. He still owned the draper's on Regent Street, but had recently left the running of his shop to more ambitious sorts and retired to his farmstead. His legs were failing him. The walking stick I'd carved for him a year earlier, one of my first commissions, was no longer enough. Now he wanted me to carve the mouldings, banisters and curtain rails throughout his house.

'If I'm to spend the rest of my damn life here,' he said, 'I might as well have something interesting to look at.'

On a blank index card I explained to him how much time I was wasting going back and forth from my hut and in payment he offered me a piece of land twenty minutes' ride from Marumaru. Until I'd built my house I could sleep in his barn.

'I get the impression this is a luxury with which you are acquainted,' he said with a half-smile.

And so for a number of weeks old man Donaldson spent his days in an easy chair on the porch, watching me work out there on his lawn.

'You are a fine worker, Mr Doig,' he told me one day as I sanded a piece of totara I had shaped into a fleur-de-lis. The motif was his suggestion, this particular piece destined for the end of a curtain rail. 'Every employer dreams of an employee who cannot speak back,' he said, almost shouting, eager for me to hear him over the sissle of my sandpaper. 'Even in my business, I'll bet you could sell twice as many gloves as a pretty young thing who just loves to chat.'

I smiled, still looking down at my work.

He called for his daughter, Maggie, to help him down from the porch. She was not in good health herself, a woman well into her spinsterhood, though I suppose she was not much older than I was.

The fleur-de-lis was ready for staining by the time Donaldson was arranged in his seat on the lawn. The tartan rug over his lap was tucked so tightly there seemed no space for legs beneath. Maggie stood for a moment, waiting for a word of thanks that was not forthcoming. Only once she was back inside the farmstead did Donaldson begin speaking.

'I'm going to give you some advice, Mr Doig. Never explain yourself to anyone. People who explain are always at a disadvantage. Can I see those cue cards you keep in your pockets?'

I retrieved the set from my left trouser pocket and handed them to him. His reading glasses hung from a cord around his neck and he lifted them to his eyes.

'See this. This is no good.' He tore the first index card in half. 'I don't need to know you've lost your voice. I can work that out myself.'

He let the two halves fall to the ground and took up the next card. 'Half the men on this island are Scotsmen,' he said and tore this card as well. 'It hardly rates a mention. And it is not as if you have to apologise for your accent, is it?'

The next card he held up and said, 'Questions are fine. I love a good question. Let the other bastard say too much.'

He worked his way through my cards, tearing up the answers and leaving the questions. When he'd finished, he asked, 'And what about the other pocket?'

I shrugged and handed him my second stash of index cards.

'No,' he said, as he tore the first of this new set in half. 'You did think of everything, didn't you Mr Doig? Well, you should think less. Ah, see this?' He waved a card. 'Technically this is a question, but it's a sap's question. It is better to ask forgiveness than permission, Mr Doig. That's my epitaph right there. Though Maggie probably wouldn't stand for it.' He looked down at the remaining cards in his hands and ran the tip of his tongue over his top lip. After a long pause his eyes shot up and he gave a weak laugh.

He rushed through this second lot of cards saying, 'No, yes, no,' and littering his rug and the grass around his chair with torn cardboard.

'Last one,' he said, brandishing the card. 'It's an answer, so I suggest you tear it up, but people have such attachments to names. I'll let you decide if you want to keep this one.'

He handed me the card. It said: *My name is Gabriel Doig.*

Donaldson's red-rimmed eyes seemed reduced rather than magnified by the lenses of his glasses. They looked like brass buttons. I couldn't decide if he was the kindest person I'd met on the mainland or the most cold-hearted. It is only now I consider the possibility that he could have been both.

What did I do with this last card? I tore it up.

It wasn't long before people in town were calling me The Carpenter, even those who knew my name. The only person who persisted in calling me Mr Doig was the man in the post office, though there were no longer any letters for me.

As I spent more time in Marumaru I was able to use timbers that grew in other parts of the country: tawa, silver beech, black maire and of course kauri, which I knew well from the castaway depot. On the land I got from Donaldson I built my own house and workshop from as many sorts of wood I could lay my hands on. I hated the act of building as much as I'd hated the work of a ship's carpenter. If you ever get to visit, you'll see the walls are not quite square, which means the roof is oddly shaped and the doors all stick in their jambs, but it has done me well these past twenty years. Never leaked, that's one thing I can say for it. But you can keep your spirit levels and your planes. I am a carpenter in name only.

I visited Donaldson once a week, long after he'd run out of things for me to carve. We'd sit in his drawing room and Maggie would bring us milky tea and dense sponge cakes. Whenever she entered it was as if the sun had gone behind a cloud. On one of these visits Donaldson told me about the new department store that was opening in town.

'I shouldn't tell you, since they'll be my competition, but I reckon there's a lot of work going in a place like that for a man like you. Besides, what do I care what happens to my shop? It's not as if I have a grandchild to pass it on to.'

In came poor Maggie at this very moment, bringing her gloom. She banged the china plate down on the table and left.

'I wish she'd take to the drink, poor girl,' he said.

I, of course, said nothing, but I thought I understood.

When Donaldson died not long after, I wrote Maggie a short letter about the respect I had had for her father and how, to an outsider, it had been clear that he cared for her, though he had a strange way of showing it. I handed this to her at the funeral. The look on her face! I'd broken her father's commandments. Never explain. Never expose yourself to weakness. In her eyes I had betrayed him. Only she was worthy. I imagine Maggie tore my letter in two when she got home. My only hope is this act gave her some satisfaction.

I began working for Hercus & Barling, the new department store. At first they wanted me to assist with the cabinetry, but I knew such work wasn't for me. Ever since that headless mannequin in Bernstone's tailor shop I'd been thinking about these figures. In Dunedin they had been little more than clothes hangers or dressmaker's dummies, nothing resembling a ship's figurehead. But in the window of Donaldson's, the mannequins began to look more human. I'm not sure if your father knows this, but he's partly to blame for me starting to make mannequins. I didn't tell Hercus that I was making a mannequin in my workshop, didn't ask permission. I knew that once he saw it, that would be enough. And it was.

I haven't said a lot about Vengeance. I left her here in New Splinterlands when I moved nearer the town, but I wasn't abandoning her.

I'd still come up here when I needed to clear my head. The last time was two or three years ago, when the war was still going on. The town, like every other town, was sending its lads to the other side of the world and all we got in return was bad news. It seemed madness to me: all the time and effort spent raising these boys, feeding them, educating them, just to fritter them away like coins.

Vengeance was still here, this last time. The worse for wear, but her expression remained fierce.

When we arrived here last month, however, she was gone, along with the sign for *New Splinterlands*. Where is she? I've looked around this bowl, in all the nooks and crooks along the way to the stream, but I haven't found her. I trust she's been taken by someone who will appreciate her. Or perhaps she finally gathered the courage to leave of her own volition.

Time will tell.

When I first wrote down my history for John Bollons I learnt that you are seldom the best person to tell your own stories. Especially not so soon after the event, when it is as difficult to put a name to the wild herb you ate as to the emotion it conjured inside you. Better to leave all the evidence and let someone else piece things together without me imposing my own blind spots and prejudices on the tale. But I'm sure you're still wondering, after all this time, why I brought you here. I owe you an explanation, Avis, however garbled it might come out.

I was there in the crowd on New Year's Eve when you were first unveiled. Your father had been talking up his latest works for some time. An evolutionary leap in artistry, he called it. The future of window displays—and a hundred other highfalutin' things.

I've never said a word to your father, I've written him no letters, shown him no index cards. For his part, he's said nothing to me. I have, however, looked into his eyes. I saw from the first that I was his rival. I understood this, accepted it. After all, I was the newcomer. And I was better than him—a better carver, anyway. It may sound immodest but I had spent my life—barring a few short intervals—working with wood. While your father relied on engines and gizmos to create movement and a sense of drama, I knew that all you needed to do was hint at it.

It's curious that the one figurehead to follow me around the world was Vengeance, my first piece, full of imperfections and daft ideas, but even then I understood how to create drama. The turned cheek, the hidden arm, the ambiguous expression. Your father's figures improved with practice, but he was still fighting the wood. You could see it. He was imposing his own geometry on the block, rather than letting the block find its form. But that is neither here nor there.

At some point, several years ago, he seemed to have given up. Instead of a new figure every one or two months, he only produced one or two a year, then none at all. His displays changed with the seasons, but rehashed old themes. He reused the same mechanical gimmicks. I had been making mannequins at a prolific rate, but I slowed as well. There was no demand. And then the war began and everyone went into their shells.

So it was strange when half of the windows at Donaldson's went black and signs were put up promoting a new display. Perhaps this was all part of your father's plan, to lull the town, to lull me, before revealing his masterpieces.

And what masterpieces you were.

I stood looking at these two figures of perfection—both beautiful and lifelike; the two don't necessarily go together—from the moment the curtain came up until the moment it dropped that first night. I couldn't believe my eyes. Here were two mannequins from the hand of Colton Kemp full of drama and movement and life.

Two young lovers—let us pretend, Avis, that I am still as ignorant about your true identity as I was that day—were strolling along the street, sharing their own New Year's Eve. I was on the edges of the crowd to begin with, so my first thoughts were about the overall arrangement. In earlier days your father might have been tempted to run the street in his window parallel with the street beyond it. But here he had it running perpendicular to Regent Street. These two figures were about to intersect with the real world. They faced forward, but their expressions suggested they were lost in their own happiness, absorbed. It seemed at any moment they would walk straight into the glass.

The female figure wore a dramatic green dress. The sort of dress that was new to Marumaru but instantly desirable, as if the window of Donaldson's were a window to the Champs Élysées. Your father had always been a better window dresser, in the most literal sense, than I was. He wisely chose the clothes his mannequins would wear. He understood that the primary purpose of the window was to sell garments. On the other hand I'd come from carving the clothes directly onto figureheads. Real fabric was difficult to work with. It was harder to hint at a navel beneath a real tunic. Impossible to create the sense of rapid movement with a heavy dress that hung straight down. I was always looking for new fabrics that would fit the image in my head, rather than starting with a garment and working from there.

As that first evening progressed I managed to get closer to the glass and was struck anew by the magnificence of the scene. The way her hand rested in his, the slight flattening of the flesh between the first and second knuckle on her index finger. The hair, my goodness. It was real hair, human hair. I'm sure the rest of the townsfolk were transfixed by the golden locks that tumbled over the girl's shoulders and down her back, but I was more amazed by the boy's curls. The work it must have taken to arrange each hair. It was the controlled chaos I'd fought to create with wood and yet here it was being achieved with hair.

And, of course, there was the breathtaking, heart-stopping beauty of both figures. His strength and her poise. The way the electric light did not blanch the life from their cheeks. They seemed to radiate light themselves. Light, youth, confidence, excitement, beauty. *Och*, I thought, *if my poor father could see these figures.*

How had Kemp done it? I went home that night and considered everything. Had he been honing his skills in secret all these years? Had he paid someone else to carve these figures? Was it carving at all? Perhaps he'd cast the figures in Bakelite or some other new substance. Perhaps it was an optical illusion, something to do with the window pane: a photograph in three dimensions, if such a thing was possible. Or perhaps they were living models. This last thought seemed at once the most obvious and the most implausible. I had stood there from nine until midnight and never saw these figures blink or twitch or sway. Admittedly I stood in a jostling crowd, craning on my tippertoes for the most part, but still, it seemed impossible. Impossible.

I returned the next day and the next. When the curtain rose on a new scene, not only had the background and the costumes changed, but the mannequins held new poses, their faces new expressions. And yet these were the same figures. The girl had the same golden mane, the same delicate nose, the same kauri-sparkled irises. The boy had the same broad chest, the same network of veins on his forearms, the same curly hair. Had Kemp carved dozens of interchangeable parts? That these were living creatures seemed the only explanation but their chests never rose or fell, their eyes never fluttered. But why else would the curtain need to come down every three or four hours?

The longer the display went on the more disturbed I became. I wondered why no one else was worried about what Kemp had done. I can only guess that they did not know how impossible it was to achieve this scene with any other material known to man but flesh itself. It was the first great thing to happen in Marumaru for many years. Donaldson's window transported the townsfolk back to a time when the rivalry between your father and me was at its peak and the streets were filled with colour. Why would they want to pick and prod at this sweet illusion in the window?

I continued my vigil, trying to work out how human beings could be made into such perfect mannequins.

Were they cadavers? There seemed to be no putrefaction as the days went by and no makeup could have replicated the flush of life I saw on those cheeks.

Were they in a kind of trance? Had they taken some sort of drug that freezes a person in place? When the curtain was down I researched mesmerism and spoke with Fricker, the pharmacist. Both options seemed unlikely.

And then, on the fifth day, the man from Ballantynes arrived. Your father made much of his presence, but the man spent the morning on the edge of the crowd, his head tilted to one side. Here was someone else, I thought, who could see the things I saw, who would know something was awry. Here was someone who could say something, get to the bottom of the mystery, put a stop to it.

After the curtain rose on the afternoon display, Kemp fetched the man, and a few minutes later they were standing in the window. I saw him weighing the girl's hair in his hand, lifting the boy's coat, prodding their flesh. He seemed unperturbed. Whatever Kemp had said to him, he had been convincing.

It is said a magician's sleight of hand is nothing without a persuasive tongue. Was I the only one who had not fallen under his spell?

I decided that it was up to me to catch out these models. I considered trying to surprise them, to trigger an involuntary movement that would give them away. But I worried Kemp would intercede and bar me from the window. I decided instead to focus on the girl's eyes. She must blink if she was alive. And if she was conscious, her eyes would give her away.

We make such resolutions when lying in our beds, but it is quite another thing in the light of day. I could swear I saw the girl's eyes move, but I know how easy it is to fool people into believing that the eyes of a statue or a painting are following them around a room. The longer I stared into her eyes, the more I felt I was slipping back into the kind of delirium in which Vengeance had spoken to me. It was as if a spirit inhabited this figure. A member of the Seelie Court who could only scratch her nose or pull the hair from her eyes when no one was looking.

Kemp announced that he was heading north to Christchurch to prepare a window for Ballantynes. He did not say that he would use his newest figures in this display—this might cause Marumaru to revolt—but I knew that he had to. If I was to uncover his secret, I had only a few days.

For a long time something had been bothering me about the boy. I had been neglecting him as I focused on the girl's eyes, but the moment I first saw him I was struck by a sense of familiarity, as if I had seen him before. And then, finally, I remembered.

It was your final scene: the girl standing on a pedestal, holding a statue's pose, one hand to her forehead. The boy knelt before her, Pygmalion to her Galatea. But there was another echo. That play I had seen, all those years ago. *The Winter's Tale*. While that Hermione had wobbled and blinked her way through the scene, Kemp's was perfectly still. I looked at the boy once more and saw it. That chest, those biceps, those calf muscles, that posture. It was Sandow. Not the man himself, and not the plaster statue that I was told to place in my window, but another of his followers.

I would like to say that everything fell into place after this, but I did not have all the answers that afternoon when the curtain did not descend. It was only a few days later, once we were up here, that I made the connection between the time Sandow had visited Marumaru, the ages of you and your brother and the death of Kemp's wife—always a thing to be whispered about in town. You were his children. He was a monster. But we must be careful of such pronouncements.

Even now, my dear, we do not have the full story.

All I knew when I stood there, watching the sun go down in the reflection of the glass and you and your brother valiantly holding your poses, was that these were human beings and that something was terribly wrong.

I left the window to find answers. I went to Kemp's property, hoping to find his sister-in-law, but the house was deserted.

You have asked often about Flossie, but I'm sorry I cannot say. I went into the barn, which was evidently where your father worked, and saw empty pedestals and strange contraptions, but the space was unoccupied. I did, however, find a set of keys hanging conspicuously by the door that I hoped might get me into Donaldson's and into the window.

I returned to town with Susan, my current horse—Galahad passed away several years ago, poor beast—and the dray I used to bring in my own mannequins for the window. The curtain was still up at Donaldson's, the figures still standing. I rifled through Kemp's keys and finally got inside the store and made my way in the near dark to the window.

As soon as I touched your skin, I knew you were flesh and blood. And yet you refused to move. For the first time in many years I wished I could speak—to tell you that you could move, that everything would be all right.

At first I intended to rescue you both. But I am not as strong as I once was. It was difficult to find the exit again and I was unnerved by the way you held your pose even as I clattered you against the racks of clothes. I could feel the heat of the blood coursing beneath your skin, the subterranean muscles hard as steel bobstay cables. When I got you onto the dray, I still hadn't resolved the mystery of who you were and what spell you were under. Whatever the case, I felt the lad could protect himself. He was strong. He could stand there all night, if necessary. He could evade any captor. And so I left him there in the window.

I'm sorry for imposing this separation between you and your brother. It must be difficult. But it is wise of you to have stayed with me this long, especially in your condition. I cannot predict what your father will do. Nor what the authorities will say, where you will be taken.

Now we have both spent time in Splinterlands, trying to adjust to a new world. For my part, I hope you will stay a wee bit longer—that your father does not break down my door now that I've reached the end of my story. Until then, you are welcome to stay. Now that you have taught me to cook, it can only get better.

God bless you, my child. My dear, dear Avis.

The shining cuckoo.

Part four

The Mannequin Speaks

*'The last act is bloody, however fine
the rest of the play.'*

I.

———————

Every winter I'm surprised when the wattle blooms. This year even more so for the battering we took in May and June. But somehow the buds clung to their branches as the easterlies clobbered the coast and our waves, shunted on by the king tide, gouged the beach from Collaroy baths to North Narrabeen.

I arrived in Sydney on the eve of one of these storms. The year was 1920. My first forty-eight hours in the city were spent hunkered in a hotel room until the sun broke through. I wanted to be on the coast. We'd grown up so close to the waves and yet the sight had been denied us. Now that I'd put many miles between myself and Marumaru I wished to see and hear and smell the breakers for the rest of my life.

Collaroy Beach was no postcard that first day. Houses and sheds teetered on the edge of the storm scarp. What was left of the beach was littered with sandbags and timber. I felt I'd missed something. A catastrophe. A spectacle. Two young ladies wheeled their bicycles around obstacles and through puddles, not looking at all devastated. Beyond them, men were pushing barrows, shovelling sand and shoring up the supports of one of these wooden buildings. It was the surf club.

People talk these days about the service I have given the club, beginning that day after the storm, but I think of it another way:

all those years of service the club has given me. The mateship, the sense of purpose, the routine. That's another thing the young guns like to go on about: old Sandy's routines. Though hardly anyone has ever seen me climbing to McLean's Lookout in the dark—good luck getting the ratbags up before nine—even the nippers know I go there to limber up of a morning. I do my exercises to the cawing of the crows and watch the orange band of daylight break over the sea, the waves, the sand, the pines, the shops, the tarsealed streets, the phoenix palms and banksias, the bungalows and unit blocks—until it finally reaches me, up there on Collaroy Plateau. Daylight brings the people out of doors, perfect miniatures walking with purpose. No one dawdles in the early hours. I watch them walk their dogs, duck into cars, paddle their longboards out for a few waves before work while I do my exercises. These days I'm mostly just stretching, checking every muscle is still there, that none have buggered off in the night.

The old body's hanging in there. I reckon I could still win the odd flag race, but I don't want to embarrass the younger blokes. Let them think they're untouchable—it only lasts so long. Besides, those few times I've gone out into the surf for a rescue in recent years, it's been all the members can talk about for weeks afterward.

'How do you keep in such good shape, Sandy?' they ask.

'This is my shape,' I say. I hold out my arms, resigned, before adding, 'And I don't intend losing it.'

About this time last year I found myself talking to the television. I'd never had much time for the idiot box. I was either training, on patrol or at the surf club. I used to go weeks without spending a single evening in my flat, with all the committees and balls and what have you. But they don't have balls any more and I've filled every committee post three times over. 'You've done enough,' they all tell me, but what they mean is, 'You've done your dash, old man.'

And so the television got called for duty more and more to fill the silence.

One day I started answering Tony Barber's questions on *The Great Temptation*, my own voice drowning out the answers of the contestants. Soon I was complimenting Barbie Rogers on her dresses.

Brian Henderson would read the nightly news and in the pauses between stories I'd add my two cents.

The Australian Embassy Platoon has withdrawn from Vietnam: 'About bloody time.'

The government has spent big bikkies on a paint-splattered canvas: 'You call that art?'

Another doom and gloom update on the oil crisis: 'Let them keep their oil, eh Hendo? Walking never hurt anyone.'

'I never owned a car in my life,' I found myself saying into the mirror as I brushed my teeth. 'Never saw the need.'

I began to yarn with the walls, regale the ceiling tiles. I didn't need the TV to drown the silence any more.

'I met June Hervey at the championships at Manly, many moons ago . . .'

'The first time I saw Collaroy Beach, the surf club was nearly falling into the sea . . .'

'There was once a man who talked to a figurehead . . .'

I forget about the wattles when they're not in bloom. They're just like other trees. But when they wake in the middle of winter and fill the front yards with yellow they seem to be saying, 'You've forgotten I was here. But I'm here. I'm here.'

The time has come for me to wake. To speak for myself.

My name is Eugen Kemp. The world may have forgotten me. But I'm here. I'm here.

I left New Zealand with Avis's diary and The Carpenter's tale, not knowing quite what I carried. Back then, I could only read sheet music. I was curious, but also terrified by the prospect of those pages. I didn't want to know what had been going on in that hut in the weeks it took to find them, didn't want to relive what happened once we finally tracked them down.

When I got to Collaroy I was seventeen, dumb, strong and handsome. It was easy enough to find young women willing to spend time with me. Easy enough to admit I didn't know my letters and to let them school me. I never told them where I'd come from, not exactly, or what I might read when I was able.

'What's your name?' one of the blokes asked me when I offered to help clean up the surf club that day in 1920.

'Sandow,' I said. 'John Sandow.'

I was handed a shovel and I stripped down to my waist. I began clearing sand and soon realised the others were leaning on their tools, watching me.

'You sure have a lot of muscles there, Sandy,' one joker said. I've been Sandy ever since.

'They come in handy,' I said.

Though none of the blokes at the club quite matched my physique, they weren't the pale weaklings I'd seen in Marumaru. We had the surf club shipshape in no time.

I'd never swum before, but I soon learnt.

After a couple of months in Collaroy, I was the first choice to run out into the surf with the lifebelt. We routed North Narrabeen and Manly in the reel, line and belt rescue at that year's championships and I was assured my pick of freckled tutors.

I have known love. I have known happiness. They may not have been constants in my life, but I have known them. Don't think the events I must return to have consigned me to a life of misery. However devastating the storm, the flotsam is always cleared, the beach returns, the swimmers venture back into the water. When someone gets into strife, a lifeguard trundles out to rescue them.

II.

_____

There I was, down on one knee, looking up at my masterpiece long after the sun went down. I didn't move when The Carpenter came, lifted Avis from her pedestal and carried her from the window. I'd let her go, but my expression didn't change. I kept my eyes trained to the spot where her head had been. I thought: if I hold this pose until the morning, perhaps the early risers will think this disappearing act is the next tableau. That's what I told my father when he returned later that morning, but the truth is I didn't care what they thought on the other side of the window. Not since I'd seen them out there: gangly, stooped, gaunt, fat, grey, reddened by eczema and acne, shrunken by age or malnutrition. At least on New Year's Eve their clothes had been crisp and well tailored. In the following days they'd exchanged their finest dresses and suits for duller, more frayed versions, better matches for the neglect they'd shown their bodies.

As with Avis, I'd been disturbed by the number of children, but also the lack of young men. There seemed no place for me on the other side of the glass.

I'd moped for days until my father raised the possibility of Christchurch.

We'd been raised to believe that beauty must go hand in

hand with fortitude, perseverance, grace—things that can't be proven in an instant. Physical perfection came first—the people of Marumaru had already failed on this count—but character was the real test. I believed I was better than Marumaru, but if I broke pose I'd be letting myself down. It didn't matter that it was the middle of the night, The Carpenter had raided the window and the street was most likely deserted: I held my pose. I thought about all the other sixteen-year-old boys at that moment—in Christchurch, Wellington, Auckland—who were midway though their seasons in the window. But they were asleep in their anterooms, dreaming of Sandow Developers that stretch and stretch and stretch without ever pinging back. They couldn't have lasted this long in the window. Even if I had no witness, I'd know what I'd done.

And so I held my pose.

The pain in my knee ebbed and flowed. It felt as if the floor were moving. A haze descended but I kept my eyes open and unmoving.

Avis describes in her diary how we managed to stand so still— the way we learnt to rearrange ourselves, our muscles, in tiny, imperceptible ways. One thing she neglects to explain, however, is blinking.

One of my earliest memories is of my father's face hard up against mine. His eyes drilling into my eyes. If I blinked, he'd slap my cheek. He would alternate cheeks—he was a slave to symmetry—and I remember feeling the burn of the last slap on one side of my face and the burn of anticipation on the other.

These weren't proper staring contests: I couldn't slap him if he blinked. He blinked often. More often than he thought he did. It was bloody distracting.

I was told that, as babies, Avis and I had blinked once every couple of minutes. I guess it has something to do with the moistness of an infant's eyes, the lack of exertion. As we grew, we disappointed our father by blinking more frequently. Sandow had suggested that the eyelids could be trained. If anyone knew muscles it was him. And yet there I was, two or three years old, struggling to go a minute without blinking, even with the threat of another slap across the cheek.

According to Sandow's System, the mind is the most important muscle. Exercise, he preached, is of little value without the judicious use of willpower (I still hear people say the same thing, all these years later, though they use different words). Is it any surprise, then, that a toddler can't control his eyelids with a half-developed brain?

My father eventually realised this and focused our training elsewhere for the next few years. When his attention returned to our eyelids, we improved rapidly, able to stare without blinking— without any eye movement whatsoever—for two minutes, sometimes three. But we'd always blink in the end.

The truth is, you can't deny your eyelids for longer than three minutes. The tension builds in the lids, they become heavier and heavier. You might be able to hold it for another thirty seconds, but by this point you're swaying, your chest is pumping, the illusion is ruined—and you're still going to blink. It's inevitable. The key is to control your blinking so that it cannot be detected. Just as we learnt to breathe shallow, unseen breaths, we trained ourselves to blink so fast, so efficiently, that our father, an inch away, couldn't be sure our lids had moved. Stretch that distance out to six feet and add a sheet of plate glass and you have your illusion. But even then, it wouldn't work if we were blinking every few seconds. The secret is the rhythm. We learnt to blink once every forty seconds and staggered our rhythms so we weren't blinking at the same time. Forty seconds is regular enough to keep the eyes moist and relieve tension in the lids but infrequent enough that the onlooker is never sure what they've seen. Perhaps they see a flutter of the lashes. But did they really? They focus hard for another thirty seconds, their certainty fading all the while, their own eyelids clapping like castanets.

Long after I left the window, left New Zealand, I was still blinking faster than the shutter of a camera, still stuck to the same forty-second rhythm while at rest. It helped me with my tutors. When it was time to put away my books and look into their eyes, they felt as if they had my full attention. My father may have raised us to be mannequins—with no thought about what would happen after the window—but he had inadvertently trained me in the art of seduction.

My father returned from Christchurch on the morning train to find a crowd of people gathered around the window of Donaldson's. His window. It was before nine, too early for the curtain to be raised. He pushed his way through the crowd and saw me, kneeling before the empty pedestal. He came right up to the glass and slapped his palms upon it. I couldn't see him, of course, but I was startled by the sound. I don't think he meant to get my attention. He didn't want me to turn.

He left the street, made his way to the anteroom and lowered the curtain. I felt his hand on my shoulder and let myself fall onto my side. I'd been posing for nearly twenty hours without a drop of water, without a hiccup or a yawn.

'Eugen, what are you doing?' He shook me.

I couldn't answer.

'Why are you in the window this early? Where's Avis? Where's,' he paused, 'your mother?'

I managed to shake my head.

He lifted me by the open collar of my sculptor's shirt. I opened my eyes. His face was clean shaven.

'What is it, boy?'

'She's not my mother,' I said. It felt as if my throat were full of sand.

'Where's Avis?' he repeated. 'What are you doing in the window?'

'The curtain. It never fell.'

His frown deepened as he tried to make sense of my words.

'You've been here all night? Posing?'

I closed my eyes again—a long, luxurious, never-ending

blink. He let go of my shirt and I dropped back to the floor. I heard his footsteps as he went to the anteroom. After some time he returned and stood over me. My eyes remained closed and he stomped off once more. He came back with a glass of water, lifted me up and held it to my lips.

When I was done drinking, he continued to hold me, my shoulders against his chest, my head against his shoulder. 'And you,' I said, 'are not my father.'

'Of course I am.' His voice was different.

'Sandow,' I said.

I felt his laughter shudder through me.

'Come on,' he said, 'let's get you home.'

I slept on the stretcher bed in the anteroom while he made his preparations. He didn't return home during this time, as I'd supposed when he first left me. I know because he didn't fetch the horses, Emily and Charlotte, and the covered wagon. I know because I saw his face when we returned to the barn.

When he shook me, I didn't really wake. I felt him dressing me. Even if it had registered that I was being put into a dress—to hide the development of my legs—I wouldn't have had the strength to resist. A shawl covered my broad shoulders, a hat my short, curly hair. He was lucky, I suppose, that Donaldson's still hadn't opened for the day. We made our way to the side door, me leaning heavily on my father's shoulder, my sandalled feet dragging on the polished wooden floors. When I opened my eyes everything was in soft focus. The longer I kept them open, the blurrier things became.

In the alleyway we were met by a rumbling motor car. I'd only seen a handful of these contraptions rolling past the window. Noisy, smoky things that seemed no faster than a bicycle. At the wheel sat a tall, lean bloke in a red and black hunting cap with the earflaps down. I would later learn this was my father's friend, Jolly Bannerman, the ironmonger.

My father propped me against the side of the car.

'You bring her back from the big smoke, Col?' Bannerman asked.

'Shut up, Jolly,' he said and tossed a duffle bag up onto the back seat of the car. He climbed onto the running board and pulled me up and into the back seat.

'She's blotto,' Bannerman said. 'I'd know that look anywhere.'

'Just get us home.'

I shut my eyes. The car jerked forward.

'It's a demon that must be fought,' Bannerman shouted from the driver's seat. 'And there's glory in the victory.'

In motion, the car was even noisier than I'd expected. Bannerman's driving was erratic. I kept my head buried in my father's shoulder.

'Don't get down,' he told Bannerman when we stopped. 'I've got her.'

'You sure there, Col?'

'I'm sure.'

'Give my love to Flossie.'

'And mine to Milly.'

As the car drove off I started feeling better. Halfway up the drive I was able to walk unsupported, though the dress made it difficult. I stopped and looked down. Why was I clothed like this? What had I missed?

'Come on, Eugen,' my father said.

He didn't go to the house, but headed straight for his workshop and waited for me outside the closed door. Did he know what we might find? Did he have an inkling? Is that why he needed me there when he pulled the door open? Perhaps it was just the dramatist in him. Gathering the audience for the big revelation.

When I reached him he was jangling the unlocked padlock and its chain in his hand. His face said, 'Fancy that?' He crouched and lifted the door up to make it easier to pull open. I stepped to the side as he brought the door back and rested it against the side of the barn.

And there she was, in the gloom, dangling from the joist. The woman who'd raised me as her own child. The sister of my true mother. The accomplice of my father.

Flossie's face was grey, her hands limp at her sides. Her

slippers had fallen to the floor and the toes of her bare feet pointed to the ground. I stood on the threshold, hoping that my eyes deceived me, but the blurriness had gone. I could see the dust particles spinning in the light from the open door. My father stood one step to the side and one step behind me. We held our poses while Flossie twisted and swayed in the breeze like a pine needle hanging from a strand of busted spider web.

My father stepped into the barn. He took his hatchet from the tool bench, righted the chair Flossie had kicked away and climbed onto it. He grabbed her around the thighs so that her head lifted and the rope bulged out. He ran the edge of the hatchet across the rope a few times until her upper half was let loose and lurched over his shoulder and down his back in a kind of fireman's carry. His knees buckled but he kept his balance.

He managed to step down from the chair and gently lay Flossie on the floor of the barn. He turned to me and ran his hand from his forehead down over his eyes, his nose, his mouth, pulling his chin down and exposing his lower teeth, his tongue.

'So,' the old bastard said, pretending he wasn't as shaken as I was, 'that answers where Flossie was. Now, what about Avis?'

'The old man,' I said.

'The Carpenter?'

I shrugged.

'What about him?'

'He came into the window,' I said. 'He took Avis.'

III.

Gabriel Doig lied to my sister. Near the end of his account he describes how, before he took Avis from the window, he went to our property in search of Flossie. He even says he checked the barn and found it deserted. 'Empty pedestals and strange contraptions,' he says, clearly having peered inside, 'but the space was unoccupied.' By the time my father cut Flossie down, she was stiff and colourless. My guess is that she hadn't lowered the curtain at five o'clock the previous day because she was already dead. When Doig went to the barn after nightfall, he'd have seen her. He must have.

This really got under my skin when I was first able to read his story. If he'd lied here, what other lies had he told? What use was everything that went before if he was a liar? Was it all a kind of elaborate seduction?

But I've read his final pages many times since then. Each time, his words seem more and more deliberate. 'You have asked often about Flossie,' he writes, 'but I'm sorry I cannot say.' Not that he doesn't know what happened to her, only that he can't say. Is it that he doesn't want to cause my sister sadness? Or that he doesn't want to ruin their cosy time together?

And the phrase 'The space was unoccupied' strikes me as odd. Does a dead body occupy a room? I've thought about this question more than I care to admit.

It's strange to think that I am now a decade older than Doig was when he took my sister into the hills and wrote his tale of figureheads and castaways. In my mind he's always been an old codger dabbing the edges of his mouth with a handkerchief. To think of what he and Avis got up to in that hut—even if it was just writing notes to one another—it seemed unnatural. A sin and a waste, according to my father's morality. Beauty, strength and character deserve beauty, strength and character in return. But he was only fifty-nine. What I wouldn't give to be *only* fifty-nine! I'd sleep with as many beautiful girls as I could. (That's the difference between Doig and me, I guess.) Even now, my looks are hanging in there, my shape is holding. But no, what am I thinking?

It would be nice, though, to spend some time with a pretty girl. A schoolgirl. We could talk about swimming and sunbathing, about her HSCs, the books she has read for English and the books she reads for herself. She could ask me questions and I would tell her anything, anything. Wouldn't that be something? An old bloke and a young girl, talking. They'd lock me up. I wouldn't need to touch her. They'd only need to see my eyes, wide and unblinking. My years of service at the surf club would be brought against me. What's in it for him? What's he really checking out when he scans the beach? Oh yes, it'd be an open and shut case. But you know what? It might all be worth it.

To my father's credit, if credit can be extended to one so far gone, he didn't delay reporting Flossie's death as he did my real mother's. Over the years he'd become an expert liar and knew that it wasn't the size of the lie but how many lies you were juggling that led to your downfall.

The complete truth, of course, was not possible.

The Carpenter had taken Avis, thwarting my father's hopes of taking us to Christchurch and leaving their twenty-year rivalry in his dust.

My father didn't strike me or even raise his voice, though he seemed always on the verge of lashing out. He sat me down and told me what I was to say before he took Flossie into town in the covered wagon and brought the constable back to inspect the barn, the rope, the joist, the chair.

'And this, constable,' he said, ushering me forward and into the barn, 'is John, the other witness I mentioned.'

In his absence I'd changed into my own clothes, drunk four gallons of water, eaten a loaf of bread and rested. The officer eyed me up and down. He was somewhere in age between me and my father. It was hard to tell what sort of muscles he had beneath his stiff uniform. It wasn't clear if he recognised me from the window. I didn't even know if Marumaru had its own police station.

'Where do you fit in?' he asked.

'He is a performer of *tableaux vivants*,' my father said, stepping between me and the constable.

'What?' he asked.

'Still lifes. Like a painting, but with real figures. You've seen my window displays of late, surely?'

The constable said nothing. He looked down at his notepad.

'There was another performer,' my father said. 'A girl. She's been kidnapped.'

'Kidnapped, you say?' The constable tapped his pencil against the spine of his notepad. 'Busy day for you lot, isn't it? Does he speak?' he asked, prodding the chewed end of his pencil at me.

'I speak,' I said.

'What is your relationship to this man?'

'He is not my father,' I said.

'Oh? And why would he be your father?'

'What he means to say—' my father began.

'Let the boy speak.'

'It's as he said. I am a performer of tableaux. He runs the window where I perform.'

My father was pleased by this response, but I wasn't trying to make him happy. I was trying to twist the knife by asserting that he was not my father. I still believed that I was the son of Eugen Sandow, the only man I knew of who matched my physique. I saw this as my opportunity to break from the man who'd raised me in this poky town, trained me for its paltry window, when I deserved better. I didn't care that my season in the window had come to a premature end. I wanted to find Sandow and reclaim my position as the heir to his empire, to take his place on the covers of magazines and tins of powdered milk.

'The man they call The Carpenter tampered with my display,' my father said. 'He is the kidnapper.'

'Do you have a name?'

My father looked away. 'No.'

The constable smiled for the first time. 'Come on, Kemp. He's been your rival for how many years and you don't even know his name?'

I looked at the rope that was draped over the back of the chair in the centre of the barn. Was Flossie so soon forgotten?

'Well, what is his name then?' my father asked.

It was the constable's turn to look away.

To my knowledge, Flossie didn't leave a note. My father told me to stay at home while he helped the police track down Avis and The Carpenter, leaving me plenty of time to fossick for one. I couldn't even find her diary. Though I wasn't able to read a word, it seemed important that someone was still thinking about her.

It didn't help that neither Avis nor I had ever set eyes on her diary. But I knew the difference between type and handwriting. I searched every room, between every volume on the bookshelf, rifled through the woodpile, the workshop, the laundry, the hedges—everywhere. I found nothing. Perhaps, I decided, she destroyed her diary before taking her life. There was nothing in the range but ashes. Or perhaps my father had found the diary before I could.

I believe Flossie agreed to act as a mother to Avis and me because she had a kind heart and thought highly of my father, too highly. She was only seventeen when her sister died so suddenly. She was a relative newcomer to Marumaru and had no other family to speak of. She must have been bemused by Colton's request that she mustn't speak of the children in town, but probably thought it was temporary. I suspect she thought that once the grief at Louisa's passing subsided, he would let her into his heart and they would marry. He may well have promised this much. When his strange behaviour continued, she found herself in a bind. He couldn't raise Avis and me alone. She was needed to counteract his growing obsession with physical training, to nurture us, show us love and teach us a little of the world beyond the hedges. As the years passed and she came to understand my father's plan, it was too late to stop him. She was culpable. Seeing us in the window—and cooped up in the anteroom—still disconnected from the world, from reality, was the final straw.

This is my version of events at least. At times my thoughts have gone to darker places. I've made more sinister connections that reach back before Louisa's death, but no good ever comes of such thinking. Better to return to the affection I felt for Flossie as a young boy and let that wash over everything.

IV.

Every day that my father returned home no closer to finding Avis was a day closer to violence. He left long pauses between his words, during which I could see the muscles in his neck twitching. As I got ready for bed I could hear him down the hall, exhaling through his nose in short bursts like an impatient horse. I could easily overpower him if the need arose, but I didn't want him to remove the stopper from his rage.

His thoughts centred on Avis. He needed to find her. I wanted her to be found too. After all, this was the first time we'd ever been apart. But I'd been preparing myself for our separation at the end of our season in the window. The way in which it happened was a surprise, but she was a tough girl. She could have fought off The Carpenter. She was smart, too. Smarter than me, that's for sure.

These are the things I told myself.

When I look back upon our childhood together, the changes that came as we prepared for the window, I feel as if I'm standing on the edge of a storm scarp, that my memories are a ledge of unsupported sand that might give way at any moment. The only static thing from this time is Avis's diary, though I feel just as precarious when I enter its world.

Early on she writes about how she longs for a day when

she might have an exciting life that contains events to conceal from her family. We must remember she was giving these entries to Flossie to read and that our father had taught us the art of misdirection.

We'd always been curious about each other's bodies as we sponged down outside the washhouse before starting our exercises each morning. We were trained to monitor every muscle, to target our development to ensure there were no weaknesses, no imbalance. It seemed natural to monitor my sister's progress, not just my own, and for her to take an interest in mine.

Avis was the first to enter puberty. It was no secret. Our father had warned us about the changes in store and how to work with them, how they were necessary, but the budding breasts and the shock of springy, rust-coloured hair that appeared between her legs seemed like glaring imperfections. Gone was the uniform smoothness of her skin. Gone, the definition of her chest.

Avis, wise soul that she was, bore her changes with pride.

'I am becoming a woman, Eugen,' she told me once after I'd said something snide about her new body. 'One day, if you are lucky, you will become a man.'

I know now, of course, that it is odd for a brother and sister, even twins, to spend so much time in each other's presence, naked, but we knew no other way. Our property was a kind of Eden. Long after our morning routine, I would walk around the garden in the nude. We didn't know shame. Instead, we took pride in our bodies. We took charge of their development. If it had stopped at this, perhaps I would feel no shame, even now.

I had to wait until I was almost fourteen for my skin to grow oily and my voice to judder. I began to get erections for no apparent reason. I didn't know about masturbation and had little time alone to experiment. Instead, I tried to focus this strange new drive on my exercises with dumb-bell and developer and, by night, on the piano keys. For the most part I was successful.

Avis assumed the role of older sibling during this time, observing the changes to my body without comment.

By the time I turned fifteen, the worst of the changes were over. I was taller, stronger. My cheeks had tautened and my face took on a harder edge. I was fortunate that my pimply skin didn't last long and left no permanent marks. Each night our father gave us both an ointment that smelt of cut grass and this, combined with the religious bathing, day and night, probably helped.

This was around the time he began to teach us the poses for our first few tableaux, which meant we spent a lot of time staring into each other's eyes, pretending to be lovers. It was less than a year until our season in the window and my excitement was growing. Avis seemed excited too, as if she'd woken from a long slumber. She began to pay my body extra attention as we bathed. I'd learnt the best way to avoid an embarrassing erection was to concentrate on my own body, the work I had ahead of me that day, the improvement that would result. But she had a way of catching my eye with her movements or her own protracted stare.

One night she crawled into my bed.

'I can always tell when you're not asleep,' she whispered. 'You don't make a sound.' I was lying on my back. She was on her side, perched on the edge of the mattress. Her hand reached across my chest and took hold of my shoulder. 'I wonder how quiet you can be.' She ran her hand down my arm to the wrist, then across to my hip and, soon enough, to my pubic hair. She took hold of my penis. 'How did I know it would be like this?' she whispered, pouring her words into my ear. Her fingers were cold and I let out a little groan. It was better than a wet sponge after a hard workout on a hot afternoon. She tightened her grip, then loosened it. Tightened and loosened. 'I'm just playing,' she said. 'Do you mind?'

'No,' I whispered.

'Do you want me to stop?'

'No.'

She toyed with my penis and balls for a long, blissful time, though she never worked up enough rhythm or force to make me come. (At the time I didn't know such a thing was possible.) I kept my arms at my sides. Eventually her hand rose from my crotch, this time tracing a line up the centre of my body until she pressed down on my chest and lifted her head and shoulder. 'Goodnight, Eugen,' she said and kissed me on the forehead.

She returned to my bed the next night and my hand found a breast, small and soft, and its captivating nipple. When she wrapped her fingers around my penis I placed my other hand down there, around her hand, squeezing tighter.

'Do you like that?' she asked.

I groaned and began to move her hand.

The next night she guided my hand between her legs.

So our education progressed by degrees. By day we stared at each other like lovers, our father watching for any movement, reviewing our postures. By night we were alone and continued our play-acting.

One night I took the initiative and crawled into her bed.

'No,' she said.

'Why not.'

'Because Mother is on the other side of this wall.' My bed, however, was next to an external wall. 'Goodnight, Eugen,' she said coldly and waited for me to go. She didn't visit me that night, though the hope of it kept me awake and vigilant.

It seemed she wouldn't come across the next night either, but eventually I heard her peel back her bedclothes and the soft sticking and unsticking of her feet on the floorboards.

A few nights later the time came. She rolled onto her back and whispered, 'Put it in me.' I obliged. We had to remain quiet with Flossie in the next room and our father down the hall. I felt a torrent surging within my chest. I wanted to become a snarling beast, but I knew that would put an end to everything. We'd started leaving a small gap in the curtains so that any moonlight would help illuminate the room. As I began to thrust, slowly, I saw Avis bite her bottom lip and close her eyes. I worried that I was hurting her, that we were doing something wrong, that I was doing her irreparable damage, but I couldn't hold back the raging waters.

We didn't speak afterwards. I worried that our nightly sessions were over now. At morning routine the next day she wouldn't meet my eye. She broke pose twice in two hours under the electric light, which brought our father's wrath.

But that night she came back to my bed.

We'd always felt a connection bordering on the physical. Sometimes it was as if we could read each other's minds. I didn't learn to read in part because she'd learnt. She didn't play the piano because I could play. This new connection we'd discovered felt natural and yet we knew to guard it from the two people who claimed to be our parents. Perhaps it was because we'd never seen any affection pass between them. Perhaps it was something that had been drummed into us as small children, not to play with ourselves, not to play with each other. But our days and nights were charged with adrenaline. Our time in the window was hurtling toward us, we were doing everything we could to ensure we caused a sensation and, on top of this, we had a secret.

By this time we knew all about how the window worked, how we were destined to be married to other people and live separate lives. But somehow this didn't bother me. It was as if I believed I could have both fates: a successful season in the window leading to a marriage with the most eligible girl in the land and my sister always in the bed next to mine when I snuffed out the candle.

But Avis could see. Avis knew.

'We have to stop,' she told me one day as I fed Juniper a handful of chickweed. We were at the far corner of the property. I could smell bread baking in the kitchen and hear the clanging sound of my father hammering metal in his workshop. I looked up at Avis and the goat nipped my fingers. I pulled my hand away and stuck it under my armpit.

'Here,' she said, 'let me look.'

I turned to face the hedge.

'Eugen.' She placed her hand on my shoulder. 'You know it

can't go on forever. You will have a wife soon. I'm sure she will make you very happy.'

'I don't want a wife,' I said. Juniper began to nudge my hip, eager for something else to eat. 'All right, Juney,' I said and patted her side. 'No more biting my fingers, though.'

'Eugen?' Avis placed the backs of her fingers on my cheek but I brushed her hand away.

'Leave me alone.'

As I expected she didn't climb into my bed that night. I stayed in mine. There were two months left until we turned sixteen and took to the window. If we were going to be wrenched apart, I told myself, it was best to start now. The next morning I turned away from her as we bathed. The only time I'd look into her eyes was while posing. I spent more time in the garden talking to Juniper. I only played the piano when she wasn't in the room.

During those final weeks, we barely spoke.

V.

One week after I left the window, I found myself standing at the end of our driveway with nothing to stop me taking another step. The police had questioned everyone in town about Avis's kidnapping—or so they claimed—and had no leads. My father continued to set out every morning in search of answers, though I knew answers alone wouldn't be enough. I feared what would happen when he finally found Avis and The Carpenter. I hadn't found Flossie's diary, but another quest had presented itself: finding my true father.

I couldn't see any sign of the town from the end of our driveway, just paddocks and trees. I thought back to the night we were taken to the window, lying on our backs with a blanket over our heads: that first turn had been to the right.

The road I found myself walking along was dry and narrow and lined with blackberry tangles, thorny matagouri and dog daisies—pests that never lasted long on our property. Soon I saw a spire. Then another. The town of Marumaru came into view. I had seen it before, of course, through the window, but it was like being shown a photograph when you've asked for a map. Only now could I see how far Regent Street stretched in either direction. Most interesting to me was what I saw beyond the buildings: the blue-black line of the horizon, the green-grey water sliding toward the land. I walked into town and found myself one street back from the main road and a few hundred yards from the beach. The houses I passed were on tiny plots of land and further cramped by their ragged gardens. Cottages covered in jasmine and honeysuckle, overshadowed by oaks and birches. I felt sorry for the children raised on these properties. I would have gone mad waiting for the window if confined to such a small space. And with the world so near!

When buildings weren't hidden by hedges, when they fronted the street, their windows were boarded up. Why would these people shut themselves away, I wondered, when the world was so wide, so open? Then I realised fathers were probably preparing these windows for their children's sixteenth birthdays.

Further down the road I saw a row of bicycles—contraptions I'd become accustomed to seeing through my own window—outside a store. I could see the value a bicycle may have in working the quadriceps, calf muscles and, of course, the gluteus, but the static handlebars seemed a lost opportunity. I had no concept of money so didn't feel its lack as I walked quickly toward the bicycles, eager to try one out—how hard could it be?—but my path was blocked by an elderly couple. The plait of hair looped across the woman's head made me think if I pulled it I could lift her like a bucket.

'Bill, look who it is,' she said.

'Oh yes,' said the man. His short-brimmed hat looked as if it might be on backwards.

'It's the boy from the window.'

'Is it now?'

'You are, aren't you?'

I leant to one side to look at the row of bicycles and remembered my true purpose. 'I'm looking for Eugen Sandow,' I said.

The woman grabbed my upper arm. 'Feel that, Bill. Firm as cast iron.'

'Is it?' The man pulled a yellowed handkerchief from the pocket of his single-breasted coat. He went to blow his nose and I took a step back.

'Where's the girlie?' the woman asked.

'Where is Sandow?' I said.

'Is he foreign?' the man asked.

'You're a Yank,' the woman said, 'aren't you? That's what the paper said. Off to Christchurch soon, I expect.'

It was as if their brains were as deficient as their bodies. I stepped around them and started on down the road.

'Fancy that,' I heard the woman say. 'Without as much as a nod farewell.'

'That's Yanks for you.'

'He wasn't even wearing a hat.'

I walked up and down the row of bicycles, inspecting each machine in order to select the one that best matched my height and physique.

'I've seen you.' A skinny man came out of the shop. 'You'd best move along. I've seen you eyeing them bicycles.' He flicked his hand out as if shooing a fly.

'I'd like to try one,' I said.

'You'd like to try one? That's rich,' the man said. He reached inside the door for a broom. 'Go on now,' he said, waving it near my head, 'move along. No trouble here today.'

My knuckles clenched but I decided it best to walk away.

'Sandow,' I told myself. 'I'm after Sandow.'

I turned right onto a street that led to the ocean and was stopped by a red-haired bloke in an open waistcoat, its turquoise lining flashing as he swung his arm forward to shake my hand. I was worried about skin diseases, but I had little choice than to follow this custom I'd seen through the window.

'Do you know Eugen Sandow?' I asked.

The man chuckled and ran the back of his wrist beneath his nose while sniffing deeply. 'Good one,' he said. 'Will I see you down the Criterion this afternoon?'

Next it was a group of young women, probably not much older than I was. The first had deeply sunken eyes, the second a slight palsy of the face, the third was blessed with enormous breasts and an equally large behind that ensured she didn't topple over. They bowed their heads and tittered and found it difficult to address me directly. When I asked about Sandow, they shook their heads. How superior Avis was to these creatures!

Sandow always said that his system could improve the weakest man, woman or child. When my father read the strongman's gospel to Avis and me, he and Flossie were our only comparisons. I'd always considered my father a weakling, but compared with the people of Marumaru he was a beacon of vitality.

I continued down the street, expecting at any moment to see another boy or girl my age performing in the window, but these windows were packed with junk – bottles, balls of wool, pieces of furniture.

Outside a large stone building with a prominent verandah I came across a man about my father's age holding a watering can and humming to himself. I suspected he was mentally retarded, even more so than the others I'd met, and decided to keep walking. As I passed, however, he stopped humming and dinged the watering can with his knuckles. 'You're the fella from the window,' he said.

I turned. 'I'm looking for Eugen Sandow.'

The man looked up at the front of the verandah. I guessed that he was reading the words across the building's facade. The characters meant nothing to me. 'You'd best talk to Jesse,' he said.

'Jesse?'

He nodded. 'He knows your man Sandow. He'd be keen to talk to you too, I suspect. Never been shy of a conversation and now he's got it into his head to run for mayor . . .' The man put his free hand on his hip and shook his head. 'You wouldn't know it to look at Jesse now, but he was almost your match when he arrived in town. A duskier shade, mind, but plenty strong. Would you mind holding this for a moment?' He handed me his watering can, which turned out to be empty. He pulled a handkerchief from his trouser pocket and blew his nose before I even had a chance to step back.

'Hayfever,' he said. 'Any day the sun is shining.'

I resisted quoting Sandow on the link between physical strength and resistance to disease and asked instead, 'Where can I find him?'

He pointed toward Regent Street and the sea beyond. 'The old signwriter's shop. Go to the end of this street and turn right. It's just past the bank. You'll see it.'

'Thank you.' I handed the man his watering can.

The sick and feeble continued to step in my path as I walked down the street, but I sidestepped them now. I couldn't read and had never seen a bank before—I was imagining the base of some hill—but at least I knew my right from left. When I reached the junction I was so intent on finding the signwriter's shop that I almost didn't recognise the church on the far side.

I stopped dead.

I've been here before.

Another step and I'll enter the frame.

Part of me believed I was still in the window. That, while posing for so long the night Avis was stolen, my consciousness had separated and I'd been living out the last week as a kind of fantasy. Without looking to my right I crossed the road to the churchyard. Only then did I gaze upon the window.

How small it was!

There were, in fact, two windows of equal size, either side of double glass doors, all beneath a black awning. The window to the right of the doors must have been our window because there was nowhere for the anteroom on the other side. The curtain was down, showing the plush red velvet we never got to see.

There was, however, a scene in the second window. Two shoddy figures stood draped in heavy gowns. I could tell they were wooden from across the street. What would possess anyone to place these things in a perfectly good window? Were there no other sixteen-year-olds in this town?

It was so unremarkable. All of it. Most people walked past without stopping. Some pushed their way through the glass doors and entered, I guessed, the giant wardrobe. I looked up at the square building, its tall windows in three rows above the awning.

I realised my abdominal muscles were tensing. Was this the arrival of Avis's worm? I felt behind me and leant upon the wrought-iron church gate, my head tilted to the clouds.

'Are you all right?'

I looked down and saw an orphan boy. His cheeks were freckled and fat. Perhaps his parents had only died recently.

'What is that place?' I asked.

'That place?' he asked, pointing at the window, the giant wardrobe. 'That's Donaldson's.'

I slumped down so that I was now sitting on the footpath, my back pressed against the gate.

'What is it?'

'Are you all right?' he asked again. 'My mother's just in Donaldson's. The department store. I can get her if you feel sick.'

'Your mother?'

The boy nodded.

'No,' I said quickly and shook my head. I hadn't expected the town to be like this. To be baffled at every turn. Nothing made sense except that I'd been lied to. The world was nothing like what my father had led me to believe.

I stood up and took a large breath so that my chest reached its full expansion. 'I'm fine. I don't need your mother. I'm looking for the signwriter's shop.'

'It's next to the bank.'

'Where's the bank?'

The boy cocked his head. 'Right there.' He pointed to the building with stone pillars next to Donaldson's.

'So that,' I said, pointing at the next building along, 'is the signwriter's?'

The store's window was covered in elaborate squiggles that were meaningless to me. Once across the street I noticed the white paint was beginning to flake toward the bottom of the glass, suggesting these letters had been painted some time ago.

Before I could enter, the door opened and a familiar face emerged. Or, should I say, a familiar belly. It was the fat, well-dressed man we'd seen so often through the window.

'It moves,' the man said and chuckled. Up close, I realised he wasn't nearly as old as I'd imagined. The skin of his face was smooth, untouched by wrinkles or pockmarks, and the warm colour of honey. His thick moustache ran out to the vertical creases that appeared in his face when he smiled, which was often. 'I read about you two in the paper,' he said, 'but I scarcely believed it. But here you are, eh?' He stepped forward and his hand found its way into mine, his other hand gripping my triceps while he pumped up and down and looked into my eyes.

'Jesse Hikuroa, the next mayor of Marumaru,' he said. 'I'm sorry, I don't I think I caught your name.'

'John,' I said, looking down at his hand, still pumping mine. His belly, straining the buttons of his waistcoat and the gold chain of his pocket watch, was nearly touching mine. I squeezed his hand tighter until he let go.

'Strong grip you have there,' he said, but didn't nurse his hand, just laid it to rest on his belly.

'I'm looking for Eugen Sandow.'

'Sandow? You might just give him a run for his money, though he's getting on in years now, eh?' He placed a hand in the small of my back and led me inside the store. He walked with a kind of wobble, not a limp so much as an exaggerated swaying of the upper half of his body. No wonder I'd thought he was an old bugger. 'The number of men that used to challenge him.' He shook his head. We passed the counter and entered the back room, which contained a large wooden desk covered in papers, two chairs and little else. 'He always refused. The first few times I thought it a bit cowardly.' He pointed at one of the chairs. 'Sit down.' He removed his hat and sat on the other side of the desk. 'But he couldn't possibly arm wrestle every joker who'd bought one of his dumb-bells. He'd never get anywhere that way.'

The air smelt of suet and recently snuffed candles. There were a number of framed photographs on the walls.

'It will be nice to move into the council chambers in May. All things going to plan. Ah,' he said and hoisted himself to his feet. He walked over to a photo and lifted it from the wall. 'Here's me and Sandow.' He huffed on the glass, wiped it with the triangle of shirt that had come untucked from his trousers and handed it to me.

There was Sandow as I'd seen him many times, wearing just a loincloth and Roman sandals, the waxed tips of his moustache swooping upward, his arms folded across his pectorals, a thick vein running from elbow to wrist on each forearm. To the right of Sandow stood a boy, slimmer and slightly shorter but still quite impressive, holding the same pose and staring at the same point in the distance. I looked back at Jesse.

'All right, all right,' he said, reaching for the photo, 'no need to squint. I admit I've let myself go these past few years.'

I looked at his outstretched hand, the fingers wiggling, and pulled the frame closer to my chest. For a moment he left his hand there, his eyes drilling into mine, before he sighed and slumped back into his chair.

I turned the frame around so the image was facing him. 'How old are you in this?'

'I must have been, oh, sixteen. It was taken in Wellington, just before we caught the ferry to Christchurch. How old are you, if you don't mind me asking?'

'Sixteen,' I said.

'A confluence of coincidences.' He opened a drawer. 'You look much older,' he said, his head down, rummaging through the drawer. 'Take it as a compliment.'

'How old do I look?' I asked.

'Old enough to vote.' He placed a pipe and a tin of tobacco on the desk and sighed. 'You don't see many twenty-one-year-olds around Marumaru these days.'

'Why is that?'

He looked up at me and narrowed his eyes.

'I helped raise the funds for the memorial clock tower,' he began stuffing tobacco in his pipe, 'but workmen are hard to find. Every bleeding town wants a tower or an obelisk or a fountain. I love this town dearly, but as a guest you will understand how we must wait in line for our bigger brothers to receive their portion before we can step up to the table.'

He lit his pipe and drew on it a few times. He must have seen my expression. 'John, let me tell you something your hero told me the first day I laid eyes on him. He enjoyed a cigar, did old Sandow. "One small pleasure a day is sufficient," that's what he said. Not that you've asked, but here's what I say: the only thing better than one small pleasure is two small pleasures.' He laughed. 'Or one big pleasure, I suppose. Oh, come on boy, it's as if you've never seen a man smoke a pipe before.'

I had, but only through the window. The smell was something else.

'At the risk of offending you for a third time in quick succession, may I say that you don't sound particularly American?'

'You may,' I said.

He laughed again.

'Tell me about Sandow,' I said, still pressing the photograph to my chest. 'When was he last in Marumaru?'

'Just after that photograph was taken.'

'He has only been here once?'

'Just the once. Last I heard he was still calling Britannia home.'

'Tell me about the time he came here.'

Jesse's eyes widened. 'You know what the folks out there will tell you?' He nodded toward the street. 'The best way to lose an afternoon is to ask me to tell you a story.' He laughed again, his hands bouncing on his belly.

'I have all afternoon,' I said and leant back in my chair.

Jesse told the story of his arrival in Marumaru, how he got off the train at the wrong station with Sandow's plaster statue and had to convince Harry Rickards to put on a show in the town.

He went on to explain the revelry afterwards that culminated in him losing his virginity with his dear sweet Julia. Sandow hardly featured and I was frequently confused, but there was something thrilling about listening to him talk.

When he finally checked his pocket watch he announced, 'True to my word as always. Your afternoon, sir, has been soundly squandered.'

'No,' I said. 'It hasn't been a waste at all. I only wish you would continue.'

'Perhaps another day.' He smoothed the edges of his moustache with his thumb and forefinger. 'Mrs Hikuroa controls the vote in the domestic sphere and I am expected home.'

'Tomorrow,' I said, rising from my seat.

He laughed. 'Well, I can't guarantee I will be free, but there's no harm stopping by.'

'Thank you,' I said and held out my hand for him to shake it.

My father was waiting for me when I got home.

'Where the bloody hell have you been?'

'To town,' I said and folded my arms.

'I thought I told you to stay put?'

'I don't see why I need to hide away any more. I'm not going back in that window. They're talking about us in the newspaper.'

'Who've you been talking to?'

'No one. Just a bunch of wheezing, snivelling invalids. I need to wash my hands.'

'Eugen,' he said sharply. I stopped and turned back to face him. 'Did you find out anything about your sister?'

'No.'

'What about The Carpenter?'

'I thought that was your job. I thought that's what you were doing. If you wanted me to help, you should have asked me. I'm not useless, you know. You may have tried, but you didn't raise a fool. And I'm stronger than any man in this crummy town.'

For a moment I thought he would come for me, finally. But he just said, 'Go on, wash your hands.'

'You've lied to me.'

'When?'

'Always. You and her.' I pointed to the barn, though Flossie's body was long gone. 'The world is nothing like you said. Don't think I don't know. It's your fault Avis is missing.'

He hadn't shaved since returning from Christchurch and he rubbed the dark but patchy beard that was developing. 'You're right,' he said. 'It *is* my fault. It's up to me to get Avis back, to make things right. But I could use your help. How about helping me tomorrow? I'm going to talk to Maggie Donaldson. I think she might know where The Carpenter is hiding.'

'I'll think about it,' I said and walked away.

VI.

I didn't go with my father to Maggie Donaldson's the next day, or wherever his search took him the day after that.

The only place where things seemed to hold together was in Jesse's company. When he wasn't free, I sat on the beach, watched the rollers and slowly let my dream of being Sandow's heir dissolve and disperse. Funny to think about it now, but I never even got my toes wet.

Though I had many questions for Jesse, when I was with him I found myself leaning back in my chair, closing my eyes and letting him tell his stories: Sandow inspecting his troop in Wanganui; Jesse joining Rickards' company and leaving his mother in Kai Iwi; his decision to return to Marumaru and Julia after Sandow's tour ended in Invercargill; his work as a signwriter's apprentice; joining the army at the start of the war against Julia's wishes and the accident at Sockburn Camp that gave him his waddle and kept him from shipping out.

'I don't think Smithy was aiming for me,' he said. 'I just hope he was a better shot in the field, or else Lord help his battalion, eh? After that, I was a real misery guts. Julia had gone. I'd always been this strapping young lad. Now I was useless. Couldn't even climb a ladder. There went my livelihood. But I was still in my twenties. I just wanted to be useful. I saw all my friends shipping off to Europe and I couldn't help. Eventually I stuck a bung in that barrel of pity and looked around for another way to be useful. That's when I met Josephine, the future Mrs Hikuroa, and blossomed into a politician,' he said, his hands rising out above his belly, his lips pursing, a twinkle in his eye.

News of the war hadn't reached our property. I didn't fully understand the seriousness of it as I sat in the back room of the signwriter's. Come the Second World War, however, I would get a taste of combat—of men biting into their own biceps to forget the pain, the smell of cauterised flesh, the concussive blast of shells striking you long after you've seen them explode. I was thirty-six when that one started, still fit as anyone, quick as a panther, strong as an ox. But individual speed and strength didn't count for much any more. The war, in Europe at least, was all about machines. What they wanted was an army of reel-turners, never anyone to run into the surf and come back alive.

All that was beyond me, though, when I was sixteen and fresh out of the window.

Everything my father had said about the window and the custom of arranged marriages was a lie, I knew that soon enough, but I couldn't see the reason for this deception. Standing in front of Donaldson's other window, the one with the two wooden figures, didn't bring any answers. But when I finally walked down Regent Street and saw the window of the town's other department store it was as if the wind had vanished and everything had gone silent. The figures in this window—four females of different ages, dressed as though they were all off to separate events—were still made of wood, but they possessed the grace and beauty that Avis and I had aspired to. They were not alive, I could tell that, but they seemed about to move.

'Admiring the competition?'

I turned and saw Jesse smiling, his hands resting on his belly.

'I'm told you've been here for over two hours. I wondered what you got up to when I wasn't boring you.'

'You don't bore me.'

'What about the young lady?' he asked. It took me a moment to realise he meant Avis. I hadn't told him she was my sister, or that Colton Kemp was our father, though I'm sure he suspected the stories in the newspaper weren't completely accurate. 'Is she still missing?' he persisted. 'I never quite understood: did she run away, or was it something more sinister?'

'The police are looking for her,' I said.

'And you're happy leaving it to them?'

I turned back to the window. 'Who made these?'

'You know that, surely. These are The Carpenter's beauties. Not a patch on—'

'This Carpenter,' I interrupted, 'is he old? Short?'

'That's the one. Been around this town longer than I have. He was the bloke who carried the statue of Sandow from the train station.'

'What do you call these?' I pointed at the figures.

'Mannequins, I suppose.'

Mannequins. I remembered the man from Christchurch using this word when he inspected us in the window.

'Where does he live?'

'The Carpenter? He has a place on Pukehine Hill. I'm sure the police have paid him a visit already.'

'Yes, I'm sure they have. Can you take me there?'

'He hasn't been seen—' Jesse began.

'Please. Take me there.'

'I'm not sure I should get any more involved than I am.'

'Then tell me how to get there.'

Jesse waddled off and told me to follow him. At the junction he said, 'This street here is Albert. You see that hill there, behind those buildings, that's Pukehine. I've never been up to his place myself, but you can see it from Stirling Road. You won't get up to any mischief, will you? Not with an election in a couple of months.'

'I just want to take a look.'

'Of course you do.'

The hill had been partly cleared for grazing. I could see no structures at first. Then I noticed an oddly sloped iron roof on the portion of hill that was still given over to scrub. I'd imagined at least two buildings, a house and a workshop like my father had, but then we had a larger family and more to hide. When I got further up the hill, it became clear that there was only this one building, which appeared to slump to one side. The timbers of the outer walls varied in colour from almost black to a light brown that was nearly blond. The two sides I could see were dominated by large windows, each made from six smaller panes. I followed the path around to the door. A busted padlock dangled from the latch. The bolt was withdrawn. My father and the constable had been here. But I wasn't here to find The Carpenter or Avis. I just wanted to understand.

I opened the door. There was no hallway. There were no internal walls at all. From the threshold I could see each of the four windows streaming with daylight, the small bed, the stove, the armchair, the rows and rows of books, the tool bench, the sawhorses, the saws, gouges, sandpaper—the same implements that occupied my father's workshop and I'd spent so long staring at while Avis and I practised posing. The floor of The Carpenter's house was covered with a fine layer of sawdust. The air smelt of honey and gasoline.

It's true, I thought. The Carpenter wanted to fool people, just like my father.

There were no full mannequins—he must have stored his finished pieces at the department store—but there were blocks of wood of various sizes in the far corner. Some were still square, as if fresh from the mill, while others had seen the gouge's edge.

A single block about the size of an oil can sat alone on the workbench. I crept closer and saw that it was covered with pencil. Closer still, I recognised the image. How could I not, having spent so long staring at that same face?

VII.

When I got home my father asked me the same question he'd asked the last four days: 'What have you been doing?'

I gave him the same response: 'Searching for Avis.'

For once this wasn't a lie.

'And?'

'The Carpenter took her. He was obsessed with her.'

'I could have told you that. Come on,' he said, tucking his shirt into his trousers, 'we're going back to talk to Maggie Donaldson.'

'Why do you need me?'

'I don't need to explain myself to you, do I, John?' He said the name with spite.

'No, you don't. But I don't need to obey you any more. And my name isn't John, it's Eugen.'

'It's John as long as I say it's John.'

'Best of luck with Maggie Donaldson,' I said and untied a bootlace.

He grabbed one of my ears and twisted it, pulling me back up until our eyes were level. I could have knocked the arm away. I could have hit him in the solar plexus. I could have caved his skull in. But I concentrated instead on not wincing. I kept my expression plain, my eyes cool and unblinking, my chest held out at its full extension.

He barely opened his mouth to speak. 'You'll do what I say.'

I held my pose, but second by second my defiance became more and more like acceptance.

'Good lad,' he said and let go of my ear.

We rode to Donaldson's farm, both of us on the same struggling horse, my father holding the reins, my arms around his chest and one side of my face planted into his back. I'd never learnt to ride a horse. It didn't seem like something people did: Emily and Charlotte were made for pulling carts and wagons, not for sitting upon. Another lie of omission from my father to keep us pinned to our property.

The Donaldson farmstead was a two-storey wooden affair with a corrugated iron roof fronted by a wide porch. The house was painted the colour of creamed spinach, though the elements were at work, bubbling and flaking the paint and revealing the whitish undercoat.

I followed my father onto the porch and stood behind him as he knocked on the door. I heard movement inside, but it was a full minute before the door opened.

Maggie Donaldson was wearing a black dress with a large square lace collar. Her face was criss-crossed with wrinkles.

'Mr Kemp,' she said. 'Two visits in one week after so long without the pleasure of your company. I am truly fortunate.'

My father placed his hand on the door frame, as if to pull himself inside the house, but she didn't move.

'I'm told your father gave The Carpenter the land on Pukehine Hill,' he said.

'I believe he did.'

'Why?'

'Oh, you poor thing,' she said. 'It must be very confusing for you. The founder of your precious store and your great rival . . . in cahoots.'

'Why?' he repeated.

She turned to the side and swung her hand down the hall. 'A few steps inside and you'll see.'

My father entered. I followed. To the right of the passage was a staircase with a balustrade of rich brown wood, the length of it carved with an intricate pattern featuring what looked like leaves and shoots. The banisters were carved in this same style, though you could tell on first glance that each was a slightly different pattern. The final post was capped by a sphere that wasn't perfectly smooth, but featured raised, undulating blobs surrounded by hundreds of tiny peaks. I didn't recognise it as a globe at the time, never having seen one.

My father stepped forward and ran his hand over the finial, his lips slightly parted.

Maggie Donaldson went into the first room off the passage. 'I'm frightful with dates,' she said, expecting us to follow, 'but he did this for my father before that other store opened.'

My father and I entered the drawing room. We both raised our eyes to the carved curtain rails and cornices.

'You mustn't feel too betrayed, dear boy,' the woman said. I thought she was addressing me for the first time, but I saw she was staring at my father.

'He did all this,' he said, still surveying the room.

'Yes, I thought we had established that. My father was a cruel man at heart, but he had a soft spot for Mr Doig. I believe he helped him get his job at Hercus & Barling.'

'Doig?' he asked.

'Yes. Gabriel Doig. I thought the man's name was common knowledge in town and that nickname of his was just some kind of elaborate parlour game.'

'Gabriel Doig,' he repeated. 'Why didn't you tell me any of this the other day?'

'Please, Mr Kemp, I am an old spinster. I am liable to feel threatened if you continue to raise your voice.'

He closed his eyes but I could see his neck muscles twitching.

'Do you know where we can find Mr Doig?' I asked.

She looked at me properly for the first time. 'If I didn't know better, Mr Kemp, I'd say you and this lad bore a family resemblance, however faint.'

'Doig has my sister,' I said. 'Where can we find them?'

'In all honesty, I cannot say. This island is not so small when you want to disappear.'

'Where did he live before your father gave him the land?' my father asked.

'Inland,' she said.

'Due west?'

'I am not a compass, Mr Kemp. I know that Doig used to come down from the hills. It was a day's ride, according to my father. When he carried out all this work,' she waved her hand in the air dismissively, 'he camped out in our barn to save him the journey.'

'A day's ride,' my father repeated.

'Of course, Mr Doig never said anything for himself. All I have is what my dear departed father told me. I would be awfully sorry if I end up sending you two on a wild goose chase.'

'I understand,' he said. 'Thank you, Mrs Donaldson.'

'*Miss* Donaldson,' she corrected.

'Yes, of course. Come, John, we have much to consider.'

VIII.

The next day we set out for the hinterland. My father rode Emily and I took Charlotte. Though neither horse was used to a saddle or a rider, they were so old they could scarcely muster the energy to throw us off. I found it easy enough to stay upright, pinching Charlotte's flanks with my strong legs. I'd pay for this technique the first few days whenever I dismounted, but I soon learnt to balance without tensing every muscle.

Ours was to be a deliberate pace—one of many niggles for my father—but it left me plenty of time to observe all the new plants and birds I hadn't seen before.

'What's that?' I'd ask whenever my father seemed up to responding.

'A hawk,' he'd say. 'A willow.' 'The river.'

The town of Marumaru—first glimpsed through the window and later explored on foot—had been a great disappointment, but the world beyond the town was infinitely richer and more fascinating than I could have ever imagined.

My father hoped to find people along the way who could direct us, or at least narrow our search, and that we'd have Avis home in a couple of days. I saw that he packed my sister's diary, though I'm not sure if he thought it would help guide our search or if he brought it for sentimental reasons. I never saw him reading it. For provisions we had a small camp oven, a sack of flour, some glass jars containing other powders and spices, several tins of sardines, a tin of biscuits, two canteens of fresh water each and a basket of apples that drove the poor horses crazy. From Bannerman, my father had borrowed two swags, a green tarpaulin for shelter if it rained, a hunting rifle and a box of cartridges. He kept the rifle slung over his back as he rode, the butt bouncing against the saddle, the muzzle pointed to the sky.

This weapon was a disturbing development. I could no longer be sure of overpowering my father when he finally turned to violence. I'm sure he told himself he was just bringing it along to scare Doig, but I didn't trust what he might do with his temper up.

After several hours we stopped to stretch our legs and eat a biscuit. 'We'd best follow the river,' he said.

'Where does the water come from?'

'From the mountains.'

'Why is it this colour?'

He grunted.

'The sea,' I persisted, 'is not this colour. A glass of water has no colour at all. And yet this river—?'

'It's melted snow.'

'Will it snow where we are going?' I asked, excited.

'It's the middle of summer, boy. There'll still be snow on the Alps because they're so high, but we're not going that far. Doig is holed up a day's ride from the coast. There's bound to be a settlement somewhere along the river. That's where they'll be, or that's where we'll find someone who knows where they are.'

He indicated that it was time to get back in the saddle. I pulled myself onto Charlotte with ease and watched as my father struggled to lift his foot into the stirrup. When he was finally up and had readjusted Bannerman's rifle, I asked, 'How many times has Sandow been to Marumaru?'

He flicked the reins and Emily started to amble forward. Charlotte snorted and decided to follow without any guidance from me.

'I don't remember.'

'You don't remember? You are always telling us about meeting Sandow. I had the impression you were in regular contact with the man.'

I'd finally drawn level and he turned to look at me.

'Who have you been talking to?'

'Jesse Hikuroa.'

'Jesse?'

'The next mayor of Marumaru.'

He snorted.

'*He* performed with Sandow.'

'He told you that, did he?'

'I saw a photograph.'

'There are photographs of you and Avis, you know? Performing in the window. They were in newspapers from Invercargill to Auckland.' His hands clenched tighter on the reins and I could tell another rant about The Carpenter was coming. 'We could have—'

He pressed his lips together and gazed at the crest of the hills on the other side of the milky river.

'I thought Sandow was my father,' I said. 'I couldn't see any of myself in you or . . . or Flossie. But I was looking for physical development, forgetting that it must be achieved, forgetting all the hours of work that went into being this strong.' I took one hand from the reins and rubbed the back of my head. 'I only hope there's some truth in what we have been taught. That a person's character can be trained as well. That it can be improved through hard work and diligence. Because I don't want to end up anything like you.'

My father reached forward and patted Emily's neck, then looked up at me. 'That's the first sensible thing you've said all day.'

We stopped at a couple of farmsteads that afternoon but no one had heard of Gabriel Doig or The Carpenter. They seemed unimpressed with us 'townies', as they called us, interrupting their day with our problems.

Toward the end of the afternoon I caught my first glimpse of the Southern Alps. Until this point, they'd been hidden by the rolling hills of the hinterland. These dark green lumps had seemed quite large and filled me with dread should we decide to drive Emily and Charlotte up their slopes, but the Alps, good God. They loomed dark as charcoal, dark as the far edge of the ocean. We set up camp in the lee of a string of willows, filled our bellies with damper, unrolled our swags and climbed inside. We both lay on our backs in silence, staring up through the willow branches at the slowly shifting stars.

'We'll press on in the morning,' my father said. 'We didn't make great time today, but that's to be expected if we're to stop so often.' His voice grew quieter, as if he were now talking to himself. 'People will be more helpful tomorrow. We'll find them soon,' he said. 'We'll bloody find them soon.'

Avis and I used to sleep under the stars once or twice every summer. We were allowed to take our bedclothes out onto the back lawn as long as we washed them ourselves afterwards. I wonder now what kind of surveillance my father carried out on us. Did he stay awake all night to ensure we didn't sneak through the hedges? Or did he make Flossie do it, since she'd told us we could sleep outside in the first place?

We'd lie on our backs, counting the stars, talking about the boy in the moon. On one of these nights we decided that he must have had a poor season in the window.

'He forgot to use the lav beforehand,' I said, 'and wet his pants during the first performance.'

'The townspeople laughed at him and turned away,' Avis said, 'consigning him to a life of solitude.'

'Knowing he would never find a wife,' I added, 'he built a skyrocket and strapped himself to it. Only he'd forgotten to light the fuse.'

'His arms were bound and he could not free himself. There he remained, strapped to his skyrocket, for seven days and nights.'

'Until,' I said, eager to push the story on, 'a forest fire swept through the town, killing everyone—'

'Except the boy strapped to the skyrocket. The fire lit his fuse and he was shot to the moon, where he remains to this day.'

'When the moon is full,' I said, 'you can still see the scars on his face from the fire.'

'But he survived,' Avis insisted.

'Yes. He had the last laugh. The crescent moon is actually his smile, if you tilt your head.'

'A happy ending.'

'So long as you tilt your head the right way.'

That first night on the trail with my father, the moon had just begun to wane. It would be another week before the boy's smile began to show. The next day we continued west, following the river, stopping at every house to ask about Doig and returning to the trail each time none the wiser.

'They can't have made it this far west,' my father said some time after midday. We'd come to a stretch where the river widened into dozens of smaller streams and rivulets after passing through a bush-clad gorge. Some of the islands in the river were so large they had their own narrow forests of tea tree and fern. 'We're too far south. That's the problem.'

In the last three weeks my world had expanded from a few acres to include the town of Marumaru and now this sweeping landscape only partly tamed by man. I felt we could search for the rest of our lives and never find Avis. Part of me would have been all right with this. The world seemed full of wonder, teeming with space, ripe for adventure.

'Yes,' I said. 'I'm sure someone will help us further north.'

It was harder going once we left the river. The trails were overgrown and hilly. We spent a lot of time on foot leading our mounts, tugging at their reins.

We didn't encounter another soul the whole of our third day. It was no use trying to make conversation with my father as he was so often out of breath and in a permanent huff.

Late on the morning of our fourth day we joined a larger trail and soon came across a team of bullocks, their driver walking beside them. He seemed full of energy and carried a whip attached to a stick that was six or seven feet long. We got down from our horses and the bullock driver pulled on the yoke of the front pair with his free hand and the team drew to a stop.

'Morning,' he said, brushing off his shirtsleeves and rubbing his hands together.

'I haven't seen a team like this since I was a boy,' my father said.

'Not every road is a highway,' the man said. 'Not yet.' By the sound of his voice, it seemed my father was already offside with him.

'We're looking for a man by the name of Gabriel Doig. Some people know him as The Carpenter. He has a place a day's ride from the coast.'

'The coast.' The man turned to look at me, then back to my father.

'Do you know of this man?' my father asked.

He shook his head. 'I've been running this team back and forth a dozen years, never heard the name Doig.'

'Yes, well, he mightn't have been round here much in that time. But he lived up here eighteen, twenty years ago.'

'What have you got against this man?' The driver's eyes drifted up the barrel of Bannerman's rifle that showed above my father's shoulder.

'He has my daughter.'

'This is the place you'd run off to,' he said and brushed the dust off the thighs of his heavy trousers. 'I'm sorry I can't be of any help to you blokes.' My father nodded.

The man cracked his whip and the bullocks swung their heads forward. They began to trudge up the trail, the driver letting each pair pass until the dray, loaded with heavy bales, came level with him. He stuck a hand out, caught one of the ropes that secured the load and pulled himself up so that one foot rested on the frame of the dray and the other swung free. 'Best of luck finding your daughter.'

My father raised his hand to the brim of his hat. 'He knows something,' he said under his breath. 'We're on the right track, boy. Come on.'

I tended to fall in behind my father on the trail, which meant Bannerman's rifle was always right there in front of me: the dents in the rich wood of the stock, as if it had been struck with a tiny hammer; the way the trigger guard stretched down the base of the weapon and ended in the kind of wrought iron scroll that decorated our front gate; the sights sticking up like errant teeth at either end of the barrel.

We encountered more people along the trail that day. A woman picking raspberries, a lone priest riding south, a team of small boys swimming in a dark pond ringed with lime green algae. Each time they claimed not to recognise the name Gabriel Doig and each time my father decided they were lying.

'We're getting closer,' he told me. 'I can feel it. I can see it on their faces. I can hear it in their voices.'

'I'm glad you can,' I said. 'All I see are the glances they give that rifle.'

'You think they'd stop and talk to us without it?'

'Perhaps,' I said.

'Listen, I'm not going to use it. It's not even loaded.'

'What about when we find Doig?'

'It'll give him a fright, won't it?'

'It won't be loaded?'

'No.'

'And you don't want me to rough him up a bit? I thought that was the only reason you brought me along.'

'You're a part of this too, boy. We're getting your sister back.'

'Have you thought about what he's doing to her up here, Father?'

'Of course I have. It's all I think about.'

'And what if it's true? What if he's defiled her?'

'Eugen—'

'What if he's killed her? Are you telling me you won't reach for the cartridges?'

'That's enough, Eugen.'

We rode further north before bearing toward the Alps once more. The next day we backtracked and proceeded further east, back toward the coast, though I never saw anything that faintly resembled Marumaru. By this time we'd established a new routine. The rhythm of our horses plodding forward, the hastily cooked meals, the time spent lying beneath the stars, each with our own thoughts. We were yet to encounter rain, but by the dry and crumbling trails, the parched paddocks and earth-coloured sheep, it was clear the good weather had begun well before we took to our horses.

Though we continued to break new ground every day, the landscape became more familiar to me. There was less and less to ask my father about and eventually my thoughts returned to Marumaru.

'Tell me about Louisa,' I said one day toward the end of our first week or the beginning of our second.

My horse was level with my father's, but he turned his head down and away from me.

'She was our mother. That's what Flossie told us.'

'I don't want to talk about such things.'

'But I do,' I said. 'I have a right to know.'

I saw his Adam's apple rise and fall as he swallowed. 'When did Flossie tell you?'

'In the anteroom. The last time we saw her.'

'I see.'

'She said our mother died giving birth to us.'

'She's dead,' he said.

'Do you blame us? Is that it?'

'Eugen—'

'What is it?'

He turned to me, the lower rims of his eyelids red and glistening. He shook his head. 'We'll not talk of such things.'

That night, as I lay awake, looking at the crescent moon, my father spoke.

'I loved Louisa very much,' he said faintly.

I wriggled down in my swag so that my ear was closer to him.

'She could draw anything. I would pass her a pencil and it became a part of her. It did what she wanted it to do. She encouraged me to make my own mannequins.' He gave a bitter laugh. 'If she knew how much it would madden me, the tools, the wood, she may have kept her mouth shut. But she believed in me.'

He said nothing more that night, though I stayed still, my ear level with his mouth, waiting for another word.

The next morning he was his gruff self. *Saddle the horses, fill the canteens, wipe the ashes off the camp oven*—as if he hadn't spoken a word about my mother. He met the day's frustrations— the blank faces of the locals, the horses stopping to feast upon every budding fern—with the same set jaw and white knuckles. But that night, he spoke again.

'Her father didn't approve of me. I understand why. My father was very old by the time I was born. I didn't grow up cultured. I wasn't pampered. But I loved her. I loved her so much that it was impossible for her to refuse me. Her face. I still see it every time I close my eyes. The thin eyebrows. The cleft in her chin. The big eyes. I tried to carve it so many times, but it was beyond me.'

Over the next twelve nights, he told the story of how he met my mother on a buying trip to Christchurch with Old Man Donaldson. He explained how she'd sketched the plans for his window displays. How her parents had attended the mayor's picnic in the Cashmere Hills, the sudden hailstorm that overtook them, the influenza and deaths that followed.

He spoke about the last day of 1902 and the first of 1903. I've tried to piece them together to explain to myself what took him down his dark path, but even I'm not completely satisfied by the explanation. A full account might stretch back to his own childhood, or the life his itinerant father led before arriving in Marumaru, or the life of his father's father.

I understood the contract I'd entered into with my father on those nights beneath the stars. If I wished to learn more, if I wanted the stories to continue, I had to keep silent. I hoped that unburdening himself at night would ease the tension he showed during the day, but it didn't appear to work this way. In the dark, though, he was just a voice. In the dark, he possessed a chilling calm.

'I'm a broken man,' he began one night. 'I have a black heart. It doesn't make it any easier to know this. It makes it worse.

'I walked around Marumaru for forty-eight hours pretending Louisa was still alive. After that, I pretended my children were dead. In the middle of all this, I went to a show. A vaudeville show with sopranos and dancing ponies.

'When I saw Sandow, something twigged. Something broke. I couldn't keep failing. If I could unveil the perfect mannequins, if I could trump The Carpenter, perhaps I could recover Louisa, or at least honour her. I found McCann, the troupe's accordion player who doubled as vet and doctor, and brought him back to my property to make sure the two of you would survive. Would have a chance to grow up strong. McCann left Marumaru with the rest of the company and took my secret with him.'

He let out a long, crackling sigh.

'It cannot end well for me. But I've been play-acting. All this time. Ever since that day. None of it has felt completely real to me. It's no excuse.

'I convinced myself that if we could just get to Christchurch, to the window of Ballantynes, everything would be all right. But it was just something to distract me from the fact I was running headlong for the edge of the cliff.

'I know how it will end, because I was there when it ended. This is all a long dream. For some, a nightmare. When you wake, when you see the full horror of it, there's no forgiveness. Don't wait for it to arrive. Time doesn't soften a man. Time can't restore what has been lost. In fairy tales, perhaps. On a stage or through a window, perhaps. But not in life.'

IX.

'Quiet fellow?' he asked.

'Yes.'

'Short bloke?'

'Yes!'

My father took the old farmer's shoulder in his hand. We'd been searching the hinterland for three weeks. Our biscuits and flour were long gone and we'd resorted to raiding plum trees and even eating raw crabapples. Rabbits were common at dusk, though my father only ever managed to shoot one, running the bullet through its gut and tainting the meat. Though he held his facade during daylight, I suspected the fire had gone out of his endeavours. He'd even started leaving Bannerman's rifle strapped to his horse for his interrogations. But, all at once, he was in full flame.

'Father,' I said, worried what he might do to the farmer.

'Where is he? Where is Doig?'

The man looked up into the sky. 'Used to see him around these parts,' he said, his voice trying hard not to waver. He was fat-faced, but otherwise malnourished. 'Caught him stealing scrap behind my barn one time. Thought he was sneaking round with one of my daughters.' He snorted. 'Thought he was just a boy. Short fellow. Big hands, though. Up close, you could see the wrinkles.'

'Where is he?' my father asked again.

'Didn't see him round here for years and years. My daughters have all moved away, you know. Then just recently, I saw him. The years haven't been kind to either of us, it seems. He's a little stooped now. Always a pity when you have no stature to begin with. Me, I can barely make a fist.' He held out his gnarled hand to demonstrate.

I peeled my father's hand from the old man's shoulder. 'Sir,' I said, 'where can we find Mr Doig?'

'I've never seen it, but apparently there's a hut up Crossman's Gully.'

'How do we get there?' I asked.

'Is he all right?' He nodded at my father.

'He's fine. Could you draw us a map?'

The man took a step back across his threshold.

'A map,' I repeated, 'then we'll be gone.'

He lowered his head and disappeared inside the house.

'Doig,' my father said, looking back at the old man's gate. 'Doig.'

After a couple of minutes the old farmer returned with a piece of paper. 'You'll be better setting out in the morning,' he said and handed me the map he'd drawn. 'Crossman's Gully isn't too far as the crow flies, but I believe it's still a rough ride.'

'We'll go tonight,' my father shouted from the verandah.

I looked at the map. Lines, squiggles and two rudimentary house shapes—triangles on squares—with some writing beneath them.

'Where are we now?' I asked.

'Here,' the man said, pointing at the house at the bottom left-hand corner. He looked up at me, squinting. 'That's the river, there. You'll need to get back on the main road here,' he said, tapping the paper. 'You'll see the cliffs from the road. I've never been further than that myself.'

I thanked him.

'Good, good. You sure your partner's all right?'

'Right as he'll ever be,' I said.

I didn't get a sense of the scale of the rough map until we were back on the trail. The sun was behind the hills already and we only had an hour or so until dark, though it promised to be one of those late summer nights that clung to the heat of the day.

'We can't make it there tonight,' I said, consulting the map again as Emily and Charlotte plodded on.

'What do you expect me to do?' my father shouted from in front of me. 'Lie down and tell campfire stories with *them* just over the next rise?' He pulled hard on Emily's reins.

'It's further than that,' I said, drawing level with him. 'I think it's another hour's ride at least. The horses are tired. We don't know the area. If we get lost or one of us falls—'

'Give me the map.' He snatched for it.

I pulled it away and began to fold the piece of paper. 'I say we set up camp down there by the stream. We can start again at sunrise.' Charlotte began to wheel around, turning me away from my father.

'I'll not spend another night on this trail, do you hear me?'

'I hear you,' I said. 'I hear you at night, too.' I reined Charlotte in and turned back to him.

He brought his hand up to his cheek and scraped his fingernails through the bristles of his beard. 'You think that gives you some power over me, don't you? Knowledge is power, isn't that what they say?'

I'd never heard the phrase before, but it seemed to make sense. Before the window I may have questioned it. Wasn't strength power? Wasn't possession? But I was learning how easily things could be snatched away from you. How the only way to get them back, the only way to retain the smallest piece, was knowledge. I pressed the folded map to my chest.

'You know nothing,' he continued.

'And whose fault is that?'

'You never once sneaked out to see what was waiting outside. What kind of boy shows so little curiosity?'

'How do you know I never sneaked out?'

'What kind of boy waits a week before he walks past the front gate when there's nothing left for him at home?'

'You told me—'

'What kind of boy does what he's told?'

I got down from the saddle and began loosening the straps that fastened my swag. 'Go on, then,' I said. 'If you want to find them tonight, I wish you all the luck in the world. But Charlotte and I need a rest.'

'Give me the map, Eugen.'

'You'll have to come down and get it.' I patted my shirt pocket and puffed out my chest. 'I warn you, though. I may not know anything, but I'm strong. I'm willing to pit my strength against your knowledge. Then we'll see what power really is.'

My father glared at me for a moment. Then he flicked the reins, dug his heels into Emily and the pair of them ambled away.

That night the moon was nearly full and I could see the scars on the boy's face. Had there been a time when he was strapped to the rocket and the flames of the forest fire were overtaking him and he thought the rocket wouldn't work? Perhaps the fuse was too long and he would be a cinder before he was propelled into space. Could he hear the screams of his parents inside the house as they were burnt alive? His neighbours? The same people who'd left him strapped to a rocket for seven days and nights because he'd wet his pants in the window. Was it worth it: being burnt to hear them burning? What did he think when the fuse finally burned down and the powder exploded and he was thrust up and away from his lousy town?

X.

I must have slept because when I woke in the morning the temperature had dropped, the sky had clouded over and the first spits of rain were starting to fall. I hoped to catch up with my father before he made it to Doig's hut, but his trail was soon washed away by the rain. It took me over two hours to find the sandstone cliffs at the start of Crossman's Gully. I only spotted them because of the map, because I was looking for them. We may well have ridden past that spot once before. My decision to wait for the morning had been the right one, but there was still a chance my father had made it. That he was there ahead of me.

Long grass, heavy from the persistent drizzle, almost covered the narrow track that ran beside the cliffs. Charlotte's hoofs made no noise against the ground but I could hear the swish of her shins against the vegetation. I considered what I might find when I arrived at the hut. The Carpenter's body in a pool of his own blood. Avis in my father's arms. My father with his back straight, his chin resting on the top of my sister's golden head. Rescuer. Murderer. But if he wasn't there, I could rescue Avis, negotiate with Doig, let him ride away and escape my father's wrath. 'Let him come at me,' I'd say. 'Let's see him overpower me.'

As the gully narrowed, I realised there might be no other way out. Perhaps there'd be no escape for The Carpenter. I could send him on his way, only for him to be met by my father and killed. Perhaps he could scramble up the cliff face.

I entered the clearing. A grey mare was grazing a hundred feet away. Behind her a hut, small and rickety. The door was shut and there were no windows on the side facing me. Behind it the cliffs came together in a dark crease. As I drew nearer, I saw a small dray parked beside the hut; a metal drum and other pieces of scrap littered the ground.

There was no sign of my father or his horse. No smoke wafted from the hut's mud brick chimney. This must have been the place the old farmer had told me about. He'd seen Doig recently. But that didn't mean he and Avis were still inside.

I dismounted and walked the final few yards to the hut. There was a sign on the door. I ran my finger up and down and up the groove of the first letter. The wood was untreated, freshly carved.

There were tiny gaps between the timbers of the walls and a smell came through that was moist and sour, rank and enticing. I closed my eyes and saw Avis in the moonlight, her hair tumbling onto my chest, her lips just leaving my skin, her eyes looking into mine. I looked at the door knob. It had been carved, too, though this piece had been varnished and handled many times. It was a face. A boy, soft-cheeked, thin-lipped, his eyes averted. I placed my palm over this face and turned.

Light entered the small space. In front of me was a man slouched in an armchair, his head and torso covered by a brown wool coat. The Carpenter's suit. The Carpenter.

He'd heard the door, detected the morning light coming through the entrance. He roused himself and slowly lowered the coat from his face until it slipped to the floor. He was bare-chested and not wearing any trousers. I hardly recognised the old man.

Over the corner of the armchair I noticed the white chiffon of Avis's dress.

There was movement to my left: Avis sitting up in the single bed.

She looked at me, briefly, before turning to Doig. Their eyes locked. No one spoke.

Avis held the heavy grey blanket across her chest.

'Eugen,' she said at last.

'Father is coming,' I said.

'Eugen,' she said, her eyes wide, 'you've found us!' Although she still held the blanket I could see the side of her flimsy white slip, the lines of her ribcage appearing and disappearing as she breathed.

'Get up,' I shouted. 'Both of you.'

'Please, Eugen, calm down.'

'Get up,' I said again. 'Father is coming.'

Doig remained silent. For a moment it was as if he were deaf as well as dumb.

'Up,' I said, gesturing with my finger.

He pushed himself up from the armchair with some effort. He stood there in his yellowed drawers. The scars that ringed his ankles and wrists were like earthworms.

They must have known I was coming, I thought. Perhaps they'd heard Charlotte's approach and Doig had leapt from the bed and taken up his position in the armchair. They took me for a fool. I'd seen the look they shared.

'What have you done to her?' I asked.

He held out his palms, his eyes as wide as my sister's.

'Please, Eugen, calm down.'

'Don't defend him, Avis.' I stepped nearer to Doig, an arm's length away.

'He doesn't need defending. It's the truth.'

I turned to Avis, still sitting in the bed. Her eyes dropped down to my waist. At first I thought she was too ashamed to meet my gaze. Then I realised she was looking at my fists, clenching and unclenching invisible spring-grip dumb-bells.

'Please, Eugen, calm down.'

'Get out of the bed,' I said. I shook my head. 'You disgust me. Both of you.' I walked over, tore the blanket away and threw it across the room. 'Up,' I told her.

As she lowered her legs to the floor the smooth white skin of her shins caught the light from the open door. She took a step toward Doig, her arms folded across her chest. Her hair seemed darker, wilder.

'Aren't you going to run to me?' I asked.

'Eugen,' she said. 'Please calm down.'

'I am calm.' I unclenched my fists and wriggled my fingers. 'I'm calm. You're lucky that I've found you and not Father.'

They were shoulder to shoulder now. Doig's hand moved behind my sister's back.

'No,' I shouted. 'There will be none of that. Step apart.'

'Eugen.'

'Step apart!'

Doig hung his head and cupped his hands over his privates, as if his drawers no longer offered enough protection.

Avis placed her dress over her arm and picked up The Carpenter's trousers.

'Leave those,' I said.

'At least let us get dressed.'

'You should have thought about that before you got undressed.'

'Eugen,' she said, exasperated, 'you know how warm it was last night. Gabriel slept in the chair and let me have his bed. You saw.'

'I know what you do in other men's beds.'

'For goodness' sake. Take a deep breath and then let's start this over again.' She handed Doig his trousers and went back for his shirt.

'Leave it,' I said.

Doig looked up, one leg already in his trousers.

Avis picked up the shirt and held it to her chest. 'Don't worry about him, Gabriel. He's just worked up.'

'Worked up?'

'Let us get dressed and we can talk.'

'What is there to talk about? You're coming back with me.'

'And what about Gabriel?'

He buttoned his trousers and Avis handed him his shirt.

'If he had any sense he'd be halfway down the gully by now.'

'Half naked?'

'That's not my fault.'

'We were at opposite ends of the hut. Asleep.'

'So you say.' I narrowed my eyes. 'Sun's been up a long time, Avis. Whatever life you've been leading up here, it doesn't become you. Look at your arms.'

'What is wrong with them?'

'Nothing, if you're happy with sausages for arms.'

I saw her neck redden and noticed she was still wearing the seashell necklace my father had given her. I stepped forward and took it in my hand.

'Everything we worked for,' I said, so close to Avis I could feel her breath. 'You know it was a lie, don't you?'

She blinked deliberately.

'The world is full of weaklings and invalids.' I looked at Doig, who was still holding his shirt in two hands, as if he were about to throw it over a smouldering fire to snuff the flames. 'We're better than them, Avis. We can be better than them.'

'We're not leaving.'

'We? Is there room enough for three in that fine bed of yours?'

'I'm not ready to leave,' she said. 'I want to stay here with Gabriel a little longer. I'm—'

'What are you telling me? That you'd rather be with this shrunken old man than me?'

'Eugen.'

'Stop saying my name like that.'

'What am I supposed to say?'

'Say it's not what it seems. Say you were kidnapped and he forced himself on you. Say you're pleased to see me.'

'I am pleased to see you.'

'That's a start. Now act as if you mean it.'

'But we haven't . . .' She let her dress drop to the floor. She breathed deeply and the silk slip shimmered. 'Gabriel hasn't forced me to do anything. He's the sweetest—'

'No,' I said and grabbed her shoulders. I could feel the pricks of her gooseflesh. She lowered her head.

'He stole you from the window.'

'He rescued me. We'd been left there all afternoon and evening. The curtain was never coming down.'

'Look at me. You don't have to stay here. We don't have to go back to the way things were, either. We can't. But we can do whatever we want. We can go anywhere. Don't worry about Father. I can handle him. I'll bend the barrel of Bannerman's rifle if necessary.' I let go of her shoulders and stooped to pick up her dress. 'Put this on.'

She took the dress and pressed it to her body.

I placed my hand on Doig's chest. 'I don't know what you've told her. Or how—'

'Here,' Avis said, taking a pile of pages from beneath the bed. 'Here's everything you need to know.'

She knew I couldn't read any of it. She was showing me how separate we had become, how helpless I was without her. I batted the pages away, the stack striking the wall and fanning out across the floor. Doig reached down to pick up a page that had slid near his feet, but I grabbed him by the wrist. The scarred flesh was cool and surprisingly smooth in my grip.

I shook my head. Still holding his wrist, I turned to Avis. 'Get dressed.'

'Why?' she asked. I could see her nipples through the slip. As with her hair, they seemed much darker. Perhaps it was the dimness of the hut, I thought. Or an effect of the pearlescent silk, or the fact she'd been kept inside for weeks.

She let the dress drop to the floor for a second time and pulled the slip over her head. 'You've seen me unencumbered almost every day of our lives. You know my body, outside and in.'

I let go of Doig's wrist and looked into his eyes. He knew. She'd told him everything.

'There's really nothing to be ashamed of,' she continued in a sing-song voice.

'Stop it!'

'Stop what, Eugen?'

I slapped her with the back of my hand.

She held her cheek and looked at me, her eyes suddenly cold. I waited for her to blink but she refused. I raised my hand as if to slap her again but Doig stepped between us and caught my elbow. 'Get off me, old man,' I said and pushed him to the floor.

'Eugen, please.'

'You've got fat,' I said. 'You disgust me.'

'I'm not fat, Eugen. I'm pregnant.' That tone. That damned know-it-all tone.

Doig had raised himself onto one knee but his head hung down in shame or exhaustion. When he raised his eyes to mine I felt something give way within me. An almost physical shudder.

I heard myself say, 'You bastard,' and watched as my foot swung toward his head, making contact with his jaw and folding his body back awkwardly.

Avis continued to scream my name, but I was on top of Doig now, my fingers around his leathery neck, his head trying to shake but struggling in my grip. I seemed to have so much time. I saw him through the window in his brown suit, ogling Avis. I saw his wooden figures, his *mannequins*, in the window of Hercus & Barling, each in their own little world. I saw the inside of Doig's house, the block of wood on the workbench, his pencil sketch of my sister. His mouth opened and I looked into his dark gullet. I closed my eyes and listened to the crackle from his throat as he tried to talk, tried to breathe, tried to wrest my hands from his neck. I saw Avis and me through The Carpenter's eyes, posing in the window, still as wood, dead as iron. I felt Avis pulling at my shoulders, beating against my back, but it was nothing to me. She'd grown weak. Her hands were fluttering moths. I felt his windpipe pop and let my fingers tighten more, let them plunge deeper into him until I was no longer hearing noises.

I opened my eyes and gave one final squeeze.

XI.

I've saved many more lives than I've taken, but the ledger will never leave the red. There's always that doubt after you've brought someone in from the surf that they might have made it out themselves, or that another swimmer would have come to their rescue. Sometimes, it's as if they got into trouble only because they knew the beach was patrolled.

But there's nothing more definitive than taking a life. You can tell yourself he was old and probably would have died in a couple of years, or that there was another man about to burst into the scene who might have killed him anyway—*might* have—but the fact remains: you did it with your own two hands.

I was still sitting on Doig's chest when my father came through the open door. I turned and saw him standing there. His hands were empty. The barrel of Bannerman's rifle didn't show above his shoulder. He didn't look like some avenging angel, a force of nature. He seemed in those first seconds like a confused little boy.

Avis got up from the floor, where she'd been sobbing, ran to him and they embraced: my father dressed in the same grubby undershirt and trousers he'd worn the last three weeks, my sister completely naked.

She tried to talk through her tears. 'Calm down,' my father told her. 'Take a breath. I'm here now, Avis. I'm here.'

'He,' she said and took a deep breath, 'killed him.'

He placed his chin on the top of her head and looked at me. I got to my feet.

'He's dead,' I said.

'I,' he paused, 'I can see that.'

Avis pushed herself away from my father. 'Is that all you're going to say? Don't you care?'

. He reached down for her slip. 'Put this on.'

'You don't understand. Neither of you do.'

He tried to place his hand on her shoulder but she shrugged it off.

'You don't have to talk about it, Avis, if you don't want to. We can never speak about what Doig did to you, if that's your wish. It's my fault you were taken. I should never have left you in the window.'

'You don't understand,' she repeated and finally snatched the slip from his hand. 'Gabriel *rescued* me. He never touched me. But you two . . .' She started crying again as she dragged the slip over her head.

My father turned to me. 'What happened here?'

'I beat you to it,' I said.

'You can't just kill a man,' he said slowly. 'What happened? Why?'

I shrugged. 'Don't say you wouldn't have done the same thing.'

Avis was pulling on the hem of her slip and swaying gently.

'He didn't touch you?' my father asked her. 'Why'd he bring you up here? Why were you naked?'

'He rescued me. And Eugen killed him.'

'All right, all right,' my father said. 'We can sort this out.'

'How?' Avis wailed. 'Gabriel's dead.' She slipped past my father and ran out the door.

My father called her name and went after her. I stood over Doig for a moment. His eyes were still open, but they were cloudy and lifeless, like the eyes of a fish out of the sea for too long.

Outside, the drizzle had stopped but the ground was still damp.

'Stay away from me,' I heard my sister shout. 'You're a monster. You're both monsters.'

I came around the corner and saw her waving what looked like a gouge at my father.

'Put it down, Avis,' he said dismissively.

'It's your fault,' she said, her face red and puffy. 'It's your fault we're like this. It's your fault he's dead.'

'Flossie,' I said, remembering her for the first time since finding the hut.

'What about her?' Avis asked, the fear evident on her face.

I shook my head. 'It's just the three of us now.'

She let the gouge drop to the ground. 'She's dead?'

'Eugen,' my father said. 'Just . . . Just clear off for a minute. You're not helping.'

Avis was on her knees now, in the mud, her head in her hands. 'I don't want this. I don't want any of this.'

My father placed his hand on her head. 'I know, I know.'

'I can't do it,' she said, hysterical now. 'I don't want this. I don't want this child.'

'Child?' My father turned to me.

'Now do you understand—' I began.

'It's yours, Eugen,' she said. 'It's yours.'

'No. You're wrong. It's Doig's.' I looked up at my father. 'I saw them together. Well, not *together*. But Father, it's as we suspected.'

Avis stood up. The way she held her hips forward, her belly caught the light. It was only a small bulge but it was there.

'I can't believe this made me happy,' she said, rubbing her belly. 'Even when I knew all of the lies, this made me happy.' She sobbed again.

My father turned to me. 'You defiled your sister?'

'It's not my child,' I said. 'It can't be.'

'You stupid boy.' He struck me across the face with the back of his hand.

I took two handfuls of undershirt and pinned him against the wall of the hut. 'Don't touch me,' I spat. He was shaking his head. 'Don't you ever touch me again.' I shook him and let him drop to the mud.

I turned and saw Avis running down the slope, past the horses. 'Avis?' I shouted but she kept running, the morning sun shimmering on the patches of her silk slip that weren't covered in mud. Her feet were bare but she didn't seem worried about sharp stones or rabbit holes.

I set off after her. It felt good to run, to work my legs, my arms, my chest, without violence.

Avis looked over her shoulder and saw me in pursuit. She must have realised then that she could never outrun me because she veered toward a pile of rocks and boulders at the base of the cliffs and started climbing.

'Come on now, Avis,' I called. 'You're in a state. Be careful.'

She was swiftly on top of the first boulder and leant against the trunk of a cabbage tree as she pushed herself higher.

'We can work something out,' I said from the base of the rock fall. 'We can start new lives.' She kept climbing without looking down. 'You know I could come up there and get you. You're going to hurt yourself.' I pulled myself up the first boulder. 'Avis? Come on now. Please. I'm sorry.'

She'd reached the end of the rock fall and was met with the vertical cliff face. Without pausing she slipped her fingers into one of the pock marks that riddled the rock and lifted herself up.

'Avis,' my father called from the grass below. 'Eugen, get her down from there.'

I made it to the cliff face and found my first hold. Though I wasn't used to climbing like this, I was fit and strong. She was about ten feet above me, but I would catch her.

'If you stop there,' I said, leaning out from the rock, 'I can help you climb back down.'

'No.'

I took it as a good sign that she was talking to me again. I pulled myself up a few more feet, then a few more. I could almost reach her ankle. I looked up and saw that she was still a way from the top. The pock marks had run out, leaving her nowhere to put her hands.

I reached up and gently took her heel between my thumb and forefinger. 'Got you,' I said.

She shook herself free and lunged for a hold far to her right. I couldn't see if her fingers had latched onto anything, but for a moment she hung there, still, and it looked as though she'd made it. But then her feet began to scrabble against the smooth rock, trying to find a ledge, a seam, anything to take her weight. She brought her free arm up to meet her other hand, but, rather than steady her, this manoeuvre sent her sliding down the rock face.

I thrust out my hand but she was too far across and I caught nothing but air.

I remember hearing my father call her name as she fell, but for the life of me I can't remember if she made a sound.

XII.

My father got on his horse, rode to the nearest township with a constable and brought the force back to Crossman's Gully. I wasn't there when they returned. Charlotte and I were plodding north with a small purse of money and my sister's diary—parting gifts from my father. I also had the pages Gabriel Doig had written, the ones Avis had promised would explain everything. We made Christchurch in a couple of days. I bought a pile of newspapers and asked the landlady of my lodging house to read me anything about murder, suicide or tragic accidents.

'You don't look like the murdering kind,' she said, rubbing my upper arm.

'It's not me,' I said. 'But I heard an upsetting rumour about a friend.'

According to the papers, Colton Kemp, a window dresser from Marumaru, had admitted to murdering his rival, Gabriel Doig, in the hinterland. He also admitted that Avis was his daughter and blamed himself for her falling to her death. He showed compunction, the papers said, but may still face the hangman's noose. There was no mention of a son or a brother.

I quickly ran out of money, but my landlady and I came to an arrangement. Funny, but I can hardly remember her. I can't see her face or hear her voice. Good riddance.

A year went by in a blur of disappointment. Sometimes I'd walk past Ballantynes and catch my reflection in the glass. I was becoming grey and shrunken like the rest of the population. I returned to my routines, morning and evening, and started to feel better. Then the news of my father's prison sentence found me. Perhaps it was my landlady who told me. I remember asking her for the money to go abroad. She must have refused. She probably felt betrayed. This wouldn't have been helped by the fact I stole some of her jewellery. That's how I paid for my passage aboard the *Moeraki*, how I came to Sydney, to Collaroy, to the top of the escarpment at MacLeans Lookout, where I survey the Pacific. Sometimes I see all the way down to Antipodes Island. Sometimes back to Marumaru, back to that day in 1903 when Sandow came to town. Sometimes I see my father in prison, tracing my mother's face with his finger on the wall of his cell. He's dead now. He must be.

'What are you running from?' June Hervey asked me on more than one occasion. She was the best of my tutors, the greatest of my Collaroy loves.

'I'm not running,' I'd say. 'I'm staying put.'

'That's not what I mean, Sandy.'

I couldn't tell her. I didn't want to lose her. And I didn't, not for a long while.

As I've said, I've known love and I've known happiness, both in Marumaru and in Collaroy. What does it take to find happiness after you've felt another man's windpipe pop beneath your grip and seen his eyes roll back into his skull? After you've laid your sister's broken body on the ground and walked away? After years of being visited in dreams by golden-haired children who claim you're their father? It takes strength. It takes fortitude. Perseverance. Maybe even grace. It's a test of character befitting my father's window. Some mornings it's physical, a great weight bearing down on me as I trudge up to Collaroy Plateau. I'm a creature of habit, a slave to symmetry. I'm saved daily by simple routines.

The bronzed young things at the surf club are always asking, 'How do you keep in such good shape, Sandy?'

'I stick to my routines,' I say. 'This is my shape. This is who I am.'

Acknowledgments

This book started with an idea—two ideas, actually—that needed to take place in the past: a time of department stores and sailing ships, a time without television or aeroplanes. Because I started with these ideas, these fictions, and because I'd never written anything set before the year of my birth, I began with a rather cavalier attitude to history. I disliked the term 'historical fiction', as it seemed to have things backwards. The Italians say it better: *romanzi storici*. The fiction comes first and the history is just the wallpaper. This seemed true, at least, for the novel I was working on. But I soon learnt that I couldn't provide that wallpaper by myself and I gave in to the charms of research.

The following sources proved the best company over the past few years and have all made their mark on the book you now hold: the stories, gossip columns and ads offered up by Papers Past (www.paperspast.natlib.govt.nz/), and its Australian counterpart (www.trove.nla.gov.au); *Leisure and Pleasure: Reshaping and Revealing the New Zealand Body 1900–1960* by Caroline Daley (Auckland University Press, 2003); *Houdini, Tarzan, and the Perfect Man: The White Male Body and The Challenge of Modernity in America* by John F. Kasson (Hill and Wang, 2001); Eugen Sandow's own books and booklets; Helen B. Laurenson's *Going Up, Going Down: The Rise and Fall of the*

Department Store (Auckland University Press, 2005); *Scotland: A Concise Cultural History* edited by Paul H. Scott (Mainstream, 1993); Inverclyde Council's history pages on its website (www. inverclyde.gov.uk/community-life-and-leisure/local-history-and-heritage); *Wood-Carving, Design and Workmanship* by George Jack (D. Appleton and Company, 1903), *Figureheads and Ship Carving* by Michael Stammers (Naval Inst. Press, 2005); *Ships' Figure Heads in Australia* by Gordon de L. Marshall (Tangee, 2003); *Tall Ships* by Philip McCutchan (Crown, 1976); *Along the Clipper Way* by Francis Chichester (Coward-McCann, 1966); *Straight Through from London: The Antipodes and Bounty Islands, New Zealand* by Rowley Taylor (Heritage Expeditions, 2006); and *Vigilant and Victorious: A Community History of the Collaroy Surf Life Saving Club 1911–1995* by Sean Brawley (Collaroy SLSC, 1995).

Although at times it seemed like writing this novel was a solitary experience, I didn't spend the last three years solely in my office. Thanks are due to friends and family who've acted as sounding boards, boosters or much-needed distractions, my writing group for their comments and support, Harriet Allan for her patience and belief and Anna Rogers for her eye for the anachronistic.

If it wasn't for the Ministry of Education, who let me vary my hours, and Creative NZ, who supplied a writer's stipend in 2011, goodness knows how much longer this project would have taken.

Special thanks to Michael Fitzgerald, Andrea Hearfield and Sara Guthrie at Te Papa, without whom I'd never have felt a castaway suit or seen a scale model of the *Hinemoa*. Thanks to Andy Peters from www.maritimawoodcarving.co.uk for answering my questions in between trips to Sweden, and the real Dr Stanley for the Lead Poisoning 101.

Last, largest and longest thanks to my wife, Marisa. Thank you for not tolerating laziness. Thank you for reading this book too many times and never complaining. Thank you for knowing the difference between me and the stuff I make up.

Darren Cliff

Craig Cliff is the author of *A Man Melting*, a collection of short stories, which was previously published in New Zealand and won the 2011 Commonwealth Writers' Prize for Best First Book. In 2012 he was a judge for the inaugural Commonwealth Story Prize, and he is the recipient of a Robert Burns Fellowship at the University of Otago. He lives in Wellington, New Zealand.

Founded as a nonprofit organization in 1980, Milkweed
Editions is an independent publisher. Our mission is to identify,
nurture and publish transformative literature, and build
an engaged community around it.

milkweed.org